The Lingerie Designer

The Lingerie Designer

SIOBHÁN MCKENNA

POOLBEG

Published 2012
by Poolbeg Press Ltd
123 Grange Hill, Baldoyle
Dublin 13, Ireland
E-mail: poolbeg@poolbeg.com
www.poolbeg.com

1

A catalogue record for this book is available from the British Library.

ISBN 978-1-84223-495-2

Typeset by Patricia Hope in Sabon
Printed and bound by CPI Group (UK) Ltd, Croydon, CR0 4YY

www.poolbeg.com

ABOUT THE AUTHOR

After a career in the international clothing markets, Siobhán McKenna now works as a writer and lecturer in stress management and meditation, through her association with The Chopra Centre. She is a cousin of renowned Irish actress, Siobhán McKenna, and she hopes, through her writing, she will continue the family tradition of entertaining a wide audience. Siobhán lives in County Dublin. Visit her at **www.siobhanmckenna.ie** and **www.perfecthealth.ie**.

ACKNOWLEDGEMENTS

Many people helped me in small or big ways on the road to getting *The Lingerie Designer* to print.

Thanks to my family: April, Sophie, Mum, Jacqueline and Elaine and Bobby.

To my Chopra Centre family, with special gratitude to Deepak Chopra and David Greenspan. To Jackie Bresnan for encouraging me to enter the *Write a Bestseller Competition*. Seán Doran for fine-tuning the details of the Vietnam War. Howard Davis for his friendship and encouragement. Jonathon Williams for sharing his vast bank of knowledge and mentoring. June Barrett for her friendship and putting up with me in Vietnam. Also, Joe O'Sullivan, Fred Schelbaum, Michael Keating, Amy Green and Sallyann Collier.

All at TV3, especially *The Morning Show* and to the team at Poolbeg, especially Paula Campbell. Thank you for choosing me and making the experience so positive. To Gaye Shortland, for her eagle eye and patience – you are fantastic – thank you.

To you, the reader, for picking up my first book. I hope it takes you on the universal journey it took me on, and that it touches your life through laughter or tears and opens your heart to the possibilities that synchronicity brings you.

Finally, there are those who were as dedicated to this book as I was. Marie McKenna – Mum, who personifies a mother's love. Graziano Boldrini, for the never-ending support and pure belief in me – you never once left my side – *Only the Brave*. Hannah Tobin, whose loyalty and friendship knows no bounds and, despite being a time-strapped international woman of mystery, still found the time to read, edit and bring me to rugby matches along the way. My guides, Dad, Daniel, Archangel Michael, and my guardian angel, Emma – *Aham Brahmasmi. Namaste.*

> *There is an endless net of threads throughout the universe.*
> *The horizontal threads are in space.*
> *The vertical threads are in time.*
> *At every crossing of the threads,*
> *There is an individual.*
> *And every individual is a crystal bead*
> *And every crystal bead reflects*
> *Not only the light from every other crystal in the net*
> *But also every other reflection throughout the entire universe.*

THE RIG VEDA

This book is dedicated to my women. My mother, Marie. My daughters, April and Sophie. My sisters, Elaine and Jacqueline – and my virtual sister, Hannah Tobin.

In Loving Memory of Dad, John B McKenna, who taught me to dream.

1

Everyone has a secret. Maybe two. No one was more aware of this than Helen Devine. Lingerie designers know how to hide women's less sinful secrets by designing underwear that makes boobs bigger and tummies smaller. There's the padded push-up bra that has left many a man and boob deflated upon its unclasping. There's the "point & lift" bra, which is akin to a straitjacket and can take a small man's eye out on a packed Tube ride if he gets too close.

Then there's the lingerie that's designed purely to be removed. It screams sex and is sold up and down the high street in its tens of thousands in the run-up to Christmas, to men eagerly awaiting Santa's coming. Red is the biggest seller at Christmas. It also accounts for the most returns to store in January when women exchange the red micro-floss "I'm a nymphomaniac sex goddess" lingerie, for white functional "I'm going to go to the gym every day and I *will* lose fourteen pounds" New Year's Resolution type underwear.

Christmas is also statistically a time of relationship meltdown, often caused by office-party sexcapades or nights of guzzling fourteen pints with the lads. The pints, of course, are washed down with a chicken curry and an extra portion of chips before the party reveller heads home for some loving. Alas, the mouth is writing cheques that the body cannot cash – in reality, the celebrator ends

1

up passing out and farting instead of performing sex. And that's just the women.

Yes, Helen knew all this from both professional and personal experience. Therefore, she made sure her employer's stores, Eden, were filled with red, black, sequined or feathered high-priced garments in December, to be replaced with sensible and comfy three-for-the-price-of-two pieces in January.

She considered this as she sat in her design studio in London's West End. Twirling a piece of marabou fluff around her fingers, she wondered how she could reinvent the wheel or, in this case, the knicker. Get it right and her design would become a bestseller – get it wrong and it would end up in the bargain-basement sales.

"Do you think the dye kills any possible germs?" she asked, blowing on the entwined, delicate red feathers.

Sarah Ross, Helen's assistant, wiped her fringe out of her eyes – tiny beads of sweat had formed on her hairline. She fanned herself with a fabric swatch. "We really ought to have air-con." She eyed Helen over the pile of lace and ribbon samples strewn between them. It was true: the studio was airless, stuffed full of rolls of fabric and endless rails of garment samples. Sketches, memos and pattern pieces were pinned to every inch of wall space.

Without responding, Helen walked over to a large sash window and pushed it up. "Ah . . . an Indian summer breeze!" she said, inhaling.

The design room filled with the din of London traffic and the putrid smell of a dumpster in the narrow street three floors down.

"Welcome to the real rag trade, Sarah," Helen said, trying not to breathe too deeply. "Anyway, we're lucky to still be in this building, unlike our competitors who work out of a state-of-the-art concrete block near Heathrow." She returned to her desk. "Hopefully, Eden won't follow suit."

"Wouldn't you like that convenience though?" Sarah hesitated, before adding, "Don't you hot-tail it out of London every weekend, leaving the centre of the universe just as it starts heating up on a Friday night?"

"Dublin is a great city too, you know," Helen said tersely. She sometimes wondered if Sarah realised there was life beyond being a blonde, twenty-something Londoner. Or was there? Helen had been all those things – once. Maybe, unknown to herself, she was feeling the heat of the young Sarah nipping at her heels. Helen reasoned that at least she was still blonde, albeit thanks to her colourist. And she was a Londoner, sort of – surely, two out of three ain't bad?

"I prefer the Paddington Station kind of convenient, Sarah. Fifteen minutes gets you to Heathrow and at least it's located in civilisation," which loosely meant being within walking distance of fast food and a pub.

Sarah shrugged. "That fluff has been certified, by the way." She handed Helen a fax, changing the subject from the possibility of a cost-cutting relocation.

"Certified mad?" Helen smiled.

"Certified free from bird flu, because it comes from China." Sarah frowned, lightly scratching her head. "Chinatex faxed through the cert last night. Wasn't it Mad Cow Disease, not Mad Bird Disease – or was there that too?"

"No, that's right – we just needed a cert for bird flu. Unless we start making leather underwear, we don't have to worry about the cows – or pigs for that matter," Helen replied, but her smile had faded. They had hired Sarah because her portfolio had impressed Helen. The boss, Fred, on the other hand, liked her other attributes, in the form of double Ds.

"Well, at least there hasn't been a Mad Silkworm outbreak!" Sarah said, beaming.

Helen's face remained deadpan.

"That I'm aware of." Sarah bit her lower lip.

"We've a lot to get through today. Let's hope we don't have an EU directive telling us to label our Christmas stock 'Certified Bird Flu Free'. Now, that definitely wouldn't fan the flames of passion." Helen shivered. "Even the thought of more European red tape makes me feel as though someone's walking on my grave."

Before Sarah could respond, Helen's mobile buzzed under a mound of papers.

Sarah's face was still flushed from the implied rebuke as she watched Helen, who was pushing strands of fair hair behind her ear as she spoke quietly into the phone.

Helen had earned the reputation of a being a world-class lingerie designer. She had increased Eden's sales by thirty per cent with her first range for them. At the time, the company had ranked fourth in UK lingerie sales. With Helen at the helm, within two seasons Eden was the leading retailer of women's knickers across the country. Often the media referred to Eden as the UK's answer to the US lingerie moguls, Victoria's Secret.

If Helen pushed to get air-con in the office, air-con she'd get. And that's exactly why Sarah had to stick with her: she liked being on the winning team. Sarah would watch and learn or at least imitate, if the learning proved too tiresome.

She sketched a silhouette of a woman on a piece of paper. Across the desk, Helen still had the phone cradled between her ear and shoulder, reassuring someone that she'd be careful while she was in Hong Kong. It didn't take a genius to guess she was talking to her mother. Sarah discreetly studied her boss.

Physically Helen was still an attractive woman, despite being old, thought Sarah. She guessed her to be around thirty-five. Although not a conventional beauty, Helen had quite a striking appearance. Her hair, in honey-coloured waves, framed porcelain skin. But it was her emerald eyes that were most arresting. As always, in the office, she was dressed in black which gave her look the connotation of another Irish classic – a pint of Guinness.

Sarah continued drawing, pencilling the outline of a bra onto her nude and, in doing so, turning her doodling into a work in progress. "You've got to love this job," she muttered as she admired her handiwork. But her thoughts returned to Helen and what had made her a successful lingerie designer. In spite of Helen's curves, it was as if she had the mind of a bloke. Just last week, Sarah went to see a movie that Helen had recommended to her. Within five minutes of the titles rolling, twenty people got shot, blown up or decapitated. Helen had described it as terrific.

As her sketch took on its own life form, so did the movie playing in Sarah's imagination. So what did she know about Helen Devine?

She thought like a man, yet she never talked about men. She's was nearly middle-aged, yet remained unmarried. That's when it stuck her – just last week, she'd seen an email Helen had left open on her computer. Someone called Poppy had signed off with a long line of kisses. There was nothing else for it – Helen Devine must be a raving lesbo! Convinced this was now fact, Sarah wrinkled her nose. She'd be spending the next week travelling Asia pressed up against Helen, on planes, trains and automobiles. Helen on one side, Fast Fingers Fred on the other – and Sarah, the Heinz spread in their sexual sandwich.

She stood to get water from the cooler, deliberately walking with a little extra swagger in her hips. She took a quick peek over her shoulder and caught Helen checking her out.

"Sorry, Sarah, now where were we . . ." Helen had been hanging up the phone when she noticed Sarah walking rather oddly. Perhaps she'd pulled a hamstring at the gym or something. Maybe she'd been a little hard on her. Taking a friendlier approach, she said with a smile, "My mother thinks that every time I go to the Far East I'll never come out alive or I'll end up like that guy in the movie *Midnight Express*."

"*Midnight Express?*" Sarah asked blankly. Another man's movie, no doubt.

"Before your time. Never mind."

"But what about your brothers and sisters – does she fret so much about them?"

"I don't have any – just me."

"Oh."

Silence fell between them. Surely someone of Helen's age must come from the usual Irish condom-condemning family of ten?

"My dad died when I was a baby," Helen went on. "Mum never remarried – she always said that she was lucky to have found the love of her life, even if she only got to share the briefest time with him."

"Helen, that's so romantic!" Sarah said, clasping her hands over her heart.

"Funnily enough, I never thought that being made a widow at twenty-five was romantic."

"How did your father die?" Sarah asked, wide-eyed, oblivious to Helen's sarcasm.

Helen looked away, reading an email that had flashed up on her computer screen. "Fred's on his way over. He wants reassurances we're ready for Hong Kong tomorrow. He says if our baggage is overweight, we'll have to pay the excess charge ourselves."

Sarah's shoulders slumped. "But we've so many files and samples to bring, how will we fit in our own stuff?"

"Bring the lingerie designer's best friend – a chic black outfit."

"Black? That's hardly inspiring."

Helen grinned. "Trust me on this one. Twice yearly, the lingerie trade convene in Paris to forecast the hottest colours for the coming year while getting bombed on champagne from plastic cups. It'll be a convention centre of women and men in black. There will probably be a few extraterrestrials hanging about too, disguised as Italian fabric salesmen."

Sarah looked bewildered. She picked up a colour card they were working on. "So the hours of working on colour coordination is a waste of time?"

"Not at all. We coordinate the high street with a pallet of colours from the Exotic Nights forecast, or the Himalayan Plum collection, telling people what colours they should be wearing, but we the designers sit about, top to toe in mourning black."

"Do they have plums in the Himalayas?" Fred Giltrap, managing director of Eden, said, as he popped his head around the studio door.

"It doesn't matter if they do or not. Artistic licence prevails over truth," Helen replied. "You got here quickly, Fred. Your gym sessions must be paying off."

Fred sucked his stomach in, running his thumbs along the top of his strained waistband as he walked into the studio with his familiar seesaw gait.

"It's a mood board. It captures the theme for next season's collection," Sarah said.

"I don't give a rat's arse. Will it make us money?" Fred rubbed the top of his shiny head. He did that when he talked about money – as though he were summoning a genie from a lamp.

"That's the plan." Helen stood and picked up a notebook and

pen. "Fred and I are going to take a quick look around the shop floor to see how the quality looks on that last shipment from the Chinatex factory. God help them if I find any misplaced gussets."

"Helen's pet hate – misplaced gussets! And crooked knicker-elastic for that matter." Fred winked at Sarah.

She smiled at him as if she'd just swallowed a bitter pill.

Fred and Helen had only just left when the phone rang again. Sarah picked up. "Helen Devine," she said melodically, neglecting to mention to the caller she actually meant Helen Devine's phone.

"Ms Devine, Jack Taylor," a soft-spoken American voice said. "I'm one of your architects working on The Palm development in Dubai."

"Yes?" Sarah said, stretching a hand out to admire her manicure.

"The office said to give you a call. You're undecided between which unit to purchase and you want to talk to someone about layout and aspect?"

Silence.

Shit. Helen would have her guts for garters: not the kind of lingerie career she'd envisaged.

"Ms Devine?"

"I'm sorry, Mr Taylor, you must have misheard me. I'm Helen Devine's *assistant*. May I take your number and I'll get her to call you back?" The lie rolled off her tongue with ease.

Jack Taylor apologised profusely, gave his number and promptly hung up.

Sarah stretched back in Helen's high-back, leather chair with a satisfied smile, putting her stiletto heels firmly on the desk. So the boss was buying Middle East property in her spare time. That must make her the only Irish person with any money. Weren't they all broke – or was that the Greeks? What a mystery Helen was turning out to be – more complexities for Sarah to figure out. She felt a coffee break coming on. She could just see Debbie in Accounts' face when she told her about this one.

Helen and Fred stood at the elevator door waiting for the lift that led from the company offices down to its Oxford Street flagship store. Helen had her head stuck in her oversized bag, fumbling, when the doors slid open.

"I've left my mobile in the office. You go on, Fred. I'll follow you down." Swiftly, Helen retraced her steps back down the corridor to the design office.

"I forgot my phone . . . oh . . ." Helen's voice trailed off when she saw Sarah languishing on her executive chair. "Would you rob my grave as quickly?" she laughed.

Sarah bolted upright, knocking Helen's coffee mug to the floor.

"Relax, I'm only pulling your leg. I'm going to grab some food to bring back when I'm finished in the shop – do you fancy a sandwich?" Helen bent down to retrieve her mug, which read *The World's Best Friend* in big red lettering. She looked up at Sarah, whose cheeks were hot enough to fry an egg.

"No thanks, I'm watching my figure."

"Suit yourself." Helen placed the mug in its rightful place on the desk.

Having regained her composure, Sarah spoke up. "A man phoned – wants you to call him as soon as you can," she said brusquely, handing Helen a yellow note. Her clipped tone was lost on Helen, who was still fishing under scattered files for her phone.

"There it is," Helen said, picking it up. She took a quick glance at the message. "Who is Jack Taylor?"

"How would I know? All I did was take the message. Wants you to ring him back asap." Sarah sniffed, folding her arms.

"I'll call him while I'm out. Okay, I'd better go before Fred sends a search party for me. Won't be long."

Helen put her phone and the piece of paper in her bag as she was leaving. She stood in the doorway and hesitated. Breathing deeply, she pulled herself up to her full height of five-foot nine.

"Murder," she said, her back to the office.

"Excuse me?" Sarah looked up from papers she'd been shuffling.

Helen turned, looking back into the office. "My father – you asked how he died. He was murdered."

With that she left, leaving the door, and Sarah's mouth, open.

2

On Oxford Street at lunchtime, Helen joined the mêlée of office workers and tourists. The locals had phones stuck to their ears and were walking with purpose, not making eye contact with anyone. The tourists gathered in groups, meandering aimlessly, frequently checking that their bum bags were still attached and generally getting in the way of anyone trying to pass them.

The unseasonal heat in the city was making people more irritable than usual. A suit, talking loudly into his earpiece, pushed past an American tourist, knocking her out of his way lest she interrupt his pace.

"Hey, watch it, buster!" the woman shouted after him, waving her fist.

The suit was long gone and Helen hadn't been lucky enough to slip through the gap in his wake.

The American continued complaining, brushing down her red Chicago Bulls T-shirt, as if it had somehow been soiled by the touch of such a rude man.

Helen could feel her own impatience rise. The American accent grated, which she knew was hypocritical considering she had been born there. Eventually the woman waddled on, restoring one lane of pedestrian traffic, even though it was the slow lane. Helen was willing her to walk faster when the woman stopped at a souvenir stall, opening up a precious gap on the pavement.

Helen knew her irritation wasn't just about the tourist. Sarah's childish sulking, which she had chosen to ignore, was niggling her. Had they chosen the right person for the job? Then there was the matter of Sarah's direct question about her father. It had unnerved her and she didn't know why. But she knew only too well why her mother fretted so much every time her daughter left for South-East Asia, which was becoming more and more frequent as buying budgets and profit margins got tighter and tighter. She had gone and blurted out about murder, which wasn't strictly true, but, to Helen, her dad was murdered by the US government, whether they chose to call him a casualty of war or not.

Her stride was interrupted by another waddler. This one took the form of a five-year-old. *Who in their right mind takes a child for a walk on Oxford Street at lunchtime?* Probably another tourist, she guessed. As she shifted from left to right, trying to make her way past, wafts of frying beef tickled her nostrils. What the hell! If you can't beat them join them, she reasoned as she disappeared inside a burger bar. She placed her order and tried to wait patiently in line, hating not having something to do, eventually deciding to retrieve her phone from her bag. The yellow note was still stuck to it. She punched in the phone number just as her lunch was handed to her in a paper bag.

"Jack Taylor."

"Mr Taylor, Helen Devine." Helen wedged her phone between her shoulder and her ear as she opened the paper bag.

"Thank you for returning my call, Ms Devine, and please call me Jack."

Helen sighed heavily as she looked at her lunch, which she wanted to eat as quickly as possible. "What can I do for you, Jack?"

"I hope it's more about how I can help you, Ms Devine. If we can just have a quick chat about your primary use for the unit, I'll advise you of the most suitable option. I'd imagine living in London would mean you'd want to see as much sunlight as possible, escape from the English weather. Although I hear you're having a bit of an Indian summer there at the moment – is that correct?"

What was it with this man – would he ever shut up? Helen wasn't about to be sucked into a conversation about the weather.

"Long term, I plan to use the apartment as a holiday home but in the meantime it'll have to be suitable for the rental market. I'm handing it to a management company as soon as the purchase is finalised."

"I see. So you're not actually coming to Dubai to see the apartment before you make your decision?"

"Yes, Mr Taylor, that is correct. That's why I'm relying on you, as my architect, to advise me, based on my criteria." She decided to start eating anyway and hoped Mr Taylor wouldn't notice – although his voice sounded as though he might be a few years shy of wearing the 'Mr' title, which Helen usually reserved for men with a decade jump-start on herself.

"Okay." He hesitated for a moment before continuing. "In that case, if I may just ask you a few more questions?"

"Sure," Helen replied as lightly as she could muster. She sucked on a plastic straw – it made a loud slurping noise. She hadn't meant to be rude – she knew her architect was trying to be helpful but, for once, she wished she could spend lunch sitting on the grass in Hyde Park, watching the world go by. Her food looked less appetising now – she decided to bin it.

Jack Taylor placed the handset of his phone in its cradle. The call from his London client was to be his last from this office. He had explained how the apartment blueprints translated to daytime light and layouts to the woman while listening to the sounds of her trying to talk, walk and eat at the same time. He was sure he'd heard her shout "Gobshite!" at the distinctive sound of a black cab, but she had put her hand – or was it part of a burrito? – over the mouthpiece of the phone, so he wasn't sure.

Pulling back the shirt cuff, he looked at his watch. As usual, the face of the Tag Heuer chronograph timepiece had worked its way halfway around his arm. He twisted the bezel and wondered why he'd never managed to get a resizing done. It was a misfit, he reflected – a bit like the relationship with the woman who had given it to him. His gaze remained on the watch as he wondered what she was doing now. Why he continued to wear the watch she had given him, just before she had torn his world apart, eluded him. Maybe he enjoyed the pain in some perverse way.

"Why?" he muttered to himself.

"What was that?"

Jack hadn't heard the senior partner, Bill Redmond, approach his desk. The large, ginger-bearded Bostonian stood over him with a quizzical expression.

"Just talking to myself, Bill," Jack replied, as he looked up into the jolly round face.

"Sign of old age, my man, sign of old age," Bill chuckled.

"So is repeating yourself, Bill." Jack smiled back at him.

"Careful. I'm still your boss, you know – for another hour anyway, unless you've changed your mind?" Bill cocked an untamed eyebrow as he studied the young man's face. He liked the lad and, although Jack had turned the corner on thirty, he had a boyish face that he'd probably wear for a lifetime. And he was popular with his co-workers and clients. There was a quiet confidence about him, reassuring, without being cocky. Moreover, he had that great combination of a mathematical brain and artistic ability – he would be a great architect with a few more years' experience under his belt.

Jack shook his head and grinned. "Nine months in Dubai is enough for me, Bill. Hey, it's three months longer than my original contract! Besides, sand-dune surfing just doesn't cut it. I'm heading for the real thing."

"I don't know. You Ivy Leaguers – you want it all." Bill feigned a disappointed look, but he knew that Jack Taylor had never really settled in Dubai. He did look as if he'd be more at home riding waves on Huntington Beach, Southern California.

Getting back to business, Jack said, "I spoke to that Devine woman in London. She's decided on Unit 3710, at least I think she has. She said something about having to check the numbers out with her friend."

"The sales agent told me she had the money in place – that's why they were so anxious for us to ring her quickly in case she changed her mind."

"I didn't think she was talking about money when she mentioned the numbers – more of a superstition, I'd guess. Unusual name, Devine. I couldn't quite place her accent. She didn't sound English though." Jack slipped Helen's contact details back into a brown manila folder. "Wherever she's from, she seriously sounds like she needs a vacation."

"Devine, that's an Irish name, I think," Bill said, as he gazed off into the distance as if trying to recall where he'd heard the name before. Bill came from a long line of Irish-Americans – he was very proud of his heritage and loved all things Irish. "All the better if she does need some rest and relaxation. She's less likely to renege on the purchase of a new holiday home."

"Nah, I've worked with her type before. It'll end up just being an investment that she never sees. That or she'll flip it. These career-focused people have vague plans about what they'll do one day when they find the time, but they never manage to step off the hamster wheel, for fear someone will take their place." Jack dropped Helen's folder into a filing cabinet and then firmly slid the drawer shut. He paused. "I believe Ms Devine's file now clears my in-tray and therefore marks the end of my time in Allen Bernstein & Associates. The Dubai office anyway." Jack laced his fingers behind his head and stretched for added effect.

"What's your start date with the LA office?"

"December first," Jack said as he started unpinning family photos from the felt partition that had sectioned off his work station.

"But that's nearly three months away! What will you do until then? Go home to the East Coast?"

"Jeez, you sound just like my mother! No, I'm touring around Asia for a few months, taking some photos, getting a feel for the cultures."

"We must have been paying you too much," Bill said, picking up one of Jack's photos. It resembled a Kodak moment. His parents made a handsome couple – broad, even smiles, with Jack's father's arm draped around his graceful wife's shoulder as they sat on a plaid blanket. The sister, blonde and tanned, a younger female version of Jack, was hugging a Golden Retriever. The dog's tongue hung out, making it look as if he too was smiling. There was a dark, exotic-looking girl kneeling on the other side of the oversized pooch, but she didn't look like the rest of them. Bill pointed to her. "Is she one of the family?"

"No. A girl I was in school with. Amy." Jack tried to sound nonchalant and immediately regretted mentioning her name, although it felt good to do so.

"Amy. Didn't you two date before you left Boston?" Bill had an amazingly retentive memory, even for conversations that took place in ex-pat clubhouses when excess liquor had loosened ties and tongues.

"Yeah, briefly, but she was more of a buddy really," Jack said. He stood and took the photo from Bill's hand before swiftly putting it in his messenger bag.

"You can't just be buddies with a woman who looks like that!"

"Will you be at my surprise party later?"

"You know about that?" Bill looked genuinely crestfallen.

"I know everything that goes on in this office – you guys will miss me." He looped the messenger bag over his head before undoing the top button of his collar. He took a last look around the purpose-built office. It was functional and banal, filled with filing cabinets, work tables, rolled-up plans and drawings of the endless construction that was still transforming Dubai. But he wasn't really seeing it. He was just glad he had managed to avoid telling Bill what Amy really meant to him. If you catch a woman like that, you never let her go. Unless of course she lets go of you.

3

Is it possible to fall in love with someone who serves you cold soup? Lust maybe. Love? Probably not. Still, sitting in a restaurant in the Dublin seaside town of Howth, Poppy Power couldn't help but romanticise about the Latin waiter with his hair tied back and a twinkle in his eyes. Poppy blushed when he looked at her. It was as if he knew what she was thinking.

"How is the soup, ladies?" the clear-skinned waiter asked, his eyes meeting Poppy's.

Their look lingered. Blood coursed through her veins as if "Angelo", as his brass name-tag revealed, had asked her to sleep with him and not about the soup at all.

"*Molto buono*!" Poppy purred back at him, flicking her copper mane for added effect.

"*Parla Italiano*?" the waiter replied, his large brown eyes smiling.

Poppy's teenage daughter, Lily, looked up from her under-the-table texting and wished the ground would swallow her. Poppy, on the other hand, hadn't a clue what the waiter had just said but didn't care because it sounded so sexy.

"Mum, you said 'very good' in Italian," Lily hissed. "We're in a *Spanish* restaurant. He's asking do you speak Italian!" For once, Lily thought it'd be good to have a normal mum, who went to coffee mornings and fixed the hem on your school uniform when it was hanging.

Poppy giggled, a schoolgirl-crush giggle that served only to heighten Lily's ever-increasing embarrassment. She wondered if she could pretend she didn't know her mother even though they were at the same table.

"Oh – silly me! Anyway, *Angelo* . . ." Poppy made a point of directing her eyes to his chest while saying his name, "yes, the gazpacho is yum!" With that, she picked up a large pepper-grinder and started twisting the wooden top. Little sprinkles of black pepper fell on her soup.

"Can I do that for you, *signora*?" The motion of the gorgeous redhead grasping the shaft of the pepper grinder and twisting its top wasn't lost on him, and he suppressed a smile.

"That's okay – I've got it," Poppy replied, tilting her head slightly as she looked up, rapidly blinking her hazel eyes at him.

"Yes, I can see that you have." His grin broke out as he left the tableside but he couldn't help looking back over his shoulder before he went into the kitchen to cool down.

"Mum, you're such a loser! Why were you flirting with that man, or do you have a go at every Latin waiter you meet?"

"I wasn't flirting – I was just being friendly, Lily – you should try it some time," Poppy replied dryly, ignoring the caustic remark about her chequered past. She was getting weary of the scowl Lily permanently wore these days. "Anyway, it's only a bit of fun. Lighten up, Lil, maybe try a bit of flirting yourself." Poppy eyed her only daughter, the light of her life. The familiar pang of worry fluttered in her stomach. Lily, only seventeen, her shoulders hunched, as if the weight of the world was bearing down on her. She was wise beyond her years but at times it was as if Lily was the parent and Poppy the teenager. Lily appeared to have lost all zest for life.

Poppy resisted the urge to brush her daughter's hair off her face. Lily had dyed her hair jet black. She wore it straight and lankly around her pretty, albeit slightly acne-pocked, face. Poppy felt dismay as she took in what Lily was wearing: a black chunky jumper over an equally shapeless floor-skimming cotton skirt. At least the skirt hid the scruffy Doc Marten boots. Poppy realised that she was taking orders from a teenager who looked like the Grim Reaper.

"I'm not interested in flirting with men," Lily said flatly, finally feeling that she didn't have to dive under the table to avoid mortification now that the waiter was out of sight.

"Men, boys, dudes – whatever you want to call them." Poppy rolled her eyes to heaven. *Public Health Warning: parenting teenagers may cause severe financial haemorrhage, loss of sanity, and stress-related illnesses.*

"I'm not interested in the male species, period," Lily said as she rolled an olive around in a terracotta bowl with her chipped, black-nail-polished fingers.

Poppy resisted the urge to tell her to stop.

Mother and daughter sat in silence, like a couple whose days of romance had long since tarnished.

It was Lily who spoke first.

She sat up straight as if bracing herself for a punch.

"Mum – I'm a lesbian," she declared and looked at her mother defiantly.

Poppy wrinkled her brow in confusion. "But I thought you were a Gothic!"

"A *Goth*, Mum." Lily rolled her eyes at her mother's continuing attempt to be up to date with "youth culture", as she called it.

"A Goth then. Do you have to be a lesbian to be a Goth?" Poppy wasn't sure if she should laugh or cry. Looking at Lily's unsmiling face, she decided to bite her lip instead.

Lily tried to be patient with her mother but she never made it easy. Everyone loved Poppy Power – pretty, funny and kind. A bit ditsy, but that just endeared her more to those who met her. To Lily, she was endearing unless you had to live with her.

Lily softened somewhat when she saw Poppy's eyes well up. That, and the fact that the waiter had just strutted by and her mother hadn't even noticed. "It's no big deal. You like dick, I like dyke!" She smiled at her own pun.

17

"Sounds like a porn version of *Mary Poppins*," Poppy said, putting her soup spoon down. She had lost her appetite.

Poppy took in the room, warm and inviting. An aroma of garlic drifted from the kitchen. Groups of people were coming in from work for the early bird special. Couples chatted and laughed. At the table beside them sat a group of young women students, dressed up for a night on the town. One of them had three helium balloons tied to the back of her chair. Birthday cards and discarded wrapping-paper littered their table.

Poppy wondered what age the girl was – nineteen, twenty maybe? Then, horror of horrors, she wondered if Lily was checking them out. *Oh, Christ – what if she's had sex with a woman?* Poppy's stomach jumped into her mouth and she thought she'd be sick. Instead, she waved her hand to catch the waiter's attention.

She didn't have to wait long.

"*Bella donna*, can I help you? You no like the soup?" Angelo couldn't help but notice, even in the dim candlelight that the foxy little redhead suddenly lacked lustre.

"Wine, please – a bottle," Poppy said quickly. She couldn't process Lily's information sober.

"I get you the wine list."

"*No!* I mean, no need, once it's wet and red." Poppy gulped the last of the wine she'd been sipping. It was only Monday evening and she had clients booked in for therapeutic massages early the next morning, so she'd decided on having only one glass of wine with dinner. That was before images of girl-on-girl began to play on the screen of her imagination.

Angelo hesitated and considered asking whether the hot mamma, who was now decidedly lukewarm, was all right. He decided to say nothing, lest she consider him rude, and shuffled off to fetch her wine.

"Mum, you're awful quiet," Lily said, sounding a lot less defiant than a few minutes earlier.

"You reckon?" Poppy replied sarcastically. She wondered what she'd tell a client to do if they found themselves in the same circumstance. Working as a masseuse all day was physically tough work and Poppy tried to limit the amount she did. She also worked as a psychotherapist, seeing people for one-to-one therapy sessions. So what, she thought, would she advise a client to do?

Professionally, she'd heard all the stories, witnessed people's pain, and sympathised with them. Sometimes she just sat silently, giving them the space to cry or vent their anger. But now a bombshell had exploded on her own turf. Would it be possible to apply the same calm to her own life? Who counsels the counsellor? The answer came with a pop of a cork. A bottle of wine would have to be her answer for now.

"One or two glasses?" Angelo smiled broadly, proffering two.

In unison, Lily said "One" and Poppy said "Two".

He left two glasses and disappeared. Hot Mamma had turned into the Ice Queen.

"I think, darling daughter, if you're old enough to be a lesbian, you're old enough to have a drink with your mother." Poppy poured the wine, but she made Lily's a small glass.

"I can't help who I am, Poppy. It just feels right."

Poppy cringed at Lily's words but she had regained her composure somewhat.

"Do you have a girlfriend?"

"No."

"Have you had sex with a girl then?"

Lily hesitated but eventually replied, "No."

"Have you had sex with anyone then?"

"No!"

"Then you might not be queer! Lesbian, I mean!" Poppy felt a slight glimmer of light on the horizon.

Lily raised her eyes to heaven but said nothing. Poppy had won the ping-pong of words.

Mother and daughter downed the wine. The food went largely untouched. Still, by the time they called for the bill, Lily managed to crack a smile at the waiter who had kept throwing glances their way. She had the most beautiful white teeth and on the rare occasion she smiled, her whole face lit up and a spark ignited in her dark eyes.

Poppy couldn't wait to get out of the little Spanish restaurant. The wine had temporarily cooled her jets but now she was feeling claustrophobic. As she put the cash into the leatherette envelope to pay the bill, she added a generous tip. As always, more than she could afford. Counselling and holistic work weren't exactly big payers.

"Thanks," Lily said as she stood, putting on yet another layer of black – a trench coat.

Poppy knew she meant more than just thanks for the half-eaten paella. She smiled, putting a loving arm around her daughter.

"You're welcome, love. I'll do my best to understand. But there's one thing . . ." She looked at her daughter. "I may have to accept the whole female-loving thing, but I'm not quite ready to have you call me 'Poppy' – you're the only person in this world who calls me 'Mum' and I'm not ready to let that go. I'm not sure I ever will be." She swallowed hard, her voice a little shaky.

"Okay, Mum."

They left the restaurant for home.

Angelo pushed the kitchen door open with his elbow. In one hand, he balanced a tray, which held a cocoa-dusted gelato for the girl and a blue flaming sambuca for the mamma. He cupped his left hand protectively around the flame. Dessert was on the house and was sure to bring a smile back to mother and daughter. His smile faded as he looked up and saw crumpled-up napkins on the table and empty chairs where they had been sitting. He sighed in disappointment, accidentally extinguishing the flame.

4

Helen twisted the small gold ring she always wore on her little finger. She glanced up at the clock – its black hands were edging towards six o'clock.

"How are you doing with that print, Sarah?" she asked, anxious to get out of the office.

"It's frustrating. Have a look, tell me what you think." Sarah pushed her chair away from the computer monitor to let Helen see the changes she had made to the computer-aided design.

"I know it's a pain in the ass, designing a lingerie print." Helen squinted at the screen. "We'll have to limit the shades of green in that leaf." She leaned forward and clicked on the mouse.

"The colour combinations are endless," Sarah frowned.

"The more colours we use, though, the more the screen for the print will cost. We'll have to be creative, within our budget."

"But each leaf takes three shades of green. How will I manage my limit of an eight-colour print when I haven't even got to the flowers?" Sarah's voice had risen an octave.

"Just a slight change here, I think." Helen made a double tap and stood back.

"It looks great."

"It's worth tinkering over. If we get it wrong, all the stock will

end up being reduced," Helen said, looking at her modification with satisfaction.

"Okay – what will we call it?"

They looked at the forty-inch monitor, heads cocked in unison, as if looking at the floral design from a different angle might provide them with a bolt of inspiration.

"'Elizabeth'!"

"It's feminine, Sarah, but not the Queen Mother."

Sarah pursed her lips. "How about 'English Garden'? It has a mix of rosebuds and ivy, like you'd see in a cottage garden."

"Maybe. Chances are when the Chinese printers do their version of it – it'll look like an English summer garden all right – washed out."

"I'll look up the thesaurus, see what other word comes up for 'garden'." Sarah tapped the keyboard and the results appeared. "Private grounds, precinct . . ." She didn't bother reading the rest.

"I can just see the swing tag, when the stock hits the store – 'Flowery Precinct' – images of a cop-shop with hanging baskets, the new Eden marketing pitch." Helen glanced at the clock. "It's getting late. We still have to get files and samples together for the Hong Kong trip." She rubbed her face in her hands. "'The Lover's Garden'. Type that up in brush-script font or something swirly – it'll look the part." She walked away.

"Oh Helen, I didn't realise the time. I have a spray tan and manicure booked in fifteen minutes." Sarah sounded flustered.

"Go on, I'll finish up here. I've already copied whatever files I can to a USB, so that just leaves the garment samples I bought in New York to split between us." Helen pointed towards a rail of garments, covered in plastic.

"Surely there are copyright issues Eden needs to consider, before handing over designer goods to the Chinese to knock off."

"Every high-street store does it – and we call it 'inspiration'. Besides, it's one of the few perks left in the job – being paid to go to New York to shop."

"I'm just thinking about Eden's reputation," Sarah sniffed.

"Don't worry, by the time we've pared them down to budget,

they won't bear any resemblance to the originals, unfortunately. Now go. I'll see you at the airport in the morning."

Sarah hot-footed it out the door.

Helen wondered if she could make her yoga class or if she'd just pick up an Indian takeaway and go home. Either choice qualified as preparation for all things Asian, she reckoned. Of course, the pub might not be a bad option either. Decisions, decisions.

She decided on yoga, mainly because there was no one to go for a drink with. Helen half-walked, half-jogged along the pavement. A yoga mat and gym bag hung from her right shoulder. A laptop case and sample carrier hung from the left. She struggled to balance the two – the story of her life. The Hell and The Divine, as Rob, her not-quite-ex lover, liked to say – though he meant something else altogether by it. Her mobile buzzed in her pocket, just as it started to rain. She covered her head with the yoga mat in a vain attempt to save her hair from frizzafying. The mat unrolled, obscuring her view. "Fuck!" she cursed, as she battled to regain control of her belongings. The mat plopped to the ground, landing in a puddle. Her phone stopped ringing just as she managed to retrieve it.

The young flaxen-haired manager of the yoga centre looked up serenely as Helen, now resembling an electrocuted rat, clambered her way through the glass doors.

"Oh, to have automatic doors, hey!" Helen joked, resisting the urge to shake the rain off her, for fear she'd be mistaken for a dog.

"*Namaste*," the girl smiled, her hands in prayer position, giving a little bow. She wore a purple bandana and an elaborately jewelled bindi on the centre of her forehead. Incense burned in a Buddha statue beside her. "Remember the Yoga Rooms philosophy?" She looked at Helen, as if she herself was a great yogi seer talking to a moron.

"'No running to or from yoga class'," Helen reeled off the answer she gave every week, as she arrived red-faced to their door. Well, almost every week, depending on who was in the pub.

"That's right. Now, breathe deeply and really arrive."

"Okay, deep breath . . ." Helen puffed as she signed the register.

"Class starts in five minutes. We don't want to be late and disturb everyone who arrived on time, now do we?"

"What a pretty bindi you're wearing today, Sharon," Helen said. "Not many Londoners get to wear a bindi to work. Maybe it helps you stay calm, while the rest of us are so stressed."

The girl smiled tightly at Helen, unsure if the remark was a compliment or an insult.

Once in the class studio, Helen sat in half-lotus position and felt herself relax as she closed her eyes for a few minutes' meditation. Since Poppy had told her that it took years off your chronological age, she tried to do it regularly in the hope of avoiding a face lift.

A smug feeling washed over her when she heard the yoga instructor enter the room, five minutes late. "Put that in your bong and smoke it, Sharon," she muttered. She opened her eyes on hearing a silky-smooth voice gently guiding the class to a standing position.

Now *he* is fit, Helen thought as she saw the teacher – tall, dark and with big muscles, in Lycra pants.

"*Namaste*. My name is Ian – welcome to my advanced class. I look forward to connecting spiritually with each of you through yoga, breathing and meditation."

Helen thought of other ways of connection.

"Before we begin, has anyone got any injuries? Is anyone pregnant?"

"Not yet and not yet," said Helen, delighted she hadn't gone to the pub nor eaten a fatty curry. She would arrive in Asia tomorrow a glowing goddess.

Satisfied the class were fit and healthy, Ian continued.

"Let's close our eyes for a moment, putting awareness on our breath. In . . . and out . . . in . . . and out . . ."

This is positively Tantric, Helen mused.

"For today's class we'll bring the yoga limb of Yamas to our awareness. Let Yamas guide your mind away from feelings of violence, sensual indulgence and greed."

Considering the impurity of her thoughts, Helen realised she was buggered. She tried to focus on her breathing and behave, but as soon as Ian did his downward dog in those yoga pants, all thought of purity went out the window. Helen, following his lead, pushed her bum high into the air. She tried to watch what the instructor was doing through the gap between her legs. Thankfully, he could not see her face. Was she imagining it or was he checking out her upside-down cleavage?

"Excellent poise," he said, smiling at her.

Helen's phone, which she had wrapped in her sweater on the floor, shrilled and vibrated. Ian was no longer smiling.

"Sorry, sorry. Doctor on call," Helen said. It wasn't strictly a lie – some doctor, somewhere, was on call. She grabbed her phone and tried to extricate herself from the classroom with the minimum of fuss.

She stepped on a classmate's fingers.

By the time she got to the foyer, the phone had stopped ringing.

"Bugger!" Helen shouted at her phone. It was a blocked number.

"That language is unacceptable in the Yoga Rooms," Sharon snapped. She stood, hands on hips, glaring at Helen.

"I'm on call," Helen winced, and hoped she looked convincing.

"Your occupation is listed as a lingerie designer."

"Underwear has its emergencies too, you know. Haven't you heard of wardrobe malfunction? A thong riding too high, a bra-strap snapping off?" Helen clicked her fingers and smiled weakly, in an effort to appeal to Sharon's Zen side.

But the Zen had zonked.

5

Helen sat on her couch tucking into a Tikka Masala she had picked up on the way home, after being told by an arm-folded, toe-tapping Sharon that she was no longer welcome at the Yoga Rooms. Helen was barred.

Her phone buzzed again, the screen showing a blocked number.

"Helen?" Poppy's voice sounded shaky and slightly slurred.

"Poppy, are you okay? You don't sound the best." Helen felt a twinge of concern.

Over the years, Helen and Poppy had exchanged many a distraught phone call. In childhood it had been mainly about Poppy's strung-out parents: baby boomers who were into free love and drugs, yet they never managed give their love freely to their eldest daughter, whom they named after their favourite hallucinogen.

Then came the teenage years. When most girls were running up huge phone bills, gossiping about boys, Poppy rang Helen for advice on how to handle her brothers, who were running wild, drinking, and getting brought home in the back of police cars – the same brothers who now were all abroad and rarely even contacted her. Helen's advice was to join them and party, but Poppy had taken on the role of mother, father, housekeeper and spiritual-guidance teacher because her folks hadn't realised the sixties were over and it was time to grow up.

Then, of course, there was the phone call when the young Poppy had discovered she was pregnant with the daughter she'd name Lily, after Poppy's grandmother. Poppy liked the idea of upgrading her daughter on the floral chain from her own namesake, a poppy which grew wild in fields, to a lily, a flower of elegance and sophistication. So far though, Lily was a late bloomer.

"Lily says she's gay." Poppy's voice gave way to tears.

"I thought she was an Emo!" Helen replied somewhat flippantly.

"Goth."

"What's the difference?"

"Something to do with the shoes, I think." The conversation wasn't going the way Poppy had planned.

"I really should know these things," Helen said. "I wonder what kind of knickers they wear. Don't answer that! Anyway, don't worry," she went on in a matter-of-fact tone, "Lily's not gay."

Poppy felt a huge surge of relief wash over her.

"But even if she is, it's not so bad, is it?" Helen chomped on a mouthful of curry.

Poppy's temporary wave of relief came crashing down. She said quietly, "I don't know. I guess I always dreamed of a normal life for her. Get married, have kids, you know, the fairytale we never had."

"But you say all men are goons!"

"Remind me, why are you my first port of call in a crisis?"

"Because I tell you the truth," Helen replied without hesitation.

"Sometimes it might be nice to be mollycoddled, Helen."

"Call someone else then. I do enough bullshit in work, thanks. I don't need to bring it home."

Helen wondered if she should eat the free portion of chips the take-out had given her as a type of loyalty-point reward. "Anyway, as I said, I don't think she's a lesbian. You got me barred from yoga class by the way, just when I was getting the hang of it." She dipped a chip into the curry sauce.

"How can you be so sure she's not? It's not like she's ever shown any interest in boys." Poppy was fishing for Helen to throw her a lifeline.

"Because gays go through years of mental anguish, before

27

admitting to themselves that they're batting for the other team. When they finally accept themselves, they have to go through the whole torture of telling their God-fearing family. That's if they ever do. Unless, of course, they get pissed at Christmas dinner and come out over the sherry trifle. That's just the way it is, Poppy."

"Bloody hell, Helen, fifties' Ireland is well and truly gone. What universe are you living in?"

"The one where I'm the only person on the planet barred from a yoga class obviously!"

"Let me guess: the instructor is male. What did you do to him?"

"*I* didn't do anything – you did!"

"How did I manage that, considering I'm in Dublin?"

"Oh, never mind, I suppose I can't blame you for all the times my phone has interrupted the class – I should have remembered to turn the damn thing off – but tonight was obviously the straw that broke the yogi's back." Helen took a gulp of Diet Coke. "Look, Lil is young – Christ, she's still only seventeen. Yes, she might be gay and, if she is, it doesn't matter as long as she's happy. But knowing her, by next week it'll be something else. She'll probably announce she's a vegetarian and then you'll really have problems."

Poppy laughed. The crisis now in perspective, she asked, "You home this weekend or travelling?"

"I'm heading to Hong Kong in the morning. I'll be back the following weekend."

"Will I call on your mum?"

Even though Helen's mother drove her nuts at times, she worried about her on the weekends when she couldn't make it back to Dublin.

"Do you mind?"

"Don't be daft."

"Bring Lily with you – she can tell Mum about her new-found hobby."

"Yeah, I can just hear your mother now – 'That's lovely, dear. Lesbian, you say? Is that what the young people are doing these days? Would you like a custard cream?' Can't you picture it?" Poppy laughed at the imaginary scene.

"Unfortunately, yes." Helen looked down at her belly and rubbed it, wishing she hadn't eaten so much. "Right, I got to go, early start tomorrow. Tell Lily I said hi, and that she's not allowed to turn into one of those scary lesbians that people look at and wonder if they're a man or a woman. She'd better be a lipstick lesbian – the clothes are much nicer too. Bye!"

"Wait – you know, I didn't actually call you earlier – at least I don't think so – unless I'm going senile . . ."

"Hmmm . . . maybe. Tragedy it was, Poppy." Helen paused for effect. "The Universe delivered the man of my dreams, then by a cruel twist of fate took him away again, just as quickly."

"Don't worry, Helen. If he's for you, he won't pass you by."

"Goodbye, Poppy," Helen said firmly, unwilling to hear her friend's synchronicity theory again. She hung up, before Poppy got a chance to obsess again.

Helen decided she'd need to walk off the effect of the curry if she was to have any chance of sleep that night. Damn, why didn't she just say no when they offered the free portion of chips, she wondered as she pounded the pavements. But there were babies starving in Africa. It was a shame to throw good food in the bin. She wondered why it was that every time she tried to be wholesome and healthy, temptation appeared with her name emblazoned on it. This reminded her to pick up the voicemail that had caused her ejection from the yoga class – another stab at releasing her pure side squashed. It turned out Poppy wasn't to blame.

"Ms Devine, Jack Taylor from Allen Bernstein Architects. We finished our call so abruptly earlier that I forgot to tell you that today was my last day in the Dubai office. There should be no problem acquiring the specific unit you want but if you've any concerns or further questions, please call my colleague Bill Redmond. His direct line number is . . ."

Helen pressed 'end' on Jack's voicemail. I could bloody strangle him, she thought. Her architect had been the one who got her barred from yoga with his conscientious phone call. It must have been nearly midnight in Dubai when he'd called. His last day and he was still burning the midnight oil. Why wasn't he out getting drunk with his former colleagues like a normal person instead of getting her kicked out of class? Helen decided Mr Jack Taylor was definitely not her type of guy.

"All right, Helen, darling?"

She was jolted from her mental rant by her local barman, who was standing outside the pub on a fag break.

"Oh hi, Tommy, I didn't see you there – in a world of my own."

"I can see that, love. You coming in?" The old-timer barman stubbed out his cigarette. Tommy was a kindly man in his late sixties who gave up what he called his disgusting habit of smoking every Monday morning.

Helen could see that he hadn't had much success kicking the habit this week either. Maybe next week he'd fare better.

"No, Tommy, not tonight. I've an early start in the morning."

"Ah, come on, my lovely, it's quiet as a church in there, I'm bored out of my mind. Tell you what, why don't you just have a half and you can tell me all about what's troubling you?"

Helen hesitated. She did enjoy chatting with Tommy, who she'd got to know during many a lonely London night.

"Okay, I'll just have the half – to keep you company." She followed him inside.

6

Helen arrived at the Cathay Pacific desk in Heathrow's Terminal 3, wearing a large pair of black sunglasses. She was annoyed that, having successfully walked off the effect of the curry and rejection from the yoga class, she had somehow ended up in the pub. Tommy and his promise of just a half! She didn't even drink lager and well he knew it. She hadn't meant to walk in the direction of the pub – it was as though she was on automatic pilot and the pub had some sort of homing device. As she handed over her passport and e-ticket printout, she decided that the pub had Bermuda Triangle-type powers, sucking in well-intentioned walkers. Therefore it had nothing to do with her lack of willpower.

Pleased with her deduction, Helen smiled at the petite Asian check-in clerk behind the business-class desk, oblivious to the wistful glances coming from the long line of people queuing up for the economy cabin check-in.

"Thank you, Ms Devine." The airline girl stood, and with a slight bow of her head she handed Helen a boarding pass with both hands.

Helen had travelled in Asia long enough to know this was a sign of respect and cordially accepted the documents with both hands in return.

"I have allocated you seat 2A as requested, Ms Devine. Your

colleagues . . ." the girl hesitated as she glanced back at her computer monitor, "your colleagues, Mr Giltrap and Ms Ross, have not yet checked in, but I have allocated them seats on the same row as you." The girl beamed at Helen, as if she had just delivered the best news of her career. "Do you know where our lounge is?" She settled back into her seat and looked up at Helen.

"Yes, thanks, I do." Helen smiled back. She stuffed her boarding papers into her handbag and rummaged for her mobile.

"Have an enjoyable flight, Ms Devine," the Cathay Pacific girl said, but already a harried-looking businessman wearing a charcoal-grey suit and a lemon-sucking face had placed his bag on the conveyor belt. He appeared unaware that Helen was still standing at the desk. As she moved out of his way, she noticed that he was carrying an unusual briefcase: it was straw, almost a slim-line picnic basket, and it looked out of place. She shuddered, perhaps reacting to his stress levels after the staff's graciousness. It dawned on her that some of the most discourteous passengers she met travelled business class. She smiled as she thought of her mother, who had a saying for every scenario. "All fur coat and no knickers!" was one of Mary's favourite declarations, when referring to people with money but not much else.

A high-pitched voice interrupted Helen's thoughts.

"Helen!" an out-of-breath Sarah called out.

"Mother of God!" Helen said, as she looked at the trolley Sarah was attempting, to push. She'd obviously packed the kitchen sink. And was that really a yoga mat, rolled up on top of the pile?

Fred Giltrap came into view behind Sarah. He was carrying a cabin-sized black leather weekend-case, with a matching laptop holder attached to it.

"How is it men can pack so little?" Helen asked. Fred just shrugged.

"Sorry I'm late," Sarah said. "Were you worried?"

Before Helen had a chance to respond, Fred said, "I bumped into Sarah outside, good job too. Blimey, all topsy-turvy she was, may well have gone to Terminal 4 – *Terminal* 4! She could have ended up in Holland, God forbid."

"But I did! Go to Terminal 4, I mean, not Holland obviously. That's why I'm late. I got off the express train too early – then had to make my way back." Sarah paused as she looked up. "Helen, why are you wearing sunglasses – inside?" She looked around at the other passengers to see if it was some kind of fashion statement she wasn't aware of.

"Migraine," Helen sniffed, pushing the glasses higher up on the bridge of her nose.

"That's Helen's codeword for *hangover*, Sarah," Fred said.

"No, it's not." Helen took the glasses off but didn't make eye contact. "Relax, Sarah. Look, there's no one at the desk, go over and pick up your boarding pass now."

After Sarah had left, she added, "How on earth am I going to put up with your charm for the next nine days, Fred?" She put her glasses on top of her head, using them as a hair-band. "I'm going to hit the shops, I'll see you in the lounge."

"Pick me up some mints, will you, Helen?" Fred half-heartedly reached into his trouser pocket for change. "I don't want to go around stinking of garlic all week." He began sorting out some coins.

"You're all right, Fred. I think I can afford a packet of sweets. Even on the salary you're paying me."

"Honestly, the abuse I have to take!" Fred shook his head.

"I've checked in." Sarah held up her lounge pass, to prove her point.

"That was quick – I hardly noticed you go," Fred said.

"You want to come with me, Sarah, or are you staying with Fred?"

"With you! Will we still have time to go to the lounge though? I've never been in one before." She looked at the gold-coloured invitation she held.

"Don't worry, my girl, I have this walk down pat. Follow me." With that, Helen turned on her red heels and headed straight for the large yellow sign with a pointing arrow and the magic word '*Shops*'.

Once out of Fred's earshot, Helen decided that her young assistant needed to learn that there was more to the business of being a lingerie designer than knicker-elastic. If Sarah was going to last the pace, not only would she have to know where to notch a pattern, she would have to learn the art of shopping and drinking. And not necessarily in that order.

"Okay, Sarah, tactics are required. If we do this right we can get our shopping done and still have time for pre-boarding cocktails in the lounge." Helen's face said she meant business.

"But it's only ten a.m."

"Mistake number one! It is six in Hong Kong. We need to pre-empt the jetlag by getting into their time zone asap." Helen spoke as if this was gospel.

She took Sarah's elbow and guided her towards Boots.

"First things first: we stock up on every legal drug, for all possible ailments. Anti-flu capsules for the colds that will be brought on by freezing air-conditioning," she picked up a basket at the shop's entrance, "lozenges for sore throats, caused by Karaoke Night – there will be at least one of those during the trip. Cherry or lemon flavour?" She held up two packets to Sarah, who shrugged. "Good idea, we'll get both," she continued to her bewildered assistant. "And, of course, plasters for blisters from killer heels." Her basket was filling up at lightning speed. "Finally, fast-acting, double-strength Ibuprofen, for generalised pain – also known as a hangover. It is tough work, this business travel."

Helen hauled her remedy basket to the till.

"But I thought you said there were great chemists in Hong Kong?" Sarah said.

"There are. We'll restock there for Mainland China. That reminds me – you might want to buy some fake tan – all their creams have bleaching agents in them. They want to make themselves whiter, while we spend our time bronzing. Isn't the world a funny place? We always want the opposite of what we have. Okay then. Magazines and books. You'll be amazed at how much hanging around departure areas there'll be, once we hit the mainland."

"When you said shopping, I was thinking more of Monsoon and Accessorize, Helen."

Like any woman on a mission, Helen was already making a beeline for the bookstore, undeterred by the swarms of fellow travellers in the aisles. She headed to the magazine section first.

"We'll make sure we buy different ones so we can swap," she said, looking intently at the endless array of titles in front of them. "Let's start with the quality reads: *Heat* and *National Enquirer*. Which ones do you want?" She remembered all too well that when she was a trainee she considered magazines a luxury buy.

"*American Vogue*." Sarah perked up.

"Good choice." Helen grabbed the magazine, putting it on top of her pile without batting an eyelid at the price.

"Hi, Helen!" Fred popped his head over her shoulder.

She quickly placed a copy of *National Geographic* over her choice of glossies, in a lame effort to conceal her true identity. "Fred, I thought you were in the lounge," she said, looking a little embarrassed.

"I'm on my way there now. You coming?" He looked from Helen to Sarah, and back again.

"Yep, I just want to pick up a book," said Helen. "I'll follow you in."

Fred eyed the library load in Helen's arms, looking amused. "Okay, I'll see you in there, but remember it's only a twelve-hour flight."

Two pink dots appeared on Helen's cheeks.

Sarah had watched the interaction between Helen and Fred. Was there a spark between them or was it something else? Maybe she'd misread Helen on the lesbian issue. In the four months Sarah had worked with her she'd only ever seen Helen blush when she was angry or hot.

"I need two books," Helen said to Sarah, now that Fred had left them.

She headed for the "just published" aisle, picking up a James Patterson paperback without much thought, before heading to the Mind Body Spirit shelves.

"Books aren't really my thing. Maybe I should have followed Fred," Sarah muttered, taking out her mobile. "Great, now she's in the sad fucks section!" she texted Debbie in Accounts.

"Did you say something, Sarah?" Helen asked.

"Eh, can I hold something for you while you're deciding?"

"You're a star, thanks." Helen offloaded the pile of magazines and the thriller, leaving her hands free to compare two books.

"Will you get to read all this stuff? Shouldn't we get going?"

"Of course I will. I have to satisfy both the devil and angel in me, you know. I love the serial killers – Patterson never fails to provide lots of murder – always a psychopath on the loose in his books. But now I need one Mind Body Spirit type book for the development of my higher self."

Sarah went back to texting: "Confirmed, boss is a nut-job. Her father was murdered yet she buys books about bloodthirsty sickos. Glad I've got my own room in HK."

"Mind you, I'm still waiting for some of the other books I've bought on the Law of Attraction to deliver Brad Pitt, the Lotto and a villa in Marbella, but I haven't given up hope yet." Helen turned her attention to the books in hand. "*Synchrodestiny – How to Manifest Your Life's Desires.*"

Sarah raised her eyes to heaven and continued to type into her phone.

"That's a great book," a man's voice interrupted Helen's reverie. She noticed his straw briefcase. "You've read it then?" She looked up at him. It was the man who had been at the check-in desk earlier. His face looked softer now, less lemon-sucking and more peachy. She was pleasantly surprised to find a businessman revealing his interest in New Age philosophy. With his coal-black hair and unusual eyes, she had to admit he was somewhat attractive, in a shy sort of way.

Sarah noticed that Helen was blushing again. She'd seen Helen blush more this morning than she had during her whole time working for Eden. Maybe this Asian trip would be interesting, in more ways than lingerie.

"I have, and I've bought about six copies of it. I keep giving my own copy away." The man smiled as he picked up a book and turned to walk away.

"Easy gift then," Helen teased.

"Now she's attempting to flirt with some randomer – gross," Sarah continued to tap into her mobile.

"Enjoy it!" the man called back to her.

Helen decided to buy the book recommended by the elusive stranger and buy the one he had picked up as well – *Perfect Health* – both were by the same author. "*Perfect Health* – I could do with a bit of that," she said, feeling Sarah's impatience bore through her.

At the till, Helen looked around for the New Age guru again, but there was no sign of him – maybe he'd be in the business lounge? She handed over a fifty-pound note for her purchases and got little change. Looking down at the coppers and crumpled receipt, she declared, "Definitely cocktail time now!"

"Not a moment too soon." Sarah exhaled loudly.

7

In the Cathay lounge, Fred was stacking a plate high with food from the free buffet: smoked salmon, some kind of chicken on skewers, and prawns. He picked up bottle of Asian beer to wash it all down.

"Move over, Fred – the female Tom Cruise coming through!" Helen joined him at the self-service bar. "Two Bacardi cocktails, coming up!" She scanned the countertop for ingredients.

Fred stared as she poured a bizarre mix of fruit-juice and alcohol.

"What?" she asked. "This is part of Sarah's business training. I don't want to do a half-assed job." She swirled a swizzle-stick in the drinks.

Sarah sank back into a soft cream-leather armchair. She spread her fingers over the buttery leather, and checked out the room around her. Neither Helen nor Fred appeared to notice the plush surrounds. They were carrying on as if they were in the office, back in North Row. She, however, was internally hugging herself. Sarah Ross had arrived. She belonged in this world of Rolex watches and Chanel suits. These were her people.

Helen was walking slowly back to Sarah, looking like precision was of utmost importance, lest she spill a drop of alcohol.

"Get that into you!" She handed Sarah the concoction, at the

38

same time moving her elbow away from her torso to release a packet of crisps she had tucked away there. "How's that for multitasking?"

"Lovely in here, isn't it?" Sarah said, taking a sip of her drink.

"It's grand. We used to fly first-class. Damn cutbacks."

"What's the difference between business and first-class?"

"Well, in first-class you get your own masseuse, Kristal champagne and Egyptian cotton pyjamas on boarding, for a start." Helen sighed as she looked into her glass. "That was pre cheap Chinese-imported lingerie competition. I think the only people in the first-class lounge now are rock stars – and bankers of course." She picked a cashew nut from a bowl on the coffee-table. "And probably big computer-company executives. And definitely Saudi oil tycoons." Satisfied she'd covered the correct industries, she took a mouthful of her cocktail. "Wow, I may have been a little heavy-handed with Uncle Ron!" she exclaimed, making a contorted face, her eyes watering.

"Uncle Ron?" Sarah asked.

Fred, who had been making room on the small table for his food, cast his eyes to heaven. "She's talking about Ron Bacardi. Don't worry, you'll get used to her cryptic use of the English language – in about ten years, that is." He sat down and started flicking through the daily papers. "What books did you get, Helen?" he asked.

Helen tore open a packet of crisps, threw some salted peanuts on top, then shook the bag to mix everything together. She glanced around to see if the charcoal-suited man was there, aware that what she was doing wasn't exactly sophisticated. He was nowhere to be seen. The good-looking, emotionally-aware man had vanished. Proving she had been right all along – such a species only exists in fairytales.

She took the books out of the plastic shopping bag, and handed the serial-killer title to Fred, guessing that it would appeal to him more than the Mind Body Spirit ones.

"I meant to pick that one up. Mind if I borrow it?" Fred asked, discarding his newspaper.

"Sure," Helen sighed.

"That's a bit of a joke, isn't it?" Fred said.

"What?"

"You reading a book called *Perfect Health* while eating crisps and downing rum!" He broke into a hearty laugh.

Sarah couldn't help but laugh at the paradox.

"Well, I have to read it first, to see what the principles are."

"I could be wrong, but I doubt there'll be a section advocating the 'alcohol and fried-food diet'!" Fred popped another battered prawn into his mouth.

Helen took out some of her magazines and put them over the books, in an attempt to shut Fred up. Unfortunately, she hadn't realised a food magazine was top of the pile.

"I wouldn't have put you down as a cook, Helen," Sarah said as she turned the food magazine towards her.

"I like cooking!" Helen was starting to feel Sarah and Fred were ganging up on her. "Besides, Gordon Ramsay is on the cover – he's a sex-god."

Sarah and Fred looked at each other, to make sure they had heard her correctly.

"His face is a Scottish Highlands roadmap! Am I right, Sarah?"

Sarah pretended to be preoccupied with her phone.

"His face adds to his character. Plus he's got this smouldering fire inside him, never mind his body." Helen looked at Fred's gut. "Kept me awake for hours the first time I saw him take his kit off on TV." She downed the last of her drink as the lounge staff announced that their flight was boarding.

"He does have a good body," Sarah conceded.

"And he can cook and he's straight. This feature-length article on him is all I need to guarantee sweet dreams, all the way to Hong Kong. Who needs *Playgirl* when you've got Mr Ramsay?"

Sarah laughed but Fred didn't look so happy. He forcefully pushed Helen's book into his briefcase. As Helen bent down to pack up her things, her silky blouse fell away from her body exposing the top of her breast and a glimpse of red lace. Fred's eyes popped.

40

"This is so exciting!" Sarah exclaimed.

"Exciting it is, Sarah. Exciting it is indeed," Fred said, adjusting his trousers before he stood. He followed his staff as they walked to their plane.

Hong Kong bound.

8

The Eden team silently climbed into the back of a black limo, feeling a little worse for wear. Hong Kong airport is probably one of the best in the world: clean, efficient, running with clockwork precision. Unfortunately, though, reality hits once passengers leave the air-conditioned terminal building and are hit with a blast of tropical air and sunlight, a combination that serves to heighten the pain caused by too many cocktails served at 33,000 feet.

Helen reasoned it was the altitude rather than the free-pouring measures that made those few drinks so potent. She made sure she had her trusty shades at the ready once more, with the dual purpose of easing the pain of the early-morning sunlight and covering her bloodshot eyes.

Sarah wasn't in the mood for talking. She took the window seat in the car so she could grab her first glimpse of the city. The car felt as though it was gliding silently along the motorway. The heavy doors muffled any outside sounds and darkened glass prevented unwanted eyes from looking in.

They drove across a tall suspension bridge and the majestic volcanic peaks of Hong Kong Island came into view. Sarah's pulse quickened. It was as though she had stepped through the back of an old wooden wardrobe, and was seeing Narnia for the first time. Hundreds of boats of all sizes were in the water below them. It looked as though they might collide, as each one was travelling in a different direction, determinedly focused on its destination. However, it was an orderly chaos and they glided past each other effortlessly.

Sarah spied a freighter ship weighed down with steel containers. It occurred to her that one of them might hold stock bound for Eden stores. She did a mental calculation. It took twelve weeks for goods to arrive in the UK by sea. Then another three weeks to clear customs and for road distribution to the Eden central depot. Sarah counted the weeks off on her fingers but couldn't remember if she was on her third or fourth hand-count. Once in the depot, goods were picked and packed: the ratio of small sizes was higher for the city-centre stores, with provincial towns requiring a greater amount of larger sizes – the bums getting bigger the further away from a city they were. Only then were the garments delivered to the individual stores. So ships leaving Asia now, in September, were carrying next spring's stock.

She sat back into the seat. The designs on board those ships weren't hers. But next year, the ships sailing away from Hong Kong Island would be carrying Sarah Ross's creations.

She glanced at Helen, who was dozing, her head leaning towards Fred's shoulder. Fred didn't appear to notice: he was absently staring out of his darkened window while talking into his BlackBerry.

"Yes, Mr Lee, we'll be with you within the hour. We're just going to drop our bags at the hotel, then hop on the MTR over to your office."

Sarah didn't know what an MTR was, but she guessed it wasn't a limo, to which she was getting rather accustomed.

Fred pocketed his phone and shifted slightly, so that Helen's head was now resting in the hollow of his shoulder rather than on the bony bit. Though there wasn't much that was bony about Fred, not that the eye could see anyway.

The limo arrived at the Excelsior Hotel, in Causeway Bay. Three red-uniformed doormen approached the car before it stopped. Two of them pulled an oversized brass suitcase trolley towards the car.

The other doorman's white-gloved hand opened the passenger door.

"Welcome to the Excelsior," he said, tipping his peaked, gold-braided cap.

Stepping out of the air-conditioned car was like going from a plunge pool into a sauna. Two more doormen pulled open heavy glass doors in unison, ensuring their arriving guests didn't break stride as they entered the hotel's opulent lobby.

At reception a dark-suited woman approached them. "Welcome back to the Excelsior, Ms Devine. I'm Ms Lynn, your hospitality manager. As a sign of our appreciation for your continued patronage of our hotel, we have upgraded you, and your colleagues, to executive rooms with a harbour view. May I escort you there?"

Helen walked with her personal escort, looking every bit a VIP, despite the long-haul plane ride.

Sarah noticed, apart from being immaculately dressed, the guest-relations woman had the shiniest dead-straight, bob-cut. The Asian's hair obviously didn't suffer from the humidity problem.

Exiting the lift on the thirty-first floor, they agreed to meet back in the lobby in twenty minutes and went their separate ways.

Helen being the hotel's most regular guest from the Eden team, Ms Lynn accompanied her to her room.

"Breakfast is being served in the executive lounge," she said as they walked. "Would you like me to take you there first?"

"No, thanks. I have to get to a meeting on the Kowloon side."

"That is a pity. But cocktails and canapés are served there every evening so perhaps you will have time to enjoy it later." She inserted the key card to open the door. "Everything in the lounge is complimentary to guests of the executive floors of course."

The door opened to reveal a floor-to-ceiling window overlooking Victoria Harbour and the Kowloon Peninsula. Although Helen had seen the view many times, she still felt a tingle of excitement on the first glimpse.

"The New York of Asia," she said. "It never fails to take my breath away."

Ms Lynn nodded. Smiling, she gave Helen her business card,

with the customary two hands, and left the room, aware of the fine line between customer service and intrusion.

Helen stood and watched the activity on the harbour. She didn't sit on the couch that fitted snugly into the window embrasure for she knew she'd find it too hard to get up again. Instead, she did her usual routine of investigating the bathroom and the freebie toiletries.

Hanging on the door of the large marble bathroom was a long fluffy white bathrobe, *Excelsior Mandarin Oriental Hotel* embroidered in gold lurex thread on the breast pocket. Matching slippers would be left for her use in the evening during turn-down service. Helen was twisting open the shower gel, to have a sniff, when there was a gentle tap on the door. It was the bellboy with her suitcase.

Within seconds of the bellboy leaving, there was another knock.

"Bloody hell, can't I sniff in peace!" Helen mumbled.

She peered through the door's peephole. A waiter wearing a mustard-coloured uniform stood outside with an oversized basket of goodies.

"Guest relations!" the man called out.

Sure there had been a mistake, Helen opened the door slightly, leaving the key chain on. The scene reminded her of *Kill Bill*, where a gun-toting, guest-relations officer tries to blow away Uma Thurman. Helen had a healthy suspicion of unexpected visitors.

"Compliments of the hotel management, Ms Devine." He proffered the wicker hamper, containing an array of exotic fruit, wine and chocolate.

Helen opened the door to accept the gift. "And not a gun in sight! Thank you, I do love Hong Kong!"

When Helen got to the lobby twenty minutes later, it was awash with people: a mix of businessmen, airline staff and tourists. She spotted Fred and Sarah standing at a side door. A tall, burly man in a dark suit stood at the exit. He had an ear-piece nestled in his ear, which he touched every so often, in a secret-service manner. He watched everyone entering and leaving the building. His counterpart stood overseeing things from the mezzanine balcony.

"Why is there so much security around the place?" Sarah asked as Helen joined them. "Hong Kong is safe, right?"

"Yes. There are the usual scam artists roaming about, but it's no worse than any other big city. How's your room?"

Sarah's face lit up. "Oh my God! I could just sit looking out that window all day!" she said, putting her hand to her chest.

"Wait until you see it tonight when all the lights are on!" said Helen. "They say the view from the Kowloon side is better but I think it's pretty amazing whatever way you look at it."

The street they were on was narrow. Everywhere were neon-lit signs, on and off, their blinking lost in broad daylight. The bleached-white faces of Chinese models looked down at them from massive billboards. Although Chinese writing was predominant, the English translation was clearly visible too. China might be the official ruler of the former English colony, but its Western influence was still very much alive.

There was an American coffee house a few steps from the hotel's side-entrance. Once stocked up on caffeine, the three made their way to Causeway Bay underground MTR station, just a few minutes' walk along the road. On seeing the queue for the ticket-desk, Fred valiantly undertook to use the automated ticket-vendor. The station was thronged with office commuters. Sarah grasped her handbag tightly.

"The MTR is great," Helen said to her, noticing her discomfort with the crowds. "It's much the quickest way to get to Kowloon. It's trade week, the world's rag trade is in town. Don't be surprised if you start to see the same faces on the train, at the convention centre and in the bars."

"Will it take long?" Sarah asked.

"Only about ten minutes. We go two stops, change train at Admiralty. After that, it's just one stop to Tsim Sha Tsui."

"You sound like a local!"

"Just think 'Tim Sow Choy' – say it very fast and elongate the 'oy' at the end and you'll sound local too!"

Fred swayed back to them holding three small cardboard tickets. "I just got one-way tickets. I thought we'd get the Star Ferry back, since Sarah hasn't been here before."

"Ah, Fred, you big softie! Maybe you're not just Excel spreadsheets and profit margins after all." Helen affectionately patted his cheek, which caused Fred to blush.

The train was as advertised: efficient, ultra-clean and swift. As with most public transport the world over, despite getting up close and personal with fellow-commuters, no one smiled or made eye contact. Some people wore white surgical face-masks. Sarah spotted more than one Louis Vuitton handbag adorning the shoulders of elegant women, who also wore flat shoes.

At street level, Tsim Sha Tsui was an assault on the senses. Street hawkers descended on them, pushing cardboard pictures of jewellery, handbags and fake designer watches.

"Louis Vuitton, Prada, Rolex, DVD!" they shouted, with mantra rhythm.

Sensing Sarah to be an easy target, a skinny man sporting a thin moustache took hold of her elbow and steered her towards his den off the Nathan Road.

"No! Not interested," Helen interjected, regaining control of a terrified Sarah. "Don't look them in the eye, Sarah – you can't give them an opening at all."

Helen walked through the dealers, a mythical ghost through a wall.

"I don't like Kowloon," Sarah said, quivering.

The friendly smiles of the Excelsior were certainly not evident here. There was a bad odour and Sarah thought this side of Hong Kong looked a lot better from her hotel room.

"Stay close to me!" Helen shouted above the traffic and throngs of people.

"We'll take the next right!" Fred yelled. "The Chinatex office is only a couple of minutes' walk. The touts won't follow us once we leave Nathan Road!"

They turned onto Haiphong Road, leaving the chaos behind them.

In the Chinatex office, a long line of introductions began, with a lot of smiling, bowing and handshaking.

"You like some Chinese tea?" the office manager, Ms Barbara, asked.

"Yes, lovely, thank you." Helen was setting up her laptop at the boardroom table. "May I connect to your broadband, please?" she asked, twirling a connection cable in her hand. A rush of Chinatex people came to help. Within seconds she was on-line and the refreshments were on the table. Despite the elaborate introductions and mandatory small talk, less than five minutes had passed and now it was down to business.

"So, Ms Helen, Mr Fred, may we see the designs you want us to make for you?" Ms Candy, a junior executive, asked.

Although both Helen and Sarah tried not to stare, it was very hard not to. The Asian woman, true to her chosen Western name, Candy, looked like a painted doll – a plump one. Her face was plastered white, which was further set in pallid powder. Her small rosebud lips were coloured ruby red. But it was her cheekbones that held the most intrigue. It appeared she had stuck her forefinger into a pot of pink jelly and drawn two swirling circles on the apples of her cheeks. The whole look was topped off with straight orange-coloured hair – the result of a home-bleaching job.

"As you've probably guessed," Ms Candy smiled shyly, "I am responsible for the design development in Chinatex."

Helen resisted the urge to look at her colleagues. "Your artistic flare is evident, Ms Candy," she smiled.

"I think we should go through the current ranges first, the goods that are due for shipment this week," Fred said, his mouth full of blueberry muffin, which had arrived courtesy of the male office skivvy. Fred watched as the man was ordered around by his female bosses. "The world is getting very topsy-turvy," he said as he munched.

"Of course, yes, we have production samples here from the factory," Ms Barbara said, assuming Fred was referring to the order of business. "The first garments from the production line." She barked an order in Chinese to her assistants.

Helen threw Fred a look that would make hell freeze over, which he happily ignored.

Ms Candy produced a handful of baby-doll samples.

How apt.

"Ah, yes, here we have 'The Perfect Pussy Collection'." Ms Candy smiled broadly at them. Her teeth appeared yellow in contrast to the white powdered face.

Helen went pale.

Sarah turned a bright shade of crimson.

Fred began to choke.

"You mean 'The Glamour Puss Collection', don't you, Ms Candy?" Helen tried to keep the panic out of her voice, desperately reaching for the swing tag attached to the little satin pink-and-black number that would soon be Eden stock.

Sarah got to it before her. "It's okay, Helen. The graphics are correct." She held up the swing tag, showing the silver-embossed Siamese twin kittens, with S-shaped backs and almond-shaped eyes, complete with false eyelashes.

The tension eased until Helen flipped over the lacquered tag. Sure enough in beautiful, shiny, French Script font shone the words: *"The Perfect Pussy."*

Helen's horror was palpable.

The two Hong Kong women rummaged through paperwork, as if it somehow held the magical, get-out-of-jail card. They reverted to speaking Chinese, which now held a tone of panic.

"You request the change, Ms Helen," Ms Barbara finally said, waving a printout of an email.

"May I see that, please?" Helen took the piece of paper from her and tried to remain calm.

Fred took his turn at doling out the dirty looks.

Sure enough, there it was. An email, bearing the name Helen Devine, directing that the "Glamour Puss Collection" she had worked on, solidly, for two months, be now renamed "The Perfect Pussy Collection". It had been sent at 23:33 hours and the date indicated it had been a Saturday. This could only mean one thing – Rob Lawless – Helen's not-quite-ex lover.

"Helen?" Fred now reclaimed his position as boss.

All eyes were on her.

"Have the tags gone into print?" Helen asked with a calmness she didn't feel.

"Yes," the two Asian women replied in unison.

Sweet Jesus.

"All of them?"

"Yes, Ms Helen – all thirty thousand of them." Ms Candy wasn't enjoying being the bearer of bad news.

"Phone the factory immediately – tell them not to tag a single garment. How quickly can we get them reprinted?" Helen sat back down to steady herself. She had a lump in her throat and it was all she could do to keep her voice from shaking. She twisted the ring on her little finger.

Bloody Rob and his idea of a joke.

"We can get it done quickly, but it cost you extra for speedy turnaround," Ms. Barbara said. "And you pay for labour. Factory will charge for removal of tags already ticketed."

"But nothing should be ticketed," Fred weighed in. "These are supposed to be the shipping samples – first off the line for our approval *before bulk production* begins."

The Chinatex women were talking furiously. Their voices were raised.

"And can you show me the fax approving the artwork for the label, please?" Helen added, regaining her composure a little. Whatever about Rob's idea of a wine-fuelled joke, she knew the mistake should have been caught at the approval stage. Emails weren't legally binding – faxes were.

Ms Candy and Ms Barbara made a vain attempt to look for the authorisation with Helen Devine's signature and the Eden company stamp, giving them the green light for production. Everyone knew they would not find it.

"We don't appear to have the signing-off fax," Ms Barbara eventually conceded.

"That's because you proceeded with production without waiting for approval – yet again." Helen had found her bargaining chip.

"Why are the sequins melted?" Sarah held up the little baby-doll garment, adding another drama to the pot.

"That's how your original sample was received," Ms Candy said.

"Those samples are hand-made in our sample room in London – you know they are only a representation!" Helen said. "Obviously, an error by a solo machinist using too hot a hand-iron isn't to be reproduced in bulk!" She rubbed her temples.

China might be ready and willing to take the rag trade from Europe, but they still had a lot to learn.

"Factory follow sample!" Ms Barbara snapped.

"Factory no think. That why we pay you commission – *to think*!" Helen wasn't sure why she was speaking in broken English.

After an hour of haggling, agreement was reached. The Chinatex factory would replace the melted sequins with regular ones, at no cost to Eden. The Austin-Powers-inspired pussy tags would also be replaced within forty-eight hours, the two companies splitting the costs.

Ms Barbara wasn't happy. She would have gladly stayed at the negotiation table until midnight arguing over two cents. She banged files down on the table. Helen knew she would try to recoup some of her lost American dollars on the quotation she'd give for the new designs they were now starting on. It was going to be a long day and she still had to face Fred's dressing-down later. At least he hadn't belittled her in front of Sarah and the suppliers, but she didn't doubt there would be a price to pay.

9

A few streets away, yet another bewildered tourist exited Tsim Sha Tsui station – but Jack Taylor was heading in the opposite direction to Haiphong Road, towards Salisbury Road. He had picked up a city map, which he held in one hand. In the other hand was a piece of paper with his uncle's address. The New World Building, Salisbury Road, was to be his stop-over home for the next few days. He turned the map around a few times to be sure he was heading in the right direction because there were so many possible exits out of the MTR station. He took exit J, as per the instructions on his uncle's email printout, politely but firmly saying "No, thank you" to the onslaught of sellers outside.

In less than five minutes he was standing in the affluent marble lobby of the harbour-facing Renaissance Hotel, which was incorporated inside the New World Building. Jack shifted his backpack awkwardly on his shoulder – he was feeling scruffy against the backdrop of his surroundings. Checking the next lot of instructions, he found his way to the residential lobby, away from the main hotel. It was an oasis of calm after the noise of the street. The floor was high-shine granite, the long corridor adorned with rows of stone and wood wall-hangings, which stood like soldiers in line. Thinking he was alone, Jack stopped to admire the artwork and scratch his two-day-old chin-stubble. Out of the corner of his eye he noticed a uniformed man behind a small desk. The guard didn't speak but he didn't take his eyes off Jack. He stared as though Jack was scratching his balls instead of his chin.

"I'm looking for Apartment 3306."

"Name?"

"Jack Taylor, my –"

"You Mr Tom nephew. Welcome. Yes, he told me to expect you. Please, this way." He smiled, ushering Jack to an elevator, its wood-panelled façade blending with the walls. "When door open, you see small flight of stairs to right, go up steps, then left, to Mr Tom's apartment. Enjoy your stay, Mr Jack." With that the man pushed a button on the elevator control, without stepping in himself.

When the elevator arrived at the thirty-first floor, Jack tried to remember if he was to turn left or right. His brain was travel-weary. He walked along a dimly lit hallway – plush carpet muffling the sound of his footsteps. Eventually he found the right walnut-coloured door.

A petite Asian woman in a black-and-white maid's outfit opened the door. Until then, Jack had thought people dressed liked that only in movies or strip clubs.

She spoke in her mother tongue, having no English. She showed Jack around the small apartment. Because he spoke no Chinese, to save them both stress Jack nodded profusely, indicating that he'd be okay.

The housekeeper closed the door behind her with a quiet click – a sound Jack exalted in. At last he was alone. He plopped down on the pebble-coloured sofa and looked around the apartment. The furnishings were bland and functional, reminiscent of hotel rooms around the world – magnolia and yet more magnolia. It didn't matter, because from the oversized living-room window was a stunning view of Victoria Harbour and Hong Kong Island. Jack was awestruck – the sight brought renewed energy as he tried to identify the buildings. His thoughts were interrupted by the shrilling of a telephone.

"Jack, it's Tom!" his uncle's voice bellowed out into the room from the answering machine. "Stop screwing the hired help and pick up the phone!"

"Hi, Tom, how are you doing?"

"Ah, Jack, you made it, great! So are you settling in alright?"

"Great, Tom, thanks. Some place you've got here! I'm glad I took you up on your offer. I had booked a hostel near the fish market."

"Wouldn't hear of it. You're family. What do you think of the view?"

"Awesome."

"Isn't it? My work colleagues live on the Island, for prestige, but the view of the Island from the Kowloon side is unbeatable. *And* I don't have to face that God-damn sardine-tin MTR commute every day."

"You work close by then?"

"Just a five-minute cab ride. The company covers that and the apartment too of course. Speaking of which, I'd better get back to the grindstone so I can duck out early. I should get home by seven. You up for a few beers and some food about eight thirty?"

"Sounds good. I can hook up with you somewhere if you like?"

"No, I'll come home, get changed. There's something I want you to see anyway. Any plans for today?"

"I thought I'd lie down for a few hours, and then wander up Nathan Road. I've read up on some of the sights. I'd like to see the goldfish market."

"Okay, there's beer in the fridge. I told Ella to leave a key for you on the kitchen counter – did you get it?"

"Eh, let me look – yup, I have it. Is Ella the girl in the maid's costume?"

"That's her, lovely girl – no English but she gives a great service. She comes as part of the package too."

"That's a hell of a package, Uncle Tom."

"Less of the 'uncle' bit, if you don't mind. We'll eat in one of the harbour-front restaurants downstairs tonight, then head over to Wan Chai or Lan Kwai Fong, on the Island, if that's okay with you?" Tom's mobile buzzed in the background.

"Sounds good," Jack replied, but Tom had already taken the other call.

Feeling hungry, Jack examined the contents of the small refrigerator. It contained a bottle of Veuve Clicquot, two bottles of Sancerre, six beers, mayonnaise, and half a lemon with greyish fur sprouting from it. He opened a bottle of beer and took a slow swig.

He remembered how he used to look up to his uncle. So much so, in fact, that he'd become an architect, just like him. Looking around him now, he reckoned Tom hadn't changed much since they last met over ten years ago when Jack was still in Princeton. A cabin-sized travel case stood beside the door of his bedroom, as if on stand-by. Tom must be mid-fifties now and nothing had changed. No ties anywhere. There were no photos of a wife and kids. Not even a goldfish. Perhaps he would buy him one at the market later.

Jack sat on the bed. He put the bottle of cold beer on the bedside locker, leaving a watery ring on the polished surface. He pulled off his trainers and lay on the bedspread without pulling back the covers.

Soon he was drifting into a jetlagged sleep.

As he dozed off, a distant memory of his mother came to him. "Be careful what you wish for, Jack – you might just get it," she'd say, in a mother-knows-best tone. It occurred to him she was right – he had morphed into the uncle he admired so much – a rolling stone gathering no moss.

10

Helen took a sip from her sixth coffee of the day. The cream in it formed a greasy film around the cup, the liquid was stone cold. She was struggling to concentrate and silently willed Fred to call time on their meeting. And then finally, as if by telepathy, he spoke.

"Let's wrap things up and let you lovely ladies get home," he said to the Hong Kong women.

"No need, Mr Fred. I no married – I often stay in office until ten or eleven at night," Ms Candy said, her face now resembling a white-washed wall, from numerous reapplications throughout the day.

That explains it, Helen thought: no matter what time of the day she sent an email or fax she nearly always got a reply within the hour. No wonder the Chinese were set to be the next superpower.

Fred, whose eyes were now red-rimmed, ignored the comment, and looked at Helen, pleading for back-up.

"Yes, I think we're done," she said, looking at her watch. "Six thirty. That's over nine straight hours. Well done, everyone – a good day's toil." She began to gather her papers.

"You hungry – we order in more food for you?" Ms Candy offered hospitably, but her glance towards Helen's sketches gave her real motivation away.

The Eden team still had orders to place and the Chinese women knew it.

Helen glanced down at the file, before looking over at Fred. She felt they had placed enough business with Chinatex and would prefer that the remaining designs be negotiated with the other companies they planned to visit in Mainland China. But Fred was in charge of the budget.

"Give us a moment, would you, ladies?" Fred asked.

"Of course. More coffee, Ms Helen, Ms Sarah?"

"Thank you, no," Helen replied, on behalf of everyone.

Sarah was pale and looked as if she was losing the will to live.

Once they were alone, Helen asked, "You okay, Sarah?"

"Fine. Just my blood sugar feels a little erratic."

"Don't worry – the meetings won't all be like this. There will be days we'll even get lunch." She turned to Fred. "Fred, I think we've consigned enough here. I've given them styles we know they can produce well. Unless you want to try them out on something they haven't done for us before?"

"Such as?"

Helen's heart sank – at this rate they'd be there until midnight. She didn't look up, in case Fred saw her annoyance.

"Well, we still have the bras, but I don't see that as an option here. Maybe they could try the cotton ranges I'd saved for the factories in Qingdao."

"But, Helen, I thought you said each factory has a specialty?" Sarah said.

"They do. Generally, if a factory is good at producing satin, they'll make a mess of, say, cotton or stretch fabrics. Specialising in one fabric or product helps their machinists work faster. The machines don't need adjusting or the needles changed for the different fabric types."

"In other words, productivity goes up, they make more money," Fred added. "I was thinking I might squeeze some extra discount if we kept going. But sounds like we'll be buying headaches further down the assembly line." He totted up figures of the negotiated prices on his notepad. "That's settled then." He considered his calculation. "Besides, it's all on LC with Chinatex," he said, twisting the top of his pen closed.

Sarah appeared confused, unsure if that meant they were staying or leaving.

"LC – Letter of Credit," Helen explained. "We have to pay for the goods up front in US Dollars. It's costly to finance. European companies usually give you thirty days' credit, which technically means that some of the goods are actually sold at retail before we have to pay the supplier. It keeps the accountants happy."

Sarah didn't care about LCs. The bloody shops would be closed at this stage.

Fred stood up. "Sarah, be a sweetheart and get the ladies back. They can make their usual pretend offer of inviting us to dinner. We'll assure them that we're fine. Then, we can get a bloody drink that isn't from an American Coffee franchise."

But Ms Candy and Ms Barbara had already spotted Fred getting to his feet through the glass wall of the office. Ms Barbara pushed open the door.

"You leaving already?" she said with feigned surprise.

"Yes, Barbara. We have to meet some friends," said Fred, but didn't add that his friends, Jack and Daniels, were poured at hotel bars worldwide.

"Such a pity. We wanted you be our guests at dinner this evening. Perhaps next time?"

"Ms Helen?" Ms Candy reached out with both hands to her. "You leave the sketches, so I can price them for you?"

Helen closed her leather messenger. She felt like a rugby centre, dodging the opposition with the try line in sight. With a disarming smile she extended her arm to shake hands. "Thank you, Ms Candy, Ms Barbara. We got through so much today. We appreciate all you did for us."

The meeting was over, Helen Devine style.

11

Fred and Helen made the executive floor of the Excelsior Hotel before the end of cocktail hour. Sarah had excused herself an hour before, saying she needed to freshen up. By now, Helen was finishing off her second cocktail – a Singapore Sling.

"Enjoying that?" Fred asked as he swirled the ice in his Jack & Coke.

"When in Rome and all that," Helen replied. She eyed the hors d'oeuvres and decided on a red-caviar-sprinkled prawn.

"We're in Hong Kong."

"Yeah, well, it's close enough." Helen popped the bite-size snack in her mouth. "You know, I named my Golden Retriever after that." She pointed to Fred's drink.

"What – Hugo Boss?" Fred placed a hand on his stomach and flattened his shirt, to reveal a monogrammed buckle.

"I meant Jack Daniels. I used to drink it in my youth before I moved on to Bacardi and Diet Coke. I figured JD sounded more like a dog's name than Bacardi. Nowadays, I try to stick to vodka and soda. It's pure, so it must be better for my body." She ignored the look Fred was giving her. "Anyway, I couldn't see your flashy belt under your belly."

"Cheeky. At least get the term right, Helen – it's a beer gut – only women have bellies." He looked at Helen, her mouth open ready to receive another nibble.

In a reflex action, Helen pulled in her stomach but, before she could retort, her phone vibrated on the low table between them.

"That'll be my mother, with a crime and weather update." She rubbed her hands together, ridding them of crumbs. She picked up the phone.

"Hello, Helen?"

"Hi, Mum, how's things?" Helen stood to go to a quiet corner in the room. Fred inspected her plate to see what he could pinch.

"Fine, love – I'm just ringing to let you know not to phone later because I'm going to the pictures with Nuala Flynn," Mary Devine said, as always calling her friend by her full name.

"That's grand, Mum, enjoy it – what are you going to see?" Her mother liked to have a reason to call rather than admit she wanted to talk to her only daughter.

"I can't think of the name of it now. Nuala Flynn picked it out – ordered the tickets over the internet. How's the weather there?"

Here we go.

"Well, it's night-time now but it was cloudy and humid earlier."

"Well, it's a beautiful day here, blue skies, but there's rain due tomorrow." Mary Devine hesitated before continuing. "Did you see the news: a tourist was raped, tortured and strangled – over there?"

Helen wondered how on earth her mother did it. No matter where in the world Helen travelled, Mary had a local horror to tell.

"No, Mum."

"I read it in the paper – shocking business," Mary went on. "I bet the Chinese are covering it up. Didn't you tell me they black out the telly when there's an American news report they don't like?"

"That was a CNN report on the anniversary of the Tiananmen Square protests – and I was in Beijing at the time. That's different." Helen tried to remain patient. She spotted Sarah enter the room, as did most of the men. She was wearing a low-cut red-silk dress and skyscraper black-patent heels.

"Just be careful, Helen. Keep your wits about you and don't get into a taxi on your own."

Watch yourself crossing the road and wear clean underwear in case of an accident.

"I've something important to tell you, love. Not over the phone though. Will you be home this weekend?"

"Yes. Is everything okay with you, Mum. Did you check your bloods today?"

"Yes, I'm fit as a fiddle. We'll talk when you get back."

"Sounds ominous. By the way, if it's okay, Poppy and Lily will call in this weekend. I think Poppy could do with a little Devine TLC." Helen could feel her mother's spirits lift, even from halfway across the world.

"All right, love, I'll get some groceries in. Lily's a grand girl, but she has a healthy appetite. I'd better get going myself. I've a lot to do, what with the pictures tonight, and now the supermarket in the morning, as well."

Helen knew Mary was already running through the mental shopping list for drop-in visitors.

"Got to go, Mum. The others are waiting on me. Love you."

Helen rejoined Fred and Sarah.

"You look great, Sarah," she said.

Sarah simply said, "Cheers." She was more interested in the potential suitors in the business lounge than making small talk with her over-the-hill bosses. Although for the life of her she couldn't figure out how neither of them were killed with jetlag. At their age you'd imagine they'd be curled up in bed by now. Although Helen was definitely full of surprises. Having seen her flirting in the bookshop, she'd realised Helen was straight and probably just an uptight spinster in need of a lay.

"So, Fred, where to – Long Cock?" Helen asked.

See, as usual I'm right, Sarah thought.

"The table is booked for seven forty-five." He pulled back his shirt cuff. "Which means we should be there now." He drained the last of his drink, just as the waiter arrived with Sarah's order. "And Helen – let me talk to the taxi driver."

"Why?"

"Because, I know when you say Long Cock, you mean Lan Kwai Fong, but lord only knows where we'll end up if you give the instructions."

Fred guided his design team to the exit.

12

Jack was woken by Tom's arrival home. He tried to focus. He'd moved around so much recently he often woke disorientated. The glow of the digital clock beside the bed blinked 19:46.

"Jack?" Tom gave a soft knock on the bedroom door before popping his head in.

Ah . . . Hong Kong.

"Yeah, Tom – hi." Jack propped himself up on his elbow. "I must have dozed off."

"No fish market I take it. Just as well – it's a smelly old place anyway. Good to see you, boy." His smile was as broad as his hug.

Despite living thousands of miles away from any blood relative, Tom loved it when one of them stopped by his town, assuming they didn't stay too long, that is.

The hug was followed by a slightly awkward pat on the back.

"Christ, Jack, you look more like your old man each time I see you. How is my big brother anyway?"

"Good, as far as I know – I haven't been home for a while."

"Dubai kept you busy, hey! Come on, let's have a drink and you can tell me what the women wear under those burkas."

Jack followed him into the living room.

"I wouldn't know. My life for the past nine months has been pretty much work and sleep, with a lot more work than sleep. This place really is amazing." Jack was looking out of the large window again. Hong Kong Harbour looked even more impressive under a night sky.

Tom checked his watch. "Remember I told you I wanted to show you something? You'll see it in precisely four minutes. Bourbon?"

Jack wasn't a bourbon drinker. Tom was quick to pick up on the moment's hesitation.

"Champagne then – a better choice." He set about popping the cork.

"Don't open a bottle just for me, Tom – a beer is fine."

"Nonsense, I love this stuff. It's not often I get to have it at home." The cork popped. Not a drop of the golden bubbles escaped.

"I reckon you share a lot more champagne than you're letting on, Tom."

"A gentleman never tells, Jack! Not until a few more drinks, at least. Here – a toast." Tom handed Jack a crystal flute.

"To family!" Jack said, raising his glass.

"To family!"

They each took a sip.

"And happy travels!" Tom saluted him, taking a larger mouthful this time.

"And new adventures!"

"May the road to your Eastern adventures be lined with more chicks than a Louisiana chicken farm!" Tom promptly drained his glass. "Top-up?"

Tom went to refill the glasses, leaving Jack staring out the window.

"Hey, Tom! Is this what you wanted to show me?"

"Something else, isn't it?"

Jack watched as the Hong Kong skyline came alive to a symphony of lights.

"Every night at eight, the beauty of Hong Kong lights up with the laser show. I've seen it countless times – and I'm still awestruck." Tom handed Jack a fresh glass of champagne and they watched as the stunning illumination, bursting with multicoloured beams, danced above and around the skyscrapers.

"A belly dancer in a harem, and we've got the best seat in the house," Tom said.

Jack wondered where Tom got his unusual analogies.

"Hong Kong really is the New York of Asia," Jack said, as the show climaxed to its celebration finale.

"Better than New York!" Tom emptied his glass again, with a quick gulp. Hiccupping, he said, "Okay, let's rock and roll! Time you experienced Hong Kong, not watched it. New York, get set for some ass-kissing!"

13

"Now, that's what I call soakage." Fred wiped his mouth with a napkin before throwing it on top of his plate. He took an appreciative sip of his full-bodied Bordeaux.

"Desserts anyone?" his host asked.

Fred had neglected to mention to Helen and Sarah that they had accepted an invitation to dinner from a French bra supplier, Liselle. They were now making small talk with four European ex-pats living in Hong Kong and working for the well-known French label, whose factories were in Mainland China. It had been a long day.

Eager to finish the dinner service, to allow the restaurant to make its transformation into a karaoke bar, a waiter removed the last of the dinner plates and replaced them with dessert menus. Fred, who had just finished a sixteen-ounce steak, was contemplating his next course.

"This looks like it could be a fun place later," Sarah said, disappointed at the dinner: an offering of burgers, chicken-wings and man-sized steaks.

The dark interior of the restaurant-cum-bar could have been anywhere in the world. The theme was The Beatles and 60's music. Everything from the menus to the placemats and even the plates, was fashioned to the image of 33-inch vinyl LPs.

"Check out the suits." Helen gave Sarah a subtle nudge on the hip. The two women were wedged together on a red-velour couch. She was referring to a group of businessmen, propped up on barstools close by. Two of the men were Western, two were Asian. They were joined by a couple of petite Chinese women in very short skirts.

Sarah shrugged and looked at Helen as if to say, so what?

"I'll put money the story goes like this. The Asian men are suppliers – the other two are their clients. The Asians generally don't drink too much. They'll have brought the clients to a nice restaurant earlier, where the Westerners will have polished off copious amounts of wine, while the suppliers sat and sipped politely on theirs." Helen paused for effect and then knocked back her own drink. She put her elbows on the table and supported her chin with one hand, leaving the other hand free to discreetly point, emphasising her detective work. "Note how the lads are knocking back beers and shooters while the suppliers are cradling one bottle of beer, creating the illusion that they too are drinking and partying." She looked at Sarah as if that proved everything.

Sarah tried to look without being noticed, which was easy enough, as a four-piece band were setting up within feet of their table.

"Is this another lesson in designer-drinking?"

"It's all about patterns, Sarah. Paper ones are just for office hours."

"But the girls appear to be knocking back a couple of shots too, so that kind of negates your theory – whatever it is," Sarah said.

"Looking at that pair – who can blame them?" Helen made a face, as if she had just whiffed a rotten egg. She would have to spell it out for Sarah. "It's simple. The Asian men just want to go home. For God's sake, look at yer man! His eyes are glazing over. And the other one just keeps nodding agreement. The girls are the entertainment – they're the suppliers' get-out-of-jail card!"

Sarah still wasn't sure what the revelation was.

Helen went for the jugular. "They're prostitutes, for heaven's sake – corporate entertainment for the clients!"

Sarah's face slowly registered what Helen was saying. "No way!"

A look of satisfaction glowed on Helen's face. "Yes, my girl:

dinner, drinks and hookers. Welcome to the world of corporate entertainment."

Sarah wrinkled her nose. "I think I prefer the biscotti and truffle-oil hampers the Italian suppliers send us."

Helen and Sarah looked to the bar, both pretending to be studying the array of bottles behind the bartender. Both businessmen wore pinstripe suits. The first one was small with a fine bone structure. He had thick-lens glasses, his hair was thin and receding. He talked incessantly, all his attention focused on the scantily clad girl sitting beside him. He was the cat that had got the cream. His colleague also had a girl in pole position.

The second man's suit was similar, but he had finished it off with a flamboyant silk tie. He was probably someone from the Inter Textile Trade Fair that was taking place, Helen reckoned. A stocky build made him appear as though he had once played rugby, before après match and family commitments replaced the playing fields. Fat replaced fitness.

By now, a few other ladies turning tricks had wandered into the bar. These women were more classily dressed and were harder to spot, except for the over-made-up faces and the way their eyes scanned the bar for potential clients.

"You two are as thick as thieves!" Fred interrupted Helen and Sarah's reverie. "Anyone for a drink?"

"Yes, please – I'll have a shot!" Sarah piped up.

"Off you go!" Fred gestured towards the bar. "Take your pick of that lot up there." He cocked his thumb towards the impressive selection of drinks that lined the mirrored wall of the bar.

Sarah wavered.

"Put it on the Liselle tab," Fred added.

This cheered up Sarah, who swiftly offered drinks for everyone at their table. There were no takers.

Embarrassed by Fred's behaviour, Helen smiled at the sales director of Liselle, whose credit card was held behind the bar. Mark, tall and broad as an ox, had a placid manner, which had earned him the nickname of the Gentle Giant. He moved into Sarah's place. It became a tight squeeze on the couch.

"Did you say something, Helen?" he asked, leaning his ear towards her in an effort to hear now that the band was belting out cover-tunes.

"No, I'm just laughing at Fred – he never changes."

"He prefers not to move the venue – here in Abbey Road we've got food, bar and music, without having to leave our chairs."

"Correction. Despite my best efforts I did have to move to make way for the band," Fred interjected. He pushed the belt of his trousers farther under his stomach, to allow for the swelling that was taking place from the waistline up.

Sarah tried to make up her mind which drink to pick. She stood beside the businessman with the brightly coloured tie who was chatting up his corporate hooker. The man held up a wallet – an accordion of clear plastic, containing family photos, fell from it.

"This one is my eldest daughter, Laura – she's nine – and that's my son, Charlie – he's six. Then there's the baby, Chloe – she's about twenty months now."

Maybe Helen had got it wrong, Sarah thought.

The Asian girl smiled politely and nodded.

"And that's my wife. Beautiful, isn't she?"

"You have lovely family," the girl dutifully replied.

"Yes, I do. But they're back in the UK and we, baby, are here!" He squeezed her thigh.

The girl took a quick glance at her watch. She'd been paid a flat rate to give him sex. The sooner he shut up and took his trousers off, the sooner she'd get home.

"What can I get you?" the bartender asked Sarah.

She was trying to give the businessman a filthy look but he had no eyes for her.

"A shot of sambuca and a vodka and Coke," she snapped.

"Any vodka in particular?"

"That goose one, whatever it's called – that's good, right?"

"It's expensive, but yeah – I guess."

"I'll have that one then. Make it a large one."

"Anything else?" the barman asked when he'd set down the drinks.

Sarah picked up the shot and knocked it back. "Yes, put it on the Liselle tab, please." She glared at the suit and said, quite loudly, "The world is a sad place. People like that – just out to get what they can." She picked up her drink and walked away.

The lead singer of the band announced a break. They would be back for a second set, after the karaoke.

"Would anyone like to start the karaoke with a little Queen?" he called out.

Unbeknownst to Helen, earlier Fred had had a word in the lead singer's ear. Helen was set to perform whether she wanted to or not.

"She's over here!" Fred shouted, pulling Helen's arm into the air.

"A big hand, everyone, for the beautiful Helen Devine, Britain's top lingerie designer!" the lead singer announced.

"Come on Helen, we're up!"

"Not on your life!" Helen struggled to stay seated. However, the announcement had piqued a lot of male interest and the wolf-whistles and applause gained momentum.

Mark took hold of Helen's other hand. "You don't have to, Helen."

But Fred wasn't letting go.

"Oh, what the hell! We're in Hong Kong. What goes on tour stays on tour, right?" she said, allowing Fred to drag her towards the dance floor.

"Here, take a sip." Mark handed her a drink as she left the safety of the couch. "You may need some Dutch courage."

Helen and Fred started a "Bohemian Rhapsody" duet. Back to back, mikes in hand, they chorused their way through the song, until it got to the guitar solo. Then it was time for air guitar and head-banging, despite Fred being follically challenged.

"I think I'm in love!" Sarah overheard a young British guy say as he watched Helen do her Freddie Mercury impression.

"I didn't think women like that existed in real life – and a lingerie designer!" his friend added, as they continued to drink and stare.

"Actually, I work with her," Sarah interrupted.

"Shut up! There's a *team* of lingerie women here?" the first guy asked.

"Yes, Helen and I are the top designers at Eden," Sarah said coolly.

"Eden, that's the shop with that Czech model, Krystal, in its windows?"

All attention was on Sarah now.

"Yes, that's us," she said. "What has you in Hong Kong, boys?"

"Hong Kong? I thought we were in heaven!"

The lads nudged each other, laughing.

"We're on holidays," the other said when he had managed to compose himself.

"Does that mean you get to meet the models?" his friend asked.

"Yes, and dress them for the photo-shoots."

The guys' eyes bulged.

"Come, sit. I'll tell you all about a day in the life of a lingerie designer."

Helen felt dizzy as she returned to the couch. She wasn't sure whether it was the effect of the alcohol or her impromptu performance.

"Who knew you'd make such a good Freddie, Helen!" Fred said, elbowing her over. He was out of breath – his shirt wet with sweat. He wiped his brow on a chocolate-stained napkin.

"Excuse me, Fred, before you get too comfortable, I need the ladies' room." Helen tried not to slur her words but she failed miserably.

Fred moved his legs to the side but didn't stand, so he got a face-full of Helen's bosom as she wedged passed him, stumbling slightly against him.

Free from the din of the music, Helen climbed the stairs to the loo. It was occupied. A sign indicated there were more facilities on the next floor. After jigging around for a moment, she made her way along the dimly lit corridor and up a narrow stairway.

She pushed open the door to the ladies' room. Someone inside forcibly slammed it shut again, catching Helen's hand with it.

"Ouch!" she cried out and grabbed her hand in pain. Her fingers throbbed. Stunned, reactions slowed by the booze, she stood staring at the door for a moment.

Yes – it definitely had the outline of a woman on it, complete with triangular skirt, but she had caught a glimpse of a man inside.

"Get off me!" Helen heard a woman's voice through the door, followed by what sounded like a scuffle.

The fog in Helen's head cleared. She banged her palm rapidly against the door. She thought of fetching security but didn't want to leave the woman either. She continued to pound. "Is everything alright in there?" The door wasn't locked but the man had his weight pressed against it. Helen forcibly pushed it with her shoulder. This caught him off guard and he stumbled, freeing the door.

"What the hell do you think you're doing!" she glared at the man. He was short, stubby and wore a brightly coloured tie. She recognised him as one of the men she'd been commenting on earlier. She turned her attention to the Asian woman. "Are you okay?"

Cheeks streaked with mascara stains, the woman said, "Yes . . . yes." She wiped her face with the back of her hand. "Please, I just want to get out of here."

Helen stood back to let her pass. The woman paused briefly, saying, "Thank you," then bolted.

The man held his hands up in surrender. "Hey, honest mistake! I thought she was my woman. They all look the same to me."

"You racist moron!" Helen shouted.

He sneered at Helen, looking her up and down. Nodding as if to say he knew her type. He made a point of craning his head forward to look at her bum. Then he laughed but his laughter held no mirth.

Ignoring him, Helen continued, "How dare you treat any woman like that?"

"Mind your own business – fat ass," he said, as he pushed past her and started to walk away.

"Short ass," Helen tutted as she turned back towards the ladies'.

Without warning, he swung around and lunged at her, knocking her against the doorframe. He pushed her inside and into a cubicle, pinning her shoulder to the wall, using his elbow as a hinge. With his forearm across her neck, he held her other shoulder back with his hand. His wedding ring caught a low beam of light.

Adrenaline coursed through Helen's veins.

"Let go of me," she said, her tone low and even. She held eye-contact. She didn't blink. Inside she felt like jelly but she couldn't let him smell her fear. She was taller than he was but he was strong and her body wasn't propelled by the hatred levels his was high on.

He bared his teeth – his breath smelt of stale whiskey and cigarettes.

"I'll have you hauled off by the Hong Kong cops. Explain that to your office – your wife," Helen continued, holding his stare.

Something flickered in his eyes. A moment of clarity perhaps? He loosened his grip. "I wouldn't touch a fat-ass like you anyway!" he spat out but he was backing away. "Fat ass!" he continued to taunt as he stepped out of the doorway into the corridor.

Helen seized the opportunity to slam the door shut behind him, quickly bolting the lock.

"Fat-ass bitch!" he shouted through the closed door, banging it with the heel of his stumpy hand, getting the last word in before scurrying away.

Helen pressed her back against the door. She could hardly breathe. Her throat was constricted – her stomach somersaulted into her chest. There was a basin and mirror within the confines of the toilet. She pressed both hands onto the cold ceramic of the sink to steady herself. Her knees were about to buckle, she was shaking so badly. She looked in the mirror and she saw herself in a way that she hadn't in years. Behind the make-up, designer clothes, the laughs, the deal-making, she saw a frightened little girl, carefully hidden in the archive of her soul.

"What the hell are you doing, Helen?" she asked her reflection.

Slowly, her heart gave up its struggle to escape from her chest. Her hand steadied enough to allow her to let go of the sink.

She splashed her face with cold water and used the loo before making her way back downstairs. Despite what had happened, or what could have happened, she couldn't stop the same thought playing like a broken record in her head: *Is my ass really that big?*

"Helen, drink?" Fred used sign-language over the crowd.

She knew better than to tell him she was leaving. She motioned that she was going outside for a smoke. She didn't smoke but Fred was too pissed to argue.

As she waded her way over to where her host was sitting, she looked around for the suit but couldn't see him. What would she say to security anyway?

He was in the ladies' toilet.

He said my bum was big.

He threatened you, Helen! He almost raped the other woman.

She looked around again – she couldn't see the woman either.

Already she was wondering if she had exaggerated the situation in her mind.

Then she spotted him.

Not the creep from the loo – the guy from the airport, Mr Spiritually Enlightened, just walking out the door. Why hadn't she spotted him earlier? It was his straw briefcase that had caught her eye, just as he was leaving.

"Are you alright, Helen?" Mark asked. "You look upset?"

"I'm fine, Mark. Thanks for a lovely evening." She tucked her jacket under her arm so that Fred wouldn't spot it and realise she was leaving. "We've an early flight to the mainland in the morning. We'll see you the day after tomorrow – right?"

"Sure. I'll walk you to the taxi rank."

"No, you're grand – it's just down the hill. Sarah, are you coming or staying?"

"Staying." Sarah barely looked up, her attention focused on the young English tourist who was chatting her up.

Helen deftly managed her escape through the heavy velvet curtains of the bar's entrance. She wanted to catch up with the man who'd just left. Surely it was too great a coincidence? Not usually someone to believe in synchronicity, it just seemed unlikely that this man, who'd guided her to buy a book on the significance of coincidence, would appear in her bar. Could the world really be that small? Was this a sign to trust the Universe? I'm going after him, she thought. In her eagerness to get out, she smacked straight into two men who were on their way in.

"Whoa! Are you okay?" Jack Taylor said to the woman who'd just run into him with force.

Helen looked up at him, this polite stranger she'd nearly mowed down. Their eyes met for the briefest moment before she mumbled an apology and looked away, her eyes searching for something else, the man with the straw briefcase whom the Universe had conspired that she meet, she was sure of it. But he'd disappeared from sight now, valuable seconds lost by bumping into someone else to say nothing of the encounter with Mark. She looked back into the bar and wondered if she should stay. The man she'd bumped into was still smiling at her. If someone whacked into her as she had him, she doubted she'd be as forgiving. She decided to keep on going and soon melted into the throngs of people drinking on the street.

14

"Wonders will never cease – there are a couple of free seats at the bar," Tom said to his nephew.

The two men sat and ordered beer. A pretty Asian woman sat alone at the end of the bar. She held an unlit cigarette between her scarlet-painted fingernails.

She smiled at Jack.

He smiled back.

She held up her cigarette and tilted her head as if she was asking him if he had a light.

He shrugged his shoulders and shook his head – he didn't smoke.

"Excuse me," he called to the bartender. "I think that lady needs a light."

The bartender looked at him, unsmiling.

"Jeez, Jack, will you stop encouraging the hooker. They're impossible to shake off, once they spot an easy target," Tom moaned. "I'm surprised at you – being a man of the world, you should know better."

"Oh." Jack reddened slightly. "I'm really not tuned into women, or so I'm told."

"Why would you want to be? Just let them *think* you are. Their brains don't work rationally, you see. It'd be easier to tune into Andromeda using a kitchen spoon than tune into the female psyche."

"Andromeda – as in our neighbouring galaxy in the universe?"

"That's the one – two-and-a-half million light years away. Now that I think of it, that's probably where women are from too – a different species from outer space."

Jack thought that for once Tom could be right.

"Whatever happened to that girl? Weren't you engaged to her?" Tom asked, popping some peanuts into his mouth.

The question was unexpected and knocked Jack back.

"Amy." He said her name and survived it.

"Was she the one with the great rack?"

"She was my only proper girlfriend. And yes, the one with the great rack. It didn't work out." Jack drew a line in the condensation of his beer bottle.

"Slept with someone else, did she?"

No wonder Dad calls him Tactless Tom. "Something like that."

"Figures."

"Why do you say that?" Jack pushed his stool back to look at Tom full-on.

"A girl who looks like that is always on the hunt for something more. More status, more wealth, more handsome. Beauty – it's a curse, you know – for those that fall in love with it anyway."

"So you're saying all beautiful women are shallow, insincere gold-diggers?"

Tom thought for a moment or two. "Yes."

"You're incorrigible, Tom."

"I'm just saying what I've seen. Screw them by all means – just don't marry and procreate with a Playboy bunny."

"Amy doesn't look like a Playgirl! She's tall for a start, and she's . . ." Jack thought about the right word, "she's refined."

"Trust me. Paint the lips redder, and make the heels a couple of inches higher – it's the only difference – she has the basic canvas." Tom popped more nuts.

Jack was peeling off the label of his beer.

"From what I remember of her, that is," Tom added. "Trust me – you're well shot of her."

If Tom was trying to console him, it hadn't worked.

"So, how long are you in town for?" Tom asked.

Safer ground.

"A little over a week, but I'll probably head across to Mainland China for a few days of that. Then I'm hoping I can fly on to Phnom Penh from here."

"Cambodia! Have you been drinking the Kool-Aid? Why on earth would you want to go there?"

"I'm kind of hoping it's not too spoilt by tourists yet – I've always wanted to see Angkor Wat."

"Shanghai – go there. As an architect, you'll love it – not some crumbling old ruin. Besides, you'll have to get all sorts of injections against the god-awful diseases in Cambodia. Do they even have proper hotels there?" Tom's lip curled involuntarily.

"I got all my shots last month. It's not the buildings I'm going for – it's the culture, the experience." Jack ignored Tom's expression.

"I'm telling you – book into the Peninsula in Shanghai, or Beijing if you want more culture. Order room service – tune the plasma TV to the National Geographic channel. Experience all the cultures of the world via remote-control."

"Nah, it doesn't matter about the hotels, I'm backpacking. And I'll go wherever I can get the best-priced flight to. I'll figure out my way once I'm there."

"Jack, I've seen the world and managed to have white cotton sheets, cable TV and a hotel bar everywhere I've been."

"What you mean is – you've travelled the world. You can't say you've seen it until you step out of your comfort-zone, off the tour bus and mix with the locals."

"Who's talking tour buses? I've always been chauffeur-driven."

There was an awkward pause.

"Or at least a taxi," Tom conceded. "Would you even consider Shanghai?"

"Sure, I'd like to see Shanghai, probably more for the old town though."

Tom raised his eyes to heaven.

"And the super train – I would like to travel on that," Jack added.

"Thank you! I was beginning to think you weren't a Taylor at all."

"I'm just not like you and Dad."

"Correction – I'm nothing like your dad either."

"What I mean is, you and dad live and breathe construction. You with your architecture, Dad with his engineering, Dubai is your wet dream, but I just don't feel the buzz anymore."

There, he'd said it. There is more to life than big boys' Lego.

"You know, maybe this few weeks off is a good idea after all." Tom paused. "You'll be chewed up in LA unless you get your 'buzz' back and quickly. Most people would kill to have your job."

Jack knew Tom was right. Sometimes though, he wondered, if he hadn't come from a family of architects and engineers, would he have chosen a different career?

If he hadn't started dating Amy in high school, would he have experienced more of life? He'd always taken the safe road. Always was the good son, the class captain, devoted boyfriend – hardworking, reliable.

He could see his tombstone now: *Here lies Jack Taylor, Grade-A student, exemplary employee, lovingly missed by nieces and nephews. No children of his own because women are from Andromeda and he couldn't leave the office long enough to get there. Died of boredom, age forty – RIP.*

15

"Is Helen not back yet?" Fred enquired, returning from the bar.

"Gone," Mark said flatly as he stole a glance at his watch.

"Like hell she is," Fred said, putting the drinks on the table. He took his mobile out of his jeans pocket, pressing speed-dial. Helen's number rang out – he dialled it again and then again.

"She mentioned you all have an early start tomorrow," Mark said.

"Never stopped her before," Fred grumbled.

He checked the phone for texts – nothing. Maybe he could still catch her – talk her into a night-cap at the hotel bar. He swiftly bade the others goodnight and disappeared through the velvet curtains in pursuit of his target: *Helen Divine*.

Party revellers thronged the narrow streets of Lang Kwai Fong. Waiters pushed through the crowds with pitchers of beer and vodka, a popular option that maximised drinking time and minimised wading-to-the-bar time. Music flowed from the pubs' outdoor speaker systems into the hedonistic night air. Beer flowed down the cobbled street. Fred, who'd normally want to be in the thick of the action, now found it irritating, his dash to the taxi rank impeded. A group of young women dressed in saucy nurses' uniforms slowed him momentarily.

"You want a shot, mister?" one of them asked. She raised a giant vial, shaped like a surgical needle – it was full of a clear-coloured alcohol like vodka or gin. Fred hesitated for a moment until he remembered you always pay premium rates to drink with a view, be it of a harbour or an over-exposed silicone cleavage. He kept going.

"I'll take it!" a British woman shouted, dashing forward. She wore a cheap cotton sleeveless T-shirt that exposed a functional white bra-strap and an expanse of belly-flab. Bingo wings jiggled as she broke away from her friends and ran towards the fantasy nurse. The woman and her friends all looked to be in their late forties, maybe early fifties. They held tankards of beer and cocktails. Some were clumsily stepping side to side, to the beat of the music.

The nurse poured, the women laughed and started a sing-song.

Christ, if they could only see themselves! He'd go bonkers if *his* wife behaved like that! Fred saw a break in the crowd. A line of people formed a human train to keep it open and make their way down the street. He latched on at the back and a moment later was free of the congestion and making his way to the bottom of the hill.

In the taxi, the driver studied Fred in his rear-view mirror. He saw men like this every night of the week leaving Wan Chai and Lan Kwai Fong. They'd flash their cash all night, only to head back to their hotel rooms alone.

There could be commission here.

"You enjoy night?" he enquired, giving Fred a gap-tooth smile.

"It was fine." Fred was texting Helen, having decided to use the guilt card – asking her to contact him because he was worried.

Bugger it, he thought. He'd forgotten Sarah . . . thankfully Mark, the Gentle Giant, would make sure she got home safely.

"You like a woman?" the driver asked, going straight for the jugular.

"What? No! I could have picked up any amount of pros in Long Cock," Fred said, adopting Helen's idiom. Why wasn't she texting back?

"No, no – no sex – rubby-rubby. Me – I am Buddhist." The taxi driver pointed to himself and nodded repeatedly. "This very good – best massage in Hong Kong." He laughed. "You never have massage like this in your life, mister – I take you there." He eagerly awaited the nod from Fred, who was now giving him his full attention.

Fred looked at the screen of his phone – still nothing. "How far is it?" he enquired, wary of a scam.

"No far – here on the island – I no charge you for going there – okay? Just fare same as you go to Excelsior, okay?" The driver kept nodding until soon Fred was nodding too.

Within minutes, the driver was navigating the car through dark narrow streets, away from the neon signs of the main thoroughfares. All the time he was muttering to himself. "No worry – very good, very good, mister."

They came to a halt outside a dingy building. There didn't appear to be any sign of life. The driver got out of his cab and gave a quiet tap on a small window. Fred remained in the cab and watched nervously from the back seat.

The window opened slightly and the driver started talking to a woman – Fred could only see her outline. They appeared to be arguing. But, Fred thought, the Asians always sound like that. A moment later, a light came on – the door opened a tiny crack. The driver signalled furiously to Fred.

"How much?" Fred enquired of his self-appointed pimp.

"One hundred Hong Kong Dollar." The man ushered Fred quickly into a room off the hallway, for fear he'd change his mind.

The place smelt of cheap perfume and cabbage soup. Two towel-covered plinths were the only furniture. A pretty young woman smiled shyly at Fred.

She could work the knots out of him any day. *Happy days and all for less than ten quid!*

Through a doorway, a rustle heralded the arrival of another woman. She waded into the room – a real-life Chinese dragon, but a lot less hot. With a grunt, she indicated to Fred to get up on the plinth. Panic set in and just when he thought it couldn't get any worse there was another swish of the multicoloured plastic strips. Enter dragon number two. Only this one was worse. This was a Chinese Weapon of Mass Destruction – and Fred was her target.

"Which one you want?" the taxi man asked, as if courtesy dictated he should give Fred the option of Ugly or Uglier.

Fred turned to look for the pretty girl who had welcomed him but she was already slipping away, out of sight. The bait escaped – the victim caught.

"Pants down!"

The taxi man's trousers dropped to the floor, revealing spindly legs. His head was still nodding.

Closing his eyes, Fred tightly held on to his belt buckle. He prayed for deliverance.

A lot of shouting later – with Fred refusing to drop his pants which resulted in him paying the masseuses their fee plus a bonus *not* to have services rendered – he was safely back in the cab. He lit a cigarette and blew the smoke out through the top of the car window. The driver was prattling in Mandarin. Occasionally he'd bang his fist against the steering wheel, and mutter what could only be obscenities, no matter what the language.

But Fred didn't care. His focus now was on Helen. She'd just sent him a text: she was okay and back at the hotel. She'd agreed to meet him in the Dickens bar for a nightcap.

Time to move things up a notch.

16

Helen descended the steep wooden stairs to Dickens, the hotel's sports bar. She'd thought of going to bed but knew she wouldn't sleep. She'd been sitting in her room looking out at the harbour view when she'd responded to Fred's texts. A nightcap might do the trick. She spotted Fred – the bar only had a handful of clients. He wasn't hard to find. As usual, he sat at the bar as close to a bartender as possible. He had already ordered Helen's usual rum and Coke.

"Hey, I'm surprised you came back here so early." Helen tried to sound light-hearted.

"Important contracts to be negotiated tomorrow, I wanted to have a clear head."

Helen sat on the stool next to him. The split in her black skirt opened slightly, revealing the top of her thigh.

"You look different, somehow," Fred said.

"No make-up."

"Suits you – makes you look younger," he said, and meant it.

"Thanks."

"So how's Sarah working out?" It was after midnight, but Fred couldn't help but talk shop.

"Good, great actually. I think with a bit more experience under her belt, she'll be an asset to Eden. She reminds me of myself ten years ago." Helen smiled, relaxing.

"That's good to know, especially now, with us opening up an office here in Hong Kong."

"I meant to ask you about that – what's the timeframe for it being up and running?"

"In the next couple of months. They'll be looking for expertise from us of course. The new office will coordinate all factories and potential suppliers around South East Asia."

"Will it affect jobs back in London?"

"Between you and me?"

"Of course," Helen said, her pulse quickening.

"They've already asked me to relocate."

"Seriously? Hong Kong? What about your family?"

"To be honest, Helen, June and me, we're more or less living separate lives since the kids left home." Fred looked into his glass of liquor, as if it could magically fill the place of his thirty-year marriage.

"I'm sorry, Fred, I didn't realise." Helen wasn't sure what else to say.

"It's not so bad. We get along well, just like old friends. I never noticed it happening, us growing apart. It was the early days at Eden, we were building the company up, I was travelling and working crazy hours – June was at home with the kids. They got older – she had more free time, she started doing things for herself – built her own life. I'm really proud of her, you know." He looked at Helen.

"Why wouldn't you be? Even though I've only meet her a few times, she seems like a lovely woman."

"Anyway, Helen, more importantly – how do you feel about it?"

"You moving to Hong Kong? We'll certainly miss you around the office, Fred." Helen was surprised at the question.

"No, you silly! I need the right team behind me." Fred waited for an answer.

Helen laughed. "You're kidding, right? What about the London office? Who'd run things there?"

"Sarah," Fred replied.

"Sarah's not ready." Damn, why hadn't she seen that one coming!

"I can commute for a few months, to help with the setting-up. Living here permanently isn't an option right now."

"At least say you'll think about it. You'd have your own apartment overlooking the harbour, a driver and monthly flights back to the UK. Plus . . ." Fred paused, "job security."

The words hit Helen hard.

"It's only a matter of time before London is scaled down – am I right?" She knew the answer already.

"Look, as you know, I'm not on the Board but my educated guess is, yes – London jobs will go."

"I can't process this information now, Fred, not at this hour." She rubbed her temples.

"Don't give me that crap – this is when you wake up!"

She smiled. "Maybe, but it was a funny kind of night – not funny 'ha-ha' – funny as in 'weird'."

"Then we need another drink."

Two more drinks arrived and Helen found herself telling Fred about being manhandled earlier.

"Why didn't you say something – I'd have bloody well punched his lights out!" Fred was livid.

"Oh look, Fred, I'm a grown woman. Why is such a relatively small incident bothering me so much?"

"Think about what could have happened! The guy was obviously barmy, bladdered, or both." He rubbed his face, his eyes welling up.

"The funny thing is he was well dressed, respectable-looking. You think you protect yourself by not walking down dark laneways or crossing the street to avoid rough characters," she reflected.

"Drink can change a person – a lot, Helen. Add being away from home, out of the gaze of your peers, community and wife. These guys feel they can get on a plane and all the rules are off. The rules don't apply outside of their home country." He averted his gaze.

"It was probably a bit of both. He *was* well tanked up. God love the young woman he was with earlier in the bar – I hope he doesn't take his anger out on her."

"What a tosser! With any luck, the girl's pimp is Triad – they'll surely chop his todger off." He thumped the bar playfully.

"You're a *Kill Bill* fan too, I see." Helen threw her head back in laughter, enjoying the imaginary scene Fred had created. "What about brotherhood? Is that not sacrilege, to wish another man's willy to be hacked off?"

"Sod brotherhood. Actually, I'd a bit of a nasty experience myself earlier . . ." With that Fred spilt the beans on his detour to the massage parlour.

It didn't shock Helen, who despite working in the women's underwear market had got used to the fact the industry was dominated by men. Therefore most of her colleagues were male and most business trips were with men. Although that was changing. In any case, Fred's version of events certainly gave her abs a good workout, she laughed so much.

"Serves you right, you dirty old man," she said, wiping the corner of her eye.

"I'd swear it was a family business, Helen – with every generation in on the act."

"Don't start – you'll set me off again. And what had the taxi driver being Buddhist got to do with anything?"

"Search me. One thing's for sure, though – the two ladies gave Buddha himself a run for his money. Blimey, larger lassies I've rarely seen!"

"Stop!" Helen playfully punched him before lowering her voice. "Anyway, Fred, I'm left with a far more serious trauma."

Fred looked at her, puzzled at her tone.

"I refer to the Fat Ass issue – Fred, do you think my bum is big?"

"Office rules, Helen, I've never looked at your posterior – I couldn't possibly comment – that could be construed as sexual harassment, you know."

"Ah, get off your high-horse and stop talking crap!" Helen got off her stool, turned her back to Fred and stuck her butt out. "You have my permission to check out my butt – is it too big?"

"Ms Devine, I can confirm that you indeed do . . . not have a fat ass." *It looks especially good in the jeans you wear to the office on Fridays.*

"Good, in that case I'm starving – do you fancy a MacDonald's?"

"I thought you'd never ask." Fred stood, steadied himself and gallantly held his arm out to Helen.

The barman whisked up their glasses before they changed their mind. Drunk and Drunker headed back up the wooden stairs in search of the Holy Grail: a Big Mac.

Fred went to walk out the main doors of the hotel towards the taxis but Helen headed to the side door.

"Don't be such a lazy old fart! It's a five-minute walk from here!" She wouldn't usually speak to her boss like that but, as Fred said, the rules stay at home, office etiquette being one of them.

The narrow streets were wet from an earlier rain-shower. Plastic bags of rubbish were piled high against shop windows, waiting for early-morning collection. Light streamed from a Seven-Eleven convenience store. An employee brushed suds out to the path, washing away the grime of the day now his shift was over. It wasn't long before Fred and Helen found the golden arches, thankfully still beaming.

"Which do you prefer, skinny chips or fat chips?" Helen asked Fred, as she fished for the last chip, which was trying to escape through the crack at the bottom of the carton.

"All chips. Can't you tell?" Fred rubbed his belly for added effect. Having got their food they had decided to walk to the harbour and eat it with a view. "Look at this!" He waved his arm. "A slap-up meal, a killer view, and all for a few dollars – not bad, am I right?"

"Absolutely, I mean who'd want to be in one of those top-floor restaurants, paying three hundred bucks on a meal for two anyway?"

"My sentiment exactly," Fred said, missing Helen's sarcasm. "A beer would be good though."

"Or a nice chilled bottle of white."

The two looked wistful.

"Well, since we've saved the company so much money on food, why don't we crack open the minibar?" Fred asked. *With any luck, I'll be cracking open more than that.*

"Best idea you've had all night, boss. Better make it your room though. Accounts will have my not-fat ass if I charge expensive mini-bottles of booze to Eden," Helen hiccupped.

"One of the benefits of being the boss, my dear – I won't let anyone have your ass. Unless I authorise it, of course. Ass-whipping is my prerogative. Come on, let's go, it's starting to rain."

Had Helen imagined it? Was Fred being sexual or was he reaffirming his position in the food-chain of Eden management? She wondered if she should call it a night. What the hell, one little nightcap can't hurt, she convinced herself, pushing her better judgement aside.

17

"Wow, Fred, it's an impressive size!" Helen said. "I've seen a lot in my time, but never one quite this big."

Fred stretched back on the couch, feeling smug. "Nice, hey?"

"Here was me thinking I'd scored a massive room and here you were hiding this all along."

"Got talking to Ms Lynn in Guest Relations. I may have mentioned that I could direct a lot more clients their way – and what do you know – bingo, they upgraded me to a suite – free of charge. Champagne?"

"Thanks."

Fred pattered over to the minibar to retrieve the bottle and flutes. He carried them back to where he'd been sitting, in the bay of the window with his back to Hong Kong Harbour.

"Come – sit." He tapped the large comfortable couch before untwisting the champagne wire.

Helen decided to sit in an armchair opposite him, a coffee table between them. "The view is better from here. Ha, it looks like you've skyscrapers sprouting from the top of your head." She held up her phone to take a picture.

"At least there's something growing there." Fred rubbed the top of his head, disappointed Helen hadn't joined him on the couch. The cork popped with a high-pressure spray that hit Helen. They both laughed and Fred used the distraction to discreetly press a remote control, dimming the lights ever so slightly in the room. He selected a playlist he'd compiled before leaving the UK on his iPod – he'd labelled it *'seduction'*. Ambient music filled the room.

"How's your love-life, Helen, or am I allowed ask such a question?" Fred leaned across the coffee table to hand Helen her drink.

"Complicated." Was she imagining it or had it got darker in the room? She looked at Fred – he looked younger, and more relaxed, sitting framed by the glittering lights of the city. "I've been kind of seeing my ex but I don't think it's going anywhere."

"Is this the guy you left Dublin to avoid?" *Careful how you play this one, Fred.*

"That's him – Rob Lawless, the solicitor."

Then as the drink flowed, Helen poured her heart out to Fred about her doubts of Rob's genuineness. Finally, she stopped – it had felt good to talk about it. Let the secret out. No one at home knew she was seeing Rob again. Even she wasn't sure if she was.

As conversation stopped, the background music picked up tempo, as Prince belted out "Sexy Motherfucker".

Shit – it's too soon for the shag compilation. Fred was annoyed he hadn't thought to loop the earlier playlist. Until he was ready.

He broke the silence between them. "With a name like that, I hope Mr Lawless is not in criminal law."

They both creased up with laughter. When they'd calmed, Fred said, "He sounds like a dumb-nut to me. Crikey, Helen, what were you thinking? You can do so much better than that. Just look at you – attractive, successful, intelligent – any man would give his right arm to be with you – love you."

Time to enter Phase Two: close the deal.

"You know what, I *am* too good for that crap!" Helen thumped the arm of the chair before standing to walk over to the window. She paced for a moment before stopping to look out at the view. "Life is too short for wasters, Fred."

"Let's toast to that!" Fred held up the champagne bottle.

She joined him on the couch, handing him her glass. She sat on the edge, her back poker-straight, her eyes darting as she looked up towards the ceiling as though seeking divine inspiration.

"How about a toast to new beginnings?" she said.

"To new beginnings!" Fred said, clinking glasses. He looked into Helen's eyes.

She smiled back at him – she was feeling warm and kind of fuzzy.

Suddenly, Fred lunged forward, kissing her hard on the lips. Helen remained in her upright position, her eyes still on the ceiling. Her brain froze but her lips responded as Fred's tongue began exploring her mouth.

Was this a reflex reaction, alcohol inaction, or attraction?

"Helen, sweetheart, I've dreamt about this for so long – I know you have too," Fred gasped. Years of running a lingerie retail business had its benefits, because with one hand he seamlessly unclipped her bra through the thin fabric of her blouse.

This was bad. Helen's brain defrosted and sprinted to catch up with her body.

She pulled back. "I feel a little woozy – I'd better use the bathroom," she said, straightening herself up.

"You okay, pumpkin?"

"Fine, it'll just take a moment." Picking up her handbag, she made her way across the room, without looking back.

Fred checked his teeth, horse-like, in the reflective surface of the coffee table. Women and the way they had to fix themselves up first – he'd never understand them. Maybe she was checking her bag for condoms . . . He smiled as he unbuttoned his shirt. Perhaps she'd reappear, languishing against the bathroom doorframe, in just her underwear and high heels. *Oh happy, happy days!*

The stark light of the bathroom was a jolt after the dimness of the bedroom. Helen's head spun. What was she thinking! She soaked a washcloth with cold water and pressed it to her face. Unfortunately, it was impossible to avoid looking at the mirror. She bore a striking resemblance, albeit blonde, to a beehive-haired songstress, with black eyeliner anywhere but the eyes.

"You've got to get out of here," she said to her reflection. She refastened her bra. Mentally, she practised the speech she'd give Fred. Time for damage-limitation.

But re-entering the bedroom, words failed her. Fred lay prone, on his side, head propped up with his hand – in all his naked glory. She didn't know if he was completely naked as the champagne bottle obscured the view of his manhood. A picture of Julius Caesar waiting to be fed grapes popped into Helen's mind.

"Feeling better, cupcake? Here, I've poured you another glass of bubbles." Fred began to get up.

"No! Don't move!" She waved at him and swung away to spare herself the sight of a rampant Fred. "I mean, I've got to go, I'm so sorry – I don't know what we were thinking."

"You're just a little scared, peach. We can take it slowly – after all, we've waited this long."

She didn't turn around as she made for the door. If she had she'd have seen him grab up an ice bucket as he approached her.

"We'll talk tomorrow, Fred." Helen didn't know which planet Fred was on – just that it wasn't far enough away from hers. She opened the door, light from the corridor signalling her escape route.

"Okay, pancake," Fred said, close behind her.

"Goodnight, Fred."

"Au revoir, pumpkin! Until tomorrow," Fred said stepping into the corridor to watch her go, ice bucket positioned to preserve his honour, bum cheeks facing the fire exit.

Tomorrow – Christ, a three-hour plane ride, with Fred. Where's my parachute?

18

Poppy closed the door behind the last client of the day. Her body ached. She was packing in more clients than ever, working harder for less money. Local beauty salons had cut their rates – so had she.

"Have you eaten?" she asked Lily.

Lily was sitting on her bed, typing on her laptop. The TV was on but the volume was turned down as Poppy had been working. Couldn't have people come for a relaxing massage with strains of the *CSI* theme-tune filtering through the floorboards.

Lily looked up and lifted one ear of her headphones. Poppy could hear the din of rock music from where she was standing.

"What?" Lily looked agitated by the interruption.

"Food. Have you eaten?"

"Yeah." Lily replaced the cushioned pad to her ear, indicating the conversation was over.

Poppy was too tired to argue. She'd massaged fifteen people that week. The last lady was, well, rather large to say the least, so it took a lot of muscle to knead through the layers of fat. Poppy rubbed her wrists – they had started to swell.

In the kitchen, an empty pizza box indicated what Lily's dinner had been.

"Wonderful parenting, Poppy," she said to herself and opened the fridge door.

Nothing appealed to her. The familiar whirl of her Swiss cuckoo-clock began its hourly routine. The doors edged open, the bird's beak appeared: *"Cuckoo! Cuckoo! Cuckoo!"* Traditional Swiss dancers swung around in a circular dance, the only way the wooden figures could move. The bird continued to cuckoo, nine cuckoos.

Poppy reasoned it unhealthy to eat late and reached for a bottle of white wine instead. Um, probably not the healthiest option either. Just have one glass and take your vitamins – genius, she thought, happy with herself.

Milkthistle to detoxify the liver, vitamin C to replenish what the alcohol depletes and Omega 3 for healthy skin & hair. What's this one for – selenium? She couldn't remember, but added it to the stack for good measure. She downed all the pills with one gulp of wine before she settled in front of the TV.

She flicked through the channels – nothing caught her attention. She landed on a re-run of a cookery programme. Helen's favourite: Gordon Ramsay. What did she see in him? The screen flashed a shot of the celebrity chef's hairy chest and Poppy started to see the attraction.

Gordon jumped up and down as he talked. The camera took a side-angle shot of him while he prepared his puddings. Buns of steel too, Poppy thought admiringly. *Wouldn't mind getting those buns up on my countertop.*

She checked her watch and tried to figure out what time it would be in Hong Kong. She felt the urge to share with Helen the fact that she could finally see the charms of the craggy-faced Mr Ramsay. But first, to the kitchen. Looking at all that food was making her hungry.

Poppy returned to the couch with a bag of crisps, a packet of Tuc crackers and a block of cheese. She set up the picnic in front of her and topped up her wineglass: the salt of the crisps made her thirsty. The cookery programme went on ad break as she made a tower of crackers, cheese and crisps. It'd be five thirty in the morning in Hong Kong, was that right?

She started flicking again. Each station she clicked on featured couples. Couples laughing, couples kissing, couples looking happy.

She demolished the food tower and settled on vintage *Emmanuelle* – a couple making out. Boobs bop up and down. She'd be a granny now, Emmanuelle, Poppy thought. She wondered would the *Emmanuelle* actress keep the archives of her videos, with other family moments, captured on celluloid – visits to the zoo, weddings and christenings. "Look, Junior! There's Granny – star of the blue screen!"

Emmanuelle started to climax, well, that's what the camera led you to believe anyway – all you could see was her pleasured face – either that or she was having a pee, after holding it in for ages.

"Mum?" Lily yelled, coming down the stairs.

Poppy fumbled with the remote, anxious to change the channel before Lily came in. "In here!"

"I need a tenner for school, tomorrow." Lily walked into the TV room. "Since when did you get interested in fishing programmes?"

On the screen a man in a tweed hat held a giant fishing rod.

"It's rather interesting actually." Poppy pretended to be engrossed in the TV. "You off to bed?"

"Yeah, night." Lily disappeared as quickly as she'd appeared.

Poppy missed her daughter's goodnight kisses. When she thought about it, she realised she missed any kind of kiss actually. She picked up the bottle of wine – there was only a dribble left.

Poppy thought about Helen, having a bloody fabulous time in Hong Kong. Helen would be having fancy dinners, expensive wines – not drinking the Deal of the Week, from Chile. She'd probably met some tall dark stranger, in her five-star hotel, and they had made mad passionate love. She'd be lying there now, in her big luxurious bed, in his arms – or, knowing Helen, on her own, in a blissful post-orgasmic sleep because she had kicked him out already, saying she had an early start, she'd email him. Little did he know his contact details were already in the wastebasket. Poppy enjoyed the imaginary soap drama playing in her head, especially as there was nothing happening on the box.

Most of the time Poppy wished her friend would stop running from commitment. Right now she admired it. Free, no ties, plenty of money and pretty.

The fisherman was filleting his catch, Poppy changed channel again, this time landing on *Animal Planet*. Two bobcats were mating.

It's not fair – everyone is getting laid!

Poppy decided to text Helen, to see what was happening in Asia but her eyes felt heavy and she closed them, just for a moment. *How did you get here, Poppy, half-wasted, watching TV alone? Next Lily will move out and you'll end up with a cat. You'll be a cat spinster, smelling of cats.*

She began to drift, back to a time – the first of September 1978, to be exact. She was unsure how much of it was her own memory, or if they'd each recounted their version of the story so often all details fused. Whichever it was, she still remembered the feeling when she met Mary and Helen Devine for the first time.

19

1st September 1978

"Isn't this exciting Helen, your first day back at school!" Mary Devine straightened her daughter's navy polyester tie, its elastic backing hidden under the stiff starched collar of the white cotton school shirt. The little girl's bottom lip trembled – she fought to hold back the tears that were threatening to spill. How could she tell her mother that no one liked her?

"What does your daddy do?"

The words had haunted Helen all summer. The prettiest girl in the class, Natalie Porter, had asked her the question, knowing full well the answer. There were giggles and nudges from the others sitting at the table.

"My daddy is one of God's angels," Helen had replied, without looking up from her drawing. She thought it was a very cool answer.

"Well, that's no good, is it? How will you do tonight's homework – 'My Daddy's Job'? My dad is a pilot – I'll have lots to write. Karen's dad owns lots of sweet shops and –"

"Deadly! Does your daddy really own sweet shops, Karen?" a girl interrupted from the next table, pausing to wipe her nose on her jumper sleeve. "That's so cool!"

"Yes, he does!" said Karen. "And my mummy says it's my daddy's hard work that keeps single mothers and their snotty-nosed brats in clothes and a house!"

Helen didn't understand, but something told her that in some way the Devine family weren't good enough.

"May I have that thingy, please?" Helen held her hand out for the sailing-boat stencil.

"It's not your turn! Who will you give a Father's Day card to anyway?" was the girl's caustic reply.

"My mummy."

More sniggers and nudges came from around the table.

Helen waited. She left a space in the middle of her picture, big enough for the boat – she could colour around it later. She chewed her lip as the group of friends took their time drawing around the cardboard cut-out before handing it on to each other, making sure she was by-passed.

The teacher called from the top of the class. "Alright, boys and girls, it's nearly home time! Finish up your Father's Day cards now, please, and make sure you put your name on the back."

Helen's cheeks flushed red and she feverishly started to draw a sailing boat free-hand.

That was last June – it was the first of September now – but still Helen hesitated at the hall door. She turned to her mother. "I don't feel very well, Mummy."

"Now, love, we're not going to start all that again this year. Just you wait and see – this year will be better." Mary Devine licked her thumb and rubbed a non-existent spot of dirt from the child's face. "Oh my, look at the time! We don't want to be late on your first day! Come on, Helen, put on your coat." The young widow held out the gabardine coat with both hands, shield-like. Her own breath quivered.

Becoming a widow at the age of twenty-five was not something she had got used to. She wanted to hold her little girl, tell her she could stay at home with her forever, because Mary didn't want to let go any more than the child did. So she did what she did best – earlier that morning, she had distracted the two of them from the task at hand by brushing Helen's hair, plaiting two little pigtails and scrubbing her clean to within an inch of her life.

It was times like this that Mary missed her family. Had she made the right decision to move to Dublin when Jim died?

"I'm sorry for your loss, Mary, I really am. That war, 'tis an awful thing, shocking. James died way before his time, he did," Mary's brother had said. "But it doesn't change the fact you walked out on our family. Ma and Da needed your wages."

"I was always going to send money home, Liam, you know that. I dreamed of a better life for all of us!" Mary had protested into the black mouthpiece of the telephone she held so tightly.

"Better for all of us, don't make me laugh!" Liam spat. "Saving money behind all our backs for a one-way ticket to America! How was that better for all of us?"

"I'd have made it on Broadway, Liam, and then all our troubles would have been over. Acting was all I ever wanted . . ." Mary's voice trailed off, as she felt the cold feeling of failure creep through her veins.

"You were away with the fairies, Mary. Fame, my arse. And where did all your fancy notions get you, tell me that?" Liam didn't wait for an answer. "Pregnant, out of wedlock, at nineteen years of age – not in some fancy starring role. Leading-lady of the whorehouse more like."

"Jimmy and me, we were in love," Mary said. "We got married in City Hall, New York, before the baby was born. But you already know that." Although her voice was defiant, the glimmer of hope she'd had when she dialled home had faded with the mounting anger she could feel coming down the line.

"Look, Mary, the facts are you and James Devine ran off together – two rats jumping ship. You'd crazy notions above your station of being a famous actress. Ye left us here to face the gossip and shame. Neighbours whispering and laughing behind Ma's back. She stuck up for you, you know, to the point where Da stopped talking to her altogether. When you sent news of a child born, out of Catholic wedlock, that just killed him, Mary, and, well, you know the rest yourself. As far as I'm concerned, Ma didn't die of cancer, she died of a broken heart, caused by you, Mary. I will not let you do the same to Da, my da. Goodbye to you and your bastard child, you're dead to us."

With a click, the line went cold.

Poppy Power was so excited about her first day at her new school she had set two alarm clocks – just to be sure not to sleep it out. She had needed neither of them as natural adrenaline had woken her with the dawn. She had laid out her navy uniform over the back of a small wooden chair in her room. She put on each layer with care. A white cotton vest, then next came the shirt. The collar was frayed and, being her older brother's shirt, it stopped just above her knees. She tried tucking the shirt into her knickers, but that just made it look as if she was wearing an oversized nappy. Poppy frowned when she looked in the mirror. Next, she pulled the navy pinafore over her head and finally the woollen jumper with the school crest embroidered on it. The jumper was a bit bobbly from the previous owner's wear. But Poppy didn't care when she looked at her reflection. All she saw was the fancy school crest – the school to which she now belonged. Her heart soared with delight.

"Mam, get up, we're going to be late!"

A grunt and a waft of last night's alcohol greeted Poppy.

"Please, Mam, just today, bring me in. I promise I'll get the bus after today."

Poppy placed a mug of milky tea on her mother's bedside table. Beside it she carefully placed two painkillers. Just shy of eight, she was well versed in her mother's needs.

"I'll leave this here, Mam. I'll be downstairs."

Her mother didn't stir.

Unable to wait on her mother any longer and with no sign of her father, Poppy decided to make tracks. She pulled the door closed behind her. Making sure she had her copybooks and pen in her bag, she began walking along the laneway that led to their workman's cottage.

A minute later, she was startled by a familiar voice.

"Hold up there, kiddo, where you goin' without me?" Poppy's

mother hollered out the window of her battered Volkswagen bug as she flicked a cigarette butt onto the gravel.

A grinning Poppy climbed into the passenger seat.

"You look great, Pops – you're a real treasure, you know that?" Her mother affectionately brushed her thumb across her daughter's cheek.

"Thanks for coming with me, Mam – I know you're not feeling well."

"Ah, baby girl, you're a gift from the angels. Where would I be if I didn't have you? Now let's go to this den of repression and brainwashing you're so keen to be a part of!" She pushed her foot on the accelerator.

Poppy had no idea what her mother was talking about but it didn't matter – they were on their way.

"You can't sit there!" The girl stretched her hand across the Formica desk to emphasise her point. All six sets of eyes around the octagonal table stared up at Helen and Mary Devine. It was unusual for the kids to be mean in front of a parent and they waited with bated breath to see what would happen next. Another mother saw what was going on, but decided to ignore it and continued chatting – it wasn't her child who was being excluded.

"Okey-dokey, how about this chair?" Mary Devine smiled and pulled out another free chair at the same table.

"Natalie Porter is sitting there," the same child said defiantly.

"Well, it looks like we'll just have to find another table, Helen." Mary's voice had a cheery lilt. She scanned the room for a free spot.

"But I want to sit at the same table as my friends," Helen said.

Mary got down on her knees, so she could talk to her daughter face to face. "Helen, why would you want to be friends with children that are mean to you?"

Helen shrugged and looked down at her black leather brogues.

Natalie Porter walked in the door.

"Over here, Natalie – I saved your seat!" the girl called.

Natalie walked over, putting her pink Sindy bag on the desk and an excited chatter started around the table.

Natalie's mother joined the other mothers. By now, both mothers and daughters had turned their backs on the Devine family. Case closed.

"Come on, Helen – let's find a seat over here."

Helen knew she just wasn't the Sindy-bag type of girl. Any progress she had made into the group she so desperately wanted to be part of had been lost over the summer. No Daddy, no Sindy, no deal.

"Is this Sister Carmel's class?" A flame-haired woman, wearing a long cheesecloth skirt, breezed through the door, an angelic red-haired girl behind her. Everyone looked up. There was a new kid in town.

"Yes, yes, come in. Welcome to the Immaculate Conception," said the kindly middle-aged nun. She turned to the girl, who looked like a deer caught in headlamps. "You must be Poppy."

Usually there would be a scramble for the new kid to sit at your table – everyone loved the novelty – but there was something about Poppy's washed-out uniform that caused a hesitation. Poppy twisted one foot behind her leg and rubbed it on her sock. The mothers stopped their gossiping to turn and look at the newcomers. They eyed mother and daughter, then went back to their conversations, this time in hushed tones with a look of disdain etched on their faces. The new people, whoever they were, just didn't belong.

"There's a free place over here if you like," Mary Devine called out.

"Thank you, Mrs Devine, that's wonderful," Sister Carmel said, but already one of her thirty-five students was distracting her. It was more crowd control than teaching.

The bell rang loudly, signalling the start of class.

"See you, Pops. Enjoy your day in the 'Immaculate Conception'. Maybe they are into fairytales here, after all, with a name like that, hey!" Poppy's mother ruffled her child's hair then got out of the classroom as quickly as if she'd been asked to stand barefoot on burning coals.

Mary Devine looked down at the newcomer whose hair was a rich copper shade of red. "That's a lovely slide you have in your hair, dear. You look pretty," she smiled. "Where's your lunch box?"

Poppy didn't answer.

"Is your lunch in your bag?" Mary took a quick peek inside. "No? Oh my, your mum must have forgotten it – I'll try to catch her." But she hesitated when she saw the child's face.

Poppy was shaking her head vigorously, still not saying a word.

"Don't worry, love, Helen will share hers with you, won't you, pet?"

Helen nodded eagerly. "What's your name?" she asked.

"Poppy."

"Like the flower?"

"The weed, so my brother says."

"I'm Helen. Do you want to sit beside me?"

Poppy nodded. Mary Devine slipped out.

"Helen?"

"Yes?"

"Will you be my new best friend?" Poppy didn't look at her as she took a crayon from the communal pot.

Helen hesitated for a moment – no one had asked her that before.

Then she smiled. "Yes, Poppy, I will."

20

Hong Kong International Airport. Departures. They were on their way home.

Well over a week had passed since Fred's interlude with Helen. His fantasy of Helen Devine had finally come to pass. And it did just that: pass. Disappointed, he went over it all again in his head to see if there was something else he should have done or said.

He had tried talking to her before they left Hong Kong for Mainland China. "That was some night last night," he'd whispered to her.

She'd smiled seductively back, saying nothing. She didn't have to – with Helen, her emerald eyes spoke a thousand words.

"We can do it again if you like, buttercup, real soon," he'd said, putting his hand on the small of her back. But Sarah joined them before Helen could reply. Damn it, he'd planned that one-liner since she'd left his room.

Helen and Sarah had slept all the way on the plane to Northern China. On arrival, Sarah had looked like she was about to pass out. Fifty-five minutes they stood in line for immigration at Qingdao – Sarah going different shades of pale all the while, ending up an odd shade of green. Green the girl was, he thought to himself, with bright pink ears, not the most attractive look. Said it must have been the food she ate. *Food my arse, tequila slammers more like.*

He smiled, remembering her face when she realised she had to go through a body-temperature test.

"What's that for, Helen?" Sarah had asked, a bead of sweat threatening to slide down her face.

"They've been doing it since the SARS outbreak. Relax, just walk through it. It detects elevated body temperature."

A look of terror shot over Sarah's pasty face. "Oh God, they'll never let me through. Honestly, Helen, I shouldn't have eaten those prawns."

Helen had looked at Fred, amused. *Who was Sarah trying to convince?*

Sarah started to shake – her blouse was soaked through with sweat. "Please God, just let me make it through," she prayed under her breath. "I swear I won't have a one-night stand in Hong Kong or anywhere again. And I'll never drink again."

Then as if God wanted her to know he'd heard her, her stomach lurched and she started to heave.

"Next!" the guard shouted and signalled to her.

She swallowed hard and stepped forward, while Helen and Fred smirked.

That evening, in the supplier's car, Fred tried to sit beside Helen but somehow Sarah ended up between them. Their meeting hadn't been the most pleasant – a full day, no lunch breaks – again. The glamour of Hong Kong was left behind.

Things went from bad to worse when they got to their hotel. Mysteriously, one room had been cancelled.

"Check again!" Fred demanded of the desk clerk, who continued to tap on her computer keyboard.

"One single, one twin, that's what was booked and it's all we have now, sir," she replied, handing over the key cards, conversation over.

"This is ridiculous – who changed the booking?" Fred could see his planned midnight call to Helen fade.

"You heard the girl, Fred, the hotel is full," Helen said, taking one of the room keys off the counter. "Sarah and I don't mind sharing, do we, Sarah?"

Sarah shook her head, unable to speak. It was amazing she'd got through the day at all. She had excused herself on numerous occasions to be sick. She'd sprayed air freshener around the loo, to cover her tracks, the smell of which made her throw up again.

"Well, if you're sure. But I'll look into this when we're back in London," Fred said, as a vein in his temple throbbed.

And now here they were back in Hong Kong, on the way home, where Helen would transfer straight to Dublin from Heathrow. Sarah hadn't gone out again, said she was in Asia to work, not rack up Eden's bar bill. Helen agreed and spent the evenings with her holed up in their room brainstorming about the new season's collection. Only the boss in Fred was impressed.

Jack Taylor stepped out of his taxi, which had left him kerbside at the Dragonair check-in area. The airport was quiet except for a few business travellers heading home before the weekend.

"Where are you flying to, sir?" the red-uniformed clerk asked.

"Phnom Penh," Jack smiled, handing over his passport.

"It's your lucky day, sir – you've been upgraded to first class." The girl circled the boarding gate and boarding time on his boarding pass before handing it to him.

"That's awesome, thanks!" Jack grinned – he considered asking why, but decided not to, in case she changed her mind or realised she'd made a mistake.

"Wait – you'll need a pass for the business lounge." She took out a gold card and started writing his details on it.

Technically, upgrades didn't get a lounge-pass, but her supervisor was on a break. She had already broken the rules by offering the only upgrade available to a back-packer and not one of their frequent flyers or someone in a suit. But this guy had such nice dimples and hands – he had beautiful hands.

"Just follow the signs for the Cathay Pacific lounge – we're the same company," the girl explained, with a tilt of her head. "Have a pleasant flight, sir – I hope I see you again." She flashed Jack a killer smile.

Jack hesitated for a moment – was she flirting with him?

Andromeda came to mind. He picked up the golden ticket: his good luck not feeling so lucky any more. He'd just met the hottest girl in Hong Kong, and he was leaving.

"Was there something else, sir?" She pushed a strand of hair behind her ear. A queue had started to form behind Jack.

"No, thank you, I'll be going to the business lounge now, eh, thank you."

Say something, Jack – get back in the saddle!

The steward watched as Jack walked away – a cute ass too, she noted, as she called the next in line.

Helen looked up at the departures board: *Cathay Pacific to London LHR, Status: on time.* "Thank you, God." She headed straight for the departure gate, not taking any chance of missing this flight.

Jack couldn't see any signs indicating which way he should go to the business lounge. The airport appeared devoid of staff also. Then, as chance would have it, a portly man came into his line of vision.

"Helen, where are you going? The Cathay lounge is this way!" he called out, signalling to a woman ahead of him that she was going in the wrong direction.

"No, Fred, see you on the flight!" the woman called and waved.

"Excuse me, sir," Jack asked as he approached Fred. "I couldn't help but overhearing – did you say the Cathay lounge is this way?"

Fred was still looking after Helen. Distracted, he grunted at the young man. "Women, don't think I'll ever understand them," he tutted.

"My uncle has a theory that woman are from Andromeda," Jack said.

Fred looked at him, his attention back now Helen was gone. "What's Andromeda?"

"A spiral galaxy in the outer universe," Jack replied.

"Huh?" Fred thought about it. "Makes sense, sounds like a smart chap, your uncle. I think he's most likely right." He took one last look in the direction of the gate and muttered something under his breath. "Cathay, did you say? Come on, lad, follow me, I was just on my way there."

Helen sat on a narrow steel seat opposite her departure gate. She fished for a book from her bag. She pulled out the one on synchronicity. She settled back. Finally she was on the home straight. She missed her mum, she missed her dog and surprisingly, she missed Rob.

21

Helen turned the key in the lock of the wood-panelled door to her mother's home in Sutton, County Dublin. "Hello? Mum, you home?"

The familiar smell and sounds greeted her with the wave of comforting feeling that a loving parent brings. She wanted to tell her mum about the awful Hong Kong trip but she knew she couldn't, as she would worry. Instead, Helen would smile, giving her a Chinese clay teapot and souvenir packet of tea and say nothing.

From the kitchen, RTÉ Radio One was blaring out, the Joe Duffy chat-show at a volume high enough for Mary to hear it from the garden. A waft of freshly grilled bacon caused Helen's stomach to rumble.

She hung her handbag at the end of the banisters she had slid down so often as a child and walked through the blue-carpeted hallway into the sun-filled kitchen, the soul of the house. The back door was open – a warm breeze brought the Indian-summer indoors. Mary was on all fours, planting flower bulbs, the first of which would flower in January. Mary loved seeing the first snowdrops of a new year. Helen's Golden Retriever, JD, lay beside her sprawled out, soaking up the sunrays.

"Hi, Mum!" Helen called again, not wanting to give her mother a heart attack.

She turned down the volume on the radio from eardrum-shattering to just plain uncomfortably loud. Beside the radio was a posy of flowers and a rose-scented candle flickering. Mary liked to keep her home beautiful. Or was she trying to hide the evidence of fried pig?

"Mum?"

The dog's head jolted upright, ears pricking up at the sound of Helen's voice. Then he was bounding to greet his mistress.

"JD!" Helen stretched her arm out to greet her oversized pooch. "Come here, boy," she said, rubbing behind his ears. He covered her in doggy kisses. "Whoa, less of the dog breath, JD!" She pulled her face away, laughing.

"Oh, it's you, dear – I didn't hear you come in." Mary struggled to get on her feet. "How was the flight?"

"Uneventful."

"And the weather in Hong Kong?" Mary hobbled towards her daughter on pins-and-needles-affected legs.

"Humid." Helen stepped down three small steps towards her mother.

"Same as here then, I never remember the likes of it, this kind of heat in autumn. It must be that global-warming thing." Mary fanned herself.

"Was it bacon sandwiches for lunch again, Mum?"

"Oh, they weren't for me – I made them for Lily." Mary didn't make eye contact, lest Helen start lecturing on cholesterol levels.

"Really? Funny that, seeing as Poppy texted me a few days ago to say Lily has declared herself a vegetarian." Helen was still feeling smug for being proven right in that prediction.

"And she's one of those lesbians now too apparently – have you ever heard the like? We didn't have them in my day."

"There were always lesbians and gays, Mum, stop changing the subject. Did you remember to inject today?"

Mary ignored Helen's reference to her health. "I mean it, my

111

father mentioned poufters occasionally, and I saw a few in America, but I never heard about lesbians until I was a married woman."

"What are you saying? If you knew you had the option, I might not be here?"

"God rest your father, if he could hear you now he'd turn in his grave."

"If he had a grave."

James Devine's ashes still sat on the polished mahogany sideboard in the dining room. Every Christmas and family celebration, Mary dusted off the urn, and placed it at the head of the table.

"Ah sure, you can mix us together, when I'm dead and gone. Judging by the aches and pains, that'll be any day now." Mary stretched her back.

"Stop it, Mum, you're only a young one – what's all this talk about leaving me an orphan?"

"You're nearly forty, some orphan!" Her mother laughed as she gave her a warm embrace. "I don't know, between cholesterol tables, injections for blood sugar and now arthritis, dear God, if I was a dog they'd put me down."

Helen kissed her mother on her soft cheek. She smelt of Max Factor powder and Channel No. 5 and had done so for as long as Helen could remember. She loved the softness of her mother's skin, which was a physical reminder of the softness of her heart. She had a large bosom that weighed heavy on her now, which meant she regularly rubbed her lower back in pain. Thanks to her love of processed pork products, Mary's midsection was close to measuring the same size as her chest – something she disguised with free-flowing brightly coloured dresses. Today she wore a lavender blue one that finished just short of the ground.

"Would you like a cup of tea, love? I bought some of that weird infusion stuff you and Poppy like." Mobility regained, Mary made her way into the kitchen. "Or there's a bottle of white wine open in the fridge, would you prefer that?"

"How long has it been there, Mum, a week?"

"Just a couple of days, I had a visitor, you see . . ." Mary paused, as if about to elaborate. Instead, she picked up the red-framed reading glasses that hung from her neck by multicoloured beads, to check the labels on the tea packets. "Ah, now that reminds me!" She held up her index finger, as if about to conduct a symphony. "I was clearing my presses out and found this nice bottle of that Baileys you like. I left it out for you to take home – I won't use it."

"Caramel Baileys – um, I gave you that as a present," Helen said flatly, as she picked up the bottle from the kitchen counter-top.

Mary chose to ignore the comment. "And there's fancy mustard there as well, I'll definitely never use that – you may as well have that too." She removed her glasses.

Knowing her mother, Helen picked up the whole-grain mustard jar. "Best-before January 2008. What are you trying to do? Kill me, Mother dear?"

"Don't mind those silly dates – they just put them on so they can sell more stuff. I never pay heed, and I'm as fit as a fiddle."

Helen resisted the urge to point out to Mary that not five minutes ago she was about to kick the bucket.

"Right. Tea. Which one do you want, green tea with jasmine or Pur-eh – I think that one makes you skinny." Mary picked up one of the packets. "Now where did I put my glasses?"

"They're on your head."

"So they are." Mary adjusted her glasses to read the packets through the bi-focal part of the lens.

"I'll have the green tea, please, Mum, and there's no such thing as a tea that makes you skinny."

"Wait – it's just as well I put my glasses on. That's Oxtail Cuppa Soup, not tea at all. Now where did I put the tea?"

"You're very distracted, Mum – whatever is going on with you?"

"It's not my fault. I'm a Vata!"

"What?"

"Poppy explained the whole thing to me. That thingamajig she does – Ayur-something."

"Ayurveda," Helen sighed.

"Yes, that – the Indian medicine thing. Apparently we all have different body types. She did the quiz on me – I'm a Vata type, which is space and air, so I can't help it. It's my dosha!"

"Airhead more like," Helen laughed. "Maybe I'll have that glass of wine after all. It's a good excuse for JD and me to walk back tomorrow for the car. Unless of course the wine *has* actually been sitting there for a week." She eyed Mary for confirmation.

"It's been in the fridge, sure it's grand. Honest to God, your generation would never have survived in my day." Mary was glad Helen had opted for the wine – it might make it easier for her to hear what she had to tell her.

"Ah, the old days, *Angela's Ashes* style," Helen mimicked. "Ye'd no electricity or running water – the forgotten West of Ireland, left behind in the Stone Age." She squinted an eye and pushed out her chin.

Mary laughed at Helen's one-man performance. "Maybe I'm a little inclined to exaggerate," she admitted, "but it *was* rural Ireland, we had no fridge, the toilet was an outhouse at the end of the garden and I had four brothers, remember."

"Bless – the Fitzgerald clan. Those were the days when the men were men and the sheep were afraid," Helen continued with her Wild Man of the West impersonation.

"Helen Devine – wash your mouth out!" Mary said, but mother and daughter both doubled up with laughter.

"So this is where the party is!" Poppy arrived at the back door, as she had done since she was a child.

Mary wiped a tear from the corner of her eye. "Oh, there you are, love. I was just explaining that dosha thing to Helen." With that, the two of them burst into laughter again, leaving Poppy a little bewildered.

"Glad I provided the entertainment, though I'm not sure I know how," Poppy said, enveloping them in the scent of musk as she walked past. She gave Helen a hug. "So, are you all set for the morning? We need to leave here before eight to give us time to set up. It is so good to have you home!" Poppy tried to sound convincing and gave Helen her most dazzling smile, to cover up the fact that Helen hadn't actually agreed to help her out the next day.

"Are you doing a car-boot-sale thingy again, Poppy?" Mary said, barely suppressing her amusement. No matter how much Helen loved her slightly hippy, eco-warrior friend, she hated it when Poppy roped her into one of her less-than-glamorous cash-producing schemes.

Helen's face registered horror, as memories came flooding back of haggling with a six-year-old over eighty cent for a one-legged, black Barbie that once belonged to Lily. The child, relentless, had beaten her into submission, acquired the doll for fifty cent and had even got Helen to throw in an extra pair of doll-shoes, the point of which was lost on Helen, considering the doll had only one foot.

"What have I agreed to do now?"

"The Mind Body Spirit Fair, in Temple Bar. I thought you'd man my stand while I'm doing the massages . . ." Poppy's voice trailed off.

"Oh right, of course." Helen was relieved – at least it was an in-doors city-centre venue, which meant an abundant supply of decent coffee and relative warmth.

"You are the bestest mate ever, Helen, thanks a mil. We'll have fun! There are free yoga classes, I'll make sure they let you in," Poppy tapped the tip of her nose in a "mum's the word" fashion, "and Indian head-massage. If that's all a bit pure for you, we can go for a drink afterwards."

"Massage and cocktails, now that sounds like my kind of day. I may skip the yoga though." Helen raised her mug in salute, having decided the tea was the least likely option to give her food poisoning, but she had checked the expiry-date, just in case.

Mary laughed. "You two are a match made in hell, do you know that? Will ye ever grow up and settle down at all?"

Poppy and Helen looked at her in shock. "Heaven forbid!" they chorused.

The conversation switched to Hong Kong and Helen started to

rummage through the goodie bag of trinkets she'd brought back as gifts.

Mary realised the news she was so anxious to tell Helen would have to wait – for now.

22

Poppy drove along the seafront road from Raheny towards Helen's house in Howth. She'd nudge Helen into her early weekend start, offering caffeine and carbohydrates. She reckoned one of the cafés was bound to be open, even in this sleepy town. Alas, she was wrong.

She pulled into a car-park to do a U-turn. As her trusty Mini Cooper nosed back onto the road, it stalled. Restarting the ignition, she noticed a *"To Let"* sign hanging from the old stone building on the opposite side of the road. What a beautiful setting for a holistic centre! She checked her watch – she was already running late. "No time to daydream now, Poppy," she said aloud and pressed the accelerator, to get back to reality. That's when the second sign of the morning grabbed her attention – this one had the inviting word *"Café"*. Poppy didn't remember it being there before.

"Thank you, Dahlia!" Poppy tapped the dashboard of her old car, in praise. "Government Scrappage Scheme, my backside! We'll go to the knacker's yard together, old girl." Poppy climbed out of the small car, in which she'd managed to fit a fold-up table, a massage chair and boxes filled with paraphernalia required for her day ahead.

"Ciao, bella!" a thin man called out to her. He sat on a windowsill of the building, available for rent, next to the café. He had an espresso in one hand, a cigarette in the other.

Poppy approached him. "Hello, please say you are open?" she said with a grimace and looked at him with pleading eyes. Although his face was fresh, his eyes were wise and as dark as deep pools of chocolate.

"*Domani, principessa*." He blew smoke in the opposite direction before he stubbed out his half-smoked cigarette.

Poppy looked at him blankly.

"Tomorrow, I open for the first time. But, as you can see, I test the equipment, make sure everything work okay. Would you like to try?" He raised the small cup.

"It must be my lucky day," Poppy said, entering the small Italian shop. The aroma of fresh bread baking caused her stomach to growl.

"I hope everyone has that reaction to my shop – you like it?"

"Excuse me." Poppy patted her stomach. "I love it. It's little Italy."

"*Grazie, grazie*. Now, you must tell me the truth about the coffee. I make sure the machine is set up right, although the secret is all with the *barista*. What can I get you?" He went behind the counter.

Poppy pulled out a heavy wooden bar-stool. "Coffee, please – black. And one for takeaway."

"One or two shots?" He stood waiting – handle at the ready.

"It'll be a long day – go on then – make it two!"

"And the takeaway, is it for your daughter?"

The question took Poppy by surprise.

He smiled. "Ah, but you don't remember me! I am the waiter from Antonio's."

The penny dropped. He had looked familiar. He was their waiter the night Lily announced she was a lesbian. He looked different now in his paint-splattered jeans and T-shirt.

"Yes, I remember now. You look different without your clothes on – I mean the white starched shirt and tie. I thought you were Spanish?" *Nice recovery, Poppy.*

"No, I am Italian. No worries – everybody thought that. I was working in a Spanish restaurant after all." He handed Poppy a weighty white cup.

118

Poppy blew the top of the liquid to part the caramel-coloured froth – underneath: black gold. She took her first sip. "Umh, this is really good! You can make that two takeaways!"

He beamed, pleased at her approval.

"So, you're working in both places now?" Poppy asked.

"No, I finish in Antonio's, just last night. I had to keep working, help make my dream real." He waved his arm at the small interior.

"So, this is your place?"

"Yes, me and my partner. I am Angelo." He extended his hand.

"Poppy. Pleased to meet you, Angelo." She shook his hand. Had he been referring to a business partner or a life partner, she wondered.

"'Puppy' – what a beautiful name – like the flower."

"It's 'Poppy'." She laughed at Angelo 's pronunciation as she climbed off the stool. "I'd better get going." She fished for her wallet.

"No, no charge."

"But then I won't be your first customer."

"Yes, you are and this way you'll have to come back again." Angelo shrugged, holding his hands out as though saying Mass.

A warm feeling coursed through Poppy, she wasn't sure why. She often felt uncomfortable taking things from people, even though in this case she knew it was only coffee. Her wallet contained forty euro in notes, and then some change. "Tell you what, Angelo, this is an Irish tradition." She handed him a twenty. "For luck." She nodded, encouraging him to take it. She had enough left for parking today and probably wouldn't have time for lunch anyway.

"Really?" Angelo hesitated, and then smiled broadly. "Thank you, Puppy. My place will be a big success!" He climbed onto the bar's draining-board. High up, he wedged the note halfway behind his café's name – *Il Panorama Café*.

Poppy she watched her lunch money be immortalised behind the slogan: *Enter a stranger – leave a local.*

Poppy walked back to her car loaded down with the two takeaway coffees and samples of Angelo's fresh-baked bread. "You take it," he'd said to Poppy, "I'm just testing the oven – this will go in the bin. Tomorrow I will bake a fresh batch."

She placed the coffees on roof of the car as she unlocked the car door. As she sat behind the wheel she realised what she'd been doing but she couldn't help herself – even as she turned the key in the ignition, she was still doing it – grinning like a Cheshire Cat.

23

Helen spread organic cotton over Poppy's makeshift stand. She had begged it off a supplier a few seasons ago. She stood back to admire her handiwork. The fabric looked much better as a tablecloth than a nightdress.

"Okay, Poppy, tell me what I have to do today." Her eyes darted around the hall. Other stallholders were setting up. Many appeared to be wearing tie-dye T-shirts, and tie-dye trousers – on the same body: the designer in her balked. It also become apparent there was a lot of facial hair on display.

"Just be yourself, tell them what I do, hand them a leaflet and ask if they'd like to join my mailing list." Poppy smiled, her arms outstretched as if it was all child's play.

"Ah, right, see here's the thing, what exactly do you do? You're always on some course or other. You pick up new qualifications as often as other people pick up dry cleaning." She waved her hand in front of her face. "What's that smell?"

"Incense, obviously, get used to it, there'll be a lot of it around today. I'm trying to cut back on massage and counselling, concentrating instead on Ayurveda and teaching meditation." Poppy stared at Helen beneath lowered eyebrows. Helen had asked her to teach her how to meditate months ago, but had kept putting it off.

"I know I should be doing it. But it's one of those things, isn't it?

You put it off until you reach crisis point. A bit like going to the gym after you've gained ten pounds." Helen fanned out Poppy's business cards on the table.

The first of their neighbours for the day had arrived. They bowed to Helen and Poppy but didn't speak. This suited Helen just fine.

"Okay, the Ayurveda thing is: Vata – air-heads. Pitta – hot tempered. Kapha – need to lose a few pounds. Have I got it right?" she asked.

"I tell you what, why don't you leave the explaining to me?" Poppy waved to a guy with a shaved head, bar a ponytail which hung from the nape of his neck. He had something painted on his forehead and along the length of his nose.

"You know the strangest people, Poppy Power – apart from me, that is. What am I again?"

"A Vata-Pitta, creativity with passion." Poppy smiled at her. The corner beside them was filling up fast, as its occupants arrived in dribs and drabs. "Remember, Helen, the true purpose of meditation is to find out who you really are."

"Eh, you're Poppy Power."

"Very funny. I think an easy way to explain it is that meditators make better choices. They start to notice coincidences – synchronicities – throughout the day. There's no such thing as coincidence – the more you notice them, the more you know you're in Dharma." Poppy stood back and looked at the stand from the perspective of the public.

"Dharma?" Helen thought Dharma was the part-title of an old sit-com.

"Your life purpose – we all have one. We just have to figure out what it is. Synchronicities show us the way." With that, the main doors opened and people started to flood in.

"It'd be easier if I had a sample, something I could physically show them." Helen's brow furrowed with worry, then she looked like she had a light-bulb moment. "Come to think of it, I did experience an unusual coincidence when buying a book on synchronicity! It was recommended to me by a stranger."

"Go on . . ."

"Well, I saw him at the airport check-in, and then I bumped into him again in the bookshop. The thing is, he had an odd-looking briefcase that caught my eye." Helen twisted the small gold ring on her little finger as she spoke. "It didn't fit with the rest of him – with his image." She looked to see if Poppy could follow what she was saying.

Poppy was nodding like a spring-headed dog in a car rear window.

"Well, I had this nasty experience in a bar in Hong Kong. I'll tell you about it another time, I don't want to talk about it now . . . but anyway just after that I spotted the man from Heathrow, or rather I spotted his straw briefcase, just as he was going out the door of the bar."

"Please tell me you went after him?" Poppy asked, barely breathing.

"Yes, but he had disappeared. I didn't see him or his straw case during the rest of the trip so it must have meant nothing. It was just a coincidence."

"Nonsense, of course it meant something."

"What?"

"I don't know. You've got to learn to trust the Universe, Helen, have faith."

"You lose me when you start talking about the Universe, Poppy."

An elderly lady carrying a large plaid shopping bag approached the table. "What free stuff have you got?" She pushed the leaflets around the table, looking for something to claim.

"A smile," Helen beamed at her.

The woman stared, open-mouthed, her nose screwed up and lips pursed.

"And a 'positive thought for the day' card – from *The Seven Spiritual Laws of Success*. Let's see – today is Saturday – The Law of Dharma. How apt."

The woman scowled and grabbed the card from Helen before shuffling off to the next stand.

Poppy reached up and put her arm around Helen's shoulder. "See, you're a natural!"

"Give me knickers any day."

The Mind Body Spirit Fair was in full swing. On the stand beside Poppy's, a group of people wearing orange robes sat on cushions. Each of them held a different instrument, from cymbals to drums. More of them appeared to arrive every few minutes. They began their musical chorus of chanting and drumming: they had a lot of drums. To begin with, Helen found it rather soothing but by lunchtime, they still hadn't stopped. They had a relay of volunteers to ensure continuity of the beat and of course the chanting – "*Hare Hare Krishna Krishna*".

It was going to be a very long day.

Helen answered the phone on the first ring.

"Hi, it's me. I'm ready to leave the city now – I'll unload the car tomorrow. What do you fancy this evening?" It was Poppy. She had sent Helen home at four o'clock, saying she'd manage alone. The show had quietened down, bar a few stragglers and Helen had looked like she was losing the will to live.

"Oh, Poppy, I forgot to tell you, I've a date with Keifer." Helen yawned to emphasise she had no intention of going out.

"Keifer?"

"Sutherland."

"Don't tell me, Helen, you're staying in on a Saturday night, watching psychopathic murderers?"

"Yes, I think of it as a healthy way to release my dark side. So I don't actually cause bodily harm to my fellow commuters on the Tube. Anyway, that's what God invented Sky Plus for – I've a whole two weeks of quality programmes to catch up on."

"But it's Saturday night."

"Exactly, amateur night on the town – the last thing I need is to feel like I'm old enough to be everyone's mother." Helen adjusted a cushion behind her head while balancing her mobile between her shoulder and ear. She stretched her legs along the dark purple couch. In perfect harmony, her Golden Retriever mirrored her action, on the deep-pile carpet. She had positioned everything just perfectly to be within reach of her horizontal position on the settee. The circular glass and stainless-steel table was within arm's reach. On it, the remote control, a cordless phone (although the only one who ever rang her on the land-line was her mother) and a bottle-cooler containing a bottle of New Zealand's finest. She placed the wineglass on the table as softly as possible – it made the all too familiar clink sound.

"You're drinking wine already, aren't you?" Poppy was dismayed to realise she was competing with wine.

"I just opened it a few minutes ago," Helen said defensively. "Besides, I've had a tough week – I may not even have a job on Monday, after snogging the boss and running away. On top of which I'm refusing to run away with him to join Eden Hong Kong. He may well show me the door. I need to chill out."

"Meditate then, don't sit and drink wine at home. Alone." Poppy cringed internally at her own double standard.

"Jeez, all this time I thought you were telling me to *medicate*. If you're so concerned with my mental state, come over, and then I won't be alone."

JD looked up with dewy eyes.

"Besides, I'm not alone. I've got JD here to keep me company." Truth was, the Hare Krishna drums were still ringing in her ears and Helen just felt like canine company this evening. She lowered her leg to rub JD's soft blonde belly with her bare foot. She giggled as his hair tickled her toes. The movement caused her dressing gown to fall away from her body. And then she saw it.

Panic-stricken, she choked, "Oh my dear God!"

"Helen? Helen – is everything okay?"

"*Noooooooo*!" she wailed.

"What's wrong? What's happened –"

"Granny pubes, that's what!" Helen sobbed. If she could see the tiny grey hair in the muted lighting of her living room, imagine how it'd look in stark bathroom lighting!

"What the hell are you on about?"

"My black box isn't looking so black any more, that's what. It's more a paler shade of grey." Helen's voice quivered.

"Please tell me you aren't examining your crotch while on the phone to me."

"This is serious, Poppy. Have you ever heard of a pilot's voice on the grey box? Do they search for the grey box? No, that's because everyone's only interested in the black box."

"You haven't answered my question and since when were you interested in pilots? I thought after that last one you met you said they were more interested in their throttle than the box, no matter what colour it is."

"No, I didn't. What I said was, some of them mistake their penis for their throttle, or whatever that thing they pull for lift-off is!"

"Take-off, you mean, unless you've bonked an astronaut and neglected to tell me that as well?"

"A cowboy, maybe – fly-by-nights, definitely – astronauts, no – I've never heard that line on the chat-up circuit. Listen, I've got to go, I've just the thing for such an emergency." Helen was on the move.

"If that's your idea of an emergency, remind me never to call you in a crisis," Poppy said, hearing Helen running up the stairs. "Do you remember that time in New York, and the Irish President was in town? Those Secret Service guys gave us their cards. Do you still have them? Secret Service is nearly as good as an astronaut. I wonder were we considered a threat to national security after we rumbled them?" Poppy rambled on, to sounds of Helen ransacking her house. "That was a great night. Pre 9/11 mind. Probably wouldn't happen these days." Poppy sighed at the memory and wondered should she hang up.

"It's in here somewhere," Helen mumbled. "Here we go . . . The Black Betty!"

"Black Betty?"

"Yep, I was going to go for The Pink Betty, but it reminded me of that *Sex and the City* episode where Samantha ended up looking like Bozo the Clown."

"Right." Poppy was often in bed by watershed time and only

126

recently, thanks to Lily's protests, claiming she was a disadvantaged teen due to lack of Reality TV, had she succumbed and installed cable. Of course she'd heard of the programme, but she still had no idea what Helen was talking about.

Hiding her annoyance at her satellite-inept friend, Helen elaborated. "The last time I was in getting my Brazilian wax, they had this hair-dye stuff on sale at reception, called The Betty."

"I'm nearly afraid to ask . . .?"

"Well, it's especially formulated for the hair-down-there. Red for a heart-shape, pink for, em, I don't know, maybe a fluffy box. They even had duck-egg blue for a Tiffany box. I was tempted by all of them, but then, as I said, memories of that *Sex and the City* episode come back to haunt me, so I decided to play it safe."

"But why didn't you go for blonde? To match your hair? Why black? I don't know why –"

"Okay, so they were out of stock of Blonde Betty! And to be honest, it's hard enough keeping up with highlights on my head, never mind anywhere else!"

"But black – when you're blonde –"

"Oh, shut up, Poppy! I'd noticed a grey hair down there – I plucked it out of course but I bought the stuff just in case. Do you think I got more greys because I plucked one out? I seem to remember an old-wives' tale: if you pluck one grey hair, seven grow back in its place." Helen was getting worried as she remembered she had actually plucked three hairs.

"Helen, you're an intelligent woman, well, at least you are most of the time, and that's nonsense. But I'm sorry to tell you – you've brought this upon yourself." Poppy sniffed.

"How?"

"You believed that you were going to go grey, so the Universe delivered. It's the Law of Attraction: *As the mind goes, energy flows.*" Poppy was sounding rather smug.

"How do I un-manifest what the Universe has manifested then, oh Wise One?"

"Positive thoughts and meditation – but seeing as the grey is already there you may want to try your Betty-whatever in the meantime. Hang on . . ." There were muffled voices in the background as Poppy put her hand over the mouthpiece – then she was back. "Much as I'd love to stay and chat about your fanny, Helen, the Hare Krishna group have just invited me to join them for tofu and a cup of ginger tea. Saturday night with a difference – at least it solves the problem of drink driving – Dahlia can stay with me."

Helen was pleased to be off the hook.

"Don't forget about tomorrow, I'll call you to make arrangements," Poppy said.

"What on earth now – can't I even get Sunday off?"

"Relax, it's that mystic appointment we've waited so long to get."

"Appointment? What –"

"I've room for one in my car!" Poppy shouted at the Hare Krishnas, who were trying to sort out drums, squeezeboxes and lifts.

"Poppy, please don't go joining a new group – dragging you out of a kibbutz once in this lifetime was enough."

"For God's sake, I was eighteen and you'll never let me hear the end of it, will you?" Poppy exhaled noisily.

"No." One of Helen's favourite pastimes was winding Poppy up – she made it so easy to do.

"Look on the bright side." Poppy cheered up. "The psychic – he'll be able to tell you if you're sacked or not – save you an early-morning flight on Monday."

With that, Poppy hung up.

Having lain down spread-eagled on a pile of old towels for thirty minutes, Helen hosed herself down with the shower nozzle. She looked in the mirror and admired her handiwork. The black box was back and it was blacker than she'd seen it in years. She was feeling warm and the familiar tingle of growing excitement ran through her body. She wasn't sure if it was caused by the gushes of water, or the glass of wine she'd consumed. Or maybe Poppy was right and wherever you put your attention, energy flows. She'd been dying down below but now she could definitely feel the energy there.

Then, even though she knew she shouldn't, she reached for her phone and began to text.

"Hi Rob, how r u? At home, bored. U got any exciting gossip r juicy bits 4 me?" It was an unashamed textual flirtation, with a man whose number she knew she should delete, along with their relationship. Within seconds, her phone bleeped.

"I've got something big and juicy all right. Have u eaten? @"

The "@" symbol at the end of the text was Rob's way of sticking his tongue out at her.

She smiled and typed, "I'm out of batteries." She waited ten minutes before she pressed send, lest she appear too eager.

Again, she received Rob's reply by return: "Be there in twenty."

24

Rob pressed the bell next to Helen's bright red-lacquered door. He ran his fingers through his thick dark hair. As he heard her footstep approaching, a shot of adrenaline hit him.

"Hey, Rob!" Helen half-opened the door. He could just see her face, blonde waves falling loosely around it. Bee-stung lips, glossed, berry-red.

Helen liked red.

Anticipation replaced adrenaline. He couldn't take his eyes off her mouth – that was until he stepped inside and saw the rest of her.

"Wow, you look great, Helen!" was all he could manage to say. She wore a tantalising black silk robe. Its low cut revealed smooth olive skin and the curve of her cleavage.

"Pleased to see me?" Rob moved closer and nuzzled the side of her neck.

Helen shivered as she felt his warm breath on her skin.

"Come on, baby, let's take this upstairs, I'm HD-Ready." Rob whispered his usual catch-phrase, comparing Helen's initials to high-definition television.

His words had an unexpected effect. Maybe she shouldn't have texted Rob – she pulled away slightly.

"Slow down there, soldier – what happened to pleasantries like 'How are you?'"

"We can do those later," Rob muttered. With one arm, he pulled her towards him and swiftly entwined her in a tango-like move. Behind her now, he wrapped his arms around her waist – pressing his hardness against her.

"I think it's *you* who's pleased to see me," Helen giggled, weakening.

"You smell so good," Rob said, inhaling deeply. He moved a hand under her robe to caress her breast, the other he slid between her thighs.

Desire replaced Helen's fleeting attempt to have a conversation before sex – she turned her face to meet his, their kissing becoming more urgent as they explored each other's bodies.

Helen closed her eyes and allowed herself to be elevated to a place she believed only Rob could take her. He slipped off his jacket, placed it on the polished oak floor and lowered her onto it. She reached up, releasing his belt.

Rob moved down her body. He knew every inch of her, what made her shudder – what made her tick. He lowered his mouth to her dark nipple and began flicking it with his tongue. She groaned as he began to suck. Licking his way down past her belly button until his head was between her legs, he spread them apart as he buried his face in what he called the origin of the universe.

He felt her melt in his mouth as he listened to the sound of her shallow breath, his ability to seduce her making him even harder. He could feel her body tense and, as she climaxed, he thrust himself deep inside her, moving to her rhythm – their rhythm.

They lay still, not saying anything, both waiting for their breathing to abate. Rob rolled off and lay beside her on the hall floor.

Helen was glad the housekeeper had been yesterday.

"Is that wine I see?" she said, as she propped herself up on one elbow.

"Very astute – one white, one red – take your pick. Hey, doggie!" Rob jumped to his feet and pulled up his jeans as JD waddled over to him.

"Hells, your dog was about to lick my butt." Rob made a face.

"Just as well you can't talk, boy." Rob tickled the dog under his chin. He sniffed his hand after rubbing JD and looked displeased. "Have you any anti-bacterial hand-wash in here?" he asked, as he headed for the downstairs loo.

Helen looked at JD and raised her eyes to heaven. The dog turned and went back to his bed in the kitchen and watched her from there. The silent treatment. Who says dogs can't talk? You just have to tune in to them, at the right frequency.

Rob wasn't one for pillow talk, but seeing as they hadn't made it far past the front door, it wasn't an option anyway. Helen knew it would be the same even if they had made it to the bedroom. Rob was expert at meeting her physical needs but emotionally he was a stranger.

By the time he emerged from the toilet, Helen had changed from her seductress silken wear into a fluffy baby-blue robe with matching slippers which she wore to shuffle around the kitchen.

"Excuse me – did you see where Helen went?" he said, his brow knitted in confusion.

"What are you on about, Rob? Do you want red or white?" She held up both bottles of wine.

"Helen, Helen? Is that you? I thought it was your long-estranged grandmother. I go to the jacks for five-minutes and my sexy vamp morphs into dowdy gramp!"

"Very funny."

"I've got the car, so a Diet Coke will do me."

Helen busied herself with the corkscrew in an effort to simmer down the irritation that was bubbling.

"You're welcome to stay," she said, trying to sound carefree. The familiar pattern emerged – friction replaced sexual tension, giving rise to a potential argument.

Rob's expression darkened. "You know I prefer my own bed – besides, I have to work in the morning." He looked away, having laid the seed for his escape.

"You're working on a Sunday?" Helen's voice was tight – she looked him in the eye. *Damn! Why can't you just let it go, Helen?*

"Yes, unfortunately. No rest for the wicked. I'm working on

contracts for a merger between two multinationals. It's worth a fortune in fees, so merits a few Sunday hours." Rob's eyes came to life again. "It'll firmly place us on the map, as the top corporate law firm in the country." He pushed both his hands deep into the front pockets of his jeans. "I can't say too much, but you'll be reading about it in the papers in the coming weeks."

"As long as it's not Eden, or one of our competitors, I really don't give a toss." Helen wouldn't look up at him, twisting the gold ring on her little finger instead.

"Eden is small-fry by comparison. These are the big boys. Maybe I will have that glass of wine – it's been a long week." Rob leant against the kitchen counter, his ankles crossed and his body relaxed. He enjoyed talking about work, especially with someone outside of the office.

"Did you see the season finale of *24*?" She handed him his wine.

"No, do you have it?" Rob's night was getting better by the minute.

It was Helen's turn to act smug. "I bought the box-set in a market in Shanghai. I got you the entire James Bond collection too: every Bond movie ever made." She quickly added, "It was really cheap, it would have been a shame to pass it up."

"Helen Devine, you are, without doubt, every man's wet-dream." Rob planted a kiss on her forehead. "Now, if you'd just agree to some girl-on-girl action, I'd die a happy man."

"Come on, Don Juan, grab the wine. I'll get the popcorn. I'm not ready for you to die – just yet."

Rob drained the last drop of red wine into their glasses. They had polished off the bottle of white sometime earlier, neither noticing, engrossed in the heart-stopping action on the small screen.

"Told you he was a baddie!" Helen declared when the credits rolled. It was one of their favourite pastimes – trying to out-guess each other in spotting the plot line or the secret villain.

"I knew that," Rob said, dismissing her comment.

"Yeah, yeah." Helen flicked the off button on the remote-control. The light in the room softened without the glare from the

TV. Now, the only illumination came from a sandalwood candle and a small table-lamp. With a click of another control, low strains of New Age ambient music filled the air. Rob kicked back and sank deeper into the couch. He swirled his wine around the glass, lost in thought.

"A penny for them," Helen traced the tip of her forefinger along his temple.

Not needing further encouragement, Rob talked about what he always talked about, his work, which Helen understood was his life. And that was okay. His face relaxed so much as he talked, he looked years younger. He loved what he did – she envied him. Her passion for Eden was waning, she couldn't deny it. Previously, if she wasn't working, she was talking about work. She ate, slept and breathed lingerie. She had always been on the lookout for fresh ideas and new designs, no matter where she was. It could be watching TV and she'd notice a subtle curve of a seam. Or in a restaurant, perhaps a colour would catch her eye. She kept a small sketchpad in her handbag at all times in case she saw something that she could translate into a new bestseller – she still did but it wasn't as crammed with inspiration as before. Maybe if she could get back to being more of a designer and less of an administrator it would fan the flames of her creativity again. But a niggling voice inside her told her it was more than that.

They continued to talk into the night and at one point they retrieved Mary's re-gifted bottle of caramel Baileys. Rob liked his over ice – Helen took hers straight up.

"I don't know how you drink it like that," Rob said.

"I don't like ice any more – Poppy says it's better to drink liquids warm or at least at room temperature. You're a Pitta, that's why you like the ice."

"Here we go!" Rob rolled his eyes. "Poppy and her mumbo-jumbo – no doubt Pitta is something bad – that woman hates me. How is the daft witch anyway?"

"Rob! Don't be so mean. Poppy doesn't hate you – she just hates what you did to me." Helen immediately regretted what she had said as the atmosphere in the room chilled. "Actually Pittas are great leaders and have a fiery passion." She rubbed her foot along his groin and let it linger, but got little response.

There was a silence, then he said, "So, what's the story at Eden? Are you ready to fly the nest, start up your own business, rather than raking the money in for them?"

"Don't start at me, Rob. The company has been very good to me over the years. Besides, after last week's Hong Kong trip, I'll be lucky if I even have a job on Monday and you certainly didn't help things with that *Perfect Pussy* prank of yours – I could have lost my job! Fred had a right go at me over that." She flinched as she said Fred's name.

"What did he say?" Rob didn't wait for a reply before continuing and so dismissing any retribution for his practical joke. "Legally, it'd be difficult for them to terminate your contract, based on the number of years you have been with them, unless you did something completely unethical. Did you? Embezzle funds? Supply the competitors with next season's designs?"

"Rejected the advances of the managing director?" Helen said, leaving out the bit about the kiss.

"What, Fat Fred?" Rob burst into laughter. "Fred would never be able for a woman like you!" He had met Fred once, in London, during one of the brief on-again periods he and Helen shared. "Jesus, did he make a lunge for you? Between your tits and his belly you would have just bounced off each other." He whooped loudly.

Helen playfully thumped him. "Oh shut up, you – it could have been yin and yang."

"Please – no more Poppy-isms!"

"Needless to say, I'm dreading seeing him in the office. Fred can be great fun and good to work with, as long as he's getting his own way. He can also be a nasty piece of work. I could be wrong, but I often got the impression he manipulates people, situations."

"What exactly did happen between you two?" Rob suddenly looked serious.

"Nothing actually happened," Helen said, looking at the floor, "but I'm sure he's offended. I don't think I'm going to brush this one aside too easily."

"Bullshit. You're exaggerating things again, Helen. They need you and they know it. You were the one who brought them out of the ha'penny place and into the big league."

"Maybe, but I think I've lost my mojo. I don't feel the excitement any more when it comes to designing. My job is more about cost-cutting, EU red-tape and bloody Chinese factories."

Silence fell between them for a moment.

"Maybe if I'd made the move to come home and set up on my own a few years ago, it'd have worked out. Let's face it, who nowadays is voluntarily leaving a six-figure salary with pension, healthcare and perks?"

Rob's eyes narrowed. "You have a point there – how much are you on?"

Helen shifted uncomfortably. Her success was somehow a bone of contention between them – it always had been. "Plus, there's this girl I'm working with now, Sarah. I have to admit she's good. She's young, enthusiastic, has a first-class honours degree in design. She lacks cop-on but they love her – and she costs about a quarter of my salary."

"Is she hot?"

"Shut up!" Helen poked him a little harder this time.

"Ouch! That's assault!" Rob rubbed his belly. "Sarah is exactly why you should think about being your own boss. Okay, so she hasn't got your experience but she'll be nipping at your heels. It's only a matter of time before they try to oust you and your big pay cheque. Let's hope Sarah's not willing to shag Fred, or it could be sooner than you think."

Helen looked troubled – was that really a possibility?

Rob cheerily added, "Don't worry – we'll sue their asses."

"But the thing is – I think I'm knickered out of it. To start my own business I'd have to have drive, passion and belief in what I'm doing. Lingerie isn't doing that for me any more. It's time for phase two of my career. But what's next? I feel like I should be doing more with my life but I don't know what that is. Can I reinvent myself or will I forever be the lingerie designer?"

The conversation was getting far too deep for Rob's liking.

"I've still got plenty of passion for your lingerie, baby, but if you're ready to get out of knickers, I'm here to help." He grabbed her hand and put it on his penis, which was stiffening again.

Helen took a sip of her Baileys and moved closer to him. She kissed him and, as he opened his mouth to receive her, she slowly released a trickle of the creamy liquor onto his tongue. She straddled him and with their lips still locked, she eased herself on top of him. They gently rocked, their lovemaking more sensual and slower than it had been hours earlier. He undid the belt of her robe and let it fall to the floor, leaving her naked. Her breasts were level with his face – he licked and teased each nipple to hardness. Her hair fell onto his face. It smelt of amber. He inhaled her scent as he softly groaned for the second time that evening.

Rob looked at her – his eyes glistened as he brushed her hair off her face. "God, you are the most beautiful woman, Helen. You're an angel, with a devilish glint, my 'Hell in the Divine'."

Maybe it was the lovemaking that made her want to talk. It was gentler than their usual WWF style (wrestling, not wildlife). Or was it the wine that loosened her tongue? Somewhere, subconsciously she knew it was because there had been that rare glimpse of a tender moment between them, like the ones they shared so routinely when they were younger. So routinely, they assumed that it would last forever. It didn't.

"Do you ever think about the baby? He'd be a young man now," she said softly as Rob held her in his arms. She knew she was treading on a minefield. She felt him tense.

"Stop it, Helen. We've been through this a million times before. We did the best we could – under the circumstances." Rob's voice was cold, firm.

A tear escaped from Helen's eye, she quickly wiped it away. "But was it the right thing? I thought there'd be plenty of time for children, but here I am nearly forty and guess what, Rob – no child."

Rob pushed her away and stood to leave. *Damn Helen, why did she always start this shit just as he was starting to relax?*

"So that's what this is about, Helen – your biological clock."

"Maybe, but I've felt this way for nearly twenty years, so it's unlikely." Fighting back more tears, she continued, "You always say this crap, Rob – I'm your ideal woman, you could never feel about anyone the way you feel for me. But here we are – middle-aged – and what have we got to show for it? Nothing! We're alone, for fuck sake, look at us. How did we go from being soul-mates to fuck-buddies?" She tried to catch her breath.

Rob went to the hall, picked his jacket off the floor where it still lay crumpled from earlier.

"I thought you were staying tonight," she said, following him.

"I never said I was staying, you assumed that I would. Assumption, Helen, is the mother of all fuck-ups."

"You can't drive, you're over the limit."

"I'll get a taxi."

"Why do you always scurry off, like you're suddenly standing on a bed of nails?"

"I am not! It's after three in the morning – I've a lot on tomorrow." Rob's words hung like stale air. Then he changed tack in an effort to expedite his exit. He put his hands on Helen's shoulders and looked down at her from arm's length. "Look, we did the right thing. We were a couple of kids, still in college – we could barely look after ourselves, never mind a baby."

"Mum would have helped us," Helen said weakly, unable to look up.

"And what? You drop out of uni. Me working to make ends meet. Look where we are now. You're design director in one of the UK's top retail-chains. You've travelled the world ten times over. I've built the most respected law firm in the country. Do you think we'd have all this if we'd become parents barely out of our teens?"

"Maybe we'd still have each other." She looked him squarely in the eye.

Rob swallowed and thought for a moment, his Adam's apple bobbing up and down. "We still have each other," he said softly.

"This isn't together, Rob. This is sex. I can't even tell my best friend that we're together and, as for my mum, she'd have a canary."

138

"Ah, Mary – how is the old bat?"

"Shut up, Rob. I mean it. I need more than this. Maybe we should start dating again, stop sneaking around behind people's backs. Talk to each other. Christ, we're not even using condoms! How do I know you're not having sex with other people?"

"Because we discussed it, Helen, we agreed we'd be sexually exclusive."

Helen thought of her brief response to Fred's kiss. Christ, had aliens kidnapped her brain, for those few moments, or was it Uncle Ron Bacardi? She considered telling Rob, but he'd always been so jealous of her around other men. Would he understand?

"It seems that's all we have, Rob. It's as if you want to have your cake and eat it. I don't know who your friends are, what you do with your time during the week."

"I seem to remember when we started this whole thing that it suited you just fine. You even laughed that your idea of commitment was to own a dog!"

"That is a big commitment. At least it shows I'm capable of caring for another living creature, other than myself."

"Look, we have it good here, Helen. If it ain't broke, why fix it? You're in London all week – you've got your travel on top of that. Can you imagine a boyfriend whingeing at you that you don't have time for him? Then there's the singles scene, getting to know someone, dating, having to teach them what you like." Rob smirked.

"Okay, so sexually we work. I'm not questioning that. All I'm saying is: I'm ready for more."

"Helen, we were always fighting. This way you get all the good bits of a relationship – without the drawbacks."

When Rob spoke, he had a way of making anything sound reasonable.

"I don't know, Rob – I'm starting to think all that couple crap might be nice to try."

Rob had known this moment would come sooner or later, but their arrangement suited him fine. Still, the thought of losing Helen didn't appeal to him.

"I tell you what. After I finish the paperwork tomorrow, why don't I take you to dinner, my treat?"

"I'd like that." Helen yawned – they'd made some headway. "I'll book somewhere local – how about that new fish place on the pier?"

"How about we go into Dublin?"

"Oh, all right so. I'm on the red-eye on Monday, but I haven't been out in town in ages, so why not?" Helen got on her tippy-toes to give him a kiss on the cheek. "Will I call you a cab?"

"No, it's fine, I'll just hail one down on the main road, cheaper than calling one."

Outside, Rob waited for a few minutes. When Helen's bedroom light went out, he turned the key in his ignition. Thankfully, as always, he had parked a few metres down the road rather than in the driveway. He'd be damned if he was forking out for a taxi after only a few glasses of wine and hours ago at that, but it wasn't worth arguing with Helen about. He was pleased at how he'd handled her when she'd started to go off on one.

That's what makes you so damn good in the courtroom, old boy! he thought as he drove into the night.

25

Despite the late hour getting to bed, Helen woke early on Sunday morning. She looked out the window and noticed there was no sign of Rob's car. He's up early, she thought. She pulled on a pair of black track-suit bottoms and tied her hair back in a pony-tail, before running downstairs.

"Come on, JD, the beach awaits!" Helen called as she went into the kitchen to wake the dog.

JD bounced around in excitement, his tail wagging so furiously he knocked over several free-standing photos on a low windowsill. Helen loved her beachside home. She had the best of both worlds: city-life on weekdays, and escape from the rat race at weekends.

Helen and JD ran along the beach which Helen could access from the back of her townhouse. A light breeze was on their backs, sunshine on their faces. Thirty minutes of pure abandonment, where nothing else existed.

Getting back to the house, Helen put her key in the lock and opened the back door, just a fraction. "No chance, JD, you can stay out there until you dry off." The tide was in, and the dog had swum in the sea. As if to protest, he shook his whole body vigorously, spraying Helen with sea water and dog hair. When he'd finished, he looked like he'd stuck his paw in a light socket.

Helen brushed the sand off, made a coffee and booted up her

other baby, her white iMac laptop. This was her time: no phone, no people, just her, her coffee and her Mac. JD pressed his wet nose against the window but Helen didn't budge. She was in her world of time-wasting internet sites, another Sunday indulgence.

There was something about looking at shopping websites, consuming caffeine and a week's worth of cholesterol with one laden pastry, that made it all the better. She wandered onto her Facebook page, and laughed at some of the silly photos and comments her friends had up-loaded. A link at the side of the side of the computer screen caught her eye: *Find Friends on Facebook. Start the search button and Facebook will identify friends from your email lists."*

She clicked on it. Dozens of profiles popped up on the screen. Poppy's daughter, Lily, was one of them. Helen decided to send her a friend request, which she knew Lily would reject – how embarrassing being friends with your godmother! She pressed send anyway, if there's one thing she enjoyed almost as much as annoying Poppy, it was annoying her daughter.

She was about to log off when another profile name caught her eye. For a moment, her world stood still.

She directed the cursor over the silhouetted faceless picture.

Sam Fisher the name said, but it had come up attached to Rob's private email address.

"Sam Fisher only shares information with his friends. Click here to request Sam as a friend" the pop-up message box read back.

She double-checked. It was definitely Rob's email all right: lawbreaker007@ . . . But he had used a false name. Hardly surprising. Rob swore he wouldn't be caught dead on a social networking site. His profile was set to private but Helen could still see his friends.

He had only one.

And she was beautiful.

Her sparkling eyes and blinding white smile taunted Helen. Was she imagining it or did the girl look like she had, over fifteen years ago?

Nadia Rossi.

Helen wanted to slam her laptop shut. Instead, with a lump in her throat, the cursor appeared to glide across the screen of its own volition as she voyaged into Ms Perfect's life. She could be anyone, Helen told herself. A work colleague of Rob's – but if that was the case why did he hide his identity? Helen wanted to stop but she kept on delving. And then, as she'd feared, Helen saw the photo she had hoped she'd never see – Rob and another woman, heads tilted together, all shiny happy couple.

Helen closed the laptop and sat for a moment, dazed, not knowing what to think.

All the usual excuses came to her.

She's just a friend.

Rob wouldn't sleep with someone else.

And just as quickly, the counter arguments started.

She's his lover.

He probably was sleeping with her.

Wanting to wash the Facebook image and negative thoughts from her mind, Helen stripped, to shower. As she removed her underwear, she could still smell Rob's scent on her skin. She looked at her naked body in a full-length mirror – all she saw were flaws.

She turned the water pressure onto the highest setting and let the water beat down on her head, hoping the power of the water would wash everything away. But her thoughts just kept going back to Rob, the only man she'd ever fallen in love with.

26

Helen and Rob: 1990

"Rob, I'm pregnant," Helen whispered.

"How the fuck did that happen?" Rob shouted down the phone.

Helen began to sob. She had just done the home pregnancy test in the girls' toilet of her college. Now she was on the public phone in the corridor. She twisted the curly cable around her finger. Rob's reaction wasn't what she'd hoped to hear.

"I don't know . . . I must have messed up the pill or something." Helen struggled to regain control. The phone started to beep – it needed more money. Calling mobiles was expensive.

"Okay, look, calm down, we'll work it out." Rob's tone was softer.

They met up later that night. Helen's eyes were red and swollen from crying.

Rob took her in his arms. "It's going to be okay, Helen, don't worry. You didn't tell your mother, did you?"

Helen shook her head. "No, I'm not going to spoil her first holiday in years – it can wait till she gets back. What are we going to do, Rob?"

"Well, are you sure? I mean, did you get the result confirmed by a doctor?"

"No."

"Then there's no point panicking until we do that. Sure, it could all be a false alarm." He was upbeat – he made Helen relax.

"Do you want something to eat, have you come straight from lectures?" she asked.

"Yeah, I have for all the good they were – I couldn't take my mind off you all day." He kissed her gently before pulling back. "But I can't stop. It's training night and if I'm a no-show Coach won't give me my game on Saturday."

"Rob, please miss rugby, just tonight. I don't want to be alone."

"You never do, Helen. You're always at this, trying to get me to skip training. It's not a competition between you and the club."

"Why does it feel like it is then?"

"Look, Helen, I've had the day from hell – I need to unwind. I'm going training." Rob opened the hall door he'd stepped through just minutes previously. He paused. "I tell you what, I'll drop by afterwards, instead of going for a pint with the lads. I've really got to go, beautiful."

He left.

The next day came and despite holding on to a thin thread of hope, the doctor's test confirmed Helen was indeed pregnant. A week passed. They had screaming matches that turned to lovemaking then back to screaming matches again.

"Marry me, Helen," Rob said, as they lay in bed.

That evening had been calm. They'd watched a movie, eaten ice cream and gone to bed early. Mary would be returning from her two-week sun holiday tomorrow, so it was their last night in the same bed for a while.

"Are you mad?" Helen laughed.

"I mean it, Helen, why not? You're the love of my life, I always thought I'd marry you some day – we'll just be getting married a bit earlier than I'd planned."

"Bloody hell, Rob, I haven't thought about it. I mean, I always thought when we were older, sure, but I've still got another three years in college and your finals are coming up."

"So? We've been together years now. And besides, I've never set eyes on a more beautiful woman in my life." He gave her a crooked smile.

Helen blushed at the compliment, her heart skipping a beat.

"We would never forgive ourselves if we don't have this baby. Terminating it, for me, just isn't an option, Helen."

Helen thought about what Rob was saying, realising she felt the same. Why, since she'd realised she was pregnant, had she stopped drinking coffee, and started taking folic acid, while at the same time saying abortion was their only option? Who was she trying to kid?

Rob jumped out of bed, naked as the day he was born. He got down on one knee and took her hand in his.

She giggled. "Get up, you big oaf!"

"Helen Devine, will you marry me?" He looked into her eyes.

She could see that he meant it and then, to her surprise, Helen heard herself say, "Yes."

Rob didn't want to wait and decided they should wed in the USA.

"We're going to Vegas, Hells! Dad stumped up the cash!" Rob proudly produced two airline tickets.

"Las Vegas?" Mary Devine, who had returned from her holiday wearing a sombrero and carrying an over-sized straw donkey under her arm, was still reeling from Sangria withdrawal and the news she'd soon be a grandmother. "That's in America." Mary's face reddened. She hoped she'd get the money together in time.

"Geography is obviously your strong point, Mary!" Rob laughed, putting his arm around her.

"It's very far," Mary said. Thank God for the Credit Union.

"Another brilliant observation, Mary. That's why Helen and I are going – on Saturday. It's far from this place and its red tape. We can get married and have a quick honeymoon, all in one."

"This Saturday!" Helen and Mary said in unison.

"Rob, can I talk to you – alone, please?" Helen said.

Mary was happy to oblige. It might only be three in the afternoon but she needed a stiff brandy.

"Rob, this is all happening so fast," Helen said, as soon as Mary had left the room.

"You're not getting cold feet on me, are you, Hells?"

"No, it's just, it's all so much. I need to slow down – it's a whirlwind. I can't catch my breath." Helen patted her chest, willing air to fill her lungs.

"Helen – I love you. I want to spend the rest of my life with you – it's that simple," he put his hand on her stomach, "and our baby too. As David Soul once said, 'Don't give up on us, baby.'" He broke into song but he had tears in his eyes. He was begging the woman he loved.

"Please, no singing, Mum's crystal can't take it," Helen joked. She cleared her throat, "So, you're really sure about this, Rob?"

"Helen Devine, I've never been so sure of anything in my life."

Helen and Mary spent the next few days in a flurry of excitement. They chose a simple, pale-pink dress for Helen to get married in. As always, Helen spent most of her time trying to choose the perfect underwear. After hours of shopping, the two women sat in Bewleys café, surrounded by shopping bags. On their table sat mugs of steaming hot coffee and warm scones with melted butter, whipped cream and strawberry jam.

"I shouldn't be doing this really," Helen said.

"Then don't, love," Mary jumped in. "It's so far away, and you won't have anyone with you. Wait until after the baby is born. If it's meant to be, you and Rob can still get married then."

"I was talking about the coffee, Mum."

"Oh."

"I know you and Poppy are disappointed you can't be there, Mum. And, to be honest, I had my doubts too. But Rob's been so supportive – it will be okay. Besides, when do you think I'll ever get another freebie from tight-fisted Old Man Lawless?"

Mary wasn't convinced, but put on a brave face. "Too true, love, too true," she said, not looking up, putting extra butter on her scone instead. After a moment or two, she appeared brighter. "History repeats itself, and another Devine woman will wed in the States. So, if you're sure, Helen, there's nothing more for me to say except *'Bon voyage'*!"

Mother and daughter clinked mugs of coffee in salutation.

Later, as Helen had packed the last of her clothes and sat on her suitcase to try and close it, something didn't feel right. She hadn't heard from Rob all day. She had called him a few times but his mobile phone was off. Then she started to ring his parents' house. His aloof mother said she'd pass on Helen's numerous messages, when she saw him.

By the time Helen was going to bed, Rob still hadn't returned her calls. A knot formed in Helen's stomach. What if there's been in an accident? she reasoned, but she knew that wasn't the source of her fear. She tried to settle down to sleep – they had to leave for the airport early in the morning. She looked around her childhood room – it was hard to believe she would come back to it a married woman.

She had cleared out a load of old clothes and junk from her wardrobe to make room in her closet, and life, for her new husband, whom Mary was willing to welcome into her home, for they were to live with her for the first years of their married life.

It was nearly one in the morning when Helen heard the doorbell chime.

She jumped out of bed, ran to the top of the stairs, and was relieved to see Rob's silhouette through the glass of the door.

"Who is it?" Mary called out.

"It's okay, Mum, go back to sleep." Helen dashed down to open the door, and thanked God for answering her prayers.

That was until she saw Rob's face.

"Rob, what's wrong?" She pulled her dressing gown tightly around her, feeling a chill.

"I can't do it, Helen, I'm sorry!" Rob blurted out.

"What?"

"I can't marry you, Helen. It's all too much. I want to be a lawyer – it's all I've ever wanted. I can't do that if I get married now. I need to qualify and have at least a few years working before I consider settling down."

Reeling, Helen sat on the bottom step of the stairs.

"But I thought the same thing – you convinced me I was wrong. What changed all that?"

"No one," Rob said, thrusting his hands deep into his pockets.

"I didn't ask *who*."

"Look, I'll still help out with the baby and everything, you don't have to worry."

"It's your parents, isn't it?" Helen asked, but it was more of a statement than a question.

"My folks are just looking out for me, Helen, I can see that now and you will too – when you've had time to digest this."

"'Digest this'!" Helen spat.

She was on her feet, anger ripping through her body. She wanted to smack him across the face. But she didn't. She had learnt years ago, when faced with condescending neighbours or stuck-up class mates, that hiding her true feelings, such as anger, worked better than showing weakness. It helped her survive. Charles Darwin's Theory of Evolution – survival of the fittest, Helen Devine style.

"We'll talk about this tomorrow, Rob, I'm too tired now," she managed to say calmly. "We've a twelve-hour plane trip ahead of us – we'll talk then."

"Ah, well, here's the thing – Dad managed to change the name on your ticket. We reckoned, with you being pregnant and us needing some time out . . ." Rob looked at his shoes as he stepped awkwardly from side to side.

"You're going to Vegas – without me?"

"We couldn't get a refund, but they allowed us a name change. Helen, I'm not discussing this now." He tried to regain control. "One of the lads from the club was able to come up with the cash for the ticket." He looked pleased but his smile soon faded.

"I think you should leave now, Rob." Mary Devine stood at the top of the stairs.

"Mum, stay out of it!"

"No, I've stayed out of it long enough." She started down the stairs.

Rob saw it as his signal to exit.

"I'm sorry, Helen, Mary. We'll talk when I get back. This doesn't mean we have to break up, just not get married – yet." He swallowed hard.

Her earlier control disappeared and Helen lunged at Rob. "You miserable fucking prick!"

Rob jumped back – frightened Helen would hit him.

Mary held her back. "Don't let yourself down, love, he's not worth it!" She glared at Rob, before slamming the door shut, but he was already halfway down the drive.

Helen buried her face into her mother's chest and sobbed. Mary rocked her, whispering words of comfort while struggling to control her own tears. She kissed the top of her daughter's head, wishing she could somehow take away Helen's pain.

Rob didn't contact Helen while he was in Vegas, but his mother did, or at least she put something in the Devine household letterbox. Helen saw her car pull away from the house in the early morning hours, the day Helen should have been getting married. She had got up to pee, which she needed to do every few hours now.

She went downstairs and retrieved the large, brown, manila envelope which had landed on the mat. On it, the block letters read: HELEN DEVINE. Inside there was five-hundred punts in cash, an Aer Lingus airline ticket to Heathrow, and an elegantly written note with the name and address of an abortion clinic. A yellow Post-It was stuck on the note. Scribbled on it was a date and time of an appointment, made in Helen's name. Abortion being illegal in Ireland, many a young girl found herself "on the boat to England" as it was referred to. More often than not they were alone, afraid and full of shame. It was as though, if people couldn't see them, hear them or speak about them, they didn't exist. The Lawless family had money – Helen could travel by aeroplane. Rob's mother had decided that her grandchild be terminated the next day, at two o'clock.

A few days after returning from the States, Rob reckoned it was time to face the music, but contacting Helen was proving harder than he'd thought. He tried phoning the house a few times, but Mary had answered so he hung up. He let a few weeks pass before he stopped by her campus – it was an easier option than facing

Mary Devine's wrath. One of Helen's classmates told him Helen hadn't been around – rumour was she'd dropped-out. Rob stewed on it for a while, eventually biting the bullet and calling to Poppy Power's house. Being into all that spiritual crap, she was bound to be more understanding. Boy, had he been wrong!

"She's gone," Poppy had said coolly. "Helen has moved to England to pursue her passion for fashion, or lingerie to be exact. Apparently, the only place offering a lingerie design course is in England."

"What, she's packed up her business degree in Trinity to learn how to make knickers in London?"

Poppy hadn't said London, but Rob was hoping to whittle down his search.

Poppy's eyes narrowed – she was on to him. "Let her go, Rob, leave her with that much." She closed the door on him before he had a chance to walk away.

He stood staring at Poppy's door for a few minutes, feeling completely at a loss, stunned as he realised that Helen must have got rid of the baby: his baby. Briefly, a wave of guilt swept over him but then he convinced himself there was nothing he could have done – he wasn't to blame. How could she do such a thing to him? But the truth was he already missed Helen. He had started working in a well-known law firm. The hours were cruel – he had hardly any free time, not even for rugby. So maybe he'd give Helen some time to calm down, come to her senses. She was his woman, he had never doubted that, but he had other things to do in life – surely Helen could see that too?

They could start afresh, once he found her. Rob straightened up to his full height, and brushed his fingers through his hair. He was feeling better already. It will all work out, he told himself as he walked away from Poppy's house. Helen will come back, she always does.

27

Helen decided to get out of the shower before she single-handedly caused a drought in the greater Dublin area. She had bought Mary the Sunday papers on the way back from her run – what better way to take her mind off Rob than spend an hour or two with her mum, in their family home?

She pulled her car in at her mother's house and, on seeing the rows of pretty flowers and hanging baskets bursting with autumnal colour, she felt able to breathe again.

She rang the bell, then opened the door. "This will always be your home, dear – you don't need to ring the doorbell," Mary Devine always said but, out of respect, Helen usually rang the bell anyway before she opened the door.

"Mum, it's only me!" she called out.

The house was in darkness, the curtains still drawn. The alarm wasn't set. Mary always set the alarm when she went to bed. Helen looked at her watch – it was after eleven in the morning.

That's strange, maybe she's gone to Mass, she thought. She pulled back the heavy cream curtains to check if Mary's little red convertible was in the driveway. She had been too preoccupied to notice. It was.

"Mum?" Helen called louder this time, her heart pumping hard as memories of finding her mother in a diabetic black-out last winter came flooding back.

"Oh, God, please let her be okay." Helen started up the stairs. Then she heard it, a faint groan. She took the stairs two at a time – bursting into her mother's bedroom expecting to find her mother laid flat on the floor.

She was flat out all right.

Helen screamed.

Mary screamed.

The old grey man with the crinkly bottom screamed.

"Helen! What are you doing?" Mary scrambled to pull up the duvet for cover but inadvertently further exposed the mystery visitor. Helen wished her mother hadn't done that – as now she had seen an old willy too.

"Oh God, sorry, I thought you were in a coma." Helen covered her eyes – she'd seen enough negative images to last a lifetime. "I brought the papers, they're downstairs." Her hand shielded her face. "Nice to meet you." She nodded her head although her gaze remained averted. She closed the bedroom door behind her. *Nice to meet you! Where did that come from?*

"Helen, wait!" Mary struggled to get out of bed but Helen was already halfway down the stairs. She hadn't seen her mother's boobs since she was in kindergarten, and she'd no intention of seeing them again now.

"Just wait for me in the kitchen, Helen, please – I'll only be a moment."

A few minutes later, Mary Devine came into the sun-filled kitchen. Helen was leaning against the counter with her arms crossed.

"I'm sorry you had to see that, love," Mary said, as she smoothed down her bed-head hair.

"So am I."

There was an awkward silence – then they started to talk at the same time.

"Cyril is a very dear friend – I meant to tell you, love, but you've

been so preoccupied lately and there's been so much going on –"
Mary stopped short.

"Look, Mum, you're free to live your life." Helen drummed her
fingers on the marble-top. "Who the hell is he anyway? How long
have you been seeing him and I can't believe I'm saying this but I
hope you are using protection."

"Cyril, three months and none of your business, madam."
Mary's cheeks burned with two dots of pink.

Helen sighed. Her mother was right. "I'm off, Mum – I'll call
you later." She managed a weak smile.

"Okay, love, and despite this little setback, I still want you to use
your key in future. This is your home too and always will be, as
long as I'm alive."

Helen looked at her mother as if she'd announced she was
running off to join the circus.

"Oh, for heaven's sake, Helen, it's just sex – it's the most natural
thing in the world." Mary tried laughing it off.

"You're pushing for the bus-pass and he looks like he should be
pushing a Zimmer-frame!" *Just sex indeed.*

Mary fiddled with her hair again. "Sixty is the new fifty, and I
can assure you Cyril's very able-bodied – he's seventy-five, you
know."

"Agh, enough!" Helen covered her ears, but that didn't erase the
picture.

Crinkly bottom,

Crinkly bottom,

Crinkly bottom . . .

"Most people get a roast dinner when they visit their parents on
a Sunday. Look what I get – I'm scarred for life, Mother!"

"Stop being melodramatic, Helen, you're forty years of age – get
over it!" Mary retorted.

"Thirty-nine, and you should have been level with me!"

The onslaught just kept on coming.

"Is it safe to come in?" A hand waving a white handkerchief
appeared at the kitchen door.

154

Great, now I have to deal with Casanova.

"You must be Helen – you're even more beautiful than your photos," Cyril said as he entered the room. He held his hand out, and smiled broadly.

And Don Juan.

Cyril didn't look so creased with his clothes on and he had a twinkle in his old blue eyes that glistened with gentleness. Helen shook his hand.

"Who fancies a cuppa?" Mary feigned normality as she put the kettle on.

"Not for me, I was only dropping off the papers. I've arranged to meet Poppy for lunch." Helen smiled and tried not to look at the wall clock. They all knew it was a fib but they went along with it. No one wanted to discuss the big pink hippopotamus in the room.

Helen got into her car, and waved goodbye to her mum and Cyril who had come to the door to see her off.

Crinkly bottom,

Crinkly bottom,

Crinkly bottom . . .

She pressed hard on the accelerator in the hopes it would beam her up to a planet far from "Pensioners-on-Viagra-Ville". She set her sights on safe-haven number two: Poppy's house.

"Helen, I wasn't expecting you, this is a nice surprise," Poppy said, pulling her dressing gown tightly around her body.

"It's nearly lunch-time, are you only getting up now?" Helen's eyes wandered towards the bird's nest masquerading as Poppy's hair. "I thought you got up with the dawn every morning to meditate or something."

Poppy stepped back to let Helen into the house. "I try to keep my body aligned with the circadian rhythms, it's healthier, but lie-ins have their benefits too. It's all about balance."

Here we go, Helen thought, and ignored Poppy's attempt at education.

"Is Lily here?"

"No, she went into town last night – slept-over at her friend's place."

"What's wrong with you? You seem tense." Helen pointedly looked at Poppy who was tugging on a strand of hair. Poppy immediately stopped and looked wide-eyed back at Helen. Too late. The hair-pulling was, as always, a dead give-away. There was no need to answer.

"*Namaste*," said the bare-chested Hare Krishna, as he lazily shuffled down the stairs.

"Morning," Helen waved, her words a statement, not a greeting.

"*Akasha*, okay if I make us some peppermint tea?" The Hare Krishna yawned, giving Poppy a gentle kiss on her forehead, while at the same time scratching his manhood through his orange harem pants.

"Of course, Ry, you know where everything is. We'll follow you in," Poppy smiled, ignoring Helen's glare. "Make some for Helen too."

Ry, the Hare Krishna, seemed about to ask Helen what her infusion of choice was, but obviously thought better of it and trundled through to the kitchen without a word.

"Ry?"

Poppy put her forefinger to her lips before whispering. "He's very sensitive about that. His full name is Henry, reckons his parents had hopes he'd be an accountant."

Helen threw her hands up in the air. "You only met him yesterday – it looks like he's moved in!" she hissed under her breath. "And what the hell does *akasha* mean anyway?"

"*Akasha* – Universal Spirit, space, air, angel." Poppy let out a sigh of contentment. "Ry thinks it's the perfect name to embrace my true essence."

"Well, he's got that right – space-cadet."

"Oh Helen, always the cynic. Come on, have a cup of tea with us – you'll like him." Poppy hooked her arm through Helen's to lead her to the kitchen.

"He drove me nuts, banging those bloody drums all day

yesterday, so no thanks, I'll pass. Isn't casual sex against his cult anyway?"

"Sshh! It's not a cult – honestly, Helen, you're unbelievable!"

"Me! I'm not the one who's bonking a monk." Helen refused to lower her voice.

The visit to Poppy's house wasn't going quite the way she had planned.

"He's not a monk and we didn't have S-E-X. I found their music yesterday entrancing and they were all so peaceful. We got talking, then we went to that little vegetarian restaurant on Wicklow Street and, well, it went on from there. What's got into you anyway? It's not like you to take the higher moral ground." Poppy noticed Helen's normally smiling face was looking decidedly glum.

"Nothing, apart from Mum is having sex with Hugh Hefner, Rob is having sex with a barely legal nymphomaniac and you're having sex with someone who's married to God – how will that affect your karma theory by the way? Will you come back as a frog or something?"

"I didn't have sex with him!" Poppy hissed. "And who the hell is Hugh Hefner – is he the man from the drama society? And why on earth would you give a toss about who the hell Rob Lawless is sleeping with? I assume it is that prick we're talking about?"

"Tea's ready." Ry appeared in the doorway, bringing with him a whiff of incense.

"Nice to meet you again, Ryvita, eh, sorry, Ry." Helen was delighted the interruption gave her the chance to escape. *There –* she'd said it again – *nice to meet you. What was it, this Sunday morning, with its strange men and tea-making? What happened to going to Mass?* She gave Poppy a kiss on the check. "Give me a shout later when you've finished playing doctors and nurses – sorry, I meant goddesses and priests." She gave her friend a friendly wink.

Poppy hugged her. "Will do – don't forget we've got that appointment with the medium in Meath this afternoon."

"I'd completely forgotten about it." Helen brightened. She'd been sceptical when Poppy mentioned it. But now, the timing was perfect.

"I'll pick you up about two – we can stop and have a coffee in the tearooms at Tara afterwards."

"I'll collect you," Helen added quickly and avoided looking at the clapped-out old mini in the driveway. She feared old Dahlia would splutter and die halfway up the motorway.

Despite the rocky start to her day, Helen cheered up. Whatever about the medium, she loved going to Tara, there was something about the energy there – it always brought her peace.

Maybe she wasn't such a non-believer after all.

28

"What if he tells me something I don't want to hear?" Helen chewed the inside of her cheek.

"I wouldn't worry about it, Helen – you never listen to stuff you don't want to hear," Poppy chirped.

"According to this printout, his house should be just up here on the left!" Lily called out from the back seat.

"I think we're lost," Helen said flatly, tapping her mobile phone, which was currently doubling-up as a GPS. She slowed the car to take in where they were. The rolling green hills of County Meath stretched out before them. The sky was grey with dark clouds moving rapidly, as if being chased. A unique Irish sky that most people only saw as dreary, but in that moment looked mystical. A black-and-white cow stood in a field – she paused in her munching to look at the car, before she raised her tail and deposited a huge mound of dung.

"What a great life – eat, crap, sleep. I'm coming back as a cow in the next life," Lily said as she watched her.

"Sounds pretty much like your life now, if you ask me," Helen said.

Poppy shot her a warning look but Lily ignored the dig.

"Maybe a cow in India – I hear they're sacred there and people treat them like royalty." Lily looked as though she was wistfully imagining her ideal life as a holy cow.

"As I said, no change then – apart from the India bit." Helen looked out the window at the ever-darkening skies. "I think I'll get a nice piece of fillet steak tonight. All this talk of cows is making me rather peckish," she said as the first drops of rain hit the windscreen. She flicked on the wipers.

Lily gave Helen a filthy look, but it was wasted on the back of her head.

"There on the left – where that wooden post is – I bet that's it." Poppy waved frantically as she spotted the barely visible gateway.

Helen edged the car forward and sure enough, leading from the small country road was a driveway to a modern bungalow.

"Doesn't look like a wizard's house," Helen said, driving up the gravel entrance.

Whatever had got into Helen that morning, Poppy wasn't finding her easy.

"He's a healer and a medium, Helen – I thought you said you had an open mind?"

"I have. I'm just saying, that's all." Helen stopped the car.

"You said he was a druid or a witch or something like that, Mum," Lily piped up.

Poppy threw her eyes to heaven. "Don't be silly, Lily!" She gave her daughter a look that could have frozen hell over.

With that, a bearded man dressed in jeans and a white T-shirt appeared.

"There he is," Poppy said, giving him a wave. "You go first, Helen, he's expecting you."

"A bit sceptical, are we?" the medium, Jeff, said without looking up. He shuffled a deck of tarot cards.

"I like to call it open-minded," Helen said, determined not to say too much lest she make his job easier. She felt strangely comfortable in his room though. It was warm and welcoming. One plain white candle burned on the desk. There were bookshelves stuffed with books: it looked like a personal library. Jeff was around fifty, Helen guessed. He had a full head of curly, salt-and-pepper hair and a beard. Not a wizard-type beard though, Helen smiled to herself, an everyday run-of-the-mill beard.

"You've a red aura. Strong energy. You're a fighter, with a strong Mars influence." He continued to shuffle. "You live life in the fast lane. I see orange too. You're a highly sexual person and apart from your physical appearance you have a strong sexual energy that draws both men and women to you."

Helen opened her mouth to speak but Jeff raised his hand.

"I'll answer all your questions, Helen, but for now just let it flow. Your spirit guide is here with you."

Helen shifted a little uncomfortably in the chair, resisting the temptation to look behind her.

"He's standing on your left," Jeff continued. "There is also a young man with a crew-cut. He's wearing some sort of uniform."

"My father!" The words escaped her lips despite herself. A shiver ran down her spine. How could he know that? She struggled for her practical mind to find the answer but her heart longed for contact with her father.

"There's another name coming through . . . begins with B, no it's R, a lover of yours maybe?" Jeff stopped shuffling.

"My, em . . ." Helen couldn't find the right word, she wasn't sure if there was a right word, "friend."

"You don't have sex with friends. Tread carefully around him. Having sex with him is stunting you."

Helen sat in silence. One thing was for sure, Jeff had her attention now.

Jeff laid down the tarot cards, one by one, unravelling her life and secrets with each one. "Your creative side is suppressed, that's not good for you. You need to develop your creativity – you're stagnating in work. Someone is jealous of you – watch your back."

Helen regained her composure. He was wrong – her job was flying, they wanted her to help set up office in Hong Kong, for God's sake.

"Beware of the wolf in sheep's clothing."

Now he's just being cryptic.

He lay down another card – the Grim Reaper.

161

"There are a lot of changes on foot for you. You need to decide what you want and where you want to be. Open yourself up. Now would be a good time to go on holiday, somewhere you haven't been before, experience something new, clear your head, consider your habits – drinking and sex. You use sex as a barrier to intimacy. Alcohol is masking your true feelings, making it appear as though you're happy. You need to make important decisions that you've been postponing."

Helen wondered if her spirit guide and dead father had been in the room while she was having sex. Were they ever there when she was on the loo?

God, Helen, think of a worthwhile question! Her mind raced with inconsequential thoughts.

"The spirit world is very respectful of the living, you know," Jeff said.

Was he a mind-reader as well?

It felt like only five minutes had passed when he asked her if she had any questions – she'd been sitting with him for over an hour. She studied the small gold ring on her little finger. The ring that her father had kept for her – it had belonged to his mother.

"So my father, he's with me?"

"Yes. You have support from the angels and your spirit guides. But you also have free will. They'll only help if you call upon them and ask them to."

Helen Devine was not one to ask for help. She wondered if she could start now. She made a mental note not to think about her spirit guides when in the bathroom though, especially if she was Betty-fying, lest they appear at an inappropriate time.

She stood to leave, unable to ask the one question that burned. She thanked Jeff and wondered if her dad would leave with her.

"Helen?" Jeff said as she opened the door.

"Your dad asked me to tell you. Your son – he's doing fine."

29

Helen and Lily sat in the car while Poppy had her reading.

"You okay, Helen? You look kind of freaked out?" Lily hadn't gone for a reading. Jeff had thought, because she was still a teen, a healing would be more appropriate.

Helen stopped scribbling in her notebook. She looked up – her eyes were clear and alive. "Sorry, Lil, I'm not much company, am I? I wanted to write down every little word Jeff said to me – I'm already beginning to forget some things."

It had been a long time since she'd been alone with her goddaughter. When Poppy rang her with yet another worry about Lily, Helen sometimes felt irritated, thinking the teen just needed a good kick up the arse. She felt a pang of guilt now for that.

"He said my father was in the room with me, he could even describe what he looked like," she told Lily.

"Savage! Did you get to talk to him?"

"No, well, sort of – through Jeff – he told me things I needed to hear." She put the notebook down. "What about the healing – how does that work?"

"Pretty cool, all I did was lie down on the plinth – Jeff covered me in blankets. He said he was doing Reiki, clearing energy centres or something. His hands hovered over me – the heat from them was amazing. He just touched my feet, head and shoulders though.

Strange thing was I felt all warm and fuzzy. I think I fell asleep 'cos it was all over too soon." Lily yawned as she tugged at the sleeves of her black hoody, conscious of the marks on her arms.

"Why did you cut yourself, Lily?"

"You wouldn't understand," Lily said, looking away.

"Try me."

Silence fell, while Lily struggled to find the words to explain why she'd been self-harming.

"The pain inside gets so bad, I can't bear it. When I cut myself, it relieves it, lets it out."

Helen didn't understand, but she wanted to. "Do you hate yourself, is that the pain?"

"I guess so. Jeez, Helen – even my own family hardly know I exist. Other girls in my class, their grandparents want to spend time with them, buy them stuff their parents won't. Mine, if I did see them, would probably ask what my name was and offer me a spliff." Lily looked at Helen for confirmation, before rubbing one of her heavy black-kohl eyes. She pulled down the passenger sun-visor and started to apply more of the dark liner to the inner rim of her eyes.

Helen shrugged – she couldn't deny it. She said nothing.

Encouraged, Lily continued. "I've no father. All Poppy knows is that his name was Massimo and he was working as a pizza waiter in Florence during his summer holidays."

Helen winced slightly, remembering one of the first holidays she'd been on with Poppy, without Mary. "We were young and foolish. I think it was looking at all those naked statues – penises were everywhere you looked in Florence. That and the heat had us high on life. After we had been to see the Statue of David, we stopped at a pizzeria on the piazza."

"I know. I've heard the story like a million times. Massimo was studying art, he'd beautiful big brown eyes and the pizza he served was sublime. The combination of which was intoxicating – *blah blah*. One night of passion, a burst condom and bingo! Nine months later, I pop out."

"She told you about the condom then?" Helen said, rubbing her forehead.

"Yes, too much information, but Poppy's all about open communication as you know," Lily sighed.

Helen was stuck for words. Poppy had made an effort to contact Massimo but he was off the radar. The restaurant had paid him in cash – he was a casual summer worker from another town. Without a surname or address, he'd been impossible to trace.

Lily appeared not to notice Helen's silence because she continued, "I've no brothers or sisters that I know of. My classmates think I'm weird and kind of avoid me. I think half of them are scared of me, to be honest." She rubbed the corner of her mouth to fix a smudge on her Angel-of-Death lipstick. She popped the visor back up.

"That might be the whole dressing-in-black, being-angry-at-the-world vibe, Lil." Helen was treading on dangerous waters. "You've got your mum, she's better than most mums and dads put together."

Lily stared out at the rain.

"Then there's me and Mary – you're the grandchild I never gave her." Helen's stomach tightened as she uttered those words, but she continued, "We're not even blood and we want you around, so that has to say something, hey?"

"Yeah, it does – you're just as weird."

"Seriously, Lil, there are times you wreck my head but I love you – tell me what I can do to help." She brushed Lily's hair back off her face.

"I'm seeing a therapist now, she's great. And, maybe it's my imagination but after that Reiki session I feel good." Lily smiled at Helen, a little shyly.

"Good, you deserve to feel better, Lily." She took the girl's hand in hers.

"What's with the PDA?" Lily laughed.

Helen was puzzled. "The iPhone?"

Lily rolled her eyes, "PDA – Public Display of Affection – it's not like you."

"I can have my tender moments. Just don't tell anyone – especially not your mother. She'll see it as a sign to help me release my inner child or some baloney. I've got a Hard-nosed Bitch image to protect!"

Lily creased up with laughter.

"I'm not joking." Helen tried to sound serious, but failed.

In the rear-view mirror, they could see Poppy approaching the car – her long emerald skirt billowing in the wind, her eyes red-rimmed from crying.

"That was fantastic!" she declared as she opened the car door.

"You don't *look* fantastic," Lily frowned.

"Oh, I'm just so happy. Let's go," Poppy said, blowing her nose.

"Tara?" Helen asked, turning the key in the ignition and driving off, not waiting for an answer.

30

It was late – the tourist buses had left. They were the only three on the Hill of Tara, except for the sheep.

"It's amazing here." Lily was looking all around her, taking in the layers of peaks and valleys, as far as the eye could see.

"It's bloody cold is what it is," Helen said, pulling her leather jacket tightly around her, trying to protect herself from the wind. "But do I love this place." She took hold of Lily's arm and huddled into her for added body heat.

"Ancient mythology says Tara was the entrance to other worlds of eternal youth, abundance and joy!" Poppy shouted above the noise of the wind.

"I should come here more often then – save myself a fortune on Botox," Helen laughed.

"St Patrick came here to drive out the pagan gods where they were at their most powerful. Come on, let's each make a wish." Poppy took a deep breath, closed her eyes and tilted her face towards the dying sun.

Helen and Lily looked at each other, unsure what to do.

"I wish for love," Poppy said.

"I wish for a new friendship," Lily said, looking at Poppy to see was that the kind of wish she had in mind. Poppy's eyes remained closed. Instead, Helen gave Lily the thumbs-up.

"I wish to be my own boss and be more Zen but still earn big bucks and be a sex goddess," said Helen. "I also wish to lose ten pounds and fall in love with a really nice hunk, who adores me and isn't a shit."

"Helen!"

"What?"

Poppy decided to let her off. "Now release your wishes, send them to the Universe, the gods and goddesses, and let them take care of the details."

"I like that," Helen said. "Let someone else work out the details."

The sun was a setting fireball – some grey clouds striped across it gave it an ethereal look. Darkness was descending on the hill. Sheep continued to graze, unperturbed by the people and their drums.

Drums.

"You know it's the darndest thing, I swear I can still hear those Krishna drums ringing in my ears." Helen rapidly rubbed her index fingers against her ears.

"I think that's probably what you're hearing, Helen." Lily pointed in the direction of three silhouettes that were coming their way.

"What on earth are they wearing?" Helen double-blinked to make sure she wasn't hallucinating.

"Cloaks," Poppy said.

"Cloaks – as in witches' cloaks?" Helen asked, her voice rivalling a soprano's.

"Maybe they're real-life druids?" Lily was wide-eyed.

"No, druids' cloaks would be white – I'd say they're Wiccan."

"Wiccan, as in . . . " Helen swallowed hard.

"Witches," Lily and Poppy said together with jubilance.

Poppy has finally lost it, Helen thought, and wondered would they catch up with her via broomsticks if she made a bolt for it.

"Merry meet!" a cloaked man called out.

He wore a regal cape and carried a staff made from a tree branch. He stabbed it into the muddy grass with each step. With him were two women. All were apparently in their late fifties and, apart from their outfits, they looked like members of a book club. One of the ladies had a small bodhrán under her cloak. She was drumming as she walked.

"Ah, would you look at who it is! Poppy Power, great to see you," the man said, adjusting his glasses as he approached them. "How've you been?"

"Barney, it's yourself, sure I should have known! What are you celebrating?" Poppy gave him a warm hug.

They weren't as Helen imagined witches should look. She couldn't picture them having naked orgies on stone altars. Mind you, until this morning she wouldn't have thought of her mother having sex either – gross, as Lily might say.

"It's Mabon – the autumn equinox. We were giving thanks to Mother Earth, for the harvest." He nodded hello to Helen and Lily. "Must be my lucky day, all you lovely ladies to myself. Will you join us for a cuppa?"

"We'd love to, wouldn't we, girls?" Poppy didn't wait for them to answer. "We were just on our way to the coffee-shop ourselves."

Helen wished the pagan gods or St Patrick himself would come through the veiled world, and swallow her up right now. She wasn't sure whether she was intrigued, mortified or scared.

The others chatted as they were slip-sliding off the Hill of Tara, towards the coffee-shop. Helen looked around her. It was rather dark now. A sheep bleated, causing her to jump. She decided Poppy and her band of witches were the lesser of two evils. She made after them, seesawing her arms as a balancing pole in an effort to remain vertical as she shimmied down the hilly mudslide. She thought about the people she'd met today: Ryvita, sorry, Ry, the Hare Krishna, Jeff the *"I talk to dead people"* and Barney the witch. Helen wondered who on earth Poppy would introduce her to next: Puff the Magic Dragon? Suddenly, life in London was looking very mundane.

A small light glowed from inside Maguire's cottage-like coffee-shop close to Tara's entrance. The owner laid out a big pot of tea and a selection of cakes on a round, wooden table. In the centre of the table lay a tied bunch of purple heather and a candle. He wouldn't take any payment, saying that the cakes were left over at the end of the day anyway and he was glad not to have given them all to the crows. The group chatted happily for while but, aware the owner was waiting to lock up, they didn't linger too long. As they left, Helen thought they must have looked like an odd bunch of people to anyone who might be passing by, but surprisingly she didn't care. It was probably just as well that Poppy hadn't brought the Hare Krishna along though.

"That was fierce," Lily said, climbing into the back of Helen's car.

"Fierce is good – right?" Helen asked Poppy, who nodded.

Lily had bought a book on the way out of the coffee-shop. "*A Guide to Witchcraft,*" she read the title out loud. "Mum, I think I'd like to become a witch."

A vegetarian, Goth, lesbian witch, Helen thought – *and she wonders why she doesn't fit in?* She looked around at Lily, who had already started reading the book, and decided to say nothing. She looked happy, so if that's what made her happy who was she to judge?

"You never told me what Jeff said to you," Poppy said as Helen steered off the slip road and onto the motorway.

"You never told me you had friends in a coven!"

"They're not a coven. Anyway, could you imagine your reaction if I said, 'Oh, I was just talking to Barney, he's the witch by the way.' You'd have had me locked up! Now that you've met them, you can see there's nothing odd about it. People just fear what they don't know, and propaganda has them painted as crooked-nose, green-faced hags." Poppy stared out at the line of white car lights coming from the opposite direction, lost in thought.

"He said lots – Jeff." Helen broke into her reverie. "He said it'd be a good time for me to travel, re-think my life at Eden. I've decided I'd like to go to Vietnam, see where Dad was killed."

"Vietnam, imagine. God, I'd love to go there," Poppy said.

"Go with her then." Lily piped up from the back seat, without looking up from her book.

"How could I possibly take off to Vietnam? You're back in school for a start." Poppy turned to Lily. "And it is Leaving Cert year so I can't take you out. Besides, where would I get the money?" She slumped back around in the front seat – her wishful thinking had gone flat.

"Poppy, the best things in life are free – '*for everything else, there's a MasterCard*'," Helen said.

"I'll stay with Marma. I could do with a few decent dinners anyway," Lily giggled.

"It's true. Mary is always asking her to stay. Remember when she was doing her Junior Cert, Lily moved in for three weeks, to get away from the noise in your house." Helen was thinking it might also put a hold on her mother's libido.

"My chanting and drumming circles aren't noise!" Poppy was indignant. "But, Helen, do you really think it possible? You're just back from Hong Kong." She was getting her hopes up again.

"That was work! I haven't had more than a few days' leave in nearly two years. Are you sure, if we can sort the details, that you'd be okay, Lil?" It could be just what everyone needed.

"Go for it – just don't come back with a little Vietnamese man tucked into your suitcase, Mum." Lily was definitely sounding like her old self again.

"Right, that's sorted then," said Helen. "Wishful thinking on the Hill of Tara is all well and good but I prefer to be in the driving seat of my life. If Mary's happy to have Lily and JD stay with her, first thing tomorrow morning I'm telling Fred I'm taking a long-overdue holiday." It would also be the perfect smokescreen to avoid the whole other mess with Fred. She was getting masterful at dodging him.

Poppy opened the car window to shout at passing traffic.

"*Yeehaw! Vietnam, here we come!*"

31

"Of course, I'd love Lily to stay here – I'd be delighted in fact," Mary Devine had said when Helen arrived later that evening to drop off JD to his Monday-through-Friday home. "It'll do you and Poppy the world of good." She paused for a moment. "Just don't go driving off the Grand Canyon."

After leaving her mother's house Helen checked her phone. Two missed calls from Rob. He hadn't left a voicemail, opting instead to send a text, which simply read "?". Initially, Helen had no intention of keeping their date but realised if she ignored him she was repeating their familiar pattern of game-playing, each determined to get the upper hand by staying out of contact for weeks or sometimes months at a time.

She phoned him and, after a lot of coaxing, he had eventually agreed to meet her locally, in the new café overlooking Howth Harbour. As always, he was late.

"A glass of white wine, please. House will be fine, as long as it's not Chardonnay." Helen unbuckled her coat. She settled on a high stool that looked out onto the harbour. The wind was causing the ropes of the sailing boats to chime. The last of the day trippers had left and the locals had gone home in preparation for the start of the working week.

"One glass of Italy's finest," Angelo said as he placed her glass on the counter. He had also brought a small bowl of green olives.

"That's very kind, thank you. I like your place. My friend, Poppy, suggested that I come here." Helen picked up an olive.

"Ah, Puppy, she was my first customer and she's my first regular. She's been twice already!"

Helen laughed, immediately warming to Angelo. "Are you still serving food? I know it's a little late?"

"*Sí*, no problem, I bring you the menu."

Rob walked in with a strong gust of sea air on his tail. "It's a dirty old night out there." He shook out his coat before looking up at the blackboard to study the wines on offer. "A glass of Valpolicella, my man," he said to Angelo. "Small in here, isn't it?" He pulled out a stool, his back to the wall, so he could survey the small interior and anyone that might enter. Helen had to swivel to face him, giving up her view of the harbour.

"And a menu," Angelo said as he returned to them.

"I'm not eating much, Helen." Rob lifted his arm up in an exaggerated gesture to check his watch. He looked displeased.

"How about a mixed meat and cheese platter, for two?" she asked. Taking Rob's barely perceptible nod as a yes, she handed both menus back to Angelo.

"I don't see why we couldn't have just ordered a takeaway to your place," said Rob. "This town dies a death come nine on a Sunday. They did a good job on this place, how long is it open?"

"I don't know, just today I think. Look, Rob, there's something I need to say . . ."

"How much was the lease on this place?" Rob shouted across to Angelo.

"I only make the coffee," Angelo rolled off without looking away from the meat-slicer.

"The thing is, Rob, this idea we had about us dating again . . ."

"I believe that was your idea, Helen."

"Right, I'll cut to the chase, shall I? I came across you on Facebook today – you know, the social networking site that you said you wouldn't be seen dead on?"

"I don't know what you're on about," he laughed, avoiding eye contact.

"It's definitely you, Rob."

"Not me, it must be someone else. How's the white?"

"It's fine. Rob, I found you, Lord knows I wish I hadn't because I wasn't looking to. You've just got one friend on it – a very pretty friend . . ." Her voice trailed off.

Rob's jaw visibly tensed as he pretended to clear his throat from an imaginary tickle.

Helen's heart felt like it was literally sinking.

Rob continued to cough. Angelo poured him a glass of water.

"I just need some fresh air, back in a tick," Rob managed to splutter out. He patted his chest for added effect.

Angelo placed the platter for two on the marble countertop. Helen smiled at him, feeling a little embarrassed.

"It's this weather, like summer one day and winter the next. A lot of people get sick," he said, smiling at her.

Helen nodded. A beam of car headlamps flashed through the window from the harbour car park. She rubbed her hands together: her palms were sweating. Five minutes passed by. Rob didn't return. Helen went to the door to look for him. There were only three cars in the car park, none of which belonged to Rob.

She walked back into the café and fumbled in her bag. "May I have the bill, please?" Her cheeks burned.

"You don't like the food?" Angelo asked.

"No, it looks lovely, it's just there's been a change of plan, I'm sorry." Helen was unable to make eye contact.

"He's gone?"

"Afraid so," Helen sighed.

"*Testa di cazzo*," Angelo mumbled. "Will you do me a favour?"

The question surprised Helen. She looked up and nodded.

"I work all day. I like to sit, have a glass of wine and eat some food. The platter for two – is on the house but I eat it with you."

"There's no need, honestly. I'm fine. He's done this before."

"I don't like to eat alone and I close the shop now anyway. Plus . . ."

Helen cocked an eyebrow questioningly.

174

"Maybe you can tell me more about Puppy, what's she like, you know . . ." Now it was Angelo's turn to look a little shy.

Helen laughed. So Poppy had an admirer who was actually normal and there wasn't a drum in sight. Of course, this probably meant he hadn't a hope in hell.

32

Helen's alarm beeped at four thirty and she rolled out of bed to start her Monday-morning ritual of heading back to London and her lingerie life. This morning, though, there was a spring in her step – she could face Fred with a smile.

"Good morning, Sarah. How was your weekend?" Helen said as Sarah arrived at the office at nine thirty.

"Oh hi, I wasn't expecting you to be here already. Sorry I'm late." Sarah plopped her handbag on the floor beside her desk. Her shoulders slumped when she saw the amount of paperwork piled up in front of her.

"It's not as bad as it looks, Sarah. Nearly two weeks with both of us gone just means a backlog of sign-offs."

Sarah thumbed through the paper edges, fanning them. Her eyes had dark rings under them.

"Jetlag, hey?" Helen smiled at her.

"I feel I've been hit by a train. I've slept all weekend except it was during the day, then come night-time I was wide awake." She yawned to emphasise her point. "You look very fresh, Helen," she paused, "and cheerful."

Helen tapped a handful of files on her desktop. "Really, aren't I always? Actually don't answer that." She laughed. "Tell you what

– I'll go get us a couple of strong coffees. I've got to stop by Fred's office anyway." She grabbed the edge of her desk and pushed back her chair, then she paused without taking her hands off the desk. The gesture made it look like she was bracing herself.

Sarah frowned, wondering if Helen was just going to sit there or get the damn coffee. "Cheers, black no sugar," she said. She turned her attention to her computer screen as she booted up, marking the start of a new working week.

Helen tapped lightly on Fred's office door before she popped her head in. "Have you got a mo, Fred?"

Fred was on the phone but rapidly gestured for Helen to come in and sit. She sat in a chair opposite him, thankful there was a heavy oak desk between them. He sounded eager to end his conversation. He cast his eyes to heaven and held the handset away from his ear, pulling a face at her. She smiled and rubbed imaginary flecks off her black trousers. Fred winked at her. This wasn't going to be easy.

"Sorry about that – the CEO breathing down my neck, looking for figures and what not. More importantly, how are you, honey bun? You're looking ravishing this morning, I might add." Fred stood and rounded his desk with his seesaw-like gait.

For a moment, she thought he was going to kiss her but, thankfully, he opted to lean against the desk instead. Helen remained seated, Fred's groin now in her line of vision. She felt claustrophobic.

"I was just on my way down to get coffee and muffins – maybe we could walk and talk?" she said.

"I've got a better idea," Fred said, leaning forward. "Why don't I order them up? We can chat in private – just the two of us."

Helen decided to get straight to the point. "Fred, I've come to tell you I'm taking a holiday – asap. I'll be gone for about three weeks and I'm hoping to go within a couple of weeks from now." She looked at him, head tilted upwards.

"That's impossible!" Fred exploded. "We're coming into our busiest season and there's no one to man your workload. I'm sorry, Helen, but leave right now is simply out of the question."

What happened to "Honey bun"?

He returned to his high-back leather chair and sat down with force, which caused a hissing sound under his backside. Fred's face was redder than an Amsterdam light-bulb.

"It's the busiest time of year in the warehouse and the shop floor, not the design office," she said. "And only last week you said Sarah was ready to step into my shoes. Why has that suddenly changed?"

Fred didn't look up – he put on his glasses and pretended to be engrossed in a spreadsheet printout.

"Fred?" she sighed.

Fred held up his palm to her. "This conversation is over, Helen. You know annual leave has to be applied for at the beginning of the calendar year. If I'm not mistaken, you haven't done that. Come back to me in January – we'll sort something out then. If you're still in London, that is."

Ouch!

Helen's plans for a holiday were going down the toilet faster than a lingerie model's breakfast. Time for a change of tack.

"Fred, I really need this holiday," she said, her voice soft.

"It's not my call, Helen, and I'd help you if I could but the Board would have a canary if senior management started to take off looking after their own personal needs ahead of Eden's." The blood vessels in Fred's neck pulsated like popping corn.

"But, Fred, we both know in a few weeks I'll be called to the executive suite and asked to head up the new design team in Eden's Hong Kong office. That's a big decision to make – going to Hong Kong to live."

Fred appeared to relax a little.

Bingo!

"It would also give us a chance to get a test run in with Sarah, see how she copes with managing the office."

Fred remained silent but she could see the cogs in his brain turning.

"The short notice would mean a lot of overtime for both you and Sarah." He stared at her over his glasses.

"I plan to stay in London until I go, so I can even work

weekends. As for Sarah, she'll jump at the chance to head the office for a few weeks. She's eager to learn and she won't have expected such a golden opportunity this early in her time with Eden – she'll bite my hand off."

Fred continued to look tight-lipped. Eventually he broke the tension. "I don't know, Helen. Certainly three weeks' absence is out of the question."

"Two then."

"Where were you thinking of going?"

"Vietnam."

Fred's top lip twitched but he said nothing.

"It's where my father was killed. I've always been curious about the country."

Fred's eyes became gentle. "Would you consider visiting a potential supplier or two while you're there, maybe a factory also?" He cocked an eyebrow.

"One factory and make it three weeks."

"Two and a half weeks and that's my final offer."

"Done!" Helen stood and held out her hand to shake on the deal.

Fred took hold of it and looked up into her eyes. "Drink after work this evening?"

The office phone beeped. "Mr Giltrap, your ten o'clock is here," his PA's voice echoed through the intercom.

"Sorry, Fred, I'll be working late tonight – every night in fact," said Helen hastily. "It'll be worth it, got to look at the bigger picture, hey? Speaking of which, I'd better get cracking." She headed towards the door. As she opened it, she turned and said, "Thanks, Fred, you won't regret this." She closed the door gently behind her.

Fred stared at the door. He sighed heavily, already regretting letting Helen go.

Helen came back to her office, closed the door behind her and pressed herself against it. Although she'd shared an office for some months now, she sometimes forgot, and acted as if she were alone.

179

"Where's the coffee?" Sarah made no attempt to hide her annoyance. Helen was behaving very peculiarly indeed, almost light-heartedly. Sarah did not like it one bit.

"Oh dear, I forgot the coffee." Helen hunched her shoulders. "Sarah, I've got some great news for you and some not so great. Which do you want first?"

"The bad." Sarah folded her arms and slumped back in her chair.

"You're working late tonight and probably for the rest of the week and longer for that matter."

"What! No way, I'm exhausted already."

"Ah, but you haven't heard the good news. Come on, we'll go down to the shop's café – that way we haven't officially left the building. I'll tell you all about it there." Helen opened the door and made a swiping motion with her arm. "After you."

"Fine," Sarah replied, trying to remain impassive . . . but there was something about Helen's demeanour that said this could work out very well indeed for Sarah.

33

Jack sat on his backpack at the side of a dusty road in the Northeast Province, Cambodia. He was heading to a transport stop to pick up a minibus ride. Where to, he'd yet to decide. He flicked through the images on the digital screen of his Nikon. He smiled as the pictures he had taken since he arrived in Cambodia flashed up at him, the mighty temples and wats in the Siem Reap Province to the vivid orange robes worn by the Buddhist monks. He stopped at one picture and zoomed in, so far his favourite snapshot of his trip – Angkor Wat. His first visit to the temple had been at dawn. Although majestic at any time of day, the image he had captured of the towers framed by a rising sun was breathtaking. He had spent three days exploring the area and temples, marvelling at the intricate detail. It had reawakened a love of architecture he'd forgotten he ever had. Seeing what the Khmer architects had created back in the twelfth century had mesmerised him in all its magnificent glory. It was truly humbling.

He was jolted back to reality by the sound of music. A large group of people was heading his way, a procession of young and old walking down the street. They carried brightly coloured umbrellas, trays of food and pitchers of juice. Two young men held a silver tray between them, on it a large head of a very dead pig. Jack jumped up before he was trampled on – the boys laughed as

181

he brushed off his trousers. The sight of a beautiful young woman dressed in a flamboyantly coloured sampot, the traditional Cambodian wrap skirt, told Jack there was a wedding feast taking place. One of the older men gestured to him to join in with the celebration. Jack shook his head but held his camera up to indicate he'd like to take some pictures. The man smiled and nodded, Jack started to shoot.

"Come, have fun!" A Western woman pulled at his elbow as she danced past him. Jack found himself being dragged into the flow. She laughed at him as she took his hand and began to sway. Much to Jack's relief the wedding party started to turn into a building and began to lay down the platters for the feast, cutting short his dance routine.

"English?" his hijacker asked – she had beautiful dark eyes.

"American."

"Ah," she nodded as if that explained everything. She smiled. "I'm Carine."

"Jack. You're French, right?" He smiled at her.

Carine was petite and pretty in a quirky sort of way. She had a blue bandana on her head and two more knotted around her neck. She wore an assortment of bracelets on both arms that jingled each time she moved. She wasn't wearing a bra.

"Yes, from Montpellier. Where are you going, Jacques?"

"I don't know. I was just on my way to the travel stop. I'll check out what's available and go there." He was trying not to look at her breasts.

"Good, I'm going that way too, we'll walk together." Carine picked up her backpack and pulled the padded handles over her shoulders. Thankfully, this covered her protruding nipples. The local women had shied away from her, the men just stared and some pre-teen boys had giggled behind cupped hands before their mother shooed them along.

In the ten minutes' walk to the stop, Carine managed to give Jack a detailed account of her twenty-four years on the planet. He even knew she owned a black and white cat named Casper. She spoke fluent English and her accent was sexy as hell, which was just as well considering the amount she talked. Her voice disappeared in the din of chaos as they arrived at the travel stop. Touts vied for their business, guiding them towards their rusty white vehicles, which were in various states of disrepair. Jack's camera shutter whirred as he captured as much of it as possible.

"Would you like to share my taxi, Jacques?" Carine used her hand as a sun-visor as she looked up at him.

"But I don't know where you're going." Jack squinted, lowering his lens.

"But neither do you know where you are going."

She had a point.

"I'm going to the volcano lake," she said. "We can swim. You can swim, Jacques, no?" Carine had adopted the role of little girl lost.

"Sure. Why not?"

She skipped in her delight and to the delight of her admirers who watched, fascinated, as she bobbed up and down.

The shared taxi to Banlung was with four other passengers plus the driver. Carine jumped on Jack's lap to make more room for everyone. She clasped her arms around his neck and talked to the passenger sitting next to him. As her conversation became more animated, she began to tell her stories in scooping arm gestures which meant Jack got an eyeful of breast as her loose T-shirt fell away from her body. She had nice breasts, small and firm – her skin kissed golden by the sun. They reminded him of Amy's before she'd had breast implants. He lightly twisted the back of Carine's shirt – thereafter when she moved he only saw her armpit.

Jack and Carine got out of the shared taxi, laughing.

"I did not know it was possible to fit so many people into one tiny car!" Carine giggled. "Let us eat some lunch, Jacques, before the lake, huh?"

Jack never remembered hearing his name sound so damn good, and he was happy to oblige. They ran across the road to the first restaurant they saw. Not looking at the menu, they ordered two bottles of Angkor, the local beer. He was enjoying Carine's company – she did talk an awful lot but she didn't ask questions.

She was happy to talk about herself and her travels, which suited Jack just fine. And she was nothing like Amy. He wiped beads of sweat from the top of his lip.

"Are you listening to me, Jacques?"

"Excuse me?"

"I said we should find somewhere to stay in town tonight before we go out to the lake." She pursed her lips and brought the long-neck beer bottle to her mouth.

"Eh, sure." Jack cleared his throat.

"And decide which direction we go tomorrow. There is a place, three hours from here that I am thinking of. The monks meditate in little wooden huts. It is said to be very beautiful, sweet-smelling flowers everywhere. And on the walls there are paintings, how do you say it – murals?"

Jack nodded.

"Murals that tell a story of karma, Jacques." Carine smiled broadly. "They say if you speak bad of people, you will lose your tongue. If you have an affair, the pictures show what will happen to your love parts. Of course, it could never be in France – making love is our national sport!" She took a swig of beer and waited for Jack's reaction.

"Wow, I should bring my ex there – she'd be totally screwed. When can we go?"

"Tomorrow we will go – in a few days I'm leaving for South of Vietnam, before going north to see the amazing Halong Bay – do you know of Halong Bay, Jacques?"

"I've heard of it, sure. I have vague memories of it being a backdrop in a Bond movie, but I was more interested in the on-screen action than the scenery."

"I think you were distracted by the Bond girls, Jacques! You should go there – it is a natural wonder of the world after all. Perhaps we will go together, swim in the bay, you can be James Bond and I his beautiful companion." She threw her head back in laughter before jumping up. "Which reminds me, now the lake awaits! Come, let us go! We can leave finding a room until later." She pulled him up, giving him barely enough time to fish out a few dollars from his pocket to pay for their drinks.

It was getting late by the time they had hiked through some forest to get to the lake which was set in a volcanic crater. They passed local craft stalls selling woven silks that looked like rainbows. Jack tried to stop to take a photo but Carine tugged him on, saying they could stop on the way back. They quickly forgot about the stalls once they got to the water's edge. The natural beauty was haunting, the water crystal-clear and calm. A haze rose from the surface making it look as inviting as a giant hot tub.

"Ah, swimming at last!" Carine stretched her arms out. "Come, Jacques, hurry!"

Jack felt a twinge of irritation. He'd been travelling alone for a couple of weeks and, although at times he thought it might be nice to have company, he'd enjoyed his freedom.

"Just a second, I'm going to take a few shots, this light is awesome." He adjusted the lens on his camera.

"Just the light?" Carine said from behind him.

He looked over his shoulder just as she was lifting her T-shirt over her head.

"Amy, I don't think that's a good idea." Jack waved his hands at her.

"Amy? Who is this Amy? I am Carine Dupoux, and I say we swim!" With that, she unbuttoned her shorts and let them drop to the ground. Carine obviously didn't care much for underwear, as she worn none. And she liked the natural look, Jack noted. Embarrassed, he turned his attention to imaginary dust on his camera.

"Sorry, 'Amy' just slipped out – it happens sometimes in moments of panic. Carine, please put your clothes back on. They are very conservative people here – I don't think they'd appreciate . . . Oh, God, here she comes . . ."

Carine had started to skip again, this time towards Jack. She grabbed both his hands and placed them on her butt. She wiggled as she bent over and slapped his hands repeatedly against her buttcheeks. She wasn't leaving anything to his imagination. He looked towards the lake, not wanting to look at her reddening buttocks.

She let go his hands. "Don't be a stiff old man, Jacques – skinny dipping is fun!" she giggled as she ran towards the water. She stopped just before diving in to give him one last butt-shake.

She was wrong – right now, there was nothing stiff about Jack. He rubbed his face. Maybe she was right, maybe there was no one else around and he needed to lighten up. He unhooked his camera from his neck.

"Check out the broad with the great rack!"

Jack looked around, startled. Two guys had arrived.

"Man, you are one lucky dude." One of them patted him on the back.

"Hey, isn't that the crazy French chick from our hostel last night?"

Carine bobbed up and down, waving to the shore. "Boys, you came! Come, join me!" she shouted.

"Fucking A, man." One guy already had his shoes off and was running towards the water. He plunged in and Carine screeched with delight as he grabbed her by the waist and threw her up in the air. Then she wrapped her legs tightly around his waist. The other guy dived in and began to splash them, all three laughing as they frolicked in the fading light.

Jack kicked pebbles awkwardly – he wanted to get out of there but didn't want to leave Carine alone with strangers, although it didn't look as if they were exactly strangers to her.

As he feared, a National Park guard eventually arrived on the scene. He pointed to Carine and started shouting at Jack. He then shouted into his walkie-talkie.

Great! A night in a Cambodian cell coming up.

Carine laughed at first, then disappeared so that only her head was visible above the water.

Wise move, Carine.

The two guys sniggered as Jack appealed to the guard not to call for his colleagues. The guard eventually nodded but mumbled to himself. Jack offered him money, which appeared to insult him further.

"I swear, man, she's a little loco." Jack made a circular motion with his forefinger to his temple. "The water is good for her, makes her calm. I promise, no trouble. She'll put her clothes back on and we'll go. Okay? Okay?"

"You got cigarette?" the guard asked.

Jack looked over at the packet of Camels that sat on top of Carine's rumpled clothes. He walked over and picked them up. "How about twenty cigarettes?"

He handed them to the guard who gave a faint smile and popped a cigarette in his mouth. He was still mumbling but he rambled off.

"You can come out now!" Jack called to Carine who had started to laugh again, yet to discover Jack had bargained for her freedom with a pack of her cigarettes. She ignored him. "Carine, I'm going to head back to town now!" he called.

"*Au revoir*, Jacques, nice to meet you!" she shouted back.

Jack hesitated. "Will you be okay? I can wait if you want me to."

"Don't worry, I am in good hands," she said and there was another whoop of laughter.

Jack walked back the way they had come but the stalls had closed up and gone home for the night. He shifted his backpack as he began to walk towards town. He made a mental note to think twice before accepting rides from strange women again, whether they were from Andromeda or France.

34

While Helen waded through her final preparations for her holiday departure from Eden's design office in London, Poppy Power and Mary Devine went about their own ritual: their Monday lunch date. Recently, Poppy had decided that since she worked Saturdays, she should have Mondays off – taking advantage of being her own boss.

"*Buon giorno*!" Angelo called to them as they walked into the little harbour-view café, their weekly venue.

"*Buon giorno*!" they chorused back.

Mary pulled out a high-stool. "I don't know, Angelo – if I keep eating that wonderful bread of yours, you'll have to buy wider stools!"

The aroma of fresh coffee and baking wafted around them.

"And why not? You only live once, no?" Angelo gave his broadest smile.

"Not according to Poppy. She believes in reincarnation." Mary cocked her thumb in Poppy's direction.

"Yes, yes, I know. Very interesting what Puppy says. She promised to teach me meditation – one day, when I'm off." He nodded and smiled at Poppy.

Poppy blushed.

"Let me guess – two cappuccino, one carpaccio and one caprese?"

"*Sí, grazie*," Poppy replied.

"See, Mary, I teach her too!" Angelo said, before being called away by a large group, lured in by the warmth of the café.

"I just want to say again, Mary, thank you so much for agreeing to have Lily to stay."

"I'm really looking forward to it, Poppy, and, as I said, I think you and Helen need a break. Helen hasn't been herself recently, always talking about work – I'm beginning to think that company won't be happy until they've got the last drop of blood out of her. Then there was that business with Cyril. Sweet Jesus, that was downright awkward."

Angelo put the coffees in front of them. "Skinny milk, just as you like it," he said, smiling at Poppy. Their fingers brushed.

"I see next door is still up for rent, Angelo," Poppy said.

"Yes, *bella*, I think it has your name on it," Angelo clicked his tongue, "and the neighbours are very nice too." He double-tapped his nose in jest.

When Angelo was out of earshot, Mary commented, "He likes you, you know."

"Don't be daft, he's Italian, he's like that with every woman. It's in his genes, or should I say jeans," Poppy laughed.

"Watch it, Poppy, you're starting to sound like Helen."

"Maybe he does like me a little bit," Poppy conceded. "I've become very fond of him in a short time. Lily even comes in for a hot chocolate after school and he helps her with her Italian homework."

"He's a genuine lad, Poppy, you can see that. Apart from the 'Puppy' bit – I reckon he well knows how to say your name – I think he's playing with you."

"I know, but – and I know this sounds bad – he's just not my type. Once bitten twice shy, as they say. And with everything that's going on with Lily recently, the thought of starting a relationship with any man isn't something I have the head space for."

Angelo arrived with a basket of warm bread and the platters. Poppy and Mary stopped talking and smiled at him.

"*Buon appetito*," he said before leaving them alone.

"Ah bless him, how could you not fall for a face like that, Poppy?"

"Will you quit with the match-making!" Poppy drizzled balsamic glaze over her food. "I'm not interested. What's more, he smokes. I hate smoke, never mind the fact he's about ten inches shorter than me." Poppy caught Angelo's eye as he warmed up a teapot. He smiled – she felt a pang of guilt.

"Don't exaggerate – besides, the best of goods come in small parcels."

"You know what it's like single-parenting – I never remember you with a boyfriend when Helen was growing up."

"I kept to myself pretty much. I had a few dates when she was older, but no one I wanted to introduce to my daughter. Sure, look at the reaction poor old Cyril got." Mary covered her face, not wanting to think about it.

"She never said anything to me but, from what you said, I'd love to have been a fly on the wall. She'll get over it. You're an attractive woman, Mary – and young. You deserve to have a life of your own."

"I know, love – it's just there are so many changes going on. I really wanted to get to talk to Helen." Mary looked troubled.

"Look, Mary, I know Helen hasn't been home since Cyril-gate, but it genuinely is because she's working around the clock, so she can get away on holiday."

"I know that. And I'm glad – a holiday will clear her head. I'll get her on her own when ye get back."

"It's good, ladies?" Angelo was back again.

"Yummy as always, Angelo. I'll miss your coffee over the next few weeks." Poppy wiped the corners of her mouth with a napkin.

"Oh, where are you going?"

"On holiday – Vietnam."

"That's great, have a wonderful time," he said. But his voice lacked enthusiasm.

"Don't worry, Angelo, I'll still be here and Lily too," said Mary. "We'll be in every day while the other two are off gallivanting across the globe."

He took her hand in both of his and shook it gently. "Ah, Mary, thank you! I am glad some of the family stay with me." He was smiling again.

When they got up to leave, Poppy tried to catch his attention. She had started to like his three kisses every time she left his place. But Angelo was busy with other customers – he was having a laugh with them too – a table of attractive twenty-somethings. He waved over to her. "*Buone vacanze*! Send me a postcard!" he called, before turning his attention back to the young women.

Poppy left feeling disappointed, although she didn't know why.

Angelo watched her as she got into her car. As always she caught her skirt in the door. He waved and pointed to try to get her attention as she drove off, the dirt of the road already soiling the hem. Poppy didn't see him.

Send me a postcard but, please, bring your heart home to me.

35

Helen wasn't at her desk when Sarah arrived to work, although her handbag slung over the back of her chair meant she was around somewhere. Sarah checked her watch. It was eight fifteen and she was raring to get going. She'd learnt more from Helen in the past couple of weeks than in all her years of college. This was the break she needed and Sarah intended to use it fully to her advantage.

She decided to look for Helen in the small sample room where they kept the trimming and fabric samples. Floor-to-ceiling shelves covered every available inch, piled high with rag-trade treasures from around the world. She found Helen hunkered down on her knees, running a delicate ivory lace along the back of her hand.

"It's beautiful," Sarah said as she leaned against the doorframe, watching her.

"Isn't it? When I started, we used this slotted Galloon Leavers lace all the time. They still had some Leavers lace machines in the factories in Nottingham." She smiled as she looked up. "I remember visiting a bra factory in Manchester and the trainee machinists were sat around gossiping while they hand-threaded satin ribbon through the delicate holes. They whizzed along – it was amazing to watch."

Sarah knelt down next to Helen and pulled a web of lace from a container.

"Ah, another favourite of mine, black Chantilly lace!" Helen looked as though she had just met a long-lost lover.

They opened out the lace to admire the subtle needlework with its distinctive weighty thread interweaved around the delicate floral pattern.

"And this one is from Calais in France." Helen pulled out a narrow white lace that peeped over the edge of a cardboard box as if to say 'Don't forget about me!'. "I always said the best things to come from France are their lace and champagne."

"And their lingerie of course."

"That goes without saying – the lace is an art form that adds to the most sensuous of garments. Lingerie, lace and bubbles, give me that combination and I'll think I've died and gone to heaven." Helen started to roll the trimmings back up.

"They're cracking – I don't understand why don't we use them more often?"

"We can't afford them." Helen pulled herself up by grabbing onto a steel rack. "Most of the European manufacturers have either closed their doors or moved to Asia."

"Nottingham and French lace made in China?" Sarah hadn't thought much about where the components for their stock came from.

"That's it, but we still can't afford it. Most of the trims we use are made on mass-produced machines. They look pretty good, but they don't hold a candle to the originals."

Sarah joined Helen at the door. "Why do you keep them? This room would be great for file storage or we could put that monster of a laser printer in here that would free up a lot of space in our office."

Helen scrunched her face. "Lord no, these are my old friends in here. I have to come visit every so often to keep me sane, remind myself of my first love – lingerie."

Helen pulled the cord to kill the light. She closed the door behind her. "Right, back to reality, what time are the fit models booked for?"

"The Size 16 girl is booked for nine, Size 18 is coming in about ten then the Plus Size woman will be in after that, with the smaller sizes coming in after lunch."

"Great, that gives us time to have a meeting first, review where we're at, make sure we've covered all the bases before I go on holiday." Helen's lips curved to a smile as she uttered the word *holiday*.

Eden had a fitting day once a week. The models were either former fashion models that were now older or women who were well-proportioned for the size they were fitting, be it a Size 10 or a Size 20. Photographic models were only used when the goods were ready for marketing. Today was more important than the usual weekly fits as they were checking the entire range of next year's spring stock. The factories were waiting to get the green light to start production.

The models paraded in front of the designers, pattern makers and quality controllers, each team defending their corner if a bust piece didn't sit right or a garment looked plain ugly. The period after St Valentine's Day was a difficult season for lingerie. The offer in store had to be inviting, good value and fit well. And they couldn't rely on gift purchases at all once Mother's Day was over.

"I'm telling you that dart is placed incorrectly. If it's gaping on the Size 10 by the time it's graded up to the larger sizes it'll look like a funnel sticking out the side of her boob!" Helen didn't take any prisoners and wouldn't put her stamp of approval on anything less than perfect. The pattern-makers threw their eyes to heaven. "And you can bin that attitude. Go produce muck like that for the cut-price chain stores down the road but not if you want to stay part of Eden." She cocked an eyebrow at them.

The two pattern-makers jumped up and started pinning and pulling. There was a dexterity involved in placing pins with a live model. The models in turn were skilled in taking the pin-stacked samples off, without a pinprick in sight.

Sarah walked alongside Helen once the fit session was over. She felt a little taller than before. "I think the range looked good apart from a few minor problems, don't you think, Helen?"

"I'm happy with it. It's hard to tell, but I think it's a winner. Will you make a note, while I think of it? We'll use the turquoise chiffon collection for the window display and make it the main photo shoot for the season. Graphics can airbrush out the offending body parts and hair down there. Actually best if we bring nipple shields and nude thongs for the models to wear on the shoot rather than leave it to graphics alone." Helen was remembering the year one of her window displays got pulled as the standards authority deemed it "inappropriate". Since then she had avoided using see-through fabrics such as chiffon or all-over lace in her main ad campaigns but maybe Britain was ready for a bit of spice again.

"Got it, no body parts, flesh thongs," Sarah scribbled in her notebook as she tried to keep up with Helen.

"The only place I want to see a black bush is on the label of a whiskey bottle. Right, Sarah. Questions?" Helen sat behind her desk, back in the design room.

Sarah thought for a moment. Now she was on the cusp of trying on Helen's shoes, she was feeling a little apprehensive. "What if the pattern-makers tell me that a change I need can't be done? I'm not sure they'll listen to me the way they do you."

"You've had training in patterns so have confidence in yourself, Sarah. But do listen to them when it comes to sizing – grading is a skill – it's not just a matter of adding extra inches to all the patterns. It's possible a change you make to the design won't grade well for the larger sizes. Use some judgement, you'll get the hang of it."

"Should I do a fit on the mannequin if I'm not sure?"

Helen shook her head. "You can't rely on an old tailor's dummy any more. Here, let me show you." She took a measuring tape that hung around her neck and went over to a calico-covered K&L mannequin. "I saved for months to buy old Dolly here. I bought her second-hand from a dressmaker," she wrapped the measuring tape around the dummy's waist, "so Dolly is a traditional Size 10 and her waist measures . . ." Helen looked at where her thumb pinched the tape to remind herself, "twenty-two inches." She hooked the tape back over her neck. "There are very few British women with a waist that size nowadays."

She went to the sliding wardrobe in the corner of the office and pulled out flexi-plastic patterns held together with a hooked wire. "Women keep getting bigger – taller and wider. Today's Size 10 would have been considered a Size 12 years ago." She placed the pattern blocks on the large worktable in the middle of the room. "So we keep adding centimetres to the garments."

Sarah walked over to have a look at the patterns, which were marked with words like "back panel" and "shoulder piece".

"These are my blocks. I've developed them over years. Constantly adjusting and altering until I got my fits in each size right. The foundations of Eden's base lines are built from these blocks."

"That's so cool!" Sarah ran her fingers along the smooth surface of the patterns.

"And the key to our success is customer loyalty. People come back to us because they know our stock flatters their body by fitting properly." Helen looked at her watch. "Is there anything else you're concerned about before I go?"

"I think I've got a good handle on things. What about sales reps, should I accept appointments while you're gone?"

Helen bit her lip as she thought about it. "We have to be very careful who we work with – there's a lot of factories willing to use unethical work conditions in order to make more money. They have to be carefully vetted plus I don't hand over my blocks lightly." Helen lifted the pattern pieces and placed them back on the rail. "No, don't make any appointments with new people while I'm gone. Spend any free time you have occupying yourself with the blocks, get familiar with them. There's no point having wonderful designs in your head if they can't be produced to show off a woman's natural beauty."

"I never thought about designing like that. I always thought about my creation as the masterpiece with a wearer just being a canvas." It was then it dawned on Sarah why Helen Devine's designs had been so successful.

"I'll have my phone with me, Sarah. If you need to ask me anything just call, it's not a problem."

"Do you think I can develop that ability, design clothes that frame a woman to show her in her best light?" Sarah asked, showing a vulnerability she usually masked.

"Of course, Sarah, that's why you're here. You've got talent, now you've got to learn to tap into it, develop it."

"I come from old money, you know. My parents don't believe in the word *no*. If I didn't get a placement or a college I wanted, they'd buy my way in. I've never achieved anything on my own, apart from getting this job with you – and, well, getting my degree." Sarah pushed a strand of hair behind her ear.

"But when we were in the business lounges and fancy hotels you said you'd never been in places like that before?" Helen twisted her small gold ring.

"I wasn't. Mum and Dad travelled the world but I was in boarding school or else at home with the nanny – they didn't take me with them."

"You, Sarah, are going to be just fine." Helen put an arm around her shoulder.

"What's all this then, designer-bonding time?" Fred walked in, hands deep in his trouser pockets jingling loose change.

The lid slammed shut on Sarah's brief moment of honesty as she returned to her own desk.

"The office is in good hands, Fred, you'll hardly know I'm gone," Helen smiled.

Fred grunted.

"Sarah, why don't you take off?" said Helen. "It's been a long couple of weeks and we're finished here for today."

"Okay, if you're sure. Cheers, Helen!" Sarah slipped her jacket off the back of her chair. "Have a great holiday and don't worry – I'll take good care of old Dolly while you're away." She winked as she left, leaving Helen and Fred alone.

Helen sat at her computer to type her out-of-office message into her email settings. She had known this moment with Fred would arrive sooner or later.

"You're all set?" Fred continued to play with the change in his pockets.

"Yes, my friend is arriving tonight – we head out from Heathrow tomorrow," Helen said lightly.

"And you'll give serious consideration to the Hong Kong move?"

197

"I promise, Fred, I will seriously consider it," she said, using the same words she had used to him repeatedly since she'd been granted leave.

"And us?" He stopped the jingle in his trousers.

She looked up from her computer screen, her mouth open. "Fred, there is no '*us*'. There never was and there never will be."

"But the kiss . . ." Fred didn't want to hear what Helen was saying. For years he'd been building an imaginary life with her – her on top of him most of the time, that is.

"Fred, you haven't been listening to me. You're a terrific man but I just don't feel that way about you, I'm sorry." Helen looked into his eyes but Fred looked away.

"No, I get it, Helen, really I do. I know I've gained a few pounds recently . . ." He smoothed down his shirt.

Oh God, he's still not listening!

"Fred, please stop talking and think. You've got June to consider. No matter what you say, she's still your wife. Maybe the move to Hong Kong will rekindle something for you two, who knows?" Helen stood, gathered papers from her desk and pushed them into her briefcase. He wasn't going to make this easy.

"It's none of your concern how I handle my home affairs, Helen."

It's not your home affairs I'm worried about.

"Go on holiday, relax, clear your head, think about what you want," he went on. "But remember you're only as good as your last season. This industry moves at lightning speed – it waits for no man . . . or woman."

Fred turned and walked out leaving the office door open behind him.

Helen was left looking at his backside and his side-to-side shuffle walk. He barked something at one of the office clerks as he walked past, causing her to jump.

Damn Fred Giltrap and his veiled threats! Helen's fingernails dug into the palms of her fists. "I'm going to tell him to shove his job up his arse!" She started to march out the door after him. With that, her mobile phone vibrated on her desk. "Ugh!" she growled as she picked it up. It was a text message from Poppy. "Just boarded, see you in London shortly. Yippee, we're on our holliers, Hells!" The message made Helen smile – she took a deep breath and pressed the shutdown button on her computer. The office fell silent – she was on holiday time now. Pausing, she took a quick look around before flicking off the overhead florescent lighting. Fred and her job were saved by the text.

36

Helen and Poppy were on their way. The itinerary Poppy had planned was economical, using indigenous tour operators where possible, thus saving money while helping to sustain the local economy. They'd fly to Hanoi and from there they'd travel to visit the area where Helen's father died. Then they'd take a boat trip on Halong Bay, followed by trekking into the Northern Hills visiting the various tribal villages and staying in local homesteads.

"Is that okay by you? Staying in local homesteads, I mean?" Poppy had asked.

"Of course I don't mind – it sounds fun," Helen had said. "What exactly is a homestead anyway?"

"I'll send you the link – it looks amazing, really remote. We get to stay with local families, eat with them and everything. They've got communal lofts with mattresses on the floor and, well, wherever you lay your sleeping bag that's your bed for the night!"

Helen had felt Poppy's excitement down the telephone line. Silently she screamed, but she wasn't about to rain on Poppy's parade.

"Sounds like a swinger's party to me – why didn't you say that in the first place? Of course I'm in!" she replied.

Looking at Helen now, Poppy wasn't so sure it had been a good idea. The problems started with Helen automatically turning left when they boarded the plane.

"Excuse me, madam, economy passengers are this way," the steward said, guiding her to the right.

"Oops, force of habit, sorry," Helen said to Poppy a little coyly.

Matters deteriorated when the only two seats together were in the middle of a middle row, sandwiched between two rather large burka-wearing passengers.

"Can we order double Bacardis?" Helen whispered.

"Of course, why not?"

"I don't know – I don't want to offend anyone or anything." Helen tilted her head, to refer to their neighbours.

They ordered rum – singles not doubles. The crew didn't offer refills and the girls decided against clambering over seats to get to the galley for more.

Helen had slept most of the way, her sleep troubled with thoughts of Eden. She'd worked fourteen and sixteen-hour days, organising as much as possible for Sarah to run the office without hiccups. Still, Fred had grumbled and made comments about selfishness, job-cuts and company loyalty, which had led to the final unpleasant encounter with him. She'd left the office with a bad taste in her mouth.

Trying to find a comfortable position in a tight semi-upright seat, Helen's mind tossed and turned as much as her body. Was she ready to leave Eden? More accurately, was she ready to leave the security and fat salary? As if in answer to her question, the seat in front of her reclined into her lap. This is what life would be like if she left her prestigious job – shunted to the back of the bus, vying not to melt into oblivion. Could she start over from scratch at nearly forty years of age? By leaving her job would she also leave behind her self-worth? Or was she just bound to her ego? She thought of Sarah and her revelation that growing up wealthy had reduced her self-esteem. Helen had come from a loving home but she had still spent her life trying to justify her existence in this world. Why?

The other side of her brain began its counter-attack. *You could take that month-long trip to ride horses in Patagonia. You could run on the beach with JD – every day. You could open your own lingerie boutique – leave the rat race behind, leave Fred Giltrap behind. Maybe things could finally work with Rob. Stop it, woman, you're driving yourself crazy!* Helen put on her iPod, as much to quieten her own thoughts as drown out the sounds of the aeroplane.

On landing at Doha, Qatar, Poppy still hadn't admitted to Helen the length of the stopover.

"So what time's our flight to Hanoi? Do we have time for food?" Helen looked at the itinerary, a look of panic flashing across her face. "Poppy, what's the time difference here? According to this, we've a six-hour stopover?"

"Really?" Poppy tried to look innocent. "That's awful. Look at all the money we saved, though."

"Well, I'm going to spend my savings in the bar," Helen said, rolling her eyes but smiling all the same.

Until that is, they got to the bar. Or rather didn't.

"There's no friggin' bar!" Helen exclaimed, having desperately searched every nook and cranny of the airport. Doha was an alcohol-free airport.

The drink-police thwarted a cunning plan to buy duty-free. "You can collect your bags of alcohol when you board the plane," the cashier told them after they'd handed over their cash.

"Now might be a good time to teach you to meditate, Helen," Poppy said, defusing the bomb that was Helen's impatience.

Everything would be fine when they got to Hanoi.

Hopefully.

"Are you sure this is a three-star hotel?" Helen asked their local guide, Lu, who wanted to be addressed by her adopted Western name 'Sue-Ellen'.

They were standing looking into the lobby of their Hanoi hotel, which was lined with scooters.

Lu brushed off their concerns. "Yes, yes, great hotel. Don't worry – they only move scooters inside for the evening. They will put them outside again in morning. Now you go wash, get some rest, I pick you up in a few hours, we have dinner. Don't be late."

The beds were akin to a wooden board, covered with a threadbare sheet. The bathroom suite was a vomit shade of green with mildew and various fungus shapes growing out of the tile crevices.

"What do you think that smell is?" Poppy made a face.

"Don't even go there, Poppy! It'll look better after a few hours' sleep. And look at the bright side – if we get hungry we can just go to our bathroom and pick some mushrooms."

They climbed into bed fully clothed to avoid sheet-to-skin contact.

They didn't sleep.

Later that evening their guide, Lu, or 'Sue-Ellen', arrived to collect them, on a motorbike.

"Hanoi traffic very bad, this much quicker. I no use car for you," she said, thrusting a helmet at Helen. "In Vietnam, we all fit on one bike. Because you foreigners, we go on two bikes."

Helen wondered if she was referring to the size of their arses.

Sue-Ellen gave an abrupt wave to the driver of another motorbike, shouting something at him in Vietnamese – he duly took off his helmet and handed it to Poppy.

"Okay, keep knees in and no one gets hurt. We supposed to wear helmets. Not enough helmets so we avoid police. They fine me, but put money in their pocket," she said, adding what was surely a "fucking-pricks" insult in Vietnamese. She raised one arm as though calling the troops to battle, as she high-revved the throttle. "Let's go!"

Helen and Poppy were catapulted into the stream of traffic.

They rode the motorbikes through the labyrinth of the Old Quarter before weaving into the wider streets of the city. It beat any roller-coaster experience in Disney and blew away the cobwebs the long journey had left.

Dinner was in Sue-Ellen's kitchen – "A real Hanoi experience!" she had called it.

As they entered her house she startled them with a shout. "*Take off your shoes!*" Then she added more gently, "Please. Cannot wear street shoes in house." She pointed to a line of plastic flip-flops that lined the wall. They slipped their feet into the least worn-looking on offer.

Sitting around the small table, Helen wondered how she'd ended up in a stranger's kitchen, wearing a stranger's shoes, in a back street of Hanoi.

Despite the rocky start, the girls ate well. They even downed a few shots of some sort of homebrew, equivalent to poteen.

Sue-Ellen stood, indicating the meal was over. "Okay, tour over. Curfew in Hanoi tonight, I bring you back to hotel now. Tomorrow morning get yourself to airport to fly to your war tour. You no book that with me so I don't have the fly details." She shook her head and tutted.

Helen looked to Poppy for confirmation.

"Yes, she's right. I booked the tour and the flights down to Hué with another company," Poppy said, fiddling with her hair.

"I see you in a few days, back in Hanoi after your war tour. You can book more tours from me then, okay?"

"Maybe," Helen replied.

This answer did not please Sue-Ellen who tutted again.

"Why is there a curfew – it's only ten thirty?" Poppy asked.

The guide simply shrugged. "No reason, they just do it. Come on – let's go!" She was booting them out.

The hair-raising motorbike ride to the hotel was much more fun with food and a few shots of an unknown fiery substance in their stomachs. Poppy even managed to keep her eyes open this time.

37

Mary Devine spooned the last bit of fondant on a gooey chocolate-fudge cake. She stepped back to admire her handiwork. Satisfied that the cake was finished she licked the spatula – the best part of baking, no matter what your age or diabetic tendencies. She heard the familiar sound of a key in the front door, bringing with it warm memories of a previous life when Mary had been a wife, lover and mother.

"Hi, Marma!" Lily called out. A loud thumping of books hitting the floor announced her arrival home from school. "Something smells divine, Mrs Devine!" Lily followed the chocolate waft into the kitchen.

"How was school, love?" Mary asked.

Lily grunted and sat at the table.

"That good?" Mary smiled. "Here, I was going to keep this until after dinner but sure we can have a sample slice now with a cup of tea."

"I think I'll text Mum and tell her to stay in Vietnam for another week. I'm getting used to all this home cooking."

"That reminds me, Helen rang here earlier. Did your mother get you on the mobile?"

"Yep, she rang the café too. Angelo said she thought I might be there and she was hoping to save on cost by calling a land-line."

"Very wise, your mother." Mary smiled to herself. "You know you're welcome here anytime, Lily, even when your mother is back. I love cooking and it's nice to have someone to cook for."

"I wish you'd give Poppy a few lessons – she thinks cheese on toast is a gourmet meal – when she's managed not to char-grill it!" Chocolate cake melted in Lily's mouth.

Mary stifled a laugh, remembering what Poppy had said to her once, "Mary, I can cook you anything as long as you like Cajun. Cajun Chicken, Cajun Salmon, Cajun Spag-Bol." Cajun was Poppy's term for anything she cremated beyond recognition.

"Thankfully, your mother has other fantastic qualities that more than make up for the fact that she's somewhat challenged in the cooking department. Besides, you're nearly eighteen – you should be learning to cook for yourself!"

"Why would I do that when I've got you to do it for me?" Lily enjoyed the banter nearly as much as the cake.

"Independence – that's why every woman should have her own money and know how to cook. Your health is your wealth but a few bob in the bank helps too."

"I've no idea what you're on about, Marma, but you do know how to make chocolate cake, so if there's more going I'm willing to sit and listen as long as you're not going to start a lecture – I've homework to do, if you're going to start on me." Lily pressed her finger to the plate, collecting the last few crumbs.

"My lecturing days are well over, love. I tried with Helen and your mother and look where that got me." Mary cut another thick slice of cake.

"Helen's very successful, Mum too in a different way. It's not your fault they're a pair of loons."

"Oh, I don't know, it's not that marriage is the be all and end all, but if I'm being honest, I would like to see Helen and Poppy settle down and not go running off like Thelma and Louise."

"Who are Thelma and Louise? Girls they were in school with?"

"It's a movie, before your time, dear. Maybe we'll rent it one night."

"What did Helen have to say today then?"

"They're in Hanoi but they'll be heading to a small island somewhere, Cat's Paw or something." Mary shook her head. "Why she had to go to Vietnam, I'll never know – why not go somewhere normal – like Spain?" She threw her eyes to heaven.

"Who'd want to be normal?" Lily frowned. "And wasn't Helen's dad killed there? It's natural to be curious about her father."

Mary wondered if Lily was talking about herself or Helen. "Of course it is. I just never felt the need to see where Jim died. I don't want to think of him there. If I see it, it'll make it more alien. I prefer to remember him in paint-splattered overalls, Marlboro in his mouth – before he ever wore that blasted uniform."

"If you don't mind me saying, it's a bit weird how an Irishman died in an American war." Lily found the snippets of stories she'd been told about Mary and Jim Devine's life fascinating.

The only sound in the kitchen was a clock ticking and even that appeared to stand still for a moment. Mary stopped cleaning counter tops and sat down to have a sliver of cake – dinner could wait.

"I wasn't much older than you, Lily, when we got married – Jim and me." Mary twisted the plain gold wedding band that she still wore. "He was eight years older than me, tall and handsome. All the girls in the town fancied James Devine, especially when he left town to join the British army." Mary smiled, the images in her mind clear, as if she'd only seen him yesterday.

"That's odd – why not the Irish army and how come the British accepted him?"

"By joining the British he had a chance to see the world and, remember, the Irish army was still relatively new in those days – he wouldn't have got much further afield than Dublin. If you were born in Ireland before 1948, you were entitled to dual citizenship. Not that it matters because the Irish are still accepted into the British army to this day."

"Huh, I didn't know that, Marma." Lily pursed her lips.

"And he was the second son to a small farmer. The farm couldn't support all of them, so naturally it went to the eldest brother. His father was a mean drunk, who was quick to lose his temper and use his belt. Jim wanted to get as far away from him as possible. He would work at odd jobs all around the town after school. When he got a job on the big dairy farm, he'd go there before and after school each day. He said he wanted to save up enough money to go to America and never come back to this godforsaken place. I thought he worked all those hours to avoid his father and his drunken temper, myself. Jim's mother died shortly after giving birth to him and according to the town's gossips, Jim Senior took to the drink after that." Mary stared off into the distance as she spoke. "My own father worked at the farm too, that's how I got to talking to Jim. I'd find any excuse to go there, to bring my dad a packed lunch, pick up a dozen eggs for the tea. At that stage Jim thought of me as a kid but he'd sit and talk to me and tell me stories of America, where everyone was given the chance to follow their dreams." Mary fell silent, lost in the past.

"Marma?"

"Here's me, reminiscing when you've got homework to do!" Mary went to stand up.

"Please, Marma, I can do that later, I'm enjoying this. I'll even make a fresh pot of tea," Lily pleaded.

Mary didn't need much encouragement. "All right so but I'll make the tea." She went to get the teapot. "I suppose the romance started when Jim came back from the army – he was gone for nearly five years. I'd all but put him out of my head and then there he was, standing at the back of the draughty church hall, rucksack over one shoulder, his fatigues tucked into his boots." She heated the teapot. "I was leading lady in the musical society's production of *Annie Get Your Gun*. I spotted him mid-chorus of "Anything You Can Do I Can Do Better". Oh Lord, even thinking of it now! My heart beat so hard when I saw him that I thought it would leap right out of my chest! I don't know if it was the feisty Annie Oakley, the singing, or the final embrace in Buffalo Bill's arms that did it, but when we bowed to the applause, I caught Jim's eye, even all the way down the back of the hall. There was something different. I think that was the moment we fell in love."

208

Lily looked at Mary, mesmerised. Mary's face glowed, that schoolgirl falling in love, all over again.

"He waited for me in the shadows outside the hall, said he wanted to walk me home safe. We had our very first kiss that night and it felt so right, not like with the few awkward young lads I'd kissed before." Mary smiled, with a little shyness.

"Bit of a dark horse, are we, Marma? How many lads were you kissing?" Lily teased.

"It wasn't like that! Lord no, especially not with my father, a staunchly religious man. He kept a close eye on me, his only daughter. He had a rifle for shooting rabbits – the joke was it was really for shooting any lad that tried to step out with his daughter."

"How did you and Jim manage?" Lily asked.

"We kept it secret at first. We'd snatch an hour here and there – talk about America. Jim had been giving me his money for some time, asked me to hide it for him. His dad would tear the house apart looking for it, so he could buy more booze. I shared with Jim that I dreamt of being a New York actress, on Broadway – I felt I could say it to him, you see, I knew he wouldn't laugh. So we'd kiss and cuddle and talk about our life together – I never remember feeling as alive as I did on those long summer days." Mary paused again, lost in her own world.

"So what happened?" Lily urged her on.

"The inevitable when you live in a small town – we got caught."

"But what was so wrong with it – didn't you say you were seventeen?" Lily looked confused.

"Yes, but that didn't matter to my father. He hit the roof saying that Jim didn't come from the right side of town and that he was too old for me. A soldier of his age would be expecting things from a young woman. He forbade me to see him any more."

"And?" Lily prompted.

"We just got cuter, but it was difficult. I was studying for my Leaving Cert, and Jim was working more than ever, but I think it made us realise how much we wanted to be together."

"Your dad obviously got over it, if you ended up married to Jim."

Mary blew out a deep breath. "Not my father. He wasn't exactly a reasonable man – my mother would try to get him to see sense, but he'd violently shake the Bible in her face and blame her for the Jezebel daughter – that was me, by the way." She laughed. "It came to a head eventually. As soon as I finished my exams, my father had organised for me to attend a secretarial course in Galway. I'd live with his sister, who was as much a Bible-basher as he was. My life was over." She sighed.

"What did Jim say when you told him you were being sent away?"

"His eyes welled up. I'd never seen a grown man cry before. I didn't think they knew how to cry – until then." She smiled. "That's when he asked me to marry him and I accepted." She put both hands on her lap.

Lily stretched back in the chair. "Your father must have been happy about that then – you'd be a respectable married woman after all."

Mary laughed. "Did I leave out the part where we had to go to New York first? I suppose I did. Jim had saved enough money for the two of us to go. I could audition for parts on Broadway and he wanted to study, get a qualification so he could make something of himself. He'd work too of course and then we'd get married in City Hall."

"What did Jim want to study?"

"His main aim was just to get to America although he'd started to talk about being a pilot. Even though he didn't say it, I think he missed the army – it had got into his blood. He said it didn't really matter what he did as long as he had me by his side. 'Maybe you'll be spotted on Broadway, Mary!' he'd say. 'Who knows, we might even end up moving to Hollywood – the world is our oyster!' I loved that about Jim – no matter how many times his father had bruised and battered him as a boy, it never broke his spirit. I can't be sure but I think his father continued to beat him even after he came back from the army. 'He can hurt my body, Mary, but he can't touch my dreams,' he told me."

Lily frowned. "I think your dad was very tough on him. I mean,

210

wasn't he impressed that Jim worked hard, did that not mean something?"

"It wasn't just Jim's background my father disapproved of – Jim was a Protestant. 'Drinkers and murdering heathens,' Da said of Jim's family when Mam tried to get him to see sense – then he'd hit her with the Bible. The Bible! Of all things, can you imagine? Jesus Christ himself would turn in his grave – if he had one, that is. No, there was nothing for it, we eloped to America." Mary stood up and stretched her back. "I'd better get the dinner on and you'd better get your books out, Lily."

"You can't stop there!" Lily protested. "I've never met anyone who's eloped before. I'm not even sure I know what that is actually."

"We ran off to get married, except we didn't get married straight away, we lived in sin. In America, nobody cared what we did and that felt wonderful. I did write to my mother to let her know I was all right and that I was going to be a famous actress and I'd send her an airline ticket to come and see me in my first show."

"Was she happy for you?"

"I don't know, I never heard back from her. I found out later my father hid the letters – said I was dead to them, for bringing shame on the family."

"Jeeze, that man seriously needed to lighten up."

Mary realised it must be hard for a modern teenager to understand the small-town life of rural Ireland in the sixties.

"America wasn't exactly as we expected. I got a job as a waitress and went to lots of auditions – I got a part in an off-Broadway production, to start. Eventually, I landed a role in a Broadway musical. Jim and me danced around our tiny rented living room when I got the news. *'This is it, Mary, our dreams, they're coming together! I love you, Mary, you are the most beautiful woman I ever laid my eyes on!'*"

It was only a small part. It was a start, but not enough to buy my mam a ticket to America. Jim was working on the buildings and studying at night. God love him, I'd find him asleep over his books more often than not. Little did we know everything was about to change. I got word from a friend back home that Mam had taken poorly." Mary shook her head at the memory. "I think Jim felt guilty about taking me away and not being able to provide for me. He asked me how I'd feel about him joining the US Marines . . ." She sighed. "It appeared like the perfect solution at the time. This was his way of fixing things, you see. He'd be trained by the Marines while earning a good wage too."

Mary stood and went to the dining room to retrieve an old photo album from the sideboard. Returning to the kitchen, she laid it out on the table and opened a page with a picture of Jim Devine in full dress uniform.

It didn't matter how many years had passed, the same feelings of overwhelming sadness engulfed her every time she thought of that fateful day when she arrived home to see James Devine in his blues and sporting a fresh crew-cut.

Silence fell in the kitchen – Lily didn't ask any more questions. Mary was in a different timeline, reliving the first steps of the countdown to losing the love of her life.

"Looking back it all seems like a cruel twist of fate – or karma, as you young ones say. He'd got US residency soon after we arrived, something to do with his service record in the British army – I believe that stood to him. A born Marine, they called him. Because his papers were all in order and Jim had field experience, they signed him up straight away. They'd even train him as a pilot. They saw something in my Jim, but to me he was a gentle, loving man, just my Jimmy."

A heavy silence fell between them. Lily took Mary's hands in hers, unsure of what to say.

"The thing was the Americans were already pulling out of Vietnam. The US involvement was all but over, or so we thought. I could continue my acting career – we could even visit home when we'd saved enough money. We'd give our future children the loving, comfortable home that neither of us ever had." Mary nodded her head. "Some time passed, Jim's career was flying – literally – and everything was looking up. Until I got a telegram from my brother, Liam. Mam was dying. As I was the only daughter, it was my duty to give up this American nonsense and come home. He was sure if he put in a good word for me and I apologised to our father that he'd find it in his Christian heart to forgive me. That's what Christ would do and he was sure Da would do the same." Mary's expression darkened.

"What did you do?"

"I wrote back, told them I'd be home as soon as I could, to nurse Mam. Jim had already sorted out the money. I told them to be prepared because, well, by then I was a mother myself." Mary paused.

"Wow, when did that happen? I can imagine your old man's face when he read that!" Lily clapped excitedly before cutting another slice of cake from what was left of it. "This cake is awfully good for sugar-free, Marma."

"The sponge is sugarless, but the chocolate is real, I can't stand that carob stuff. I only had a little bit anyway." Mary looked contrite.

"But go on, Marma! What happened next?"

"It was a shock to Jim and me too, but we were happy. We were engaged anyway. I think we only put off marrying in the hopes my family would eventually come round. We took ourselves to City Hall, downtown New York, and got married before the baby was born. Jim said we could have a proper church wedding soon, he'd even become a Catholic, but I didn't care about any of that. I was now Mrs James Devine and soon we were to be a proper family. In spite of everything, I did miss my family, especially my mother. I never did make it home before she died though."

"Oh no!" Lily's eyes filled with tears. "You never saw your mam again?"

"No. I got a phone call from her, much to my father's disapproval, but the family priest had got him to see it was a dying woman's wish. Mam said my brother had showed her all the letters Father had hidden from her. She thanked me for not forgetting her and she was sorry for not standing up to my father better. For once, he was silent in the background. Then she said I wasn't to waste my money coming back to Ireland because she wouldn't last and my life was in America now. 'There's nothing here for bright lights like you and Jim,' she said. 'Cherish your child, Mary, they're a gift from God' . . . and that was it, she died that night."

Both Lily and Mary blew their noses.

"That's beautiful, it's just so sad!" Lily smiled through her tears.

"It was – it broke my heart. I got a letter from my eldest brother saying she passed away peacefully. When he'd told Da that I was on my way and I had a chiseller, his reaction wasn't the Christ-like one we'd hoped for. My father said it was I who'd killed my mother with my carry-on – she couldn't bear the looks of disgust from the neighbours. Mam's engagement and wedding rings were wrapped in a tissue with the letter." Mary looked down at her hand where she still wore her mother's rings. "He reckoned Da would kill him when he realised they were missing, but he thought it was fitting I should have them. And then he said goodbye, that he wasn't much of a letter-writer and he didn't have a phone in his new house. He said he didn't want to upset Father and have him die too, so he hoped I understood, but I wouldn't hear from him again either."

"Prick," Lily said.

"Lily, mind your language!" Mary scolded. "Ah, sure, I was never that close to any of my brothers anyway and I'd other things on my mind. Jim was going to Vietnam again."

They sat for a moment, before Mary patted the back of Lily's hands in reassurance.

"It must have been hard, when he was killed – on you and Helen, I mean."

"Helen was just a baby. He came back from his first tour without a bother. That's when that photo was taken, on Long Island." Mary pointed to a black-and-white photo of herself and Jim. Jim had one arm around his wife, the other proudly holding his baby girl. "He idolised Helen, treated her as though she were a china doll."

Mary paused again, her expression so deeply sad that Lily kept quiet.

"Second time around we weren't so lucky. Jim was on a search and rescue mission for downed B-52 crews. But his Huey was shot

214

down by Viet Cong guerrillas – he was killed instantly, I was told."

"Huey?" Lily bit her lower lip.

"It's the nickname for the helicopters they used. You know, the ones you see in all those Vietnam films." Mary turned the page of the album and pointed to a different picture. "That was the last photo taken of him."

This photo was colour. Jim Devine was kneeling down beside Helen, who sat holding an ice-cream cone and squinting at the camera. She wore a white cotton dress and a large satin bow in her hair.

Mary closed the album, which brought them both back to the present, leaving Jim frozen in time.

"Jim was amongst the last of the US casualties in Vietnam. Without Jim, there was nothing for a young widow and her child in New York, so I packed up our home and moved back to Ireland."

"Back to your family?" Lily asked.

Mary laughed. "Not at all, girl. I moved to Dublin. I wrote to my family to let them know what had happened though no doubt they already knew. I got a single-page reply from my eldest brother saying that nothing had changed but he wished me well and hoped the Americans would look after me financially, which they did. I rang home when I got settled in Dublin, gave the reconciliation one last shot. But my family had frozen me out."

"So that was it!" Lily, said, stunned by the unfairness of it all.

"That was it. No more America, no more Broadway, but I had Helen and a bank of happy memories."

A shiver ran down Lily's spine. The light was fading and the evening chilled. "I just can't imagine what that must have been like – I mean Ireland looked seriously depressing in those days." She rubbed her hands together to get some warmth into her.

"It wasn't the worst." Mary looked away. She remembered the suspicion, the aloofness of her new neighbours, who didn't know what to make of the new, single mother who'd come from nowhere. She might as well have beamed down from Mars in their eyes. "But all's well that ends well – it all worked out in the end."

The doorbell chimed.

Mary jumped, startled by the sound. "That'll be Cyril and I haven't a spud peeled!"

"I can hardly move with all that cake." Lily rubbed her belly.

Mary turned the lights, heating and radio on after she let Cyril in. "Myself and Lily, we completely lost track of time, Cyril." She winked at Lily as she moved over to the sink to peel the vegetables.

"Do you know, Cyril, you've got one hell of a great lady?" said Lily as she started to clear away the remains of the cake and the cold teacups.

"Indeed I do, Lily, and a younger woman at that too!" He laughed. "Mary, can I give you a hand with that?"

Lily put the teacups in the sink and gave Mary a hug.

"No, Cyril, you sit down and keep me company," said Mary. "And what was the hug for, Lily?"

"Just for being you. I'll be upstairs, leave you two alone." She gave Cyril a cheeky smile.

Mary continued with her peeling while Cyril chatted about his day. He turned the pages of his newspaper as he talked. He'd been so busy running errands he hadn't had a chance to read it.

Mary savoured the moment. Her home was alive again, with youth and happiness. She'd come through all the heartaches and even found love again, as she approached her sunset years.

But best of all was who had knocked on her door. Her secret visitor – a gift from God. She was bursting to share her news, but she'd have to talk to Helen first, face to face, as soon as she got back from Vietnam.

Yes, life was coming together for the Devine family, a happy ending at last.

38

On arrival at Phu Bai airfield, Helen was very quiet. When Poppy asked if she was okay, she simply yawned and claimed jetlag.

"It's humid, isn't it?" She pulled at her shirt collar.

"Yes, hopefully the sun will make an appearance, I could do with a bit of colour." Poppy rolled up her sleeves.

Helen looked into the sky and squinted. "Doubt it."

"Listen, Helen, I know this isn't easy for you . . ."

Helen shrugged and feigned a look of confusion. "I'm fine."

"Well, I know time was tight but I managed to do a bit of research." Poppy took a deep breath. "There are a lot of Vietnam War tours on offer and, em, to be honest, they looked kind of tacky. I wasn't sure they'd be your cup of tea."

Helen eyed her. "I told you, Pops, it's fine and I promise I won't smack any rubber-neckers." She took out her phone to see if she had signal.

"Ah, see, there's the thing. I thought it'd be hard for you to handle tourists gawking, taking photos and buying war memorabilia from roadside hawkers. People that maybe are a little insensitive to someone whose life was directly affected by the war."

"That someone being me, I suppose."

"Obviously." Poppy rolled her eyes. "So we're joining a group from the States for part of their trip. They're mainly returning veterans and their families."

"Devine, Power, party of two! Devine, Power!" a man holding a clipboard called out.

"That's us, Helen Devine, Poppy Power." Poppy waved before she turned back to Helen. "It has a ring to it, doesn't it? *Devine Power!*" she laughed.

"Yeah, we sound like a girl band."

The stocky man extended his hand to greet them. "Mike King, this way please."

He strode ahead of them. He had a mop of white hair that was cut tight to his tanned neck and despite having a twenty-year head-start on Helen, his body fat percentage was probably lower than her UK shoe size.

As they boarded a dark green minivan, Helen felt a tinge of trepidation creep up on her. She'd closed off thoughts of her father being a military man, dying in a war he shouldn't have volunteered to be part of. If she was being honest, she was angry. Angry he chose to go to war, angry he died on the other side of the world, angry he left Mary alone, angry she'd no memories of a father other than a couple of faded photos. She might have said she was angry with the US politicians of the era but the fact was she was angry with Jim Devine – but she'd never admit that, not even to herself. And now she had to face it, sitting on a stuffy bus.

They watched village life as they passed through small towns in their minivan. Some people waved at them, others kept their heads down and went about their daily tasks. One woman sat barefoot as she straddled a thick bamboo stump. Bit by bit she was trimming off shavings with a handheld blade.

A little further along the van slowed down behind an ox-cart as it passed two farmers with a pig by their feet. The animal, separated from its herd, lay prone on the dirt verge. With all trotters bound together by rope, its breathing laboured hard. Poppy couldn't take her eyes off the rapid rise and fall of its belly. She wished his suffering would end and that she could in some way share the animal's burden, not leaving him alone. He looked petrified as he waited to die. Out of respect for the passing tourists, the farmers held off the kill and stood to block the view of the pig from the road. Helen covered Poppy's eyes before pulling her head into her shoulder but it was too late. Poppy had already seen too much. The bus trundled along but after just a few metres it stalled to give way to an old man cycling unsteadily at the road's edge. Then they heard a bloodcurdling shriek, an unmerciful sound. Helen held Poppy closer, willing the high-pitched scream to stop. They had never heard that noise before but they knew it was the sound of the pig dying of a severed throat.

Helen knew she would never forget that sound.

"Remind me why we decided to come to Vietnam again?" she said, trying to lighten the moment for Poppy.

Poppy pulled back, her face pale with shock, and said with utmost seriousness, "For you to connect with your dad, and get some closure."

"I don't know what I was thinking of . . ." Helen sighed as she looked out the window. "Although they make beautiful silks here. I wonder could I cut this bit short and see if I can source a new supplier . . ." She started to scroll through her phone. "I promised Fred I'd check out potential factories, I put the addresses in my phone." She showed the screen to Poppy. "Have a look – do you know if we're anywhere near there? I'm not sure if the GPS is active on this thing."

Poppy took her phone without looking at it. "There you go again. You always use your work to avoid facing up to things."

Helen tried to get her phone back but Poppy had confiscated it. Helen's efforts to dig it out of her pocket were thwarted by two elderly ladies offering them a humbug. They smiled at their fellow passengers and accepted the sweets.

"A humbug – who'd have guessed they'd name a sweet in your honour, Hells!" Poppy unwrapped the hardboiled candy and popped it in her mouth.

Helen nodded and smiled at the ladies as she discreetly thumped her friend.

They drove to the historical city of Hué, close to the old border that split Vietnam into North and South. All around was beautiful architecture. Helen felt herself relax and enjoy the holiday vibe. Their day would include visits to the Forbidden City (must be good if it's forbidden, Helen reckoned), Thien Mu pagoda and the Perfume River. But first, they'd cover the battle areas. Helen felt okay with that. This wasn't where her dad had perished – they'd travel there tomorrow.

Standing in an area outside of the city, they listened as Mike gave the history of the massacre at Hué, during the Tet offensive. It was one of the longest and bloodiest battles in the history of the war. Viet Cong guerrillas and the North Vietnam Army attacked during the Vietnamese Lunar New Year when a ceasefire was meant to be in place. Over a period of weeks, thousands of people lost their lives. Helen watched the small group of people they had joined. Many were obviously veterans returning with their wives, some with their sons. She wondered what it was like for them to come back to this place.

The two humbug ladies were linking arms. One blew her nose as the other one looked out across the land.

"That'll be us one day, two old ladies linking arms, passing sweets to strangers on a bus and worrying about our cats at home," Helen sighed.

"Too late, we're old ones already and remember you're allergic to cats. Come on, let's join them." Poppy slipped her arm through Helen's and steered her towards the humbug ladies.

"We were just talking about you gals, isn't that right, Marcie? What are a couple young 'uns like you doing here?" She dabbed her eyes.

"Helen's father was killed in Quang Tri, and I came to keep her company," Poppy replied.

"Is that right?" The lady looked at Helen with gentle eyes. "We lost our husbands here, in 1968, 2nd Battalion, 5th Marines. Isn't that right, Marcie?"

"That's right, Gracie."

Gracie eyed Helen. "You don't look old enough have lost your daddy, girl."

Helen was loving Gracie more by the minute. "I was just a baby and he died when a lot of American troops had already been withdrawn. I guess the Paris Treaty didn't come in time for us."

"That's a darn shame! Your poor mama, it must have broke her heart, isn't that right, Marcie?"

"Uh-huh, that's right, Gracie, broke her heart it must have," Marcie dutifully replied.

"Was your daddy American?" Gracie asked. "You don't sound American – unless you're from Michigan. I never know when someone talks Michiganese – it's the darndest thing – I've no ear for it. Are you from Michigan?"

"No, he had US residency though – that's how he could join the Marines. I was born in the US, grew up in Ireland but I went to college in the UK and I ended up staying there, so I'd say, Gracie, I've a mix of every accent. I'm a bit of a mongrel."

"Looking at you, I'd say you're a thoroughbred, missy!" Gracie decided to let go of Marcie and hook onto Helen instead. "An Irishman, is that right? I knew they could join the forces but there can't have been many of them died in this war?"

"Twenty-three Irishmen and one Irishwoman died in this war to be exact," Helen replied.

"Well, I'll be darned! Of the tens of thousands dead, is that all? I'd say your daddy was in the wrong place at the wrong time. God bless his soul." Gracie patted Helen's arm as they walked back to the bus.

The small group spent the evening together eating dinner and exchanging war stories. It turned out Gracie and Marcie weren't as old as they looked but both had forgotten how to be young once they lost their men. Being in the company of veterans and their families was an eye-opener for Helen.

"I never really thought about the other families. I felt distant from them – separated by more than the Atlantic Ocean," Helen said to Poppy as they went for a walk that evening.

"What do you mean?"

"I just felt bitter that my situation was different, my dad, an

Irishman, killed in the Vietnam battlefield. Like that lady said – wrong place, wrong time. But it was really cool talking to the other family members – and the men themselves, they were so interesting. I don't know, but it's as if I got to see how things must have been for my dad. Nearly as though I got to meet him – does that make any sense?"

"Totally. What about tomorrow – are you ready?"

"Absolutely. I don't know why I didn't face my demons years ago."

"What happened to your family made you who you are today. Being a hard-nosed-bitch helped you succeed," Poppy teased.

Before Helen could retort, her phone buzzed. "It's the office, I'd better take this." She put a finger up to Poppy to indicate she'd be one second.

Poppy could hear Helen giving instructions about how to work something on the Eden design software. Unfortunately, the call dragged on.

"Sorry about that, Poppy," Helen said, returning to her. "I missed three calls from Sarah, it must have been during dinner. I'll just have to go online for five minutes – she sent through an email she wants me to check." Helen was already punching something into her phone. "What were we talking about again?"

"How much being with these people has changed your attitude," Poppy replied.

"Uuh," Helen was reading her email from her phone.

"I'm going back inside. One of those veteran's son was a fine thing, I think I'll run in there, tear all his clothes off and make mad passionate love to him on the dinner table."

"Okay," Helen said, typing a reply to Sarah.

"I guess your changing attitude will have to be one step at a time, hey? Rome wasn't built in a day," Poppy sighed.

222

39

Breakfast was served at 07 hundred hours. They had to report to the hotel lobby for departure at 08 hundred hours – sharp. *You're in the army now.*

They were on the road to the Peace Bridge, the DMZ – the demilitarised zone – and Quang Tri. The area where Jim Devine died. The weather hadn't improved and the dark clouds overhead weighed heavy on them.

Poppy wondered what to say to Helen when they got there or if they should do something, mark the occasion in some way. Helen was twisting the small gold ring on her little finger. Poppy knew what that meant so she decided she'd figure out what to do once they got there. It turned out she needn't have worried. Mike King, or the Sergeant Major as they had nicknamed him, stopped Helen as she was getting off the bus.

"Would you be so kind as to let me walk with you, ma'am?"

Poppy ushered her on and hung back with Gracie and Marcie, both of whom needed help getting off the bus. Having been travelling for days before Poppy and Helen had joined in, they were feeling a little stiff.

"These old hips ain't what they used to be, isn't that right, Marcie?" Gracie called out.

"Uh uh, that's right, Gracie, not what they used to be," came the reply.

Mike and Helen walked in silence for a few moments.

"It looks like rain," Helen eventually said.

Mike looked up. "We're in for a storm – thunder is my guess, but it'll pass."

On cue, a clap of thunder rumbled and the first drop of rain fell.

"Your friend emailed with details of your father's division, to see if we could provide the right tour for you. I recognised the name immediately – Lieutenant James Devine." Mike opened up an umbrella and held it over them.

Rain pummelled the waterproof polyester, Helen's heartbeat pounded with the same force.

"You knew my father?"

"Yes. Not very well, I'm sorry to say. I was a corporal in another division but we both served in I Corp. Your father stood out – there weren't many Irish voices hanging out in Vietnam in the seventies," he smiled.

"I can't imagine there were." Helen smiled back as they continued to walk. She looked around to see where Poppy was. She was just a hundred yards behind them, the rain having made Gracie and Marcie beat a retreat back to the bus, but not Poppy. She was marching towards them, head dipped, collar up, with one hand plunged deep into her pocket, the other one tightly clasping her jacket closed.

"He served with the British army and saw action in the Aden conflict prior to joining the US military, is that correct?"

"Yes, I'm told that's why he'd no problem joining. They wanted men with field experience." Helen sighed. "What else do you remember, Mike?"

"That he had a wife and a baby girl," he looked at Helen, "and that he was a man of great integrity, a good soldier you'd want in your squad. And I was told he had a great way of telling a joke – a dry sense of humour, I believe the term was."

"Why am I not surprised?"

"That explains where you get it from so," Poppy said, now only a few feet behind.

224

"This is it." Mike stopped walking as they reached what remained of the bombed Citadel.

"Were you here when he died, Mike?" Helen asked.

He shook his head. "No, ma'am, I was on a recon team by then." He paused. "Take your time, I'll wait for you back at the vehicle." He handed Helen the umbrella and nodded to Poppy, before striding back down the muddy path in the rain. Helen looked up at the remains, overgrown now with moss and shrubs. Distractedly, she ran her thumb along the smooth gold of her ring.

"So this is it?" She looked at Poppy, who nodded but said nothing.

Helen handed Poppy the umbrella. She took a piece of narrow ribbon from her inside pocket. "I took this from the sample room on my last day in work . . . just in case . . . I got this chance." She walked over to a tree that stood near the main arch of the Citadel and tied the yellow ribbon to one of its branches. She was glad it was raining. Poppy left her alone for a while, with her thoughts, before joining her.

Helen rubbed the tears and rain off her face. "All the hatred and suffering, for what?"

"I don't know, Hells," Poppy answered, as she huddled into her friend. She raised the umbrella high, protecting both of them.

Helen started to laugh through her tears.

"What's so funny?" Poppy asked.

"I was just thinking we needn't worry about ending up like Gracie and Marcie – because you're right – we're already there!"

They turned and walked away, leaving the yellow ribbon to symbolise that the dead might be gone forever but were never forgotten, living on in the hearts of those that loved them.

Mike was right – the clouds soon began to clear, opening up to blue skies and lifting the heavy humidity.

In contrast to the Citadel they had left behind, they next visited a local market that teemed with life and colour. Ethnic minorities had come to town for market day, dressed in traditional clothing.

"Oh Poppy, look at that shade of red, it'd be perfect in a

Christmas collection!" Helen said as she snapped a photo. "I wonder if I can find somewhere I could buy a piece of fabric to bring back, try and get a Pantone colour-chart number to match. How long did Mike say we could spend here before we've to be back on the bus?"

"Oh my God, you are married to that job! Just let it go!"

Helen looked at her with puppy-dog eyes.

"Oh all right, stop looking at me like that! We'll try and track down sample swatches while real tourists buy normal things like key-rings. You've got fifty-nine minutes before you're court marshalled!"

They didn't find fabric but they did find moonshine.

An eager salesman insisted on taking them to where the firewater was made, just two minutes away at the back of the market apparently. He brought them to the home of an elderly man and his wife. The man sat smoking and drinking, while his wife crouched by a large, open fire, distilling the brew.

There were two other women present.

"Gracie and Marcie, what are you two doing here?"

"It's medicinal, isn't that right, Marcie?" Gracie proclaimed.

"That's right, Gracie, need it for our hips, we do," Marcie concurred.

The old man insisted they all sit down and have shots before they made a purchase. Nattering away in Vietnamese, he started dancing as he twisted and twirled a large wooden pole between his hands. It looked like a drunk's effort at Tai Chi. The wife muttered something crossly under her breath, before she left them to it. He insisted on teaching all of them the traditional dance.

"Ah, Helen, you make a great pole-dancer!" Gracie clapped.

"Oh look, it's not a pole at all – it's a flute!" Helen burst into laughter as the man started to blow his whistle.

Nothing would do him but one of them should blow it too.

"Gracie, blow the man's flute for him, so we can get going," Marcie said, finally finding her voice.

When the traditional dancing and music lesson was over, they each bought two half-litres of the smoky-flavoured moonshine, for a dollar a go. It was decided that Helen and Poppy should run ahead and hold the bus, although the veteran widows appeared to have a new spring in their step, albeit a little wobbly.

"I wish my boss could see me now," Helen laughed as they jogged with three minutes to go to their ETA. "I mean, how's that for sourcing? It's not only cheap knickers I can sniff out. I've got the same God-given talent for eighty-percent-proof train-survival kit." She hiccupped. "We'll have no problem sleeping on the train back to Hanoi now." She saluted Poppy.

"You might want to examine your phrasing there, Helen." Poppy looked at the liquid, enclosed in battered, discarded soda bottles: Helen's job was definitely not as secure as she presumed. "Maybe stick with the designing, Helen, and leave the sourcing to Fred. And don't tell anyone in the pub you sniff out knickers for a living. They might get the right impression of you!"

The veteran's tour dropped them off at the train station – they were continuing on with their war ways. Gracie and Marcie snored, heads together, but they managed to rouse themselves long enough to wave their goodbyes.

In the morning, Helen and Poppy would go to the beautiful Halong Bay.

Or so they thought.

40

They waited in the lobby of the hotel in Hanoi to be collected – no one showed. A phone call revealed that they were a day late for their departure to Halong Bay. Today's departure was full, tomorrow was the first available sailing.

Poppy apologised profusely for mixing up the dates. Helen assured her it was okay. However, she didn't want to spend another night in a no-star hotel where the toilet paper was individual translucent sheets of paper that stuck to your fingers when wet. Poppy stumbled over one of the mopeds parked in the foyer, which doubled as the staff's parking lot.

Within an hour, they were sitting at a large window in a café next to their new hotel. Sipping strong coffee, they watched the world go by. A visit to the tourist board in Hoan Kiem had revealed a lot. It turned out Hanoi was very easy to navigate, when you knew what you were doing. They had moved to a small hotel, the Hanoi Plaza, in the Old Quarter. It was warm, friendly and the same price as the hotel they had previously stayed in – and only a few streets away.

"You must think I'm an incompetent fool," Poppy said.

"It's all turned out great, so stop beating yourself up!"

"Maybe we should just stay here for all our Hanoi nights rather than moving to the French Quarter after Halong Bay."

228

"The French Quarter – isn't that where the hotel with the pool is though?"

Poppy nodded but didn't look convinced.

Helen tried a different tack to cheer her up.

"Every minute you spend unhappy is sixty seconds less spent being happy."

"That's very Zen of you, Helen," Poppy smiled.

"I read it on the thought-of-the-day calendar from the local taxi company." Helen indicated the reception desk. "And just think, if we hadn't messed up the dates, we'd have been stuck in that awful hotel for another few nights, none the wiser."

"You're right." Poppy perked up at last. "What will we do with our spare day in Hanoi? Do you fancy going to see the water puppets?"

"Not a chance."

"There's a Buddhist monastery, a little out of town. We can go and spend the day there, meditating, eating vegetarian food with the Buddhist nuns."

"I'd sooner stick needles in my eyes, thanks. Tell you what, Pops, why don't you go and hang out with the nuns. You can tell Ryvita the Hare Krishna all about it when you go home. There's a town just outside Hanoi, I hear there are great silks there. I may as well make use of our unexpected spare day."

"You can't work on holiday!"

"It's not work, well, not completely – you know how I like to drool over fabrics. It'll be like indulging a fetish."

Poppy exhaled loudly and they sat in silence for a moment. On the street, life shuffled on. A tourist, who struggled to protect a camera that was slung around his neck, bent over to retrieve his backpack from the rear seat of a taxi. They got a bird's-eye view of his khaki-covered tight butt for twenty seconds. With raised eyebrows, they looked at each and started to laugh.

"Dirty bitch," Helen grinned.

"I said nothing." Poppy was wearing her butter-wouldn't-melt-in-my-mouth face.

"You didn't have to – I know what you were thinking about that poor innocent traveller."

"I'd say the pot is calling the kettle black!" Poppy laughed. "Maybe it's karma that we didn't make that boat – perhaps it'll sink or something." Poppy brightened.

"To karma!" Helen raised her cup.

"To Halong Bay! Who knows, maybe we'll meet our soul mates on our re-scheduled junk. Here's to destiny!" Poppy was suddenly excited at the prospect. Her vivaciousness was back.

Helen enjoyed watching her friend daydream. But she knew better – there was no such thing as a soul mate, no such thing as destiny. Such thoughts were for dreamers.

41

The taxi dropped Poppy off at the monastery first. It was hidden behind large wooden gates in the middle of a shanty town. Barefoot children with dirty little faces stopped kicking their ball around so they could stare at the foreigners, who were unusual to see in their part of town. Shy, they giggled and watched from a distance.

"How on earth did you find this place?" Helen asked.

"Google. I'm delighted now that I contacted the nuns, even though I didn't think I'd have time to visit. I can't tempt you?"

"I'll leave the spiritual stuff to you, thanks. See you in a few hours and try not to bonk any monks – Ryvita might get jealous."

Poppy rolled her eyes and closed the car door.

Helen rolled down the window as the taxi pulled away. "And don't forget your halo!"

Poppy stuck her tongue out just as the brown-robed nun cracked open a small side gate.

Helen watched through the rear window as Poppy disappeared from sight. She chuckled to herself as she sat back into the seat. She checked her phone: the screen remained annoyingly clear. She considered calling the office until she did a mental check on the time difference. Realising it was still night-time in London made her yawn. Thankfully, the taxi driver was the silent type who drove quickly, the fare being a negotiated flat rate. Helen closed her eyes for what only felt like a moment but soon the driver announced she'd arrived at Van Phuc silk village.

One silk shop after another blazed with colour, heaven on earth for the lingerie designer. She ran her hand along the smooth textures, studying the fine jacquard weaving. She found the coveted shade of red that she'd transform from classic Vietnamese styling to an Eden classic – the Santa Claus babydoll. They wouldn't be able to afford real silk for the Eden price points but her head was racing with thoughts for a diffusion range. A high-class silk collection to capture the beauty of Vietnam, transforming it into a luxury lingerie anthology that not only looked beautiful but also felt so provocative to wear it released a woman's sensuality as it touched her skin.

It's do-able, Helen, if you can find the right supplier.

Helen stood in a narrow little shop lost in thought as she tried to figure out how she could make this work. She gazed out onto the street. The answer came to her as a man strode by holding a straw briefcase.

She put down the fabric and ran after him. The street was packed but she was determined this time he wouldn't get away. The fact it was daylight also helped. She remained focused on his briefcase.

"Excuse me!" she called out when she was within earshot. "Hello, you with the briefcase!"

The man's head tweaked slightly and, mercifully, he stopped and turned around.

Helen jogged up to him. She put her hand to her chest as she tried to catch her breath. The man simply looked at her, puzzled.

"I really need to work on my cardio," she panted and this seemed to amuse him somewhat. "You don't remember me, do you?"

He shook his head.

"Heathrow. You recommended I buy a book on synchronicity." Her breathing began to normalise as she saw a light go on in his face.

"Yes, I remember you now, what a coincidence!" he said, in elegant BBC English.

"No, that's not all – I then saw you in Hong Kong – actually I saw your straw briefcase."

"It's bamboo."

"Oh, okay, your bamboo briefcase. And now weeks later I see you in Vietnam. What do you think the odds of that are?"

He paused and appeared to be considering her question. "Are you involved in the garment industry?" he said then.

"Yes, but what has that got to do with it?"

"It's the time of year for trade fairs and contract placement. Hong Kong is the meeting point for Asia and, well, look around you." He swept his hand at the street where they stood, surrounded by fabric. "I'll admit, Vietnam adds intrigue to your theory but if it wasn't for my briefcase, the chances are we'd have passed each other by – without noticing."

His eyes were deep brown with a distinctive slant but he wasn't Asian. Mixed race, Helen guessed.

"True, I'm sorry to disturb you. I guess that book had me thinking there was something more to it than just the fact the world is a small place. And even smaller when you start talking in terms of the rag trade." Helen hunched her shoulders in jest, now feeling a little foolish. She cocked her thumb. "I'd better get back to buying silk – I've left a very disappointed trader back there." With a smile she walked away.

"Wait!" He caught up with her.

"Yes?"

He held out his hand. "I'm David Strong."

"Helen Devine." She shook his hand.

"Do you know what you're looking for, Helen?"

Helen raised her eyebrows.

David reddened slightly. "I mean in terms of silk – perhaps I can guide you?"

"That's very kind of you. I've managed to hunt down a particularly beautiful shade of red that I can use – but I'm looking for a factory – this area appears to be all retail."

"As Lady Luck would have it, there's one not five minutes from here. I'm going that way – I can show you if you like?" David smiled at her, a sparkle in his eye. His olive skin was smooth and slightly moist in the humidity. Despite that, his clothes had a smell of just-out-of-the-dryer freshness – summer meadow, as the fabric-softener ads would have you believe.

Helen tilted her head and smiled back. "Sure," she said.

"This way."

They began to walk side by side.

"What's the deal with the briefcase, David?"

"It was my grandfather's. I know it looks a little strange but it's got a lot of sentimental value."

Helen thumbed the ring on her little finger. The ring that had belonged to her grandmother.

There were a few moments of self-conscious silence as they walked, then David struck up a conversation.

"My grandmother was Vietnamese. She met my grandfather when he was here working. They lived together in the UK but our family links to Vietnam were very strong, if you'll excuse the pun. My grandfather brought as much trade here as he could – he wanted the local people to benefit from Western consumers, not just be repressed by the West." They had walked away from the crowds of the silk market and entered an industrial-looking area. "It's not much further, maybe two hundred metres."

"You were saying?" Helen coaxed him.

"Oh yes, my briefcase. I decided to come to Vietnam, continue what he had envisaged. He was too old to travel by then, so he gave me his old briefcase, said it would bring me luck. And as luck would have it, or synchrodestiny," he paused to look at Helen, "I met my wife here in the very same village my grandfather had met my grandmother."

The needle scratched across Helen's vinyl. *Great, there's a wife, why is it all the good ones are already taken?*

"Here we are." David looked up at a stone building.

"What is it that you do exactly, David?" Helen asked, her curiosity piqued despite cold water being poured on her he-must-be-my-soul-mate theory.

"I have a garment factory – this is it!" he said with a grin as he pointed at the building.

Helen laughed. Now *that* was a coincidence.

"We were hoping to expand it," he went on, his face again serious, "employ more people from the surrounding rural areas but I'm having difficulty getting in with the major players. I wanted to start in the UK, as it's the market I know. But it's all about *who* you know. They won't even take a look at our offer. 'Not currently seeking new suppliers' appears to be the tagline." He clamped his lips together tightly.

Helen wondered how often she'd heard Fred use those words.

"Could I have a look at your factory?"

"I'd be delighted." He hesitated. "What sector did you say you were in, Helen?" They both knew she hadn't said.

"I'm a designer."

"I guessed as much," David laughed. "You know, when I first saw you in London, I had you written off as a career-focused business executive. You look completely different out here – you appear relaxed and much more of the designer type."

Helen grinned. "What exactly does a designer type look like?"

"I'm not sure I can define it . . . probably nonconformist and less afraid of letting their personality shine through by what they wear. It was my limited perception that pigeon-holed you into just one category back in London but if I may say, Vietnam suits you, Helen."

"It just goes to show, David, appearances can be deceptive."

You better believe it.

David's wife sat hand-stitching a button on a prototype sample. She jumped up and started to brush rogue threads off her clothes when she realised they had company. David softly kissed her hello.

"This is Helen, she's a designer. I said she's welcome to look around the factory."

"I'm Mai, it's a pleasure to meet you, Helen. Would you like some tea?" Her English was as flawless as her complexion. She wore her hair tied back tight in a ponytail – a few strands hung loosely around her face and she tried to smooth them back in place.

"No, no – don't go to any trouble, Mai, thank you. Are these your samples?"

"Yes, David is not long back from Britain, he was showing them there – they are still a little creased from the suitcase." Mai brushed her hand along the silk garments as if that would iron out the creases.

"They are gorgeous." Helen admired a long silk dress.

"Unfortunately, not gorgeous enough," said David.

Mai and David exchanged a glance. Reassuringly, she rubbed his arm.

He opened a door and the buzz of sewing machines filled the air. He indicated to Helen and Mai to walk ahead.

"This is the heart of the place," he said as they walked through rows of machines, his voice raised to be heard above the collective whirling noise.

The workers looked up with curiosity but soon turned their attention back to their seams. There were a lot of vacant machines.

"You can see we were hoping to expand. Most of our supplies are Vietnamese, from companies we carefully vet – it also helps reduce our carbon footprint. Our staff come from the town and surrounding areas. Many of these women provide the only source of income for their family."

"It's a lovely bright building. I can see you run it well."

"It is important to us to provide good working conditions, and source components locally. We had a vision of an ethical production plant that would benefit everyone and add to the community. Many families get split up because the main income earner has to go to the large cities to find work."

"Why do you say 'had' a vision?"

"Unless I can get a foot in the door with one of the larger chains, it'll be hard to maintain. Small stores are great, we can continue to supply them but we need an anchor. If they'd just give us a try I know I could make it work." The muscles of David's face showed strain as he spoke.

"Have you considered making something other than evening dresses? That's quite a limited market."

"The machinists are skilled at handling silk, which as you know is a difficult fabric to handle," Mai replied.

"I know, which means they'd quickly learn to work with other lightweight fabrics such as chiffon or satin." Helen looked at the machines. "Your machines are suitable too. A few adjustments and finer needles and you could easily expand into a new market, a profitable market."

David and Mai looked at each other.

"Lingerie, of course!" Helen drew up her shoulders and raised her hands.

David took a sharp intake of breath. "Yes, we thought of that but the margins are very tight. Give a garment a lingerie label and the asking price goes down. Call it outerwear and you can increase your profit margin. Besides, we can't compete on price with producers who save money by exploiting the workforce or dump their dye-stuffs into rivers."

Helen looked at him with curiosity.

"I don't know how much you've seen, Helen, but trust me, there are some bad factories out there. Workers, often under age, are forced to work long hours, seven days a week in death-traps of factories. Many clients prefer to turn a blind eye and not ask questions."

"They set up a model factory – the client companies only see that," Mai added. "They keep the real workers hidden." She handed the sample she'd been sewing to the line supervisor.

"Mai, remember the mill in India that dumped all their toxic waste into the river?" said David. "They poisoned the whole town's water supply. That never even made it to the news."

"That's unbelievable!" Helen said.

"When people buy throw-away clothing they rarely stop to question where it came from and what exactly they are throwing away," Mai said, her eyes dark.

"So are you saying to be competitive you have to act unethically?"

"On the contrary," David replied. "There are plenty of low-cost suppliers that are doing a terrific job. In fact, some factories producing for the well-known brands are the biggest offenders."

"It sounds like it's down to people not caring," Helen said as they started to walk back towards the office.

"Yes, but greed also – companies profiting from the misfortunes of others. Some people are so poor they'll do anything to put food on the table."

"Maybe if the end consumer knew more about it and they started to ask more questions," said Helen, "the companies would be held accountable – no one wants bad press."

"Hopefully, because unless some kind of miracle drops in our laps, it looks like we may have to close up shop and move back to the UK." He held the door open to allow Helen and Mai to walk ahead.

In the office sat two children wearing a royal-blue school uniform. Beside them sat an elderly woman, her hands resting on her squared knees. The young children ran to Mai and David. They spoke in Vietnamese for a moment before the little boy came to Helen and said in carefully practised English, "I am very pleased to meet you." His face split in a smile that stretched from ear to ear.

Helen stooped slightly and shook his tiny hand.

"Helen, this is my mother." Mai said something to the older woman who nodded politely but looked away, bashful, then beat a hasty retreat, smiling and waving as she went. "My mother's very shy, especially around foreigners."

"And don't I know it!" David laughed. "Eight years and I think she's only starting to warm to me now. Would you like that tea now, Helen, or do you want to get back to your fabric-selecting?"

Helen pulled up a seat and sat down. "I think tea would be a good option."

David raised an eyebrow ever so slightly but he smiled and simply said, "Certainly."

"What is it that you design, Helen? Lingerie?" Mai asked as she laid the children's colouring books on the office desk. "I may be able to help you find what you need."

"Yes, lingerie, that's right. Have you heard of Eden?"

"Eden, UK?" David's tanned complexion paled, realisation dawning on him. "They've nearly five hundred stores throughout the UK – rumour is they're expanding into Europe also."

Their eyes now focused on Helen.

"David, I think your grandfather's briefcase may just deliver that miracle you've been waiting for," Helen said as she reached for her business card.

238

42

They made the three-hour trek to Halong Bay on a rickety white bus. They started out at eight. Their fellow travellers, consisting of two couples, were talking in whispers or not at all.

Helen was happy to escape Hanoi's endless traffic and market streets – for now. She knew it was time to exit the city when she saw Britney Spears's Headstone, complete with picture and memoriam on Tombstone Street.

"I think I'll start a bucket list and make Halong Bay the first item I tick off," Helen said, leaning forward as she pulled a notebook from her bag. Poppy was sitting in the seat in front of her as they had both wanted a window view and neither was particularly partial to morning natters.

Poppy's head bobbed up, and she peered over the top of the seat back. "You're still glowing from yesterday, aren't you?"

Without looking up, Helen nodded. "It's a win-win situation. I saw the factory as it really is. David, Mai and their children get to stay in their home country and Fred can take the limelight and PR for Eden's new Ethical Sourcing Campaign."

"I didn't know they had one."

"They do now." Helen rested the notebook on her lap. "To be fair, they've always been careful about their sourcing but I think this will up the ante a notch." She started to write again.

Poppy settled back down. "Will you please make that a long list, Helen. I don't want you putting the intention to the Universe that you're ready to kick the bucket too soon – we want you around for a while yet."

Helen looked down at the page where she'd just written the numbers one to ten. She quickly continued on to number twenty – that, she reckoned should see her through to the grand age of ninety-six. She wrote the words *Halong Bay* alongside the number one. She had time to think about the rest.

The bus trundled through the narrow streets of Hanoi's Old Quarter. Streams of people interweaved, going in different directions, armies of ants undeterred by distractions, focused only on their goals. Everyone in a hurry. Traders were already plying their wares. Street kitchens set up kerbside where wizened old ladies cooked local delicacies: noodle soup and *bun cha*.

Looking out from the bus, Helen felt she was watching a movie, so detached was she from the mêlée. The bus driver jerked the vehicle to a halt, which caused Helen to bump her forehead against the window. The guide cheerfully announced they were stopping to pick up further members of the tour group.

"Please God, let there be a few singles." Poppy stretched up to look over the top of the seat in front of her.

"Casual sex is allowed for the spiritually enlightened then?" Helen responded dryly, rubbing her sore head. She tried to get into a comfortable position but she was fighting a losing battle.

"Talk about a one-track mind! I meant someone we can have a laugh with, not all couples. But, now that you mention it, this could be the love of my life getting on the bus. A holiday isn't complete without a bit of romance."

"Romance my backside, you always want fireworks and roses, Poppy – I hate to burst your bubble but –" Before Helen could finish a tall attractive man boarded the bus.

"Morning," he nodded to everyone as he passed them. His accent was undoubtedly Australian. His tanned face was somewhat weather-beaten and his dark-blond hair was showing signs of receding, which only added to his charisma. He wore a khaki-coloured waistcoat with lots of little pockets, the type photographers use. He was wearing the classic Aussie leather hat, topping off his clichéd Crocodile Dundee look.

Poppy perked up a bit when she saw him and turned to peer at Helen with raised eyebrows. She didn't say anything – she didn't need to – she was claiming first dibs. Fireworks and roses were already raining down in her mind's eye.

Poppy looked like a child on Christmas Eve. Helen hid a smile and signalled to her to look again. Sure enough, clambering on the bus laden down with baggage was what could only be Mrs Dundee.

"Morning all!" the slender blonde woman called out from the top of the bus, her greeting upbeat, despite her heavy load.

"Easy come, easy go," Poppy sighed and pulled her new Red Star of Vietnam peaked cap over her eyes, signalling her return to slumber.

The enthusiastic tour guide, Huy, who didn't stop smiling even while talking, turned his microphone back on.

"Tropical Sails welcomes you, Pete and Lorraine!" He gave a little clap. "Just one more stop to pick up another gentleman and we'll be on our way to the beautiful Halong Bay!" He appeared genuinely excited.

Either that or he's a very good actor, Helen thought. She doubted if a European tour operator would carry out his duties in such a positive manner. Or was she just thinking of herself and her own attitude to Eden?

"So, now we are on Tin Street, Hang Thiec. Can anyone guess what they sell here?" Huy's shoulders bobbed up and down as he tried to contain his laughter. He didn't wait for an answer. "Tin!" His good humour was infectious and the mood on the bus was less restrained than before. He continued with his impromptu tour of the city. "In Old Town, Hanoi, all the streets are named by what was traditionally sold there. It make shopping very easy, I think." Still laughing.

"Where's Beer Street then, mate?" Pete the Aussie shouted from the back.

Huy doubled up with laughter, slapping his knee for added

effect. His eyes bunched up into his laughter-soaked face as he exposed a row of crooked white teeth and a large amount of healthy pink gum.

"Ha, ha, Pete – you funny man, we have the *bia hoi* everywhere!" Huy gave a sweep of his arm.

"'Struth, they should be called paint-stripper stalls!" said Pete, rubbing his perfectly flat stomach. "We'd a few scoops there the other night. Tell you what, mate, my tummy still isn't the better for it."

"That was the *ruou* that did that, you wombat, not the beer!" the little blonde woman sitting beside Pete piped up. "You said the *bia hoi* was water so they gave you the rice wine instead!"

"Sounds about right, now that I think of it. Had me on the dunny all night!"

"Too right! And I had to lie in bed next to you!" Thankfully, she didn't elaborate.

Helen and Poppy locked eyes: all couples or not, this boat-trip would be fun.

The banter continued until the narrow streets of the Old Quarter gave way to the wider metropolis of greater Hanoi. A traffic cop stood on a box in the middle of a seven road junction. No traffic lights, only her, a little slip of woman, in a dark uniform and pristine white gloves. A mask covered her mouth and nose to lessen the effect of the toxic emissions. Although the Vietnamese appeared to know when to stop and go, Helen closed her eyes, unable to look at the near-collisions taking place every few seconds. With her eyes closed, she stopped pressing her imaginary brake, before she put a hole in the floor of the already delicate bus.

"Here we are, our last stop, and then we're on our way!" Huy announced.

The golden letters for the Four Seasons Hotel glimmered, looking like a golden carp in a sea of minnow. The driver steered off the busy street, up the steep driveway, an oasis surrounded by abundant vegetation and manicured gardens. Huy jumped out and made his way to the entrance. Everyone was curious to see the face of the man who was staying here, Poppy and Helen included.

Helen poked Poppy's shoulder. "Check this out – we must be getting a luxury boat after all – no way someone is going to leave a Four Season's bed for a junker. You might even get diamond-loaded fireworks, Pop!"

"Sssh!" Poppy looked cross, but Helen just laughed.

The bubbly Huy came back into view, practically skipping to the bus. And then they saw him – Mr Five Star, with his multidirectional wheeled suitcase, white sport socks and sandals.

Poppy said nothing.

"I'm off men anyway, Poppy – go ahead and dibs all you want," Helen said as she put the white buds of her iPod in her ears.

The dark-haired man climbed on. His eyes darted nervously, looking for a seat, careful not to make eye contact.

Helen sensed his uneasiness and silently ticked herself off for being so judgemental. She smiled and said, "Hello," as the oversized, slightly awkward man passed by. Distracted by Helen's smile, he stumbled.

The cars, motorbikes and scooters thinned out and city buildings became sparse – replaced with dramatic green paddy fields. Workers in conical hats and rolled-up trousers bent over the crops, picture-postcard style. The road ahead was long and straight. In each direction, women walked along the side of the tarmac, bamboo sticks placed across their shoulders. Huge baskets carrying an array of produce – mangoes, oranges, and bananas weighed down each side of the bamboo, as they swung rhythmically. The women held out pieces of fruit – appealing for a sale. But the tourists rarely stopped.

The terminal at Halong Bay was chaotic.

"You buy something? You buy something from me?" the hawkers on the pier shouted, with mantra-like repetition, and thus became a vibration to which weary tourists became oblivious.

Huy had the girls and company on a feeder boat heading towards the landing dock within minutes of arriving.

Helen and Poppy were tired and not in conversation mode. But as their little boat headed out into the bay, they were rendered speechless anyhow. Words were superfluous as the beauty unfolded before their eyes. Even Crocodile Dundee shut up.

Despite so many people and boats, nothing detracted from the splendour of the karsts – colossal rock formations towering over them like dragons. Majestic and noble, they commanded speechless humility in their presence. The people were dwarfed as they entered the Valley of the Rock Giants. The two friends huddled together and watched, as the Goliath forms appeared to glide past. Helen thought many of them were rather phallic but decided not to admit where her mind had wandered.

They docked.

"Kayaks, everyone!" Huy's voice jolted them back to reality. The tour was to start with kayaking.

Helen, not a lover of water in general, was a bit dubious about the whole thing.

"I'm not sure I'll go, Poppy – I might sit this one out." She looked at the water, saddened by the slicks of oil and trash – the pollution the tourists had inadvertently brought with them.

"I'm not going on my own, come on." Poppy wasn't going to be put off.

"Come, ladies, this is your boat." Huy handed them yellow lifejackets – they smelt of must.

Helen donned her lifejacket, took hold of the paddle, and faced her fear of water.

The tour brochure had said *"Kayaking Lesson"*. The lesson consisted of Huy shouting, "Go for it, ladies!" as he pushed their vessel away from the dock.

At first, things were a bit wobbly as they tried to coordinate their paddling by taking a paddle each. They ended up going around in a circle. Then Poppy, who was sitting behind Helen, insisted on paddling solo.

"All those hours giving massage will pay off now. I've got muscles on my muscles," she declared.

Australian Pete declared a mini-Olympics. "England versus Ireland, Australia versus New Zealand. See you suckers!" He paddled furiously, leaving the wife to just hang on to her hat. He was an annoyingly macho Southern Hemisphere male, but a very likable one.

On cue, the previously quiet bus-load of strangers-turned-kayakers rose to the challenge and paddled in their respective country's honour, whooping and hollering as they went. The Irish were still going in circles though despite Poppy's solo efforts.

The banter caught the attention of neighbouring boats, of which there were too many to count. Helen felt someone watching her.

"Pops, take a rest, I've got this," she said.

"It must be a different group of muscles for paddling – my arms are knackered already." Poppy reluctantly let go.

"Let's see if all my yoga Downward Dog poses will stand to us." Helen paddled and the kayak straightened up.

"Well done, girl, but I think it's your sex positions that are standing to you," Poppy laughed.

Helen splashed her.

Something made Helen look around. A young man was watching her from another kayak. He was alone. Despite the distance between them she could see that actually he was beaming at her. Their eyes fixed on one another. For a moment, she forgot to paddle.

"Hells, what are you doing, we're losing the race!" Poppy pounded the side of the craft as if she were on a racing horse.

Helen threw an impish smile back at the guy. There was something familiar about him. Even at a distance, she could make out the curve of his mouth, the angle of his chin – distinguished, without conceit.

Eye contact was broken – she started to paddle again, only this time she made a vain attempt to look graceful.

"Check out that guy over there," she said. "He keeps staring over at us."

It didn't take Poppy long to spot him amongst the skirmish of kayaks.

"The young blond bloke? Jesus, Helen – he's about twelve!"

"I didn't say he was checking us out, for Christ sake! I just said he keeps looking over. And let's face it – he's more than smiling – he's radiating at us. It's odd."

"You most likely remind him of his mother."

"Cheers, babe, you're great for the self-esteem!"

"He probably feels sorry for us," Poppy replied flatly.

"Remind me never to go on holidays with you again!" Helen panted as she upped the pace again. "You're starting to sound like me."

"We could do with him on our boat – look how easy he makes it seem. He's a natural," Poppy said, as the man's strokes brushed through the water.

Helen flashed one of her dazzling smiles at him, as if to reassure him Mommy was okay. Water-Boy returned an even wider, porcelain smile. Or was he laughing? It was hard to make out, now that he'd gone further across the bay.

The encounter cost Helen and Poppy valuable paddle-time and Team England took advantage.

"Make a hard right, Helen, the Aussies are heading into that tunnel!" Poppy shouted, having appointed herself navigator.

"Is it a cave? It doesn't look very big if it is," Helen asked, paddling furiously.

Poppy didn't reply – she was looking up in awe at the height of the limestone islands surrounding them.

"It's some kind of channel, I think. It doesn't look very high though," Helen said, ignoring the scenery, focused on where she was trying to get to – before the English. Feeling a twinge of claustrophobia coming on, she manoeuvred the small craft as if she'd been doing this all her life. Between the hygiene, the hotels and now water and caves, Vietnam had proven to be a challenge to all her fears, on every level.

Team Australia was out of sight, having entered the mysterious tunnel moments before. Team England had forgotten about the race, instead stopping to take in the strange formations of the area they had entered, their mouths open in wonder.

An eerie silence enveloped them. But there was light at the end of the tunnel, both literally and metaphorically.

Once she'd gone far enough ahead to ensure placing for Team Ireland, Helen slowed down to see what all the fuss was about. The tunnel was low and dark – above them, icicle-like stalactites made curious forms. A droplet of water fell from one of the tips, hitting the water's surface, causing an echoing sound to vibrate around them. Like a wooden stick on a Chinese singing bowl, this was the sound of silence.

They and their new companions drifted on the still water, communicating with each other by eye contact and smiles. No one spoke. Everyone felt special to be here, in this place and time – the collective consciousness transfixed by beauty and stillness. It was a moment that would stay with a person for a lifetime.

After a short time, almost by its own volition, the kayak started to drift towards the light of the cove. Emerging from the cave-like tunnel, a beam of sunlight peeped out from behind hazy karsts.

"It's like the hand of God reaching out to touch you," Poppy whispered.

"I feel I'm in a dream, it's so unreal, yet here we are," Helen whispered back, her usual wisecracks vanished.

The water lapping the kayak was the only sound.

"Why are we whispering?" Poppy leant towards Helen.

"I don't know – it's just so humbling maybe? Or maybe we've entered the twilight zone . . ." Helen widened her eyes and wiggled her fingers hypnotically at Poppy.

They entered an enclosed cove. Akin to New York tourists, people craned their necks looking at the cloud-dotted sky visible through the circle-like formation of the giant limestone.

"Hello!" Lorraine, the Australian woman, called out, breaking the silence.

Hello, Hello, Hello, Hello! echoed all around them.

Everyone laughed. The silence was broken, but for some reason it was okay, as if it was time. Their laughter echoed as well, which caused them to laugh even more.

When they'd stopped laughing Helen turned to Poppy. "I feel so lucky to be here." She twisted the ring on her little finger.

"Me too, I'll treasure this moment forever."

"It's like, nothing else matters – nothing, before now, matters. When we paddle back out through the tunnel, I'll have been reborn in some way, given a clean slate to start again. Does that sound weird?" Helen wasn't used to the kind of words she found herself saying. Leaving her comfort zone and coming to Vietnam had opened her eyes. And now it had led to here.

"No, I understand that. It's as though we've been cleansed by witnessing such incredible beauty," Poppy said softly.

Helen looked at her oldest, dearest friend. "Thanks for sharing it with me."

Poppy smiled, no words needed.

Helen wiped her eye. "We'd better head back out – there are other kayaks about to come in – it'd be nice to let them have their chocolate-box moment." She guided the kayak towards the small rocky opening, silently thanking the Universe for whatever had just happened.

43

It was a self-established traffic system in the tunnel, incoming boats on the left, outgoing on the right. As the light of the cove receded behind Helen and Poppy, it illuminated the faces of the people in a neighbouring boat as they entered – they glowed with curiosity and marvel.

Their anticipation was tangible.

And then – he was there.

The smiling Water-Boy rowed towards the light, his kayak only feet away.

Their eyes fastened as they glided past each other.

"Hi," he said.

"Hi," was all Helen could say, like the echo she had just left. Her heart thumped. She opened her mouth to say something else – what, she didn't know – but the moment had passed and he was gone. Two ships passing in the night.

"Wasn't that the guy from earlier?" Poppy asked.

"I think so," Helen said, trying to catch her breath. She wondered why her heart was beating so fast, just from a look.

"He's older than he looked from a distance, almost within your age range, Helen," Poppy added with an air of deviousness in her voice. "He's probably about twenty-five, I reckon – pity – too old for your taste, hey?"

"Sod off, you – you can paddle back for being such a smart-arse." Helen playfully pushed the paddle to a groaning Poppy.

"The old Helen is back, I see."

"Last back has to buy the beer!" Australian Pete shouted out at them. He'd appeared out of nowhere and was energetically making his way to the dock.

Helen grabbed the paddle back from Poppy, who was happy to oblige.

"Losers!" she shouted back and quickly gained ground on him.

They pulled up to the wooden gangway. Pete and Lorraine had won by a hair's breadth – according to Poppy and Helen, that is. People from the kayak-hire company and Huy hurried over to help them disembark onto a slippery deck. The water-boat saleswomen weren't far behind.

"Lady, you buy something?" a little Vietnamese woman shouted at them, her boat overloaded with bottles of water, Coca-Cola, fruit and chocolate. Three identical boats joined in chorus, all vying for a few tourists' dollars. They accepted Dollar, Dong, Sterling and Euro, sorry, no American Express.

"How much is your Buddha beer?" Pete asked, pointing to a golden-coloured can of the Vietnamese beer.

"Two dollar." The woman quickly held up a can.

"You want anything, girls? Bound to be cheaper here than on the boat," he asked his wife, Helen and Poppy.

"We're grand thanks, Pete – anyway, I thought we were supposed to be buying the beer?" said Poppy.

"No worries, I was just kidding. It's your turn on the boat though!"

Lorraine lightly punched him on the arm. "Be nice, Pete! Ignore him, girls, he's only pulling your leg. He's delighted the Irish are on board tonight."

"Damn right, it's bound to be a right good party! Actually, throw us up six tinnies, love," he said, holding up six fingers before reaching for his wallet. With the sight of the trade, more floating shops paddled in their direction in the hope of getting some share of the bread.

250

"How do they all make a living out here?" Poppy said to Helen.

"With difficulty, I'd say," Helen replied distractedly. "We don't realise how lucky we are." She was looking back across the bay.

The group gathered and Huy did a head-count.

"Good, good, all here. Now we go by small motor-boat to your Tropical Sails Junk, *The Phoenix*." Huy cupped his hand in a sweeping motion, as though he was seeing the name in lights.

"That's apt, a bird, reborn from the flames. Maybe it's a sign of new beginnings," Poppy smiled. She had noticed Helen was very quiet.

The motor idled as passengers clambered on. Then, with a pull from the driver, it spluttered dark smoke and coughed its way to life.

The noise of the engine drowned conversation. Helen let the wind blow through her hair as they headed, at speed, away from the quay and out into Halong Bay.

She couldn't help but look back and, sure enough, she spotted him.

Water-Boy or Water-Man, as she now realised, was standing on the pier – which she had left only minutes ago. What was it about this guy that she could pick him out, his gait, his presence? It was almost as though she could sense him. The back of her neck prickled with goose bumps.

Damn, she thought. Talk about missing the boat!

"Who's for beer?" Lorraine shouted as she popped open a can.

"Yes, please!" said Poppy, eager as an under-age schoolgirl. "Isn't it funny – a laughing Buddha on the can!" She mimed as she pointed to the can, as it was hard to hear over the engine. She took a long gulp of the warm, frothy liquid. "I'm thinking the Buddha guarantees hang-over free beer!"

"Wishful thinking!" another passenger joined in.

The dark-haired man, who had joined them from the Four Seasons, smiled and laughed. He was trying to fit in – he pushed his glasses back up the bridge of his nose and stole a glance at Helen. Her fair hair was blowing back from her face, revealing a long graceful neck. She had a dreamy look on her face.

251

Twilight was settling and lights from the junks began to twinkle around the bay like fairy lights on a Christmas tree. Helen looked up high into the sky – the stars were turning on now too, winking back at her. A gust of wind caused her to shudder – she pulled her denim jacket tightly around her torso. As they reached their junk, home for the night, she looked around her – they were an eclectic group of people. And they were in for a good night.

44

05:50 a.m. Helen cautiously opened a bleary eye. Her other eye was buried deep into the pillow, as she had fallen asleep face down last night – or was it that she had collapsed face down? Her mouth, dry as the Sahara, was open, the lower lip stuck to the white cotton pillowcase. She tried to swallow but lack of saliva made it difficult. That could mean only one thing – drool. And drooling meant a black mamba of a hangover.

Before moving her head too much, she tried to assess the situation. Jerky motions now could result in a shot of searing pain to her oxygen-deprived brain. Poppy was softly snoring in the next bed, her arms outstretched like Jesus Christ on the crucifix. Helen willed herself back to sleep as, despite her cotton-wool head, she could remember that they had only stumbled down to their cabin a mere four hours previously.

"Water, I need water," she muttered like a castaway shipwrecked on a desert island. She decided she'd have to attempt moving. To her pleasant surprise, a thumping headache failed to appear.

Score, she thought. She threw back the duvet to find she had only half undressed last night. Her shoes and jeans lay strewn on the floor. As she stood, she noticed the boat had started to sway.

"I hope that's the boat and not me," she said, trying to remain vertical as she pulled on her jeans. Poppy's reply was a continuing, even snort.

Grabbing up her shoes and scooping up her packet of paracetamol, she tip-toed to the cabin door, which brought a whole new challenge: sunlight.

"Bugger!" Helen winced as she stubbed her toe on the lip of the doorframe.

"You buy something?" A voice and the sound of oars swishing through water came from the side of the boat.

"You've got to be kidding me!" Helen declared as she looked overboard to see if there really was a floating shop alongside them at the break of dawn.

Thankfully there was.

"There is a God! Water, please – a big bottle. And have you any Mars bars?" Helen called down to the Vietnamese saleswoman.

The woman handed the goods up to Helen. "Something else for you, lady? Buddha beer maybe?" she asked, head cocked innocently.

Helen wasn't ready to start the hair of the dog cure, because then she'd seriously have to question her drinking habits.

"No, that's it, thanks, how much?"

"Three dollar," the woman replied, happy to have a handsome sale so early in the day.

Helen took her supplies and headed up the stairs towards the main dining room. There were bodies everywhere – the crew slept in sleeping-bags in the dining-room-turned–staff-quarters. She continued on up to the top tier of the junk and lay back on a sun-lounger. She unscrewed the water-bottle cap, downed two paracetamol for the hangover she knew was coming, and then took a bite out of her Mars bar.

An early-morning mist enveloped the bay, giving the karsts a mystical vibration.

What a good place to have a hangover, she thought happily. She closed her eyes and listened as the sounds of solitude lulled her into a gentle slumber.

"Helen – are you up there?" Poppy shouted up the stairs, unwilling or unable to climb them.

The boat had come to life. Sounds of pots and pans clattering from the galley indicated the day had officially started.

Helen roused. "Eh, yep," she shouted down. "I've got water if you need some. I've eaten the chocolate though – sorry!" She was not a bit sorry at all.

Poppy's bed-head came into view as she climbed up.

"And the dead arose and appeared to many!" Helen laughed when she saw her friend.

"Like you can talk – have you looked in the mirror this morning?" Poppy retorted, grabbing the bottle of water.

Helen handed her the packet of pain-relievers. "Good night though, hey?" she chuckled.

"It was a laugh – I just wish we'd gone to bed a bit earlier." Poppy crunched her head from side to side. It was still attached, thank goodness.

"What the hell, we're on holiday. Anyway, this Cat Ba Island we're heading to today sounds quiet enough – we can sleep tonight." She said it as if she meant it.

"Sleep now sounds like a better idea," said Poppy as she settled herself on a sun-lounger. The aroma of baking drifted from the kitchen below. "Breakfast smells good though."

"How can you even think of eating? Coffee would be good, mind."

"Come on, let's go down before the others scoff the lot."

Helen groaned but headed down the wooden steps with Poppy.

"Good morning, ladies! How are you this morning?" Huy greeted them with his usual toothy grin and child-like enthusiasm.

"Too much karaoke last night, Huy – you know yourself," Helen said, touching her throat, blaming singing into the Tannoy until the wee hours for her delicate state of being.

Huy laughed as if it was the funniest thing he'd ever heard. He was inclined to do that – a lot.

"Yes, yes, I remember – you very good singer – Freddie Mercury!" he said, slapping his thigh.

Helen had forgotten about that bit. It reminded her of Fred, Hong Kong and of course, Eden, which she had managed to push to the back of her mind for the night.

Once Huy composed himself, he continued, "So it's just three of you go on the Cat Ba Island tour. We leave in few minutes, okay? There will be breakfast for you on the other boat."

"G'day, girls," Pete said, lifting his hat to them as he entered the room.

"'Struth, did we really drink that much!" Lorraine declared, checking through their bar bill as she walked in behind him. "Hiya, girls!" she beamed, but then her expression changed to a questioning frown. "Are you definitely leaving us then?"

"I'm afraid so – we're off to a quiet island to look at flora and fauna," Poppy said flatly.

"Is it just the two of you going? Why don't you stay here, with us?" Pete looked around the dining room – no one else appeared to be packing up.

Helen and Poppy shrugged.

"I think that English bloke mentioned he's leaving today too. You know, the quiet guy, dark hair, said he was a geography teacher or something." Lorraine counted out her cash.

Helen felt her hangover kicking in.

A quick bird bath and clothes haphazardly shoved into their bags, and Helen and Poppy were back up on deck to say their goodbyes.

Lorraine gave each of the girls a warm hug. "We'll miss you guys tonight – won't be the same without Team Ireland."

Having exchanged email addresses with their drinking buddies, Helen and Poppy got into the feeder boat where Mr Four Seasons, with the multidirectional suitcase, already waited. The group waved farewell to them from the junk's deck. The captain and crew stood on the upper deck and continued to wave until their boat was out of sight.

Helen, Poppy, Keith and Huy headed across the bay.

"Do you know much about the island, Keith?" Poppy enquired of their only other tour mate.

"Indeed I do, Poppy – I've done quite a lot of research. We're in for a treat. There's a proliferation of wildlife specific to the region that I, for one, will study in depth. And then there is Thien Long Cave – I'm very excited about that. We'll see the roots of a hundred-year-old Si tree – as long as you don't mind bats, of course." He paused to remove his glasses, which had steamed up from the Halong Bay mist.

Or was it from excitement, Poppy wondered.

"Looks like we've arrived at our new boat." Poppy fixed her hair into a pony-tail. She noticed the crew waiting to greet them starboard on a junk, similar to the one they'd just left.

"We go on here, have breakfasts, then we go on to Cat Ba," Huy briefly informed them before calling out to the crew in his native tongue.

The rope was thrown and once more they clambered off one boat and on to another.

"Oh dear, this vessel appears to be rather full of people." Keith pushed his case in front of him as they entered the dining room. "I was under the impression it would just be the three of us." He zipped up his windcheater jacket to his neck, despite the fact they were indoors.

The room quietened and conversation lulled as everyone looked up to see who was coming on board.

"Christ, I feel like a goldfish in a bowl," Helen said under her breath, as Huy walked them through the room to a reserved table.

"Please sit, you have breakfast here, then we take a smaller boat to Cat Ba."

Not another bloody boat!

"Coffee?" Huy asked.

"Definitely – no more boats without caffeine," Helen grumbled.

Huy laughed. "You're funny lady," he said before disappearing.

The interest in their boarding was short-lived and the room had returned to its chatter.

"It sounded like a fun evening last night," Keith said.

"Lord, Keith, I'm sorry, were we loud? I hope Gloria Gaynor here didn't keep you awake, singing 'I Will Survive'," Helen grinned.

Poppy kicked her under the table. "Hey, you'd an unfair advantage. You've done Asian karaoke lots of times. Why didn't you join us, Keith?"

"I'm not much of a singer, I'm afraid," Keith replied, pushing both hands, palm to palm, tightly between his thighs.

Breakfast arrived. Helen popped a bread roll into her mouth, holding it between her teeth as she gathered her hair off her face to tie it back as Poppy had already done with hers. Helen took the opportunity to survey the room. It was a carbon copy of the boat they'd just left – it was adorned with lots of brass, chandeliers and a selection of karaoke casualties. They all faded into the background, though, when her eyes fell on one blond-haired man.

And he was looking straight at her.

What were the chances?

Higher than it appeared, it would seem.

Then he was smiling again.

At her.

That beaming smile that had caught her attention across a crowded Halong Bay.

Of all the boats, in all the world, and you just happened to walk into mine.

Although, technically, she had got on *his* boat.

Typical, I look like the Wild Woman of the West after a day ploughing the fields and downing ten bottles of stout, she thought. She took the bread-roll out of her mouth. Poppy didn't appear to notice and Keith was still giving them a *National Geographic* type lesson.

Water-Boy was sitting with a group of The Beautiful People. A pretty girl was flicking her hair at him as she spoke. She whispered something in his ear. He leaned closer to hear her.

Ah well, the fantasy was nice while it lasted!

He glanced over again and she smiled at him as she would smile at a pleasant shop assistant.

"Isn't that the guy from yesterday?" Poppy whispered as Huy gathered together the Cat Ba Island tour group.

"Yep, him and his entourage of nubile bunnies, by the looks of it," Helen sniffed. She felt old and envious as she listened to the happy chatter about last night's drunken escapades from their six new companions.

"Thank goodness it's not the entire boat of people on our expedition," Keith said, sticking close to Helen and Poppy.

Helen went to the bathroom, which unfortunately had a mirror. She made a feeble attempt to apply some make-up but gave up. She would fit in very well with the Cat Ba Island wildlife with her current look.

"Where were you? I'll never remember all the names," Poppy said when Helen returned. Huy had just completed another round of introductions.

"Don't worry about it. They're as hung-over as we are, except they're about twenty years younger so it hasn't hit them in the same way. Blame the onset of Alzheimer's, if anyone gets insulted." Helen looked around, fairly sure their fellow passengers wouldn't care if they remembered their names or not.

Another boat. Another attempt at looking refined, when at any moment, embarking and disembarking, you could slip and go arse-over-elbow.

"The air is clearing my head." Poppy closed her eyes as she lifted her face to the sky. A hazy sun was trying to peek through a gauze of cloud.

Helen listened to the lapping of the water against the boat as they sailed towards the island. A peaked cap and sunglasses meant she could subtly observe The Beautiful People, without appearing stalker-like – but her eyes kept drifting back to just one person.

45

"You've got to check out the restrooms, dudes," the All-American surfer declared, as he sat back down at the lunch table.

"They can't be as bad as the ones when we docked, can they?" Poppy asked him. She had patiently held off peeing, after exiting from the last bathroom-stop gagging.

Helen stood up. "I'm going anyway. Thank God for alcohol dehydration. You're right – the last pit-stop smelt like a cross between a down-town New Delhi cesspit on a hot day and a skunk with an upset tummy."

There was silence around the table, no one sure how to react to Helen's toilet humour.

"I'll go with you, it can't be so bad here," Poppy said as she checked her bag for extra supplies of tissue. "It's a restaurant for goodness sake. The food was good and the plates were clean, sort of."

"God bless your optimism, Poppy. We're in a stilt-house, on the side of a river, in the middle of nowhere, on an island that no one I know has ever heard of," Helen reminded her. "I feel like I'm on the set of *Lost* – any moment now the Black Smoke will come to claim us." She laughed, having got over the fact that Water-Boy was unavailable. It had left her free to spend the morning in the caves, which she actually really enjoyed. Even Keith had been an interesting guide.

"Once more, I've no idea what you're on about but you really ought to watch less TV, Helen," Poppy said, stuffing tissues in her pocket.

The girls started to walk along a dusty path. They followed the makeshift, hand-written sign, cut in the shape of an arrow: "TO LET".

"What do you think they're renting?" Helen quipped. "I'm guessing it's the two-by-four wooden shed over there with the corrugated tin roof – what do you reckon?" She looked questioningly at Poppy whose brow had wrinkled into a worried frown.

"Why is there a hose and a bucket outside the door?" Poppy bit her lower lip.

With that, one of the girls from their group emerged, gasping for breath. Her face had turned a paler shade of green.

"Oh Lord . . ." Poppy was crestfallen as she felt her bladder hit her throat in protest.

"Guys, don't go in there if you value your five senses." The poor girl managed to point at the cause of the offense, despite being doubled over.

"And we've just had lunch in this joint!" said Helen.

A scrawny chicken waddled over to Helen's feet and started pecking at the bare ground.

"Yes, and you've probably just eaten her mother." Poppy, who had declared vegetarianism since seeing the pig incident, frowned at Helen.

"Who do you think you're kidding? You'll be back eating bacon butties within two weeks of getting home." Helen had seen Poppy's attempts at purity fall by the wayside on more than one occasion, usually spurred on by Helen herself. "Okay, I'm going in." She took a deep breath.

With trepidation Helen edged open the cracked, timber door. Tears sprang to her eyes as the putrid stench of stale urine punched her. Poppy looked on horrified as she watched Helen's sun-kissed face turn pallid and contorted. Yet still Helen disappeared into the abyss that was the toilet.

Helen willed herself not to breathe. She unbuttoned her light cotton trousers with one hand while trying to keep the wooden door closed, by pulling on a feeble piece of string that constituted the handle. It occurred to her she could shout to Poppy to stand guard, but that would involve breathing, a risk she was unwilling to take.

She almost lost balance when one of her shoes failed to maintain its grip on the slime either side of the hole in the ground. Squatting dangerously close to the peeing hole, Helen silently gave thanks. *Thank you, Universe, that I cannot see what it is I'm standing on. And thank you, God, that it's just a wee and nothing more.* With that, she looped her free hand around the waist of her pants, to avoid peeing on them.

Outside, Poppy edged closer to the loo. There were sizable gaps above and below the swing door, which provided ventilation but also left the occupants feeling exposed.

"You okay in there, Helen?"

Helen emerged triumphant, but still holding her breath, and trousers, which she had pulled up but hadn't fastened yet, saving precious breathing seconds.

"Hi there!" Water-Boy appeared to emerge from nowhere. "Are you sick?" A look of concern was etched on his face.

"Loo," Poppy and Helen both said.

He nodded his understanding.

"John, hurry up, Buddy's starting another card game," an attractive female companion called to him from the stilt-house.

"You guys go ahead!" he hollered back. "Sorry about that," he smiled at Helen and Poppy. "So, the restrooms, that good, hey?" He scratched his stubble, all blond and perfect.

At that moment, Helen wished she'd buttoned her trousers and she wasn't flashing her waist-high comfy travel knickers.

"John, are you and your friends staying on the island tonight?" Poppy asked.

"They're not my friends." He paused. "What I mean is I just met them last night."

This answer seemed to please Poppy. "Really? We thought you were all together. Although, now that you mention it, didn't you say you'd seen John kayaking alone across the bay yesterday, Helen?" Poppy acted confused, putting Helen on the spot.

Helen feigned a smile, which meant, *I will strangle you later, woman.* "Hmm, maybe – shouldn't we be getting back to the others?" she said with wide-eyed innocence.

"Are you sure you're okay?" he said. "You kind of look like you need CPR . . ."

Is that an offer, Blondie?

Poppy stifled a laugh, and pretended she was coughing.

Helen wondered if Water-Boy was tuned into her and Poppy's humour. She didn't know him well enough to venture there. Instead she buttoned up her trousers, discreetly tugging at her backside seam as she smiled. Now well adjusted, she lifted her chin and said, "See you back at the bus, John," before she walked away.

The coach pulled up outside a hostel in the seaside town of Cat Ba island.

"All staying in Lucky Star, please get off here. Have a good night and we'll collect you here at eight thirty tomorrow morning." Huy said, beaming even more than usual. The day had gone well and he was depositing his guests while the sun was still smiling.

The twenty-something Beautiful People got off, not looking overly enthusiastic at the sight of their accommodation. It appeared a day of caves and lack of sanitary facilities had taken their toll, even on the young, who were now facing a night in a hostel. Helen realised that just maybe being a bit older had its advantages. Water-Boy didn't get off with them.

"I have three of you in the Princess Hotel and one in Island Resort." Huy flicked through his clipboard.

The bus laboured to change direction, and set off only to stop two minutes later.

"Not exactly a big holiday resort, is it?" Helen wisecracked as she pulled her bag from the overhead bin.

"Let me get that for you." John jumped up to get the bag.

"Thanks – enjoy your evening." Helen smiled with a pinch of disappointment.

"Mr John, Miss Helen, Miss Poppy, your dinner is included in the tour. It is served between seven thirty and eight thirty, okay?" Huy looked for confirmation that they'd understood.

There is a God!

Keith, who as it turned out was actually a geography professor, looked deflated.

"You stay in the top hotel, Mr Keith – stay on bus, it is just two minutes away, up the hill."

"The Four Seasons of Cat Ba, hey, Keith?" Poppy jested. "Come to our hotel later if you feel like company – right, Helen?" She dug her elbow in Helen's ribs.

"Of course, I owe you a drink – if it wasn't for you, I'd have thought I was looking at a pile of old rocks today," Helen reassured him, which appeared to work.

They checked in.

Helen pressed the button to call the lift.

"We're in 221. Do you want to have dinner with us tonight, John?" Poppy asked as only a woman with no interest in a guy could.

Good girl, Poppy!

"Unless you're meeting up with your friends from last night, that is?"

He grinned. "No, one night was enough, thanks. Sure, I'll meet you guys in the restaurant later." The doors slid open, the three got into the tiny space. They rode in silence, watching the digital panel above the door. A ping announced the second floor.

"I'm 222 – it's a good number."

The girls looked at him.

"In case you need to call me." He adjusted his back-pack. "By the way – John, that's the name on my passport – but my friends call me Jack. Jack Taylor."

And then he was gone.

In their room Poppy looked at Helen. "Stop looking so innocent, you slapper!"

"What? I don't know what you're on about," Helen said, looking out the window at the promenade and harbour.

Poppy decided to let her friend off lightly – for now. Jack Taylor was far too young and handsome to be anything but heartache.

"It's beautiful here, let's go out and have a look around." Helen changed the subject.

Despite the lack of her usual creature comforts over the past week, Poppy hadn't seen Helen looking so relaxed in years.

They walked the promenade of the picturesque fishing village.

"Is Dublin six or seven hours behind here?" Poppy was thinking of giving Lily a call.

They were directed to the post-office for phone-calls and not surprisingly – stamps. They climbed the steps up to the entrance of the state-run building.

"Hello!" exclaimed the postmistress enthusiastically from behind the brass bars of her caged office. "Can I help you?" She was a very young and pretty postmistress.

"We want to make two calls, long distance – we were told to come here?"

The girl pushed a small piece of paper and pencil across the counter. "Write numbers here. How much you want to spend?"

"This could be manna from heaven, hey? Mary can't complain if I get cut off halfway through her weather report." Helen smiled wickedly.

"Five hundred thousand Dong for the two calls and stamps for postcards to Europe, please." Poppy counted out how many postcards they had just purchased from the boulevard shop that sold everything from locally farmed pearls to buckets and spades. She made a mental note of which one she wanted to send to Angelo. The one with the funny little monkey on it. "Twenty stamps, please!" she concluded.

"Do we know that many people?" Helen looked dubious.

"First number, your call will be in booth number six." The postmistress-cum-telephone operator pointed to a line of wooden telephone booths that stood the length of the post-office wall. It appeared they'd entered a time-warp, the scene reminiscent of an old black and white movie. Gregory Peck could appear any moment, cigarette in hand.

"Second number," she said, looking at Helen, "please go to booth three." Smiling she added, "May I wear your sunglasses while you on the phone, please?" Only the postmistress's shoulders and head were visible behind the heavy marble counter top and large brass poles. She was either very small or her chair was set low – it was probably a bit of both. Taken aback, Helen took her black oversized Prada sunglasses off her head and handed them to her before heading for the booth.

"Hi, Mum, how's it going there?"

"Helen, where are you now, love?" Mary's excited voice echoed down the line.

"A beautiful little island town. It's a bit like Howth, without the BMWs."

"Nuala!" Mary shouted out to her friend in the background. "It's Helen ringing from Vietnam – she was put through by an operator. Imagine they still have operators there! Nuala just popped in for a quick cup of tea, love – Lily popped home to pick up a few things – other than that I haven't seen anyone."

There was a lot of popping going on, it seemed. By 'anyone', Helen assumed her mother meant Cyril.

"How's the weather over there, Helen? It's raining here but it's to clear up tomorrow."

"The sun is setting now, it's just perfect."

"That's good, love, but mind yourself – wasn't it terrible what happened to that poor unfortunate tourist over there?"

"On Cat Ba Island? Seriously, Mother?"

"No, in Vietnam, I'm sure it was Vietnam, no, was it India? Nuala, where was that Sky news report from?"

The operator came on the line – they'd one minute left, saving Helen from the news report, but giving her enough time to interrupt Mary's flow and say "I love you, Mum". Sure enough, seconds later the line went dead.

Poppy and Helen emerged from their booths more or less at the same time, and laughed at what they saw: a beautiful but tiny face trying to keep designer shades on, the girl's face held high in an effort to keep them from falling off as she pursed her lips as a little girl dressing up might do, in an attempt to look sophisticated.

266

"You look good, may I take a picture?" Helen got her disposable camera at the ready – the Vietnamese girl obliged with a Hollywood pout.

Laughing, Helen and Poppy left their new friend at the post office, with a promise to post the picture. The setting sun had turned the spotless pavements golden. Fishing boats were silhouetted against a canvas of tangerine sea and a firecracker sky.

"Wow!" was all Poppy managed to say.

"I know, it's amazing."

"But I was talking about the sunset, Helen," Poppy grinned.

Helen hadn't seen Jack walking towards them.

"Hi, Jack!" She smiled broadly at him.

"Hi there, something else here, isn't it?" Poppy said to him.

"Stunning." Jack wasn't looking at the harbour.

Jack's professional-looking Nikon camera was hanging around his neck.

"Would you like us to take a photo of you?" Poppy asked, indicating the camera.

"Thanks, that'd be great. I've just come down from the mountain – I got some amazing shots." He carefully removed the camera and handed it to Poppy who equally carefully hung it around her neck. "Will you get into the picture with me, Helen?"

"Don't be silly! In a few weeks' time you'll be wondering who that stranger in the photo is." Helen brushed him off as the blood rushed to her face.

"Nah, come on, I'd like you to – please?" Jack held out his hand to her.

"Oh, okay so." Helen smoothed down her T-shirt. "Take one with mine as well, Poppy." She handed over her battered disposable camera.

Jack and Helen stood against the water's edge. Jack slipped his arm around Helen's waist and pulled her closer to him. Her shoulder fitted perfectly under his. She could smell him now, his skin scented with citrus wood cologne, and a tinge of fresh perspiration from his hike up the mountain.

"Squishy tomatoes!" Poppy shouted and snapped them with

Helen's disposable. The handsome couple before her broke into genuine smiles. If she didn't know better, she'd have thought they were life-long lovers. She handed the camera back to Helen and snapped them again with Jack's.

"Thanks for that, Poppy," he grinned.

"A pleasure. Who's for cocktails?" She handed back his camera.

"Sounds good." Jack put the lens cover back on.

"What about across the road?" Helen pointed to a bar. On its terrace were little round tables, covered with green-and-white tablecloths.

"The Green Mango – looks good," he said.

"To be honest, Jack, we did a little recce earlier and they've the best, actually the *only*, cocktail menu in town!" Poppy laughed.

"I like your style, ladies! I figured the flora and fauna of the island was its chief highlights – guess I got that wrong."

They crossed the road.

"We're more into soaking up the local culture than scenery," Helen said, enjoying the view just fine. With that, a blast of European pop music echoed from a neighbouring bar. "Except for the karaoke, that is," she added. She picked up a menu. "Don't even think about going there, Gloria," she said to Poppy, without looking up.

Thankfully, once seated, the potted plants and soft, piped music of the Green Mango protected them from the high-decibel competition.

"Welcome to the Green Mango, would you like to see our food and cocktail menu?" a portly man with impeccable English said, as they were settling into the best table on the terrace.

"Is that really a Munster rugby jersey you're wearing?" Helen asked.

"Are you Irish?" The owner's face lit up.

"Yes."

"My Cork friends sent this to me – they were on holiday here last year," he said with pride.

"*Of all the bars, in all the world . . .*" Helen laughed.

"Only the Irish," Jack laughed. "It's incredible – for such a small population, you guys get everywhere."

"Please, you must have a drink, on the house," the jovial owner said.

And so the night began.

46

They missed dinner. Willingly strong-armed into ordering a tequila cocktail, Jack raised the oversized balloon-shaped glass to his lips, taking the opportunity to observe Helen. Since he'd first spotted her, she'd been smiling. There was something about her smile that illuminated everything around her and made you want to smile with her. It was kind of infectious, he reckoned. He loved this place, this moment with this woman. Up-close he could see a few freckles across her sun-tanned cheeks. Usually quite reserved, he didn't know why he had pulled her towards him for the photo earlier, other than a sudden urge to hold her. He knew one thing though – he had to struggle to take his eyes off her.

Suddenly her eyes were on him: his stomach somersaulted. Had she noticed him looking at her? Her smile appeared more seductive than before – maybe he should slow down on the cocktails.

"So, what brings you here, Jack?" Keith's voice interrupted his reverie. They had spotted the geography professor wandering the promenade and called him in.

The candle on their table flickered in the soft breeze. He thought about Amy.

He looked into his glass, as though it held the answer. "Oh, just this and that really, I'm moving to LA – I decided to take the scenic route." He tapped his foot rhythmically under the table.

"LA via Cat Ba – I like it!" Poppy grinned.

"I suppose that would depend where you were coming from?" Keith pushed his glasses farther up his nose.

Jack shifted his weight, a little uncomfortable being the centre of attention.

"I was working in Dubai on a contract. I thought I'd like to see some of Asia, take an extended vacation. There was no plan as such – I could just as easily be in Laos now. It just happened that the flight to Hanoi had a better connection." He kicked back and rubbed the back of his head.

He looked at Helen again.

She looked back.

The fine hairs on Helen's arms stood on end. She had goose pimples. It was probably just the light wind coming in from the bay.

Until he looked at her again.

"What were you working at in Dubai?" Helen asked abruptly, breaking her rule of never asking what people did for a living.

"I'm an architect. I was working on a few new-build projects. How about you guys, what do you do back home?" Jack cleared an imaginary tickle from his throat.

"Lingerie designer with Eden, a UK chain." She scanned Jack's face. His brow furrowed as if he was trying to remember something.

"Masseuse, amongst other things." Poppy held up her hand.

"I teach geography," Keith said modestly but was unable to leave it at that – as they'd learnt earlier, Keith loved his work. "My specific area of interest is geology, the study of which dates back to ancient Greece . . . ah . . ." He stopped himself. "Perhaps the ladies should go first." He sucked hard on his straw, which caused his cheeks to hollow.

But Helen wasn't listening – the cogs in her brain were turning. *Could it be possible?* "You weren't working on The Palm Development by any chance?" she asked Jack, swallowing hard.

Jack's puzzlement gave way to his signature beaming smile. "I wondered when you mentioned the name Eden. You're Helen Devine, aren't you?" He locked eyes with her.

"Jack Taylor, my architect." Helen clasped her hand to her mouth, hiding a grin, unable to say any more.

271

Poppy and Keith looked from one to the other, as if they were watching a Wimbledon tennis final.

It was Keith who broke the silence. "You know each other?"

Poppy clapped her hands together and bounced excitedly on her chair as she waited to hear more.

"Not exactly. But I believe we spoke on the phone some weeks ago. Isn't that right, Jack?" Helen blushed, her heart pounded.

"Right – nice to meet you in person, Ms Devine!" Jack raised his glass to her.

"Have I got this right? You've worked together?" Keith looked puzzled.

"I work with an architectural firm, as one of a team. We were involved with this particular development. Helen would have dealt with the sales agents, so the connection is indirect. But she is correct – I, or rather my employer, worked on her behalf."

"The six degrees of separation theory unfolds before our eyes. What a co-incidence." Keith sat back, now all was clear in his head.

"There's no such thing as coincidence. It's the Universe telling you something – now you just have to figure what that is," Poppy announced.

"Here we go again!" Helen gave an exaggerated eye-roll.

"What age are you, Jack?" Poppy asked out of the blue.

"Thirty." Jack waited for Poppy to clarify what his age had to do with the Universe's conspiring.

Helen kicked her under the table.

Poppy ignored her, rapidly stirring her drink with a swizzle-stick. *Not the only thing she was about to stir.* "That's interesting – we reckoned you were about twenty-five. Helen's still in her thirties too." She gave her best Shirley Temple smile.

Fate sealed: Poppy Power, tourist, found hanged, drawn and quartered, proving Mary Devine's theory of crimes against tourists true. Associate Helen Devine wanted for questioning.

"This calls for a celebration!" Poppy waved the waitress over to the table. "May we have another round of these, whatever they are – the acid-green things." She made a circular motion with her forefinger.

"Green Mango specials!" the waitress smiled.

"And what's that T-shirt you've got on?" Poppy wanted to know. "*Save the Cat Ba* – what?"

"Languars – they are facing extinction." The waitress picked up the empty glasses from the table.

"That's a cool T-shirt," Poppy said, admiring it.

"They are available for sale if you like – the proceeds go to the languar fund, on the island."

Poppy decided to be generous. "We'll have one for everyone in the audience!"

The waitress returned to the table with the drinks and a bundle of flat-packed tops, in various sizes. They each pulled on a black-cotton T-shirt, with a print of an endearing primate on it.

"Here's to Universal Law and saving cute monkeys at the same time!" Poppy proposed the toast.

All four raised their glass. But only two of them let their fingertips touch.

"The T-shirt looks good on you," Jack said to Helen, as they walked back to the hotel. He looked up at the full moon.

"Yours too." Helen smiled, before looking away.

The sound of the waves crashed against the shore, below them. Up ahead, they could hear Keith and Poppy laughing.

"Does she ever stop laughing?" Jack was laughing now too.

"No, not these days – this holiday has really brought her back to her old self."

Helen looked at Jack with a new shyness, unfamiliar to her. There was a moment's silence between them. They stopped walking and looked out to sea, as the moonlight glistened on the water.

Alone for the first time.

All night, they had skirted around each other. Exchanging glances, sharing a secret language without any words, holding eye contact just a little longer and more often than they should have but not so long that anyone else would notice.

Jack looked at Helen's mouth. The light of the moon picked up tiny sparkles on her lips. He turned to face her. As he did, he noticed that Keith and Poppy had stopped walking, their two figures outlined by the stark fluorescent lighting that spilled out into the road from the hotel lobby.

Jack and Helen stood so close now, she could feel his breath on her skin.

"I think they're waiting on us." Jack tilted his head up towards the other couple.

"Oh, of course, Keith is staying further on up, he's probably waiting to say goodnight." Helen's sigh was barely audible. Forgetting that she was using her sunglasses as a hair-band, she attempted to run her fingers through her hair – and the glasses slipped off her head.

They both dived to try and save them but bumped heads instead as the glasses fell to the ground. Embarrassed and a bit stunned, Helen quickly hunkered down to retrieve them from the dark pavement.

"Got them!" She held up the glasses as a three-times-bridesmaid holds up the nuptial bouquet.

Jack held out his hand to help her back up. She reached out to clasp his forearm and began to push herself up – when her bracelet got caught – in the zip of his trousers.

"Oh my God!" Helen tugged at the bracelet.

"Whoa, let me help you!" Jack laughed, taking hold of her hand.

She peered closer, trying to see how the bracelet had attached itself.

Two hundred yards further up the road, Poppy and Keith watched what looked like Scandal of the Century in downtown Cat Ba.

"Goodness gracious, you Irish are a friendly bunch," Keith said as he pushed his tongue into his cheek to hide his smile.

Poppy decided she'd have to distract him. She kissed him – needless to say, he kissed her back.

Helen, now detached from her bracelet, pushed her hair back off her face as a chuckling Jack walked over to a streetlight to see exactly how the jangling bracelet had attached itself. He tugged at the offending charm, trying to free himself.

Helen looked on, mortified. "Maybe take your trousers off!" she called over to him. "When you get back to your room I mean!" She wasn't getting any of this right.

"I think I've got it . . ." Jack gave the bracelet a final tug. "Ah, here we go, still intact and thankfully I won't sound like Santa's sleigh." He grinned, holding out her bracelet as he walked back to her. He slipped it on her wrist and held her hand for a fraction longer than was necessary. But their moment was over.

They walked side by side back towards the hotel where Poppy and Keith's silhouettes had become one as they kissed.

Jack looked a little awkward as he pushed his hands into his pockets.

"Oh, they're snogging, right, okay, em . . ." Helen looked around her as though looking for somewhere to place a hot potato.

Jack laughed. "I wouldn't have put them together." He scratched his temple to avoid looking at Poppy and Keith.

"No, nor would I, but Poppy's very affectionate," Helen nodded, avoiding eye contact. If they were fifteen, it'd be their cue to snog too. One of those fabulous French kisses during the slow set in the school-gym-cum-dancehall. And if you were lucky (or unlucky depending on who'd asked you to dance) the DJ played "Stairway to Heaven". Unfortunately, they weren't fifteen.

"I think we're good to go," Jack said.

Helen turned to look around. Poppy had come up for air.

Helen pressed the steel button to call the lift. In the harsh light of the foyer, Jack looked tired and preoccupied. Appear casual, Helen told herself, unwilling to look like a desperate older woman lusting after a younger man. None of them spoke.

The ping of the bell indicated the second floor. The heavy steel door slid open and Jack put his arm across to hold it and allow the ladies out first.

"I'm shattered." Poppy patted her hand to her mouth and gave an exaggerated yawn. "Night, Jack, see you at breakfast." She reached up on her tippy-toes and gave him a friendly hug. In a swift movement, she had the key card in the door and was out of sight.

Jack was desperate to prolong their night and recapture some of the mood from earlier. He decided to take a chance on inviting her back to his room for a nightcap.

"Oh, damn – there's no minibar in the room!" he blurted out when he realised the small fact he'd overlooked. Trying to save face he quickly added, "It's just that I've no water, no big deal." He'd seen Helen's mood change – he should have just let the notion of recapturing the moment slide. "Thanks for a great night. See you in the morning." And, with that, he left with a friendly wave, no eye contact, not even a peck on the cheek.

I completely misread the situation, Helen scolded herself. Her stomach was in a knot and her disappointment palpable. She felt like a complete fool.

His bedroom door clicked to a close.

The night and its dreams ended.

"What are you doing here?" Poppy was getting into her Eden pyjamas. She stared at Helen.

"It's my room too, remember?"

"I thought you and lover boy were getting jiggy with it! His bedroom not public enough for you?"

"We explained all that to you and Keith!" Helen rolled her eyes as she started to undress. "And whatever gave you the idea I fancy him? I definitely don't!" It was easier to lie, than admit Jack just didn't fancy her.

"You always say that," Poppy said as she moved into the bathroom.

"You always claim not to sleep with them, Mrs Hare Krishna. And keep your voice down – he's just next door!"

"Maybe he's gay." She was trying to cheer Helen up.

"Why are we talking about me – what was that with Keith?"

"You have to kiss a lot of frogs to find a prince, Helen," Poppy said as she spat toothpaste into the sink. "I haven't given up on true love yet." She paused and thought for a moment. "That, coupled with moonlight, cocktails and trying to save your nymphomaniac ass. Besides he's a very sweet guy once he shuts up talking about his rocks."

"Well, I'm not looking for a holiday romance, particularly not one that makes me a cougar. As I said, I don't fancy him. Nice guy and all that, but too much of a baby-face for me." She sounded so convincing she started to believe it herself. "We had a great chat about Dubai – that's probably what you're picking up on. Jack said it's a fabulous apartment and I should make sure I use it as soon as it's ready rather than putting it on the long finger." She took her turn in the bathroom.

"Nah, there's something else. That's too big a synchronicity to ignore," Poppy said as she pulled back the duvet. "When it transpired you'd literally bumped into each other in Hong Kong it definitely became *synchrodestiny*. What was it he said? He remembered your dazzling green eyes." She pretended to swoon as she got into bed.

"It was probably my crow's feet he noticed – he was just being polite," Helen mumbled.

"Yeah, right. Night, Hells, sweet dreams."

"Night, Pop, sleep well."

After Helen got into bed, she lay in the dark for some time, her eyes open. Her throat felt tight.

Why did she feel sick inside?

She replayed everything in her head. The first time she saw him. The fuzzy feeling she got when he stood close to her. The whole thing didn't make sense – the strong draw to this man, who unbeknownst to him had penetrated her armour – she was putty in his hands. But he didn't want her. And now he lay just feet away, a thin wall separating them. A tear escaped as she closed her eyes to sleep.

Jack sat on the bed, his back pressed against the dividing wall. He thought about Helen – how her voice had caught his interest over the phone, all those weeks ago. How he'd thought of her as a typical stressed-out business executive. Then, in Hong Kong, she'd slammed into him but it was her eyes that knocked the breath out of him, as emerald as gemstones. Finally, when he spotted her across the bay amongst all the boats, he had felt a magnetism and was drawn to look in her direction. He couldn't believe his luck when she stepped on to his junk. The girls he'd met until now were fun but flighty and immature, Amy included. Helen had a soft confidence, something about the way she moved, laughed. *Damn, she's sexy.* He'd found it hard not to stare at her all night. She had been radiant and then she'd started looking back at him. He felt the stir of arousal, thinking about her.

So why didn't he kiss her?

Because, you take things slowly, Jack. Slowly, slowly, catchy monkey. But he knew he was only fooling himself. Amy hadn't cheated on him only the one time. He'd been suspicious about others, but he always gave her the benefit of the doubt. Only after getting caught red-handed did her web of deceit start to unravel – taking his world down with it. And so he'd started to run away, and up until now it had served him pretty well. He'd met amazing people, seen more places in the past ten months than he had done in his thirty years of life, prior to the break-up. Amy had done him a favour, in a way. Otherwise, he'd be married to her now, probably with a kid on the way, mortgage on a house in Connecticut, with a white picket-fence.

Suddenly, he felt he'd been punched in the stomach, all over again. *Would that feeling ever go away?*

Then he thought about Helen Devine. A lingerie designer, no less. He smiled when he thought of her. He realised, in the day he'd spent with Helen, the thoughts of Amy that haunted him daily were gone.

Helen had replaced the punches with flutters.

47

"Good morning, ladies!" Jack waved at the girls, bright as a morning lark. He had anxiously scanned the large dining area for them when he got out of the elevator, but there had been no sign of them. Then he noticed an outside patio area through large glass doors, where he was relieved to see Poppy's distinctive flame-coloured hair and the blonde head of her partner in crime, Helen.

"Over here, Jack!" Poppy called as she put down her coffee cup. "We kept you a seat." Which, technically wasn't true but the table was set for four so it worked out well.

Helen tried to look casual by stretching an arm out over the back of the chair next to her. Her attempts to look casual failed miserably when her arm missed the back of the chair.

"Hey." She tried to regain her composure and sound casual, hoping to God that Jack didn't notice her clumsiness.

"The cocktails still have you feeling unbalanced, hey, Helen?"

So much for him not noticing.

In the bright morning light she realised her ridiculous attraction to Jack had been a combination of the sunset, the ocean and too many cocktails. She hoped he didn't think she was a basket-case.

"Can I get you guys anything?" Jack eyed their half-finished food, to see what the breakfast buffet had on offer.

"Coffee, please, sir." Helen proffered her cup and gave Jack a cheeky smile. Sunglasses hid her eyes.

His hand brushed against hers as he took the cup from her. A bolt of static coursed through them.

Jack jumped – he had never experienced anything like that before. "Wow, did you feel that?"

"I felt it alright – I usually get static shocks from freezer doors in the supermarket, not people." Helen shook her hand to dissipate the energy charge.

Cynical Helen was back.

Poppy was more enthusiastic. "Energy charges – how exciting! You two definitely have some kind of other-dimension connection. Who knows – maybe you were Jack's mother in a past life, Helen!"

Cheers, Poppy. "That's a load of baloney." Helen raised her eyes to heaven, but caught Jack's eye instead, by a play of sunbeam, even through darkened lenses. He smiled at her.

"I'm telling you, Helen, there are too many coincidences, too many connections – it's a sign and you shouldn't ignore it." Poppy stood up, as if standing above Helen would add weight to her argument.

"What kind of sign?" Jack was listening.

"I don't know, that's up to the Universe – you'll just have to be open to the possibilities. I'm getting seconds – the bus will be here in twenty minutes and Lord knows when we'll eat again."

"I swear you've got hollow legs, Pops," Helen laughed. "It's not fair! If I ate the amount you do I'd be a blob."

Jack doubted that.

"What can I say – I'm a Vata!" Poppy popped a piece of toast into her mouth but then she stopped. "Jack, didn't you say your surname is Taylor?"

Jack nodded, Poppy raised her eyebrows. "I like it! The lingerie designer meets the Taylor." She laughed at the pun.

"Very funny, Poppy," growled Helen. "It's too early for all that. Now, either Ms Vata or Mr Electrifier, I don't care which, please refill my coffee cup before my caffeine levels drop to normal."

"Coming right up, boss." Jack gave Helen a salute as he walked back to the breakfast room, a grin on his face.

I electrify her, he thought.

48

"What time is it?" Poppy asked Helen as she woke from an uncomfortable sleep. She rubbed the back of her neck. The horns and the noise indicated they were back in Hanoi. Sadness crept over her as she looked out the window at the rain-drenched streets. Only a few hours earlier they'd bathed in sunlight, watching people tend the paddy fields wearing the by now familiar conical hats. They had stopped along the way for a photo opportunity. The other passengers clicked snapshots of workers in the fields but Poppy was transfixed by a thin-framed woman, who walked the road's edge.

The Vietnamese worked hard – in the fields and off them. This woman was loaded down with goods for sale, balanced in two baskets that hung, one either side of a long stick, which lay across her shoulders. As the woman walked, the baskets swayed with a hypnotic rhythmic motion. She was quite close before Poppy could see her face clearly – her conical hat shielded her. Poppy wondered whether she was being a typical tourist, so mesmerised by the landscape and repetitive motions of its inhabitants, that she was imagining this woman's contentment from the gentle glide of her step.

The Vietnamese woman didn't look up as another tour bus passed her, kicking up dust as it did so. Her goods weren't for them. Poppy had smiled to herself as she thought about this land of contrast: the Vietnamese who embraced capitalism in all its vulgarity by doing their best to squeeze as many dollars as possible out of foreigners, to the Vietnamese who shied away from tourists and what they brought, maybe a little distrustful of foreigners, and who could blame them? Being under attack was part of their history – Chinese, French, Japanese – all had wanted Vietnam.

For Poppy, this woman was the memory she wanted as a snapshot forever imprinted on the canvas of mind. She didn't want to use her camera. The woman's skin was smooth and even. Eyes, calm. If the eyes are the windows to the soul, this worker of the land radiated one thing: contentment.

What was indeed a heavy load, she made look as light as a feather. Her burden was physical, her work looked laborious, she had deadlines but they were largely set by the land, therefore she couldn't harness them because she could not control them. The circadian rhythm. She didn't face hours of motorway delays – her mode of transport was her feet.

They briefly made eye contact as the woman walked past, the peasant worker never missing her stride. Back and forth the baskets swung as she continued on her journey. As her silhouette became smaller, Poppy decided to take a picture after all.

"It's a tough life, isn't it?" Helen came up to Poppy, both set of eyes following the figure on the road.

"Is it though? She looked more peaceful to me than anyone back home."

"It's just the weight of all that fruit, the walking for miles. Can you imagine being bent over all day with your bare feet stuck in muddy water and all you have to show for it at the end of the week is a pittance?" Helen shook her head.

Poppy remembered the brief eye contact. "Maybe you're right, but the funny thing is, I got the feeling she felt sorry for *us*."

"Really, why would she?"

"We always want more – no matter how much we have, always looking outside ourselves for happiness." In the dry earthen road, Poppy made a figure eight with her foot. "Like going to Asia, to 'find ourselves' as if spirituality is only found in Asia, whereas it's inside us, no matter where we are in the world. We just need to tap into it." She looked at Helen.

"Hey, you're preaching to the converted!"

Poppy sighed with contentment. "I'm really loving being here, Helen. Stepping out of my life, my roles and responsibilities, just being myself, even for a couple of weeks. I do miss Lily though."

"I know you do and, hey, it is hard being a single parent – you're doing great. It's okay to take off on holiday once in a while, just be Poppy, not the mother, the therapist – the nut-job!" Helen smirked.

"Thanks, Helen, I can always rely on you to say it straight."

Another bus trundled past them.

"Hey, Team Ireland, how's it going, mates?" The Australian couple, Pete and Lorraine, waved out an open window at them. "Last one to Hanoi buys the beer!" Pete shouted, before his bus went out of earshot.

Arm in arm, Helen and Poppy got back on their coach, leaving the fields of Vietnam behind.

The bus blasted its horn at one of the hundreds of mopeds weaving in a zigzag chaos that was not for the faint-hearted. Poppy nudged Helen again to see what time it was. She never wore a watch, as she refused to live her life by one, which annoyed the hell out of her nearest and dearest, because she kept asking them to tell her the time instead.

"Nearly five o'clock," Helen whispered, not wanting to wake Jack whose head slumbered on her left shoulder. Sitting on a long lumpy seat at the back of the bus, Helen had never felt so happy to be wedged for hours beside her new American buddy – or son in a past life, if she was to listen to Poppy.

Just then Jack tried to shift around in the cramped seat but an exposed spring, jutting out from the seat in front, made it difficult. One of his butt cheeks had gone numb which he reckoned was just as well because he'd a feeling another metal coil was straining to release through the cracked imitation leather. He hoped it didn't spring while he sat there – mortally damaging his manhood.

"Are we there yet?" He wiped his mouth with the back of his hand to eliminate sleep dribble.

Helen's shoulder had made the journey tolerable. At one point, he had opened his eyes to realise how close he was to her cleavage. He felt a needling in his trousers. A spring dug into him – he decided it was safer to sleep.

The bus crawled along the narrow streets of the Old Quarter and in ones and twos people started to disembark at various hotels.

Keith stood, his head hung low, too tall to stand straight.

"Are you getting off here, Keith?" Poppy looked dubiously out at the street.

"I cancelled my reservation in the Four Seasons, decided to get a feel for the local culture after all," he said, looking rather pleased with himself.

"Good for you, Keith!" Helen said.

"Who knows, you may even see me drinking *bia hoi* at one of the street stalls. I'm looking forward to having a tipple."

The picture of six-foot-three Keith of five-star mentality, squatting down on a tiny plastic stool, at the side of the pavement, made them all smile.

"Perhaps I can tempt you to join me, Poppy?" he asked.

Poppy smiled up at him. "Sounds good but we've another few days here – I'll text you." She patted her breast pocket where earlier she'd placed Keith's business card.

"Make sure you get a picture for your album!" Helen called after him, as he made his way back down the bus.

Without turning around, he waved in acknowledgement before he was out of sight. Keith had survived 'Irish night' and was feeling all the better for it.

Poppy smiled. "Keith told me he only takes a holiday every second year. He saves so he can go somewhere exotic and stay in the best hotels."

"Maybe now he'll downgrade and take a holiday every year. It's about the experience after all, not the hotel room." Helen locked eyes with her friend – they both knew it wasn't just Keith who'd left his comfort zone and enjoyed it.

"Hong Ngoc Hotel!" Huy called out.

"That'll be me. Where are you two staying?" Jack grabbed his back-pack.

"Well, we were staying in the Hanoi Plaza, a small hotel just at the end of your street." Helen pointed in the direction of the many terraced hotels there.

"Awesome, you're only two minutes from me. I'll meet you in reception, say about seven?" Jack rubbed his back. He was anxious to get off the bus. Although he liked being close to Helen, he was feeling in need of fresh air after being cooped up for so long.

"No, we *were* staying there. We decided to move to the French Quarter – to experience a side of the city other than the Old Quarter. And have a pool." Helen looked miserable. The itinerary they'd agreed on a few weeks ago back home wasn't so appealing now.

"We'll text you to arrange a time – have we got your number?" Poppy said helpfully.

"I've no phone – I'm on sabbatical, remember? Come to my hotel, when you're ready – just ask for Mr Jack."

And then he was gone. Again. Jack disappeared a lot.

"That was a bit vague don't you think?" Helen said to Poppy, looking for reassurance.

"No, it's simple enough. We'll call to his hotel – if he's there, great, if not, I'm sure we'll bump into him in one of the usual tourist haunts. The Old Quarter is compact enough."

Helen wasn't convinced – she preferred definite planning. "I suppose so. I can't imagine switching my phone off for two months though." She checked her phone as if to emphasise the point. There were no messages from Eden or anyone for that matter.

"I think it sounds wonderful! Lord, Helen, I hope our bags were transferred to the new hotel – I'm in dire need of a change." Poppy flapped her T-shirt to create a flow of air. They had brought the bare essentials (big travel pants included) to Halong Bay, as instructed, due to the amount of jumping on and off boats that took place.

"Army Hotel!" Huy shouted about ten minutes later. "You ladies are the last! I hope you enjoyed your Tropical Sails tour!" Huy hadn't stopped smiling for two days – they'd miss him.

They looked out at a grey building, red-uniformed guards at the gate.

They bade farewell to Huy and got out.

"It's rather glum," Helen remarked, as they looked up at their new hotel.

"It's your uniform fetish we were indulging by coming here. With a pool to boot, it sounded perfect." Poppy reminded her of the logic behind their decision.

"What were we thinking? The sodding French Quarter. We can hop on the Eurostar for that," Helen grumbled.

"Oh, quit moaning, Helen."

"I can't, I'm Irish – I'm genetically programmed to moan."

The Vietnamese army, who were there in large numbers, owned the Army Hotel. Reception was large and functional as was the twin-bedded room the girls had booked. There was also a lot of bugle-blowing.

"What was that?" Helen pulled back the sheer curtain to open the patio door of their balcony. The room had a view of the pool. An army wedding was in full swing, buffet tables set up around the sun-loungers. There were red uniforms everywhere. The bride wore white.

"Guess we won't be using the pool this evening so," Poppy said.

"We've no swimsuits anyway – look, no bags."

Outside, a bugle blasted and caused them to jump.

"If he blows that bloody thing once more I'll ram it up his arse." Helen was tired and ratty.

A few phone calls revealed that their bags were still in the Hanoi Plaza.

Even Poppy, who usually saw the bright side of things, was looking frayed. "Look, it's not the end of the world – we're heading back over that side anyway." She rubbed her temples as though trying to stop a headache from taking up residence.

"But look at us! We look like bedraggled rats. I need fresh clothes, make-up even." Helen sounded as though she might cry.

So much for seduction.

Another blast of a bugle sounded. Poppy grabbed her jacket. "Come on, let's get out of here."

49

"Hello, Mr Jack! How are you this evening?" the ever-friendly reception clerk enquired.

"Great, thanks – better after a nap and shower."

"Very good, very good. Can I help you with anything?"

"I'm just going to access the internet if that's okay?" Jack cocked his thumb towards the guest computer, which sat off from the entrance lobby.

"Of course, Mr Jack, be my guest. How was Halong bay – you like?"

"Highlight of Asia so far, Quan, I loved it," Jack grinned.

"You want me to book another tour, Mr Jack, just let me know. Please." Quan nodded and motioned Jack to the computer seat.

"Any chance of a beer, Quan?"

"You got it! Coming up, anything for our favourite guest – good to have you back again, Mr Jack." Quan patted Jack's shoulder.

Jack logged on to his email. He'd promised his mom he'd make contact. "A postcard won't cut it, Jack," she'd said. "If you won't take a cell phone with you, at least email me, let me know you're safe and how and where I can get in touch with you."

Fair enough, he thought. He set about reassuring his mother of his whereabouts and painting with words the beauty of Halong Bay. That was until another email caught his eye.

Inbox

From: Amy Forbes

Subject: Hello

It hit in his stomach. Every day for the past year, he had thought about Amy. Hell, he'd moved to Dubai to try to forget her. But it hadn't worked. Jack considered pressing delete. It occurred to him with renewed force that in the last two days he hadn't been plagued with thoughts of Amy. And now, here she was with a "Hello" and all the old feelings came rushing back, as if he'd only lost her yesterday.

He opened the email.

Hey Handsome, How are you? I heard on the grapevine you're on vacation in Asia. When will you be back in New York? I miss our connection. Jack baby, I feel I've made a terrible mistake.

Helen spotted Jack's distinctive frame as soon as she entered the hotel. She felt a gush of relief that he was there. Thank you, God, she said silently.

"Can I help you, ladies?"

"Hi, we're here to meet Jack."

"Ah, Mr Jack! Of course – there he is." Quan smiled broadly, *The best bit of Asia, indeed, Mr Jack, the lucky man.*

On hearing the voices, Jack clicked the x, to shut down Amy's email. He turned and saw Helen. Little wonder he hadn't thought of Amy.

"Wow, what's with the bags?" he laughed and got up to help the girls with their load. They were still in the same clothes and were laden down with luggage.

"I know we've just met and all but I was thinking . . ." Helen teased but then reddened. *Was she imagining it, or was he distracted, disappointed to see her?*

"Don't mind her, Jack, there was a cock-up," Poppy said and she blew air on her face. "Our bags were left at our last hotel down the road. Can we borrow your room for ten minutes to change?"

"Sure, no problem." Jack rubbed the back of his head.

"This hotel is lovely – I thought you said you were backpacking around Asia," Helen said.

"I like it here and they gave me a great rate. Besides, it's good to mix it up. Little bits of comfort between the hostels. Here, let me help you with those." He picked up both bags and made for the elevator.

Quan looked on, bemused at the interaction. Mr Jack and the two pretty women disappeared out of sight, headed for Jack's room. *Lucky, lucky man.*

The lift was minuscule and Jack had to push up against Helen to fit in with the luggage. He smelt good and she could get the same scent as soon as she stepped into his room. The room was small, neat and decorated with carved dark-wood furniture, traditional Vietnamese style. There was a small balcony that looked out on the buildings opposite – pressed together they looked like crooked tubes that might crumble at the slightest touch. Yet somehow they held each other up, as a group of drunks might, TV aerials and washing lines dotted along the rooftops. The heavy red drapes and fine furnishings of the room seemed a world away from the scene outside.

Jack put the bags down. "The bathroom is in here." He flicked on the light.

"Great, thanks," Poppy said, already unzipping her bag.

Helen and Jack looked at each other. Suddenly, the double bed felt like the only item in the room. Helen sat on the end of it and loosened her ponytail. She began to brush her hair.

Jack watched her for a moment before he looked away.

"I have to finish sending an email, so take your time," he said as he headed out the door, lightly bumping into the frame. "I'll leave the key with you in case you need it."

"Thanks, Jack, fifteen minutes tops," Helen said.

" It's okay – I've got a sister – I'll see you in an hour." He smiled, closing the door behind him.

Helen looked around the room. There was a notebook, a travel journal maybe, on the nightstand, but that was all. Jack kept the room neat, evidence of personal belongings minimal. She wandered into the bathroom. Jack's wash-bag was on top of the toilet cistern – unzipped. Helen hovered over it, to see what she could see, without actually touching it. *Is that where the condoms are? Stop, Helen, be nice!*

She distracted herself by getting washed. As she brushed her teeth, her eyes wandered back to the bag. She used the handle of her toothbrush to open it up a little further, as if not touching it directly made it less of an infringement of privacy. The bag contained the usual guy stuff as far as she could make out before her conscience got the better of her and she stopped. Why she wasn't tempted to touch his diary, yet was fascinated by his toiletries, was beyond her. Until it dawned on her.

Damn it. She looked at her reflection in the mirror and the truth stared back at her. She had fallen for Jack Taylor. Fallen hard.

"What are you doing?" Poppy stood in the doorway.

Helen jumped. "Bloody hell, can I not pee in peace!"

"I'd say you were having a good old-fashioned nose around."

"I know, I know I shouldn't have." Helen spat into the sink. "He's very tidy for a bloke, isn't he?"

Poppy knew Helen well enough to know that despite her protests she liked this guy, which made what she wanted to say easier.

"Helen, would you mind if I bailed on tonight?" she said, wincing.

"Why, are you okay?"

"I'm fine, just a headache is all. I was going to say it earlier but we'd to come over to get the bags and everything."

Helen swallowed hard. "It's alright, Jack will understand. Maybe we can catch him tomorrow instead." She looked away.

"Honestly, Helen, I'm a big girl, I'd feel awful if you missed out on your night. I'd book in here in a heartbeat but we've left our day bags back in the Army. I don't want to get court-martialled."

"I'd feel weird letting you go off on your own when you're not feeling well."

"I'm grand, it's only a headache and no offence but I'm feeling out of sorts and could do with some alone time." She scrunched her face as though preparing for an onslaught of coaxing.

"Are you going to invite Keith over?"

"Lord no – in the cold light of day we both realised we weren't going to be getting our rocks off – with each other. I'll text him – he'll be cool with it."

Helen knew that though she and Poppy loved each other, being with one person, that you aren't bonking, twenty-four-seven got a bit difficult after a while.

"You're trying to get rid of me, aren't you?" She raised an eyebrow and Poppy nodded sheepishly. Helen sighed, Poppy was easygoing but once she made her mind up, she was stubborn as hell, which she often conveniently blamed on her red hair.

Jack didn't return to the computer, opting instead to wait in the bar. He thought about Amy, and all the months he'd have given his right arm to hear the words, "*I've made a mistake, I love you, and I want you back.*"

Now, when he had finally started to feel normal again, she came crashing through cyberspace, to rain on his parade. It was as if she had a sixth sense that he was interested in another woman for the first time since the break-up. Amy didn't like other women – she used to say she was more of a man's kind of woman. She was right there. Problem was – she liked all of them.

He took a gulp of beer and looked vacantly around the room, lost in his world. From the small bar, he could see into a dining area that had more wait-staff than customers. A Western woman was holding a Vietnamese baby, who looked to be about ten months old. The woman, weighed down with baby paraphernalia, was gently bouncing the baby in an effort to ease its crying. The staff tried to help her. The waiter lifted the baby and spoke gently in Vietnamese. This appeared to reassure the baby. The other waiter got something from the buffet, a local dish. Whatever it was, it worked and the baby started cooing.

"The babies here, they like this. Do you want to take some with you for the journey?" the waiter, now involved in the scenario, asked.

"Yes, thank you. That'd be great. Is it sterile though?" The woman's voice was tense. She was about forty and appeared to be alone. Presumably, the baby was her newly adopted son. It wasn't the first that Jack had seen on his travels here and wordlessly he wished them both well. The woman expressed her thanks to the staff, gave a generous tip and left.

Her exit left a void – not physically – it was something else. The waiters looked after her and waved goodbye to the baby, who watched them from over his new mother's shoulder. They stood in silence, looking out the door, long after the woman and baby were gone. It can't be easy to watch so many of your nation's babies leave, to start a new life abroad. From the look on their faces Jack detected a mix of hope and regret. Or were they his own feelings?

"There you are, Jack, thanks for the room, you're a lifesaver." Poppy handed Jack back his key.

"Why the bags? Are you not leaving them there until later?" he asked, his face not hiding his disappointment.

"I'm afraid I have to love you and leave you tonight, Jack. I'm shattered and I have a headache. Bed, my book and a chat with my daughter on the phone is all I want tonight. We've still got tomorrow night in Hanoi, so hopefully I'll catch you then." She reached up and gave him a kiss on the cheek, which he returned with a hug.

"Would you still like to hang out tonight, Helen? I mean, I'm free if you are?" Jack rubbed the back of his head.

"Of course!" Helen blinked rapidly, giving a visual hint of her heart rate.

"Right, you two go have fun but help me get these bags into a taxi first."

As she was about to get into a taxi a few minutes later, Poppy paused.

"Oh, I'll give you Keith's number," she said. "You can text him and let him know where you are." She suppressed a smile – she loved to stir it.

Helen and Jack remained as silent as two kids caught with their hand in the cookie jar.

"Didn't think so," Poppy said under her breath as she got into the taxi.

She breathed a sigh of relief as she waved goodbye. She sat back, alone at last. She shuddered though. She had an uneasy feeling she couldn't identify, and it was nothing to do with the headache. This was a feeling of apprehension that she had never felt before. She picked up her phone and called home.

50

They decided to start the evening with a drink, to take in the lights and life over by the lake, a ten-minute walk from Jack's hotel.

As they turned to go, Jack gently put his hand on the small of Helen's back. A simple touch, but it broke the nervous tension between them as they walked together.

Soon they were in a section of Hanoi where the Old Quarter was behind them, the commercial area of the Hoan Kiem district was beside them and the lake by the same name lay in front of them. That is, if they could cross an open mass of thoroughfare, fed by several roads. Cars, bikes, cyclists were honking and weaving their way from the numerous different directions that converged on this one corner. All focused on where they were going but appeared unaware of the other road-users. In the centre of the intersection, petrified tourists clung to each other paralysed with terror, rabbits caught in headlights as the traffic whizzed perilously around them.

"Oh God, I hate this bit!" Helen shouted above the roar of traffic. She stood precariously at the side of the road, edging a foot out, but stepping back again.

"It's pretty awesome." Jack was enjoying the pandemonium.

"Is 'awesome' an Americanism for certain death?"

Jack just chuckled.

"Apparently there's an art to crossing here," said Helen. "I read it in *The Rough Guide*."

"I know and it works. Here, take my hand. Whatever you do don't stop. Walk at a steady pace and keep looking straight ahead. They'll go around you, but if you stop or hesitate, you'll either get stuck in the middle of the road," he nodded towards the tourists to reiterate his point, "or you'll get knocked down."

Charming.

But Helen enjoyed playing the role of damsel in distress.

With a deep breath, and not looking left or right they stepped into the mêlée.

A local woman with two baskets of flowers hanging from her shoulders walked before them, peacefully, with a tick-tock rhythm. Apparently unperturbed by her surroundings, she reminded Helen of the women they'd seen on the country roads early that day. So alike yet it seemed to be a world away.

"Stick with us," Jack said to the stranded tourists, still rooted in the middle of the road. They followed in Jack and Helen's steps and soon all four were safe, by Hanoi standards, on the footpath. Helen took a breath of relief and thought the old saying, *Be sure to wear clean underwear in case you get knocked down crossing the road*, must have been coined in Hanoi. She thought of her mum.

Helen and Jack climbed four flights of narrow stairs to the restaurant-cum-bar. They got prime seats on the balcony, overlooking the lake and the road they'd managed to survive. They ordered two cocktails.

"They're the same price as a main course, so they won't mind us hogging a table with a view." Helen pointed out.

"You're all heart." Jack grinned at her. "I love the way you're convinced we're drinking cocktails for the good of the establishment's turnover."

"I can tell you, Jack, I've done a lot of charitable drinking in my day: charity lunches, gala balls and what not. It's tough work, but someone has to do it."

One cocktail became two, as they sat for an hour watching the world go by. They laughed at the numerous tourists negotiating the minefield below. They placed bets on which ones would make it and who would get stuck. Sometimes they sat in silence and watched the world go by. The streets were illuminated with street lights, neon signs and colourful street vendors' stalls.

"That ring you wear is pretty. It looks old – sentimental value?" Jack asked. He'd noticed Helen absently twisting it since he'd first met her.

"It was my grandmother's, on my dad's side. Apparently he said I was to have it when I came of age, whatever he meant by that." Helen held out her hand, gazing at her ring.

She looked content. Jack didn't pry.

"He died when I was just a tot. My mum gave me the ring when I . . ." Helen's voice trailed. "When I was older," she smiled. "It's after getting loose on this holiday though, look." She pulled the ring off easily. "Virtually my sole source of nutrition since I got here has been cocktails and rice." She nodded, grinning. "Yes, I simplify my diet when travelling – rice and alcohol are least likely to give me Delhi Belly – even in Hanoi."

But Jack was more interested in hearing about Helen the woman – not her strange dietary plan.

"I'm sorry about your father," Jack said simply. "Coming of age – what age is that in Ireland – sixteen, eighteen?"

"Traditionally twenty-one, but now eighteen is the legal age for voting etc. And, in fact, some have big parties for sixteenth birthdays also."

"Any excuse for a party, hey?"

"What can I say, it's Ireland," Helen conceded. "From what my mother told me about my dad, I think coming of age meant something else to him – maturity, not a chronological age."

Jack watched as Helen revealed another layer. The more time he spent with her, the more he wanted to know about her. Her phone buzzed.

"Sorry, Jack, it's the office. I want to set up a meeting for a Vietnamese factory – do you mind if I take this?" Helen pointed to the phone – Jack waved her on.

Helen stood in a quiet corner as she talked. Jack stole quick glances at her. She fiddled with her hair a lot as she spoke. He admired her commitment to her job – he reckoned it showed her loyalty. He wondered why she wasn't married – so far, what he'd seen of Helen Devine indicated she was the ideal woman. She seemed wise beyond her years yet had the vivaciousness of someone young at heart. She pressed a hand over her free ear and turned further into the corner, her back to him. And she had a cute butt too.

Helen rejoined Jack. "Where to next?"

They drained the last of their drinks as they stood.

"Fancy a jazz club?" Jack asked.

Jazz agreed on, they headed back down to street level.

"Taxi?" A cyclo-driver had pulled up beside them.

"How much to Pho Luong Van Can?" Jack haggled.

The driver – or more accurately, the cyclist – quoted a crazy price. Jack started to walk away. True to form, a minute or two later the two men agreed a price. The driver pretended to be disappointed and Jack knew he'd paid too much.

Helen and Jack climbed into the red upholstered carriage attached to the front of the bike.

"Are you sure he'll be able to move with both of us on here?" Helen was dubious.

Jack had to stoop as he sat to avoid his head hitting the flower-printed canopy. The driver's spindly legs pushed the pedals and the cyclo was propelled into the throng of the traffic, with apparent ease. The driver kept pinging the lever on the bike's bell, though it was impossible to hear it amongst the din of traffic.

"I had a bell like that on my bike when I was about five!" Helen laughed.

Soon they were back into the narrow streets of the Old Quarter. The street kitchens smelt inviting, and the driver agreed to stop to let them eat. No more Dong were required for his wait time, if they would order from his sister's stall. Agreed, they set off in the opposite direction.

"The best *bun cha* in Hanoi!" the driver reassured them, which was just as well as it turned out the only thing she served was *bun cha*, a noodle dish of vegetables and barbequed meat. Helen and Jack sat with the driver and his sister and chowed down, kerbside. Helen didn't ask what type of meat it was.

"Where you go after, I wait for you," the driver insisted as he dropped a full-bellied Jack and Helen at the jazz club.

"Thanks, man, but I intend to take my time." Jack smiled as he peeled off an extra note as a tip. The driver gave Jack a knowing smile, pinged his bell and cycled away.

"I love it!" Helen said as they hit the smoky interior of the club.

They sat on two high stools at the bar. Having had his year's supply of cocktails in the past forty-eight hours, Jack ordered a beer. Helen decided not to mix her drinks and ordered vodka, figuring it to be the basic roux of all cocktails.

"I feel like we've stepped into a time warp," Helen said with child-like enthusiasm as she scanned the room.

The clientele were an eclectic mix of genres and age groups. A young Vietnamese girl danced as if she was the only person in the room and no one was watching her. Her black hair cropped tight, it stood out in spikes thanks to strong-hold hair gel. She wore a short skirt and her feet were bare – she was lost in the beat. She reminded Helen of a pixie were it not for the cigarette in her right hand. Also Helen wasn't sure if a pixie would be stoned.

At a table next to the band sat a group of people in their mid-fifties. There was a tall, elegant Western woman in the group. Her hair was naturally grey but rather than aging her, it gave her an air of cool sophistication. She wore bohemian jewellery and clothes that hinted at a hippy-spent youth. She pulled on her cigarette and tapped her foot in time to the bass. The main man in the band appeared to have eyes only for her.

"I think it's the prohibition vibe that makes it feel old-world." Jack leaned closer to Helen. Her hair tickled his nose.

"Or Paris, in the twenties – decadence after the war years!" Helen lifted her glass. "Whatever it is, it works. I salute it."

"I'll drink to that."

They were sitting very close. Their knees touched – neither

moved away. Helen's eyes sparkled, a little girl at a funfair. She chatted, laughed and moved her hands a lot in big gestures. She was warm and funny – Jack felt at home with her, at home here.

Strange, he thought, how things can change when you least expect it. Who'd have guessed that sitting with a woman who'd been a stranger a mere two days ago, listening to Vietnamese sounds mixed with classic jazz, in a communist country, would feel like home?

51

"Yeah, Mum, sure, see you next week, eh, love you too." Lily put down the phone.

"Is your mum gone already? I was hoping to talk to Helen." Mary Devine came into the living room, drying her hands on a chequered teacloth. "She sent me a text saying she and Poppy are committing to Save the Pig. And that was all was said – what am I to make of that? I think she'd had one too many myself. Honest to God, they should have breathalysers on mobile phones, stop people sending cryptic texts like that. They've every other useless bell and whistle on them as it is, at least a breathalyser would be handy."

Lily giggled but her eyes remained on the TV.

Mary's brow creased. "Is that some kind of modern lingo – Save the Pig? I don't know what the young ones are saying half the time these days."

"Not that I know of – but Mum and Helen are kind of on their own unique wavelength. Helen wasn't there anyway. Mum stayed in because she was tired or something. I think she's homesick. She was even asking about Angelo – the coffee in Vietnam must be lousy." Lily tucked her feet under her bum and flicked on the TV remote for day-time television.

"So who's Helen out with?" Mary twisted the tea towel in her hands.

300

"Think Mum mentioned Freddie. That was it – Freddie Kruger," Lily joked, more interested in flicking between *Judge Judy* and MTV.

"Don't be so cheeky, madam!" Mary pretended to hit her with the towel. "You're not too old to get a clip around the ear."

Lily raised her arm in self-defence. "Hey, we've got Childline these days, you know!" she laughed.

"Honestly, Helen should have stayed in with your mother rather than going gallivanting around a communist capital at night. That girl will be the death of me!" Mary sighed. "Tea?"

"No thanks, Marma." Lily had resumed channel-hopping.

"Oh, I'll wait and have a cup with you in a while then." Mary liked having the teenager stay even if it meant Cyril had to take a back seat for a few weeks.

As she moved to the door, quite unexpectedly, a wave of nausea came over her and she stumbled on her feet.

"You okay, Marma?" Lily got a fright as she saw the colour drain from Mary's cheeks.

"Fine, love, just a bit dizzy." Mary steadied herself against the settee.

"Here, sit down, I'll make the tea." Lily jumped up. "Did you do your bloods today?" She took hold of Mary's arm and led her to the armchair.

"Look at you clucking like a mother hen – yes, and they're fine." Mary's colour returned. "I do quite enjoy *Judge Judy*, though. I'll just watch this one programme." She adjusted a cushion to get comfortable. "Maybe I will have that cuppa, nothing like a good cuppa to make you feel better I always say. Do you know how to make tea, love?" She looked up at Lily, who had relaxed a bit.

"Yes! I love a cup of tea when I come in from school, with a Moro dipped in it. I'm not my mother, you know – I can make tea." Lily smiled. "Though now I've been going to Angelo's place, cappuccinos are kind of what I'm into."

"Tell you what, why don't we go to Angelo's for our tea this evening?"

"Lethal." Lily left the room.

"Not too strong!" Mary called after Lily. "I like my tea weak and my men strong!"

"Too much information, Marma!" Lily shouted out, as she put the kettle on.

52

In Hanoi, the jazz club was swinging. Helen and Jack enjoyed their seats, with full view of the live band, but away from the core of the action.

"How come you're here, Jack? Are you not lonely travelling alone?"

"Sometimes. I like my own company though. I wanted to see a bit of the world before heading back to the US – I might never get the chance again. Not until I'm retired anyway." He smiled down at her.

"How come you chose to move to LA? It's a long way from New York."

"Exactly – I want to be," he said seriously.

She waited for him to expand on that but he didn't, so she sought for the right way to ask him why.

Then he grinned and added, "But it's not as far as Dubai – and they've got surfing, or so I hear!"

"Are you from the city of New York?"

"No, New York State, Nyack. Do you know New York?"

"I'll have you know, I was born in St Vincent's Hospital on 13th Street!" Helen said, tilting her chin up.

"Wow, a real live New Yorker! You are full of surprises, Helen."

Helen sipped on her drink. "Is it surfing you're chasing or a woman you're running from, maybe?" *There, she'd said it!*

"Maybe." He looked away from her and shifted a little uncomfortably. "But it's a fresh start. I don't really know anyone in California. What about you? A good-looking lingerie designer, surely you can't be single?" He tried to sound casual. *Corny, Jack.* He felt awkward flirting because he was terrible at it, or so he'd been told, but he was doing his best.

"Shocker, isn't it, but that I am. Now," Helen said.

"Now? Was it a man that had you packing your bags for Vietnam?"

"That, amongst other things."

"What's his name?"

"Rob. And the girl?"

"Amy."

They smiled at each other.

"Was it serious?" she said gently.

"Yes, for me it was anyway. We were engaged to be married." He swallowed some beer, avoiding eye contact again.

"I'm sorry, Jack, that must be tough." Helen touched his arm gently.

"It was for the best, I guess. Amy and I were childhood sweethearts, I never questioned that we wouldn't spend our whole lives together." He stopped short of telling Helen the full extent of Amy's cheating. It still made him feel inadequate. When Amy left, his confidence left with her. He wondered what another man offered her that he had been unable to provide.

"It's not your fault if she cheated," Helen said, thinking of her own situation. "I'm sorry – I don't know where that came from, Jack."

"And this Rob guy, what went wrong there?" Jack asked, steering the conversation away from Amy.

Helen shrugged. "It's complicated. Rob was married – to his job and his bachelorhood – I just couldn't see that." It was true. She had lied to herself that Rob and she had a special connection. Now, here in Hanoi, thousands of miles away from him, she realised that he was probably seeing other people all along.

"When did you guys break up?"

"About a month ago," Helen sighed, "but we weren't even properly together. As I said, it's complicated. We've a lot of history together."

Ouch, Jack thought. His heart sank.

"You guys may still work it out, Helen – it's early days."

"I don't want to sort it out. It's time to move on – I've wasted too much time on something that was never going anywhere. It's hard though, we live so close to each other, go to the same bars – when I'm back home that is, which is nearly every weekend when I'm not travelling with work."

"I know that one!"

"Hence LA?" Helen asked.

"Hence LA," Jack nodded.

As the Jazz Club filled up, they sat closer together until Jack gave his seat to a lady who was standing. He put his hand on the pillar behind Helen, his arm protecting her. Someone bumped into him and his hand ended up on Helen's shoulder. He left it there. Now his body acted as a protective shield from the good-natured, albeit high-spirited crowd. They watched as the bar around them continued to rock. Then the band did a set of pop songs. It sounded strange to hear the familiar tunes given a jazz makeover but somehow it worked.

"Do you want to dance, Jack?"

Jack looked horrified at the suggestion.

"Come on, I love this song. There's more room on the dance floor anyway."

"I've got two left feet," Jack protested.

"Excellent. Bad dancing competition, it is! I haven't done one in ages!"

She held out her hand. How could he resist?

"Just follow my lead." She pursed her lips. She wiggled her index finger and hips in exaggerated moves to a jazz version of Tom Jones's "Sex Bomb". "Get it, the worse dancer you are, the more likely you'll win Bad Dancing!"

She still looked pretty good to Jack but he stuck his butt out anyway. To his surprise, it was easy to act like a dork, and before long he was jutting and throwing as many of his body parts as possible in various directions.

John Travolta, with ants in his pants.

"See, you're a natural," she laughed as he twirled her around. "A clear winner, Jack Taylor!" She flashed a smile as she tried to catch her breath.

The lights dimmed and the music slowed in tempo. People coupled off.

Helen and Jack looked at each other.

Perfect timing.

He put his arms around her waist and pulled her towards him. They swayed gently, hip to hip. She rested her head on his chest, feeling safer than she had in the longest time – if ever before. He closed his eyes and let go of his awkward feelings. He inhaled the scent of Helen – a heady mix of exotic amber filled his nostrils. He felt the softness of her breasts pressed against his ribs.

"So what's my prize?" Jack whispered.

She looked up at him. For a moment, they held each other's gaze. Slowly, naturally, their mouths found each other. The kiss was soft, as if happening in slow motion. Tingles coursed through Jack, as he tasted Helen for the first time. Helen flicked her tongue lightly against his teeth. The kiss became deeper, hungry.

They stood in the middle of the floor, not speaking, lost in each other. Time stood still for them.

It was only a kiss – but the passion was explosive.

The cool cat on sax led his seven-man crew to a grand finale. Helen and Jack remained locked in their moment, oblivious that the slow set was over. The place erupted with applause, whistles and good-humoured demands for the band to play on. Reluctantly, Helen and Jack broke away from each other but they didn't break eye contact. Smiling they pressed their foreheads together and stood embracing as the club continued to buzz around them.

"*Bon nuit et merci*!" the velvet voice of the lead player announced. He was every bit a caricature of a jazz player, the look finished off with an oversized moustache.

The woman Helen had noticed earlier was standing now and

clapping enthusiastically. "*Encore*!" she shouted.

The lights went up and the main doors opened – the night was over.

"I'm all hyped up now," Helen said, looking at her watch, "and it's only just after midnight!"

"Come on, Cinderella!" Jack took hold of Helen's hand as he walked back to the bar.

That would make you my Prince Charming.

"Any chance of a few drinks, buddy?" Jack asked the barman.

"Sorry, we've stayed open late as it is. Curfew tonight."

"Curfew?" Jack looked at Helen to see if she knew anything about this.

"That happened to Poppy and myself the first night we were here. We were expecting a swinging nightlife, instead the whole town shut down by half past ten."

"They must have been tipped off you and Poppy were coming to town – my first few nights here were curfew-free."

They headed out into the night air.

A motorbike taxi driver approached them. "You want nightclub? Out of town – no curfew, more drink."

Helen and Jack looked at each other.

"Well, I don't really want to end up in a brothel outside city limits, but if they serve late drink I might consider it." She flashed Jack a wicked smile.

"You've definitely travelled the world, hey?"

"You better believe it. I've ended up in some very dodgy places in search of the Holy Grail."

"Holy Grail?"

"Depends on the timing – the Holy Grail is usually rum in the first half of the evening but it morphs into a Big Mac as the evening progresses," she said. "Remind me to tell you the story of when I brought a blind man to a strip-club-cum-brothel. That was my first and last attempt at charity work, before my lingerie life took over."

"You've been to more then one brothel then?"

"Yep, it appears to be a hidden talent I have – sniffing out after-hours illegal drinking in the most unusual places," she said proudly.

"The brothels just happened to be attached. Which reminds me – I've got hooch!"

"It's safe to say, Helen, I never met a girl like you before." And didn't he know it.

Helen started taxi negotiations without clarifying for Jack what exactly she meant by hooch or where she was taking him.

"So, it's the French Quarter first – you wait for me. I'll only be a few minutes, – okay?" Helen instructed the driver, arms pointing in various directions, having found her feet in the Hanoi ways.

"Okay, okay, get on!" the driver ordered.

Jack and Helen climbed on the back of a motorbike that wasn't much bigger than a moped. As the driver only had one helmet, it was decided that they'd both go without. They sped through the streets, the wind blowing Helen's long hair into Jack's face. He couldn't see a thing but was quite happy with the experience of Helen's butt wedged between his legs. On cue, Helen writhed on the saddle.

"*Yeehaw! Hello, Hanoi!*" she shouted at the empty, rain-drenched streets, throwing her arms in the air. Liberated by the Bad Dancing contest, she was free to do whatever she wanted, without worrying how she looked. Her energy was infectious and Jack joined her in greeting the sleeping city.

The driver pulled up to a side entrance of the hotel, to avoid being seen by the guard on the door, with two slightly crazy tourists on board.

"Won't be long," Helen said, disappearing into the dark grounds.

Jack and the driver sat in silence. The driver offered him a cigarette. Jack shook his head. Minutes passed. Jack tapped his foot and tried to see if Helen was coming back. It was too dark. Even though he hadn't actually agreed to whatever it was Helen was offering, so far he was enjoying the ride.

Soon after that Helen reappeared, much to Jack's relief.

"I'd ask you in," she said, "but Poppy is sleeping." She held up a couple of cans of Coke and a battered old plastic bottle, which was full of a clear liquid.

Jack was intrigued.

"Mother's milk." She sniffed the bottle and wrinkled her nose. "Devil's firewater might be more accurate actually," she admitted.

"Where now?" the driver revved the throttle.

"Hong Ngoc Hotel, please," Jack requested.

Right answer, Helen thought, the perfect answer actually.

53

Helen insisted on paying the driver and gave him closer to the original amount he requested – a combination of goodwill and inebriation, which often made Helen feel extra generous. That and the fact they hadn't ended up arrested or in Hanoi's Accident and Emergency room. Job well done, the driver sped off.

"Goodnight, Mr Jack, Miss," Quan nodded and smiled as they entered the lobby.

"Night, Quan." Jack tried to look casual as though bringing a woman to his room was no big deal. He felt a tinge of apprehension. The kiss with Helen had been firecracker hot. That excited him but also scared him somewhat, if he was being honest. They'd talked more than they drank tonight, but he didn't want her to think him presumptuous, by asking her to his hotel. She was so confident and wonderful. *What if he disappointed her?*

Helen couldn't stop thinking about the taste of Jack's kiss. Was she imagining it or was it something special? She'd thought things like that only happened in cheesy Hollywood movies. Yet, here she was, Helen Devine, cynic extraordinaire, wanting to touch her mouth, which still tingled as if sprinkled with pixie dust. This felt strange – her usual cynicism replaced by nervousness and anticipation. She liked it.

"Have you any ice?" She looked at Jack hopefully as she pulled the ring of the Coke can.

He shook his head, "I do have two plastic cups though." He went into the bathroom and retrieved them. "So are you going to tell me what we're drinking?"

"I'm not sure – call it hooch or moonshine. I bought it for a dollar from an old man at the back of a market – he made it himself, or his wife did, over an open fire. It must be organic." Helen poured the clear liquid into the cup. "Straight or with coke?"

Jack took a sniff – the pungent smell of earth, smoke and alcohol accosted his nostrils. He coughed but simply said, "Interesting."

"With Coke so," Helen offered the can. She kicked off her shoes and settled on the bed. The overhead light in the room glared. Jack turned on the TV, instead of the table lamp, to spread a gentler glow. The channel set to MTV, he pressed mute.

"How about some Coldplay?" he tapped through his iPod and the soft sounds of "In My Place" flowed from the travel-dock.

"I like it, Pussycat Dolls on visual, real musicians on audio, best of both worlds." Helen laughed.

They sipped their drinks. It was rank but neither admitted it.

"I think it's made with potatoes, so one of your five a day." She winced as she swallowed the foul-tasting hooch.

As the room was small, the only seat was the bed. Jack sat beside Helen but didn't move to kiss her. There was an awkward silence.

"Are you excited to be moving to LA?" she asked.

Jack considered this for a moment, "I don't know about 'excited' to be honest, I guess so. I love the sea and it's south of LA I'm moving to, not the city – I don't think I could handle the traffic and smog."

"I admire your courage to try new things. Me, I've stayed stuck in a job I lost interest in long ago, unwilling or unable to move on." She swished her drink in the cup.

"Now how can you say women's underwear isn't interesting?" he laughed.

"Amazing, isn't it?" Helen playfully punched at him. "I worked hard to get where I am, I thought getting to director level was what I wanted, and it was for a while. Now though, there's no challenge. It's well paid but other than that it's, well, empty."

311

"If you could do anything in the world, anything at all, if you'd no commitments, no contracts to fulfil, no financial restrictions – what would you do?"

"Gosh, part of me wants to move back to Dublin, part of me still loves lingerie and yet another part of me wants my life to account for something – to give something back to the world. I'd like a better work-life balance – as you said, actually use the Dubai apartment, enjoy the fruits of my labour." She hugged her knees in as she thought of her possibilities outside of the box. "I don't want to end up retired with nothing to show for life except a gold-plated bra – I reckon that's what I'd get instead of a gold watch – home alone, with just my cats for company."

"You've got a cat?" Jack asked, remembering how Carine, the French girl he'd met in Cambodia, had talked about her cat. If she hadn't mentioned Halong Bay, he might not have even considered coming to Vietnam. *Thanks, Carine.*

"God, no – I'm allergic. I have a dog, JD."

This appeared to please Jack. "I'm a dog person too." He observed Helen, whose glow could have lit the room – no TV required. "And what about when you were a kid? What did you dream for your life?"

"Oh my God! Would you believe, I wanted to be a nun?" She waited for his reaction.

"Not possible! I don't believe it," he teased.

"Honestly, I wanted to be closer to the Highest Power and, anyway, apart from my dad, all boys were smelly and I would never want to touch one. Especially not after Roger the Dodger, as I called him, took out his willy in the garden shed – and it had a rash on it. Imagine, the first willy I ever saw had a red rash on it from Roger wetting his pants!" She hooted with laughter at the memory she had long forgotten.

"I can't say I'd approve of you joining the convent as a career change. Maybe have a look at your other options though."

"Are you mad? I've got a massive mortgage on my place in London plus an expensive addiction to anything with the word *Prada* on it."

"I don't know, Helen, maybe it was this moonshine that had you aglow, but you should have seen your face when you talked about what you really want in life."

Jack had hit a nerve.

"I thought so many times about quitting and going off to travel the world – ride horses in Patagonia – bring Poppy to an Ashram in Kerala (and make sure she came back this time). Get on a plane to New York with Mum – take her back to the lights of her beloved 42nd Street. And then, maybe consider starting my own business." Helen sat up straight. "You know, I still love designing, it's the red tape and office politics I'm tired of. Anyway, it looks like I've missed the boat now – I should have done it a few years ago when world economies were flying high." She sighed. Settling back into the pillow, she stifled a yawn.

"I don't know, I think if you really want something you've just got to go for it."

"Is that what you do? See something you want and go for it?" Helen's question was loaded with double-meaning.

Jack wasn't sure if she was being seductive or if it was wishful thinking on his part. Rather than risk looking foolish he answered at face value.

"Pretty much. Before, I had my whole life mapped out. Good old reliable Jack. Look where it got me. Now I'm happy I moved on. Hey, I'm moving to Southern California, that can't be bad!" Despite his words, his tone lacked lustre.

Helen laid her head on her arm. She willed him to ask her to stay but she couldn't read him. Maybe she was imagining it, but it was as if the atmosphere had turned more into friendship than lovers? Something was holding him back and she couldn't figure it out. Maybe he just didn't find her attractive – there was a big age gap after all. It wouldn't be unreasonable for Jack to be with someone in their early twenties.

He carried on chatting as she studied his face. He had all the bits – good body, tanned skin, blond hair – but he didn't have chiselled good looks. His baby face gave him more of a charm than a drop-dead gorgeous appearance. Helen liked that. But, probably what

313

she found most attractive about him was his openness to life. It appeared as though no scepticism had crept up on him – whether that was to do with his age or his personality, who knew. She had a feeling with Jack Taylor that what you saw was what you got, no game-playing – unlike Rob. If she was right, then why couldn't she work out what was going through his head now? What about that kiss?

There was a moment's silence as Helen closed her eyes. Willing herself awake, she opened them wide and nipped at her drink. She scrunched her face inadvertently. "The hooch is really awful, isn't it?"

Jack had hardly touched his. "Maybe it'd be better if we had ice," he said politely.

They both laughed.

"You know, I've really enjoyed these couple of days with you," he said. "I've felt at ease. When I was stuck on Halong Bay with those guys on the junk, I started to think travelling alone wasn't such a good idea after all. But with you, I feel I've known you all my life. That sounds corny, doesn't it?" His eyes scanned Helen's face for a reaction.

"I know what you mean, Jack. It was very synchronistic. I'm glad we bumped into each other – you're a great guy." She smiled.

Jack thought now would be a good time to kiss her.

"So, before I go, tell me something, Jack – what do you want to be when you grow up?"

"Very funny. I'm a big boy now, you know." He took a gulp of his drink. "Sorry, I didn't mean it to come out like that."

"Oh yeah?" Helen's voice was slightly husky.

Jack felt hot – he was embarrassed. "A cowboy." *Where the fuck did that come from? He'd meant to kiss her, not say something so bloody dumb.*

"So where's your lasso, Cowboy?" Helen laughed as she lay back on the bed.

"Hold that thought." Jack nudged her playfully on the hip. He got up and went into the bathroom. He'd been holding off peeing for ages – it was getting to crisis point. Plus he was aroused – he needed to go now while he still had some chance of hitting the toilet bowl, instead of the ceiling.

After he used the toilet, he washed his hands and splashed water on his face. He dampened down his hair, put a tiny daub of toothpaste on his index finger, and manually cleaned his teeth. He didn't want to make it too obvious to Helen what he was doing. She could easily hear him from the bedroom. He wondered if she'd notice if he put on aftershave. He tilted the bottle onto his other index finger and put the smallest touch of fragrance on his breast bone and just below the belt of his trousers. He slipped a condom into his back pocket. Was that presumptuous? Christ, he didn't want to be disrespectful either. Why hadn't he left one in his bedside locker? He checked the expiration date on the wrapper. It was okay – he was good to go. He took a deep breath and a final look in the mirror. Had it really been a year since he'd had sex? He hadn't slept with anyone since Amy. He was ready.

Jack stood in the doorway of the bathroom trying to think of something witty to take attention away from his quick grooming. He watched Helen who was propped up against the pillows. She had her antique ring between her thumb and forefinger, and she watched it, trance-like, as she gently turned it over. He stood, soaking in the curve of her mouth, the way her hair fell in soft curls around her face. He took a deep breath and tried to rationalise the emotion he was feeling. He couldn't. She looked over at him.

"You're back then," she smiled.

Responding with just a smile, Jack walked over to the bed and snuggled in beside her as he adjusted the pillows behind their backs. He put his arm around her shoulder, pulling her closer to his body before running his fingers down her arm until his hand covered hers. She moved her fingers to mingle with his. They watched their hands exploring, as though they were blind and discovering a new lover's face. The ring, at the tip of Helen's little finger, looped around Jack's as their fingertips met. He flipped it back on hers. It moved between them, back and forth with a tick-tock motion. Its effect was hypnotic. Jack bent, kissing the top of Helen's head before kissing the nape of her neck as she pulled her hair aside. He could feel her goose bumps meeting his lips.

She shifted her leg, intertwining it with his. Slowly she slid her foot along the inside of his calf. Half-turning to him, she placed her hand on the inside of his thigh before it travelled upwards until she could feel his hardness through the heavy cotton of his jeans. She gently kneaded him before placing her hand to his face. She brushed her thumb along his cheek, as his fresh stubble tickled her. She brought her mouth to his, kissing it lightly. He responded to her kiss.

"I don't want this to end," she whispered.

"It doesn't have to, Helen." He traced his hand along her body, slipping it inside the top of her jeans, letting it linger before retracing his movements back up inside her T-shirt to the side of her breast.

She pulled away ever so slightly. "I mean it, Jack. We're literally heading in different directions the day after tomorrow."

Jack brushed away a loose strand of hair from Helen's face. "We don't have to do this, Helen. It's okay."

"I want to, it feels right. I just want it to be more than a one-night stand fuelled by jazz, cocktails and hooch."

Jack knew he couldn't say the real words that were tumbling to leave his mouth, for fear she'd think he was manipulating her. He hardly believed he could feel this way for a woman he'd only met. Yet, there they were – feelings of love, which defied logic. Instead he said, "I'm on my own timetable – which direction would you like me to go, Helen?"

Her eyes darted back and forth, searching his face.

"And I'm willing to carry the suitcases," he added.

Helen's face broke into a Pretty Woman style smile before lowering her hand. She had started to let it glide inside his T-shirt, exploring his chest, when he took hold of it.

"I mean it, Helen. You're worth waiting for."

"You'd take it slowly?"

Smiling he said, "I've waited for you my whole life, what's a while longer?"

She grinned.

"My buddies say I should have a thirty-second time-delay installed on my mouth. That sounded pretty corny, hey?"

Helen threw her head back in laughter. "No . . . well, yes, but I loved it anyway."

He pulled her to him and tickled her ribs. She resisted and the pillows fell away from the headboard. Jack wrapped his arms around her as they spooned. They lay in silence for a while, until Helen's breathing became even, her chest rising and falling in a slow rhythm. Her shoulders were bare where her T-shirt had slid off.

Jack hadn't had this strong an attraction to an older woman before. Because he'd thought his life was with Amy he hadn't thought about other woman as partners, period. Sure, he'd noticed attractive women but that was it, he'd been totally devoted to his girl. Thinking back he realised the women he'd found most interesting in the past *were* a little older than him. He looked at Helen again and it dawned on him he wasn't attracted to her because she was older, he was just attracted to her, no story. Jack Taylor had finally moved on.

Gently he pulled part of the bedcovers over her as best he could before resuming their foetal position. Instinctively, even in slumber, Helen took his hand in hers. He savoured the moment of intimacy, until he too succumbed to sleep.

54

Helen woke and tried to focus on the unfamiliar surroundings. It was the familiar feeling that business travellers often wake with, when hotels and cities start to blur into one. But this time warm memories of last night quickly replaced her confusion when she looked down and saw the strong masculine arm draped around her waist. She lay, not moving, and studied Jack Taylor's forearm: that's all she could see of him.

Helen loved a man's hands, it was the first thing she noticed – that and shoes. Jack's arms were muscular, with fine blonde curly hairs. He wore a practical, robust watch – it looked new. His hands were as a man's should be in Helen's book, strong with short-cut, spotless fingernails. She stayed in the stillness of the dawn for as long as she could and relished the moment, somehow knowing she'd remember it, always.

As time passed, she saw daylight break through the cracks in the curtains. She felt around for her phone, moving as little as possible and eventually found it under the pillow – its battery dead.

"Bugger," she muttered. She figured it to be around seven in the morning. Poppy would be worried if she woke and Helen wasn't there and hadn't even sent a text.

She nudged Jack's arm, to get a look at his watch, it read fifteen after seven.

Now Helen had a dilemma. Should she wake Jack and make mad passionate love to him, in the fresh light of a new day? Or, would she be a good friend and let Poppy know all was well and the day could go ahead as planned – once she'd had sex, that is. It was a difficult call. But then she had a brainwave.

Jack stirred and Helen turned to face him.

"Hey," was all he managed to say.

"Hey," Helen replied, playfully mimicking his Americanism.

She leant over and gently kissed him on the mouth. He responded.

"I'll be back in a minute. I've got to call Poppy, let her know where I am."

Jack edged his tongue between her lips. Helen kissed him back, before pulling away slightly.

"My phone is dead – I'll pop down to reception."

He pulled her closer to him. "Don't be long."

She felt his arousal through the bed covers – she kissed him on his forehead, and then, just as he had said to her last night, she added, "Hold that thought," as she flicked the tip of his nose with her forefinger, teasing him. She grabbed her handbag, and stood at the door for a moment looking back at him. The anxiousness from last night was gone – she felt compelled to make love to this man.

Helen sang to herself in the lift. She laughed when she thought about what Poppy would say. Poppy would get great satisfaction from being right.

The same man was on the reception desk. "Good morning, Miss." He smiled at her before shouting at some workmen in the small lobby. He turned back to her. "Some work being done today, to keep hotel nice."

Helen fumbled in her bag for the card of the Army Hotel. She retrieved it and handed it to him, with a shy smile. It was her Walk of Shame smile.

"Could you ring this number for me, please?" She produced a few notes.

"No problem." He pushed her money away. "Local calls – no need to pay, Miss. Room number?"

"It's 311. I think."

There was a crash – one of the workmen's ladders had smashed into a mirror.

Seven years' bad luck.

The poor desk clerk looked like he was about to have a heart attack. He handed Helen the receiver before he went running towards the destruction behind her.

"Helen?" Poppy's tone sent shivers down Helen's spine.

"Is everything all right, Poppy?" She pressed her hand against her ear, as she tried to cut out the hullabaloo of the argument going on behind her.

"Oh God, Helen, oh God . . ." Poppy sounded breathless.

"Poppy, can you please tell me what is going on! Are you okay?" Helen tried to keep the panic out of her voice. The workmen were all shouting at each other. She reached over the counter, picked up the phone, and brought it as far away from the din as the cord would allow.

"Where have you been? I've been trying to call you," Poppy sobbed. "There's been an accident – it's Lily. I've got to get home but no one in this fucking country can help me!"

"Poppy, stay calm," Helen said with authority. "I'll get us home. I'm on my way, Poppy. Just stay put till I get there."

Helen headed to the street to hail a cab. It flashed through her head to run back up to Jack.

She went back and tugged at the hotel clerk as she tried to be heard above the noise of everyone shouting at the same time.

"Can you give Mr Jack a message? Tell him I had to leave, an emergency. I'll call back later, okay?"

"Yes, yes, emergency, I tell him," Quan said and returned to the shouting match.

In the short journey across town, Helen struggled with a barrage of thoughts but she engaged her usual survival tactic and decided not to think too much until she had all the facts. Thankfully, she'd taken her bag down with her to call Poppy because the hotel card was in there somewhere, under make-up, headache pills, pens and the mini-sketchpad that she carried everywhere. She hadn't wanted to go rummaging in front of Jack.

Jack.

Helen opened the hotel-room door and saw Poppy's tear-streaked face as she ran to her.

"Thank God you're here, Helen!" Poppy sobbed.

Helen held her for a moment and rubbed her hair, as a mother would a child's. "Poppy, I need you to tell me exactly what's happened." Her voice was soothing but firm. "I need you to calm down. Take a deep breath. Until I know what we're dealing with I can't help you."

Poppy wiped her eyes – she looked dazed. "A garda, from home, called my mobile – only half an hour ago." She stopped as she tried to remember exactly what he'd said. "He asked if I was Lily Power's next of kin." Her eyes welled up again.

"Go on."

"He said she'd been in a traffic accident and is in intensive care. They'd been trying to contact me. I was asleep, I didn't hear my phone. She's there, alone, Helen, and I'm the other side of the world." Panic rose in her voice again. "I tried calling you, I tried Mary but her mobile is off and there's no answer at the house. I couldn't even get the bloody airlines to pick up their fucking phones!"

"Okay, look, here's what we're going to do." Helen took her friend by the shoulders. "Listen to me, Poppy. You're in shock."

She sat Poppy down and fetched a small brandy from the minibar fridge. Pouring it neat, she handed it to her.

"Mum's with Lily," she said. "That's why you can't get her at the house. You can't use mobiles in ICU. Did the gardaí leave a phone number to call?"

Poppy pointed to a number she had scribbled down.

"Good. I'm going to make the call. Then I'll call Eden's head office. It'll be open now and they'll get us on the next flight home. Okay?"

Poppy looked numb but questions raced through her mind, quicker than she could process them. But now that Helen was here, everything would be all right. Helen was already on the phone getting the details of Lily's condition, saying she was Poppy Power to avoid bureaucracy snags. Yes, there was someone at Lily's bedside. Lily was stable, for now.

True to her word, Helen had Poppy in a taxi to the airport within the hour. They'd fly from Hanoi to the Middle East and from there they could fly directly into Dublin, cutting out the excruciatingly slow transfer through Heathrow. The two women sat in the back of the taxi, in silence. Helen held Poppy's hand. There were no more reassurances to give – she just prayed the journey would go smoothly. Even with Eden's travel department behind them it would still take nearly twenty-four hours to get home.

Helen looked out the window at the by-now-familiar Hanoi traffic chaos, her thoughts returning to Jack and how life can change in the blink of an eye. She still had the scent of his skin on her. In her head she relived the last few days over and over, then she stopped, feeling guilty that Lily was in hospital and all she could think about was a man she'd just met. Lily. Please, whatever power is up there – Jesus, Buddha, Krishna – Universe – just let her be okay.

The taxi broke free of the city-centre snarl and picked up speed towards the airport. It started to drizzle as they left Hanoi behind. As she left Jack behind, Jack whom she'd never even asked for a phone number as she thought she'd all the time in the world.

55

Jack had fallen back into a semi-conscious sleep, one where he felt he was awake but he was still dreaming. He fantasised about Helen – she had blown his socks off. And in a few minutes, Helen would be back in his bed.

He stretched out his arm and realised that the bed was still empty, bar a few strands of long fair hair. How long had she been gone – five minutes? Maybe ten? He lay in bed for another few minutes before an uneasy feeling made it impossible to stay still. He looked around the room. The only sign that Helen had been there was the half-empty plastic bottle of hooch.

And the ring.

Helen's ring, the one she always twisted, was entangled in the bed-sheet. She'd be in a panic when she realised she didn't have it.

Jack pulled on a T-shirt and headed down to reception. He noticed a guy sweeping broken glass away from the main doorway.

"What's going on, Quan?" Jack asked, rubbing his head.

"Mr Jack, how are you?" Quan replied, polite as ever. "Workers broke mirror. They supposed to be here to make hotel look nice, instead it look like bomb site. Not to worry, Mr Jack, it will all be fixed soon." He smiled reassuringly.

"Quan, my friend, the tall girl, did you see her?" Jack asked uncomfortably.

Quan smiled. "You all very tall, but yes, I remember her, very lovely lady. She used the phone, then she left." Quan hesitated. *Was there something else? He couldn't remember.*

Jack looked bewildered.

"I wrote down the room number. Here, I call the hotel for you." Quan, eager to please, dialled, despite Jack's protests. Soon Quan looked as dejected as Jack did.

"They said the ladies have checked out already – sorry, Mr Jack."

Jack checked his watch: it was a little after eight in the morning. He thought it odd that the girls had checked out so early, especially since they were scheduled to be in Hanoi until tomorrow. Had he misread the situation so badly? His face burned with embarrassment.

He tried to sound casual. "No worries, man, my mistake. I'd forgotten she'd mentioned something about moving hotel." Anxious to escape Quan's sympathetic eyes, he headed back upstairs.

In the background, a phone rang.

"Mr Jack! Mr Jack!" Quan's excited voice called after him. "It's the lady – she's on the phone for you!" Quan was just short of jumping for joy, as he waved the phone, his hand over the mouthpiece.

Jack felt a rush of relief. He knew something had gone wrong. Helen wouldn't just leave like that, especially not leaving her ring behind.

Quan cleared his throat. "One moment please, madam," he said coolly before handing the phone over to Jack. With the excitement of winning the lottery, Quan nodded and winked. *Everyone loves happy ending.*

"Hello, Jack?"

Jack heard the unmistakable voice of the woman on the other end of the line.

"Amy?"

Quan resumed his duties but kept looking back at Jack, who nodded, smiled and gave him the thumbs-up, to indicate everything was good.

"Jack, you've been a hard man to trace," Jack's ex-girlfriend said softly.

"How did you find me? More importantly *why* did you find me?"

Amy sighed heavily. "Don't get mad. Your mom gave me your hotel's number. She knows how I've been trying to get hold of you. I need to see you, Jack."

Jack's mother thought Jack and Amy were a match made in heaven, despite recent events. This was obviously her idea of necessary intervention.

"Just hear me out, Jack, please." Amy's voice was strained. "I'm coming to see you. I just need you to wait in Hanoi for one more day until I get there."

"Don't be crazy, Amy. It's the other side of the world – besides, it's not exactly up to your standards." He was remembering Amy's dislike of all things non-sterile.

"Surely that tells you how serious I am. Hear me out, Jack, that's all I ask – if you decide to walk away, I'll let you go. For what we had, Jack, our childhood together. Our seven years as lovers, just give me this one little thing."

Jack twisted Helen's ring around the top of his little finger. *Where was she?*

He weakened, the hostility left his voice. "I've moved on, Amy, I met someone here." He wasn't sure if he was telling the truth.

There was a pause. Jack imagined Amy bristling – another woman.

"I'm pleased for you, Jack," she said tightly. "I've booked into the Hanoi Hilton. All I ask is that you hear me out, and then the decision is yours."

The Hanoi Hilton, how apt.

"The prison or the hotel?"

"I'm heading for my flight now. I'll be there in less than a day. Twenty-four-hours – that's all I'm asking, after all our years together."

Amy knew how to manipulate – the gentleman in Jack would not let her down.

He sighed.

"And, Jack?"

"Yes?"

"I love you."

325

56

Poppy felt like throwing up. Now back in Dublin, she wasn't sure she could hold herself together any longer.

The flights had gone smoothly enough – they had travelled first class because Helen said it would ensure minimum cock-ups. As they disembarked from one plane, they directly boarded the next. With Helen's phone dead and hers an out-of-credit pre-pay, they'd tried to swap SIM cards only to realise their phones were locked into different networks. If God was trying to test them, She was doing a sterling job of it. They got to a public phone long enough to leave a message that they were on their way. But the flight was on last call so they hung up, for fear of missing it. They'd run all the way to the gate.

Despite the tight flight connection, every minute had felt like an hour, every hour like an eternity. She had watched people laugh and felt angry that they were happy. She wanted to scream at the businessman in the row in front, who complained his duck was overcooked and his champagne not quite chilled to the correct temperature. Usually she'd have laughed at the triviality of it.

Helen had tried to get her to eat but instead she asked the air-steward to leave the full bottle of wine, in the hopes it would numb her pain or at least make her sleep for a while. It did neither.

When they landed in Dublin, a steward approached them.

"Ms Power, Ms Devine, please follow me – our VIP service has been requested for you."

Helen and Poppy were ushered from the plane to a waiting Mercedes with blacked-out windows. The other passengers gawped and whispered as they tried to figure out in which movies they'd seen either Helen or Poppy.

The black limo sped across the tarmac to a private security gate. They had their own two uniformed officials, one from passport control, and the other from customs.

"Welcome Home, Ms Power, Ms Devine," the officer said, handing them back their passports.

Bewildered, they entered the softly lit lounge.

"Eden really must value you, Helen," said Poppy. "I'll never be able to thank them enough."

That's when Helen spotted him – standing waiting.

"Rob?"

Rob Lawless came rushing forward. "Helen, Poppy. I have a driver waiting outside – we'll go straight to the hospital."

In all the years Helen had known Rob, he'd never waited on anyone.

"Poppy, they've taken Lily out of her induced coma. She responded well. She has a few broken ribs, but they'll mend. It was the knock she took to the head that was the main concern. But the swelling has gone down – she's asking for you. She's going to be fine, Poppy." Rob's expression was grave, his eyes filled with compassion.

Poppy hugged him hard – this man she'd spent so many years disliking. Relief flooded every sinew of her body.

But Helen knew Rob – his face was still etched with worry.

There was more.

"What is it, Rob? There's something you're not telling her," she asked quietly out of Poppy's earshot.

"Your phone has been off, Helen – we've been trying to reach you," he said under his breath. "Get into the car, I'll explain on the way to the hospital." He held the car door open and they climbed in.

Helen's momentary feeling of joy quickly left her as a renewed sense of dread crept back. Rob hadn't come for Poppy. He'd come for her.

"There was a bit of confusion as to who to contact," he said. "Your phone was off."

"You said that already. Christ, my battery died! Poppy left a message with the hospital." Helen tried to keep the irritation out of her voice.

"The cops didn't realise you were with Poppy. By the time we cleared up the confusion, you were over the Middle East somewhere. We decided to wait until you got here."

"Wait for what?" Helen shouted, her mouth dry.

Poppy linked Helen's arm, taking on the role of carer. "What kind of traffic accident was it, Rob?" she asked urgently.

"A car crash. Mary was driving. I'm so sorry, Helen, she's in a coma. They're waiting for you to arrive. You've got to prepare yourself." Rob put his hand over Helen's – she looked devastated. He hadn't wanted to destroy her world, with his words – again.

Her surroundings swirled out of control – she couldn't breathe.

"She's alive though, right?" Poppy clutched at straws.

Rob looked at her and gave an almost undetectable shake of his head.

Helen looked at him.

"She is alive," he said.

He hoped he was telling the truth.

Helen approached Mary's bedside. The beautiful, brave Mary Devine lay battered and broken. Her chest heaved up and down as a machine pumped oxygen in and out of her lungs. Cyril sat beside her, his eyes bloodshot.

"I'll leave you alone with your mother," he said when he saw Helen. "I'll wait outside – call me if you want anything, pet."

"Thanks for staying with her, Cyril. I'm glad she wasn't alone."

Cyril nodded and patted Helen's hand as he left.

Helen sat alone with her mother. Poppy had gone to Lily. She took Mary's hand in hers and began talking.

"Hi, Mum, it's me. Sorry I was late – it's as you always say – I'll be late for my own funeral." Helen's voice shook. "So, this was a bit of an extreme way to get me home, hey?" She thought she saw her mother's eyelids twitch. "Anyway, Vietnam was beautiful – you'd love it – I thought maybe we'd go together some day. What do you think? We could go to one of those luxury spas in Thailand along the way. Chiva Som? Wasn't that the one you always admired in magazines?" Helen continued to talk and watched for signs of recognition from Mary.

The machines continued to beep. Oxygen continued to pump. Helen counted the tubes that were keeping her mother alive. There were sixteen of them: Helen's lucky number.

"Please don't leave me, Mum," she suddenly pleaded. "I'm not ready to be alone. I've been a lousy daughter. Please, Mum, just wake up. I'll move back to Dublin, I'll do anything, just please don't die."

The beeping continued.

Two doctors approached Helen. The nurse who'd been monitoring Mary looked pleased to see them. "Here's your mother's surgeons now, Helen, they'll be able to explain everything."

The first doctor, a tall man in his mid-fifties, shook Helen's hand. "Seán Flood, cardiologist, I operated on your mother," he introduced himself. "This is Mr Paul O'Reilly, her neurologist." Their handshakes were firm and strong. Helen took comfort in that. "Your mother is a strong woman, Ms Devine." He paused. "It would appear Mary suffered a heart attack at the wheel. We managed to contain the bleeding but there were added complications. There's a room just outside the ICU. If you follow us, we can go through everything with you, in privacy."

Helen hesitated as she looked back at Mary. "I always worried about her diabetes, her having a stroke –"

"Is there someone who can come with you?" Paul O'Reilly asked. "It can be a lot of information to digest."

The nurse had gone to get Cyril. He entered the ICU as the doctor spoke. "I can go with her – if Helen would like me to, that is." He looked at Helen.

She nodded, with an almost imperceptible smile. "I'll follow you in, doctors – I'll just be a moment."

She returned to Mary and whispered something into her ear as if she was telling her a secret.

Helen finally understood how Lily had felt when she was cutting herself.

"The pain inside gets so bad, I can't bear it. When I cut myself, it relieves it, lets it out," Lily had said.

Helen had wanted to understand but couldn't. How could emotional pain be felt physically?

Now she understood. Now she wanted to cut her heart out – just to stop the feelings. Her breathing quickened as her heart-beat raced. The more she struggled to breathe, the harder it became. She sat in the small windowless room with three well-meaning men. Strangers to her. One was her mother's lover, the other two her mother's doctors.

The doctors sat opposite her, their expressions grave. Cyril sat beside her. She couldn't see his face, just his shoes, meticulously polished brown brogues. His slacks looked slightly too short, the way the men had worn them in the sixties.

Dr Seán Flood interlaced his fingers as he rested his hands on the table as though praying in a church pew. His colleague mirrored him. Their words came at Helen as if they were talking through a long foggy tunnel . . .

"Chances of full recovery are slim . . ."

Helen went further down the rabbit hole.

"Survival percentages are low . . ."

A kaleidoscope of colours whizzed around her head as she gasped for air.

"Better to prepare yourself . . ."

"She's having a panic attack."

The doctors were on their feet now.

"Ms Devine? Ms Devine, Helen, can you hear me?"

They were touching her shoulders now. She couldn't see Cyril's shoes anymore.

"Helen, relax, just breathe."

But Helen didn't want to breathe.

Poppy sat by Lily's bed. Rob was right. Lily's injuries turned out to be relatively minor. Lily had been put in a temporarily induced coma. Mary wasn't so lucky.

"You can't know how much you staying with Lily until I got here means to me, Angelo." Poppy smiled across at her Italian *barista*, her friend.

"No worries. When I heard about the crash, I wanted to be here."

Lily continued to doze. She still had concussion.

"Could I ask you one more favour?" Poppy asked.

"Of course."

"I want to check on Helen. Will you sit with Lily – I'll only be a few minutes?"

"*Via!* Go!" Angelo smiled. "I say a lot of prayer for Mary – I think she will be okay. You have a beautiful family, Poppy."

Poppy suddenly felt tearful. Angelo had called her "Poppy".

57

Helen screamed – she couldn't stop. Nor would the gut-wrenching pain in the pit of her stomach subside. It was Tuesday morning, a month after the accident, in the frozen-food section of Tesco Extra – a super-sized supermarket.

"Excuse me, dear, I just want to get to the frozen peas." A small stout woman with thick glasses had waited patiently for a few minutes for Helen to move on but instead she had stayed staring at the cabinet doors.

"Oh, I'm sorry!" Helen was flustered – thankful that her screaming was internalised, otherwise security would escort her off the premises. Or arrest her – then she'd have to call Rob to get her out of jail. He'd be the hero, she'd be the nut-job, but at least she'd have an excuse to ring him.

"Are you alright, dear?" the woman asked – the stranger in the supermarket, buying petits pois.

Tears stung Helen's eyes and for a second she considered pouring her heart out to the kindly woman. Instead, she smiled. "I'm fine – thank you. I get electric shocks from freezer doors." She pushed her shopping trolley on.

From freezer doors and a man I once met, in a previous life.

She wandered around the aisles aimlessly – screaming, still screaming. She wondered if anyone else felt the same, normal on the outside, dying on the inside.

The Dime Bar commercial came to mind, crunchy on the outside, chewy on the inside – armadillos. She was losing her mind. An armadillo disguised as a lingerie designer. Or maybe she was a Dime Bar, which she'd only seen on sale in IKEA these days. Suddenly, she fancied a Dime Bar – or Daim Bar as they called it now. Maybe Tesco did stock them. She moved on from the freezer section, fairly confident she wouldn't find them there. Poppy was right: she had wasted too much of life watching TV.

"Helen? It is you – I'm surprised to see you here." Cyril walked towards her, holding a wire basket, which contained bread, milk and broccoli.

Helen had no idea why she noticed that.

"I didn't know you liked broccoli, Cyril." A stupid thing to say but at least she'd stopped screaming.

"Your mother got me into it, said it was a super food, stop me getting cancer when I get old." He chuckled.

"Pity she smothered it with bacon bits and butter then." Helen felt guilty as soon as she uttered the words.

Cyril looked uncomfortable. "I see you like Blu Tack then . . ." he said, looking into Helen's sparse trolley.

"Always handy to have, you know, Blu Tack – it saves the walls from pinholes – great for putting up posters," Helen babbled. She hadn't put a poster on a wall since she was fifteen.

Helen's hair was unwashed – she was wearing an old tracksuit that had stains down the front of it. She wondered whether Cyril noticed.

He jiggled from side to side, looking unsure of what to do. Maybe he wanted to give her hug, mind her, while Mary couldn't. Either that or he needed to use the bathroom. Or did he just find her a little scary?

"Chickens are on special – half-price and it feeds six people according to the wrapper – I never could resist a bargain," Helen rambled.

"I tell you what. Seeing as you've got only two things in that big trolley of yours, why don't you give them here to me? We'll go home and eat the chicken and broccoli together – how does that sound?"

"Okay," Helen said simply.

Not scary at all.

They decided to cook dinner in Mary's house – it felt right. They sat at the kitchen table as the aroma of roast chicken wafted through the air.

"It's almost as if she's just out in the back garden picking herbs to make stuffing," Helen said, taking a sip from the wine Cyril had put in his basket after she'd gone to get her euro back for returning her cart. She was doing a lot of mundane things these days.

"I know, in a way it's a nice feeling but on the other hand it's quite painful, isn't it? To the wonderful Mary Devine, may she sit and eat with us, even if only in spirit!" Cyril raised his glass in a toast.

"To Mum!" Helen cleared her throat. "And if you can appear for real, Mum, that'd be great, otherwise the two of us will be eating chicken for a week."

Cyril smiled – Helen always cracked a joke.

"So, how have you been, Helen?"

"Okay, I guess, drinking too much of this stuff," Helen said as she tilted her wineglass. "The doc gave me tranquillisers but they made me feel spaced. The worst bit is waking up in the morning. You know, before your mind can focus?"

Cyril nodded.

"Everything is fine for the first few seconds, then boom! You remember and that disgusting pain punches you in the stomach and you realise it wasn't a bad dream, it is waking reality, a living bloody nightmare. And then the wine-head kicks in and I take a couple of paracetamol to ease that and hope they'll erase everything else as well. But they don't, instead they wreck your kidneys so I'll probably die of renal failure anyway." Helen sighed, relieved to be admitting to her less than flattering behaviour.

Cyril didn't lecture. "How are Poppy and Lily? I haven't seen them since last week."

"As well as can be expected, I guess. Lily had a major shock with the accident but it has brought out the survivor in her – in a good way. Poppy's been great, bringing me food and sending me healing light." Helen raised her eyes to heaven and smiled at her friend's different approach to grief. "Sometimes when I get home from the hospital, there's a weird smell around the house. Poppy has been burning sage, to get rid of negative energy or something like that." Helen fell silent. The truth was there was a strain between herself and Poppy, since that dreadful phone call in Hanoi.

"I wonder will anything ever be the same again?" She looked at Cyril.

"We can't give up hope, Helen. Poppy's doing her best – you know everyone deals with trauma differently."

"I know that. I think, even though she tried not to show it, she was angry with me that we were halfway around the world when the accident happened – I'd talked her into the holiday. Then there's the guilt."

"Guilt?"

"I know Poppy. Mum was like a mother to her, but Lily is her child. Poppy naturally would have felt a huge relief that Lily walked away from the accident, with minor injuries. That she's not the one still in a coma. What she's feeling is perfectly normal, I know. Survivor's guilt." Helen rubbed her finger, no gold ring to twist.

"And what do you feel?" Cyril asked gently.

"I want to tell her it's okay, it's not anyone's fault. Mum had a heart attack at the wheel. But then, I keep thinking if Mum hadn't been bringing Lily out for a bite to eat, she wouldn't have been driving that night and she'd still be here."

A silence fell between them.

"I know, I shouldn't think like that. I know it's unkind and I love Lily, I really do, but when the pain gets so bad all I can think of is 'what if' and part of me resents that Poppy and Lily still have each other. I feel like an outsider now. I sound horrible, don't I? I shouldn't feel this way." Helen couldn't cope with the feelings of shame, on top of all her other emotions.

"Not at all – emotions are running high at the moment, that's all. It's only been a few weeks. It sounds like a cliché but time is a great healer." Cyril took a deep breath before continuing. "I wish

I'd gone to pick them up. That was the plan, you know. Then I had to run a blasted errand, for the old folks. I rang Mary from my mobile and asked would she mind driving herself and I'd meet them there." He bowed his head as he thought about it.

"What if," Helen smiled. Cyril was a good man, in his seventies himself, but always running around after "the old folks" of his parish, picking up their prescriptions, giving them lifts to their chiropodist appointments. He went swimming in the sea, a few times a week, twelve months of the year. He reckoned that's what kept him youthful. She could see why Mary wanted to be with him. He was the first man Helen had seen her mother with since her father.

"How long is it since your wife died, Cyril?"

"Nearly ten years now. Breast cancer, God rest her soul. A good woman she was too. God always takes the good ones young. Guess I'll be around for a while longer so!" Cyril's joke was a welcome relief.

"You've a daughter living abroad somewhere, don't you?"

"Yes – Maeve – she lives in Canada, married a Canadian chap. They've three grand little ones. Ah, she's settled there now, wants me to go over for Thanksgiving, Christmas and the New Year. Says the kids should know their 'Irish grandpa'." Cyril laughed as he made inverted commas with his index fingers.

"That'd be some trip – six weeks, at least." It seemed to Helen everyone had another life to go to.

"It's too far. I couldn't be sitting on a plane for that long, I wouldn't know what to do with myself. And it gets very cold over there, snow six-feet high." He shook his head and admitted coyly, "The kids are great of course but a week is about as much as I can manage."

"So does that mean you'll be here for Christmas?"

"Yes. Listen, I know you've probably not thought about Christmas this year and I know you young ones have lots of invitations and friends, but if you don't get a better offer I'd be delighted if you, Poppy and Lily would let me cook you Christmas dinner. I make a mean cranberry sauce, you know." He looked at Helen hopefully.

"Thank you, Cyril, that's very kind of you and if I was in Dublin I'd have been honoured to share Christmas with you."

The oven-timer pinged to indicate the chicken was cooked. Cyril went to fetch an oven-glove from the counter top.

"Are you considering staying in London then?" he asked. "I thought everything more or less shuts down in offices until January the second?" He opened the oven door and a plume of steam billowed out. "Ah, looks perfect," he said, removing the crisp golden bird.

"Smells delicious." Helen felt pangs of hunger for the first time in ages.

"This is just a taster. I cook wild goose at Christmas – I'm famed for it, in fact." He set the roast bird down, to cool.

"Modest as well, I see," she teased. "Anyway, they're not big into Christmas in Asia – it's just another day actually."

"I don't understand – Eden hardly expect you to go there over Christmas, do they?" Cyril sat back down.

"Well," Helen said, shifting uncomfortably, "the company made me an offer – a promotion with more money and better job security." She poured salt on the table top and made shapes with her finger, unable to look Cyril in the eye. "The thing is – the position is in Hong Kong."

Cyril gawped at her, his mouth open.

"It's a great opportunity. I get to build a new design team from scratch – actually I'll get to design myself as well, not just all paperwork, costings and targets. I even get a fully serviced apartment overlooking Hong Kong harbour – all paid for." She bit her lip.

Cyril found his voice. "But what about your mother? She might wake up – and you'll be in Asia?"

Helen took a deep breath, finally looking up. "Don't you see, Cyril, that's just it. I don't have a choice. Mary's medical bills keep mounting up. Dad's pension isn't enough. I need to keep the health insurance – as my next-of-kin, I insured her under the Eden employee scheme. They've even agreed to pay for a return flight home once a month. It's an incredible offer."

"And you're going – permanently?"

"A two-year contract – I leave next week." Helen looked down. "I can't see any other option."

The doorbell rang.

Saved by the bell.

Helen jumped up to get it.

Through the stained-glass side-panels, Helen could see the figure of a man holding a bunch of flowers. Not more bloody flowers, she thought with annoyance. What were people thinking, Mary didn't need flowers – she needed a miracle.

"Yes?" Helen said briskly as she opened the door.

The young man stammered, looking uncomfortable. "I was looking for Mrs Devine." He twisted the small posy of deep-purple stock, nervously.

There was something oddly familiar about him. He was well-built with broad shoulders. His skin had the last remains of adolescent pimples. But it was his eyes that caught Helen's attention – so green – where had she seen him before?

"I'm sorry – I didn't mean to be rude." She felt a pang, of something, for the boy. "Would you like to come in?" She stepped aside to let him in. "I'm afraid Mary was in an accident last month." She still choked as she uttered those words.

"Oh." The boy's face went pale.

"She's in a coma. I'm her daughter – Helen."

"I know," he replied, in a soft English accent. He continued to twist the flowers to the point where petals started to fall on the floor.

"Excuse me," said Helen, perplexed, "I know I've met you before but I can't place you. It's just been crazy around here the past few weeks. It's just all a bit of a blur really. How do you know my mother?" She folded her arms as she felt a shiver.

"She is, um, my grandmother." He looked her in the eye.

"Excuse me?" Helen's head was spinning.

The eyes, now she knew why they were so familiar.

"I'm Daniel."

She saw those eyes every time she looked in a mirror.

"I'm your son."

58

"I've dreamt of this moment for so many years. I can't believe it's actually happening." Sitting opposite Daniel in the living room, Helen struggled to find something profound or even motherly to say but words were failing her. She wanted to study his face, up close, get to know every bit of it. But of course she couldn't so instead she drank in every part of him with her eyes. He had Rob's dark hair, a whole mop of it – but Daniel's had a wave – he must have got that from her. He had Rob's nose complete with the little bump on the bridge. And the mouth? Helen guessed that was one hundred per cent Daniel's own.

"Yeah, me too." Daniel wasn't faring much better in the conversation department.

Thankfully, Cyril came to the rescue. "Now, if Mary was here she'd make us all sit and have a nice cup of tea. I'll put the kettle on." Mary had been very excited recently but she'd insisted she couldn't tell him anything until she'd spoken to Helen first. "Except you, Helen – you look like you need a brandy first," he said as he opened the drinks cabinet. He handed the amber liquid to Helen. "Right, I'll leave you two to talk."

Cyril discreetly disappeared, closing the living-room door behind him.

Helen left the brandy untouched.

"I don't know where to start, Daniel. I've so much to explain, so much to ask. How are you?" She hoped she didn't sound too formal. Every fibre in her body wanted to rush over, hug the boy and cry. She wanted to cry a lot.

"I'm good, thanks. I mean, I'm shocked to hear about Mrs Devine, Mary, though." He bit his lower lip. He tapped his foot up and down, which caused more petals to fall.

"They're beautiful flowers," Helen said, looking at the half-strangled stalks. "Devine women's favourite – purple stock."

"Would you like them?" He quickly held out the heavily scented flowers.

She leant forward. "I'd love them, thank you, Daniel." As she reached out, their hands touched, for the first time since the day she'd given birth to him. And then, she couldn't help it, a tear escaped, followed by another and another.

"Please don't cry, Helen, I didn't mean to upset you. Do you want me to leave?" he asked wide-eyed, his foot tapping furiously fast.

"No! Definitely not. It's just been such a rollercoaster, but trust me, Daniel, these are tears of happiness. I just wish I'd been better dressed for the occasion!" She looked down at her scruffy runners. "I'm usually rather glamorous, would you believe?"

They laughed.

"I was wondering why I hadn't heard from Mary, thought I'd upset her or something," he said, as he studied Helen's face. "What happened?"

"It was a car accident – a heart attack which caused the accident actually. All these years I've worried about her diabetes. A heart attack didn't occurred to me."

"Will she be okay?" Daniel's eyebrows knitted, making his young face look older.

"We don't know. The odds are stacked against her. But she's holding her own, for now."

Daniel nodded.

"I don't understand though," said Helen. "How come you were in touch with Mum?"

340

"Well, you left your name and this address with the adoption board, so I could contact you when I turned eighteen, if I wanted."

She nodded – she remembered only too well the protocol. She was unable to contact her son. She could let him know where to find her, in case he wanted to find her when he reached adulthood – but it had to be his decision.

"I decided to just knock on the door, not phone or anything, but you weren't here," he continued. "Mary opened the door, and it was weird. It was like she'd been expecting me or something."

"That's Mum alright," Helen smiled.

"She said you don't live here any more, but you live close by and that you work in London and were in Hong Kong at the moment."

Helen thought back to the phone call from her mother when she'd been sitting in the hotel business lounge. *"I've something important to tell you, love. Not over the phone though. Will you be home this weekend?"* Helen had wrongly assumed that 'important' in Mary's eyes would be something to do with a nice sensible employment opportunity in Dublin that she'd spotted in her weekly scan of the recruitment section of the newspaper.

I'm so sorry Mum – I should have listened to you.

"I called a few times, while you were away. We'd hang out, she'd cook me dinner, tell me stories about you and how successful you are. And Granddad, how cool was that – fighting in the Vietnam war, I mean apart from the dying bit."

He has my way with words all right.

"My mates were very jealous. I couldn't have dreamed up a better imaginary family. A granddad fighter pilot and a lingerie-designer mum!" He shifted his feet. "I enjoyed listening to Mary. Talking to her, everything made sense – why you had me adopted, that is."

There it was, those words. *Why did I give him up – why did I?*

Every time Daniel paused it was as if there was something else he wanted to say that he couldn't quite come out with.

"I thought it was for the best, at the time," she said. "I've always wondered if I did the right thing, struggled with it actually."

"I've got a good life, Helen, honestly. I always knew my parents adopted me and that my real mother was single and a teen. Mum and Dad said it made me more special because they'd picked me especially." The words gushed out of Daniel as he sat at the edge of the seat.

"I'm glad, Daniel."

"I decided I wanted to go to uni here. I'm in Dublin City University – I started a few weeks ago." His face lit up – he was obviously enjoying his new life.

"I'm surprised Mary didn't try to get you to move in with her then!" she laughed.

"She fed me well, that's for sure," he smiled. "She even wanted me to bring my washing – must admit I thought about it."

"Don't worry about it, Daniel, I've succumbed to Mary's generosity myself in that regard at times." Helen paused. "Cyril must have gone to China for the tea." She looked around awkwardly.

Daniel just nodded.

"Did your parents know you were getting in touch?" she asked.

"Yep, we discussed it. Mum was feeling a little worried about it but she understood. Dad thought it would be healthy, but warned me you might not want to know me." His eyes searched Helen's face.

"Of course I want to know you, Daniel – it's like a dream come true. I don't exactly have a lot of blood relatives, you know." She thought it bizarre that as she was on the brink of losing her mother, the Universe gave her back her son. The law of giving and receiving, Poppy would say. Or maybe it was synchronicity.

"When I told Mum about meeting my grandmother, she felt good. Said she was glad I'd family close by, even though she's only a short hop over the Irish Sea."

"They sound like very special people, your mum and dad."

"They wreck my head at times, but yeah, they're cool. They'd two kids of their own after they adopted me, you know. They said they owed you a lot, that you changed their lives. You gave them life, a son. Reckoned they'd never have got pregnant until they adopted me. They'll always be grateful – that's why they kept the name Daniel – the name you'd given me."

These people she'd never met, yet was inextricably linked to, Helen thought, she'd changed their lives. Helen Devine had done something good – and all six foot of him was sitting in the chair opposite.

"About my father, it's just there's no record of him. I was wondering if you could tell me about him, if that's okay like." Daniel sat back in the chair now that he'd finally plucked up the courage to ask about his father.

"Of course, I should have thought – sorry, Daniel. His name is Robert Lawless – he's a corporate solicitor here in Dublin. He runs a very successful practice."

Christ, how will Rob react when he finds out?

"So, you guys are still in touch then?" Daniel's tone rose with a hint of excitement.

"We've remained friends. I'm sure you'd like me to contact him?" Her face drained.

"No rush, I mean, there's so much going on. I can't imagine what you are going through. I really hope Mary's going to be okay."

"Me too. I can only imagine how happy she was to meet you too."

"And we've got lots of time – you and me, to get to know each other, now that I'm living in Dublin if you get me. My mother, em, she's a lot older than you are. I think maybe you and me, we'll have a different kind of relationship. You're more like a big sister, hey?" He looked like a child who'd just won a trip to Disneyland.

Her heart sank – she had still to the break the news that she was moving to the other side of the world, in seven days.

59

"Helen! What a surprise! Come in." Poppy was delighted to see Helen although the strain of Mary's condition showed on her friend's face.

"I should have called first but my car just seemed to veer in this direction. What's that noise?" Helen couldn't but notice a loud humming coming from Poppy's therapy room. "Don't tell me I've interrupted sex with the monk again?"

"I didn't have sex with him, I told you. He was just a friend and, no, you haven't interrupted anything. Come on, I'll show you!" Poppy led the way towards the vibration.

"What on earth is that?"

"Ah, Helen, you disappoint me, it's the latest celebrity slimming craze!"

"Hi, Helen!" Lily shouted, her voice shaking from the giant vibrating plate she stood on.

Helen gasped, with wonderment, or was that horror as Lily's flesh jiggled up and down, at lightning speed.

"Here, have a go!" Lily jumped off the machine.

"No way, if it does that to a seventeen-year-old body, I can't imagine what it'd do to mine. Never mind the damage I'd do to the foundations of the house."

"Go on, Helen, have a go!" Poppy urged.

Helen tutted. "All right then, just for a minute, if it'll it make me skinny."

She hopped on and Lily gradually increased the speed.

"It's a bit weird, I quite like it though," Helen jiggled.

Lily pressed the button for maximum speed.

"Stop! My boobs are about to fly off!" Helen squealed as she vibrated at lightning velocity.

"Better turn it down, Lily." Poppy put her hand over her mouth to hide her laughter. "We don't want the first Irish tsunami."

Lily decreased the speed and Helen's boobs wiggled a little slower.

"That'd be some headline: *Lingerie Designer Causes Tsunami with Giant Vibrating Tits*. I can just see it on the tabloids now," Helen laughed – something she hadn't done in a while. She picked up the instruction booklet with pictures of a model in various exercise poses. "So it slims, tones and rehabilitates. Where has this machine been all my life?"

"Poppy said she got it for me to aid my recovery," said Lily and continued with devilment in her voice, "I reckon Poppy's just trying to impress her Latin Lover with new and improved biceps!"

Poppy threw Lily her best angry face. The comment didn't pass Helen.

"Latin lover, hey, what have I missed? And since when were men interested in biceps that aren't their own?" Helen looked up from her flicking through the booklet.

All eyes were on Poppy.

"Don't mind Lily – that knock on the head obviously has her deranged, delusional or both," Poppy said with flushed cheeks, but her smile gave her away.

"Mum's going on a date with Angelo, Helen!" Lily declared triumphantly.

"It's not a date – we're going for a walk, that's all. He doesn't know very many people here. I'm just being friendly – after all he did for Lily." Poppy hoped she sounded more convincing than she felt. She guessed not when she heard the whoops of laughter.

"Didn't a famous singer with a super-toned body have a young

Latin Lover – do you think your mother's modelling herself on her?" Helen said to Lily.

"That's it – I told you it's all about the biceps." Lily nodded, case proven.

"Shut up, the pair of you, what are you like?" Poppy scolded.

"We'd better shut up, before we upset your mother," said Helen. "Mind you, no wonder she was buying those conical hats in Vietnam – she probably wanted to turn them into a bra. Or maybe she's after my job at Eden!" Helen couldn't help but laugh at her own joke.

"That's it – we'll re-name her the 'Material Mum'." Lily held her stomach – laughing hurt her mending ribs.

Poppy, who had her arms crossed defensively, couldn't help but join in. "I'm still a girl, I'll have you know, young lady. And besides, Madonna is way older than me."

When the laughter died down, Helen let out a long sigh. She felt a bit guilty for laughing.

"It feels so good to laugh!" said Poppy. "I can only imagine what Mary would say, if she saw this thing." She pointed to the machine.

"She'd say, 'Poppy – a fine-looking woman like yourself – stop fannying around with giant vibrators and the like, and go out and meet a nice man for yourself!'" Helen mimicked her mother's voice and the laughter started all over again.

But Helen felt a stab of grief in her chest.

Poppy looked at Helen and said softly, "Come on, we're just about to eat and as always I've made too much."

Whatever had happened between them since the accident, the unsaid words had melted away. They'd be okay.

"All right, as long as it's not some vegetarian muck," Helen wrinkled her nose, "or are you all back to being carnivores, as God intended you to be?"

"It's fish actually. I'm trying to get as much protein as possible into Lily, help build her strength back up." Poppy busied herself warming plates – she felt uncomfortable mentioning the accident.

Lily curled her lip when she saw the fish pie.

"Go on then, eat up, Lil. I thought you'd love that," Helen said, pulling a face at her without Poppy seeing.

Lily picked at her food and then took a deep breath and said, "Actually, I'm glad you're here, Helen, because I've something to say and Mum's going to start crying, because she even cries at TV commercials. So here's the thing. Since the accident, I've done a lot of thinking and the fact is, I haven't been totally honest, with you guys or myself. I don't think . . . well, the thing is, maybe I'm not a lesbian after all. And I don't like fish either, Mum."

"I'm not sure there's a connection, I think lesbians eat fish, but just go with your gut, honey – whatever feels right." Poppy patted Lily's hand.

Helen took a bite of her fish pie – she decided silence on the subject was her safest option.

"Actually, I've an announcement of my own," she said then, without looking up from her plate. "There's no easy way to say this so I'll just say it. I've accepted a job in Hong Kong. I'm leaving next week so I'm hoping you'll take care of JD. Also, I've a son, Daniel, and he's just moved to Dublin." She took a mouthful of the pie.

The kitchen was silent.

Helen looked from mother to daughter nonchalantly. "That's all my announcements – somebody say something."

"Is he cute?" Lily broke the shock-wave.

"Not five minutes ago you were a lesbian!"

Poppy remained motionless, a picture caught in time.

"Say something." Helen's cheeks burned.

"I don't know where to start," Poppy whispered.

"Well, you knew I'd had a baby so that's not that much of a shock surely?" Helen tried to lighten the situation.

"How can you even consider going to Hong Kong to live!" Poppy didn't conceal her anger. "For Christ sake, Helen, when are you going to get in touch with reality? There's more to life than BMWs and designer clothes. Your son has just walked back into your life. Even you must see the significance of the timing." Poppy flew off in an uncharacteristic rant. She picked up the wine bottle from the table, poured a large glass and took a sizeable gulp. "For once, Helen, stop running and face some responsibility!"

Helen bit her lip as she felt her anger rising. Poppy seemed to think that because she was the spiritual one it gave her some kind of higher moral ground, the right to judge Helen's decisions. As though there was a divine hierarchy and Helen was only on the starting rung. Truth was, Helen wasn't so sure Poppy was walking her own talk.

Without warning, Lily erupted.

"Just shut up, Mum! Who are you to judge anyone? You preach about healing, love and understanding – it's bullshit! Angelo has been a rock, adores the ground you walk on. And what do you say? 'He's too short, he smokes, he's Italian, they all think with their dicks, let me just have another glass of wine while I sit here, alone at night, waiting for Mr Right to find me because I'm so bloody perfect'! You're pathetic!"

"How dare you speak to me like that – I'm your mother!" Poppy spat back.

"Yeah, well, start acting like one. I've had three parents. One is in a coma, the other is running to the other side of the world and my only blood mother is living in La La Land – and you wonder why I'm fucked up!" She flung her dinner plate across the room – it smashed into the kitchen wall.

Lily stood up but didn't leave. She panted as though she'd just run a mile. They each watched as bits of mashed potato and fish slid down the tiles.

Poppy wept silently, her shoulders shaking up and down as she buried her face.

Helen was the first to speak.

"We're all grieving, in our own way, but it's all the same thing. The trauma feels too much to bear. My going is about medical bills and negative equity on my property, not luxuries, Poppy. If I've any chance of keeping Mum alive, I need my job and its salary. I've racked my brain, looking for a solution. Daniel turning up is bitter sweet. Your universal synchronicity has thrown me a curveball, Poppy. But you and Lily, you've got each other, still."

Poppy swallowed hard and looked up at Lily. "Is that really what you think of me?"

Lily softened. "I get scared sometimes, is all. I know we're different from other families and I kind of like that but you don't seem happy inside, Mum. You keep trying new therapies and chasing something. I don't know what it is you're looking for but I feel you've got all these regrets, maybe about having me so young." She didn't look up – instead she started to peel dark polish off her fingernails. "It's as if you keep dreaming, you get distant and I can't reach you. I don't understand why you're not happy with all you've got. Instead of fantasising why not take a chance, go after your dream. How long have you dreamed of opening a holistic centre? An oasis of healing, you called it – this vision in your head. Without taking a risk, nothing is ever going to change." Lily sat down. "I know you think I'm just a kid but I know when things aren't right."

Poppy put her hand over her mouth as a gut-wrenching realisation washed over her. "I never saw it from your point of view, Lily. I'm sorry I've been so self-absorbed." She hung her head.

"We've let you down, Lily – I'm so sorry," Helen eventually said.

"You didn't, I'm really proud of you two, but now that I don't have Mary as back-up, your Dumb and Dumber double act isn't so appealing." Lily gave them a half smile.

"I don't know what to say, I feel so ashamed," Poppy whispered. "I'm sorry for the horrible things I said, Helen. I just saw things my way and I felt terrified that you won't be around. Of course we'll look after JD for you." She brushed her hair back and wiped her face.

Helen sighed – it was a moment of coroner-slab clarity. "I know I'm supposed to have trust and believe everything happens for a reason but it seems to me the Universe is playing a sick joke on me."

They nodded their agreement.

"Nonetheless, I don't know who I'm trying to kid. As soon as Daniel walked through that front door and back into my life, everything changed – again. I'm not going to Hong Kong. I'm staying right here, to continue to fuck-up everything, with you two, if you'll have me."

Helen had sparked their tsunami after all. Now they were feeling the wave of aftershock. Next would come the clean-up and rebuild. Starting with the fish-pie-decorated wall.

"I'm going to leave you two to talk – there's someone I need to see," Helen said but scooped up one last forkful of food as she stood to leave. "That really is yummy, Poppy – did you really make it yourself?"

Poppy raised her eyebrows and considered telling a fib before replying, "M&S."

"Figures." Helen pulled on her coat, happy with Poppy's reply. Enough had changed around here in the past few weeks – she didn't want Poppy morphing into a female Gordon Ramsay. Sometimes the familiar, albeit lousy cooking, was what gave the most comfort.

"Where are you going?" Poppy asked.

Helen gave Lily a hug and kissed Poppy on the cheek. "To see Rob. To tell him he's a father."

After Helen left, Poppy and Lily skirted around each other for a while, talking casually as Lily cleaned up the plate-throwing mess. Eventually, they sat and attempted to talk but both were feeling too drained so they opted to watch a rerun of *Friends* – "The One Where Ross is Fine". It made them laugh.

When Lily said she was having an early night, Poppy sat and reflected on everything, being brutally honest with herself. She picked up her phone.

"Hi, Angelo, it's me, Poppy. Yes, I'm fine, thanks. Everything is okay here, yes. Angelo, I was just wondering, about the walk. No, no, of course I don't want to cancel. I thought, maybe afterwards, we could go to see a movie?"

350

60

Helen didn't tell Rob why she needed to see him, just that it was urgent and that she needed to talk to him face to face. Rob sounded pleased to hear her voice at first – but grew suspicious when she wouldn't elaborate over the phone. He didn't like mystery, he liked facts. Now standing at his front door, she wondered if it was a good idea to be here.

Rob opened the door. "Helen, hi – come in." He wore a plain black T-shirt, pyjama bottoms and two-day-old stubble. He looked damn sexy. Out of the blue she thought of Jack Taylor, how she'd woken in his arms and wanted to make love to him.

"How have you been? I meant to call but I'm slammed at work. Please, come, sit down."

Rob moved the collection of Sunday papers out of the way to make space to sit. The fire crackled and mellow strains of jazz filled the room. A bottle of red wine sat decanting by the fireplace – beside it were two glasses.

"I'm sorry to interrupt your Sunday but there's something I need to tell you."

Helen had started to take her coat off when a woman walked through from the kitchen. Helen recognised her as Rob's one Facebook friend. She couldn't explain it but she felt a pang of jealousy when she saw another woman in Rob's home. She knew the feeling was ridiculous, but there it was just the same.

"You must be Helen, Rob's told me a lot about you. I'm Nadia." The girl swished forward in a flash of silky golden hair and white teeth to shake Helen's hand.

"Nice to meet you," Helen lied but smiled, as she wondered what Rob had said.

"May I get you something, Helen, some tea, a glass of wine maybe?" Nadia asked.

"No, thank you, I won't stay long. I just need a word with Rob." Helen wondered if they were living together. Nadia appeared very much at home. How long since she and Rob had slept together – about two months, wasn't it?

Nadia didn't show any sign of leaving the room.

"In private, Rob, please," Helen said, feeling like a bitch but not caring.

Rob had watched at the interaction between Helen and Nadia, bemused. Earlier he had even let his imagination run wild – Helen and Nadia, a blonde sandwich, with him as the filling. But now the atmosphere was anything but sexual.

Nadia looked at Rob for back-up, but got none. "Sure. No problem," she said in a clipped tone. She left the room and a moment or two later they heard the front door slam.

Rob had made no attempt to go after Nadia, who had a lot to learn about Rob Lawless. "Alright, Helen, I'm all ears." He poured two glasses of red wine and handed one to her, indicating that she should take a seat by the fire.

Helen stayed standing. She looked Rob in the eye and he held her gaze. She cherished the seconds, as she knew that in a moment their relationship, whatever it was, would never be the same again.

"We have a son, Rob. His name is Daniel and he's living here in Dublin."

That was it. Not so hard was it, Helen?

Rob didn't say anything at first, his forehead knitted in confusion.

"Excuse me?"

"The abortion your mother arranged for me, I didn't go through with it. I stayed in the UK and I had the baby – Daniel. I gave him

352

up for adoption. I know I should have told you, but you were so cruel at the time, so disinterested, and then when we got back together years later, I couldn't find the words."

Rob sat down, dazed, his eyes darted from left to right, as though he were searching for the right questions to ask.

Helen waited for his anger to emerge. It didn't come.

"Why are you telling me now, after all this time?" he asked, his face showing the strain of shock.

"Because he's here. I left my details with the adoption agency in case he wanted to look for me when he was older and he did – I met him today."

"I don't know what to say. My mother told me you had a termination. I'd no idea she was involved, let alone arranged it. You did say that?"

"Yes," she answered, shocked. "She did. You didn't know?"

"No," he whispered. He put down his wineglass as tears pricked his eyes – he pinched them between his forefinger and thumb, before resting his face in his hand. "It's one of those things blokes say, isn't it?"

"What?"

"Someone asks you – do you have any children? And you answer with a nudge and a chuckle – none that I know of."

"Well, now you do." Helen flushed, annoyed.

"Come on, Helen, you know what I mean. *This is amazing*."

Helen looked at him. She hadn't known what to expect but the possibility of joy hadn't occurred to her.

"When can I meet him? What's he like – does he look like you or me or both?"

His excitement grew and she couldn't help but smile with him.

Yes, it is fucking amazing!

Rob's phone beeped. He ignored it.

"He's very handsome actually and clever – he's studying business in DCU," she said with pride.

"That's what you started out doing, before you changed to lingerie – remember?" he reminded her.

"So it was – I haven't thought of that in years." Her face relaxed, deep in thought.

"My son, Daniel." He said the words, trying them on. "I should be angry with you, Helen, I should be asking all the practical questions but I don't want to. You've given me the best news of my life."

Rob let a tear escape and Helen saw, for the first time in years, the man she'd fallen in love with.

61

Jack Taylor sat at the end of his childhood bed. He had hung around Hanoi for a few days after Helen had left. Amy had arrived as she said she would. She looked really good. They talked and hung out a bit. She sounded as though she'd changed, she said all the right words anyway. But still, at night, he'd head back to his hotel alone, and ask if there were any messages. Quan would shake his head, looking at him with sad eyes. He felt confused, eventually deciding to cut his trip short and fly back to the East Coast of America, on the same flight as Amy. Spend some time with his family. Time with Amy? His three-month sabbatical was up. He had to make a decision.

Something bothered him – he couldn't quite put his finger on it, just an uneasy feeling that wouldn't go away. He stared at the small ring that Helen had left behind. For weeks now he'd twisted it around and around the top of his thumb as if it would give him a magic answer. What the question was, he didn't know.

One thing he did know though, the ring meant a lot to Helen, a link with her father, and he had to get it back to her.

Jack rang his old office, in Dubai. "Bill, it's Jack Taylor."

"Jack, my lad. How are you? Have you started in LA already?" Bill Redmond sounded surprised to hear from him.

"I'm good, Bill, thanks – actually I'm on the East Coast."

"Is everything all right, Jack?" Bill had already received a call

355

from the New York office, looking for a reference for Jack, so something was afoot.

Jack cut to the chase. "Bill, this is going to sound like an odd request and I know I technically don't work for you any more but I need some information."

"I see," Bill said, pausing.

"I don't have time to explain and I'm not sure you'd believe me anyway, but I need the cell number for Helen Devine, the Irishwoman who was purchasing in The Palm Development." He was hoping Bill wouldn't question him.

"You're not going rogue on me, are you, Jack? Going to a competitor or something? It's just I got a phone call a few days ago from the New York office asking for a reference for you – why would they want that if you're going to work in LA?"

Amy. I'll damn well kill her, Jack thought, as he realised his ex-girlfriend must be giving fate a helping hand by using her family connections to get him a job in New York.

"No, nothing like that, Bill. I wouldn't ask if it wasn't important – and personal."

"Okay then, Jack, but if I find out different, I'll come over there and strangle you myself."

"The Boston Strangler, suits you, Bill."

"Right, let me see," Bill tapped on his computer. "Helen Devine, yes, here it is. Oh."

"What?"

"I remember now, she pulled out of the sale. Her solicitor contacted us, said there was a family emergency. He was trying to get the deposit back. Bloody disappointing – can't shift any of them these days."

Family emergency – is that why she left so suddenly?

"She won't get a nickel of course – our legal team will probably try to force the sale."

"Her contact details, Bill?" Jack urged.

"You sure you're not working for the competition – you wouldn't be stealing a client from us now, would you, Jack?" Bill was still feeling uneasy. With the property market collapse, people were doing unscrupulous things to recoup some money.

"Bill, it's Jack you're talking to." He was frustrated at Boston Bill's suspicion.

"Alright, alright, keep your hair on. Robert Lawless Solicitors, it's a Dublin number – have you got a pen?"

"You don't have a cell number or home address for Helen?"

"Says here, all contact is to be made through her solicitor Robert Lawless and Company," he said. "Look, Jack, I've stuck my neck out giving you that much, especially when I don't know what the hell you want to know for."

Jack sighed. Bill was right but he was disappointed that after such a short time, his months of hard work and long hours, over and above the call of duty, counted for nothing. Not to mention the personal relationship he thought he and Bill shared.

"So, tell me the truth, are you considering staying on the East Coast, forgetting about the Californian sunshine?"

"No. I don't know who got the New York office to call you."

"Hmm." He still sounded sceptical. "Well, you've got the number you wanted. I hope she's worth it, Jack, whoever she is."

Jack scribbled down the solicitor's phone number and said his goodbyes to Bill. Then he started to dial the Dublin number but hung up.

"Eden design office – Sarah Ross speaking." The young woman's voice was melodic.

"Helen Devine, please." Jack took a deep breath to steady his voice – why was he shaking? *Because she'll think you're a freaking stalker, Jack, that's why.*

After Jack had got Eden's phone number from international directories, he'd paced his room, bracing himself to hear Helen's voice. He reasoned that he was doing her a favour, returning a family heirloom that she treasured.

"I'm sorry, Helen no longer works here, may I help you?" Sarah tripped off the message she'd said so often in the past week. *I'm the kingpin now, oh yeah, baby!* But she'd managed to keep that bit to herself – so far.

Jack felt deflated – he had his speech prepared. But he hadn't prepared for that.

Sarah was getting impatient. "Is there something I can help you with?"

"Sorry, I'm surprised, that's all." *Think, Jack, think.* "I'm an old friend, Jack Taylor. I lost my cell, with all my contacts. I meant to back up, but you know how it is." He tried to engage her. "Do you have a contact number for her?"

Jack Taylor, the name rang a bell but she couldn't quite place from where – although his voice sounded familiar too. Maybe he'd rung for Helen before.

"I couldn't possibly give out contact details." Sarah paused. "Even under the circumstances . . ." her voice trailed off.

"Circumstances?"

"You know – the accident?" She lowered her voice, even though she was alone in the office now Helen was gone. "I really shouldn't discuss it over the phone," she sniffed, leaving an opening. People loved hearing about the misery of others.

"I'm sorry, I haven't spoken to Helen in a few weeks, not since she was in Vietnam." Jack hoped that bit of information would loosen Sarah's tongue. He was right.

"Tragic. Poor Helen, on her first holiday in years – when she gets a call telling her that her only living relative is a vegetable, after a car crash." She paused for added effect.

She didn't need to – her words were powerful enough to knock the wind out of Jack.

"I'd no idea."

"Shocking. As you know, her father was murdered – I guess that makes her an orphan. Between you and me, I think she had a nervous breakdown because apparently she just rang up and quit – in this economy and after Eden had arranged for her to get back from Vietnam within hours. I mean, that's no way to thank them, is it?" She checked her manicure as she waited for a reaction.

"Very out of character for Helen. Wow, I don't know what to say. Sarah, was it?" Jack asked, his tone one of camaraderie.

"Yes, Sarah Ross, head designer." Sarah's cheeks flushed with pride, despite getting Helen's job in less than ideal circumstances.

"May I have her number? I need to call her immediately – under the circumstances, you understand."

"I don't have it, I'm afraid, I only had her company mobile number and that's been disconnected."

"Oh lord, what am I going to do now? I have her father's ring, you see . . . she left it behind in a hotel."

"Really, that beautiful vintage one? Oh my God, she never takes that off, she must be doubly devastated." Sarah was wide-eyed. Debbie in Accounts would love this. She had to get off the phone.

"I know. I'm in the US at the moment, I was hoping to Fed Ex it to her, but now . . ." Jack stopped short.

Sarah took the bait. "Actually, I do have her home address – I got it from personnel so I could send a condolence card." She looked at the card, which still remained on her desk, waiting for a stamp. She called the address out to Jack, adding, "Could you do something for me when you get in touch with Helen?"

"Sure."

"Will you tell her I'm sorry, I mean *really* sorry. She always looked out for me, she's a good person – she doesn't deserve any of this." She took a stamp from her drawer and stuck it on the overdue card.

"I will," Jack said, eager to get off the phone now. He felt sick at the news – he couldn't imagine how Helen must be feeling. His chest tightened at the thought of her pain. But he couldn't help but take some consolation in the fact that she hadn't deserted him lightly in Hanoi. There had been a genuine emergency.

He started pacing again. He could write a letter to Helen expressing his sympathy and include his phone number – that way she could contact him if she wanted to. If she didn't, he could put the whole thing behind him and be rid of this karma nonsense that he'd gotten into his head. Helen's mother's accident was all that mattered now. And what about Amy in all of this? Was she too late in coming back to him – or did he still have some feelings for her? He felt his head was bursting with questions as he sat to write the letter.

Dear Helen, Enclosed please find . . . *Too formal.*

Dear Helen, It's Jack from Hanoi here. *You sound like a Jack-off.*

Dear Helen . . .

Dear Helen . . .

Jack sat and looked at the blank piece of paper. An hour had passed and all he had written was '*Dear Helen*'.

There was nothing for it: he'd just have to tell her in person.

62

Fred Giltrap viewed his daily agenda. It was late in the day but he still had one more potential supplier to see. When the full extent of Helen's mother's injuries became apparent, he had told Helen to take as much time as she needed, Eden was managing fine without her. The truth was he'd worked around the clock, taking on as much of her role as possible with Sarah Ross getting a baptism of fire in the design room.

He put his elbows on the desk and rested his head in his hands. It was time he swallowed a bitter pill. Eden's London office would suffer with both himself and Helen gone.

On top of that, his wife June had thrown another spanner in the works when he announced his transfer to Hong Kong.

"I'll go with you! It'll be like starting over again – a new beginning!" she'd said.

"But what about the kids, the tennis club, your friends here?"

"Oh, Fred, the kids have grown up, they've moved on. I'm lonely in this old house without them – without you." Her face looked lost. She didn't mention the club or her mixed-doubles chum who Fred reckoned had done more than bounce his tennis balls with June over the years. But then she had brightened. "Do you remember when we were just a couple of kids starting our married life together? Everything felt like an adventure!"

Fred had nodded. "We couldn't afford heating so we'd go to bed with a bottle of Blue Nun and bonk for the evening to stay warm!"

How he'd laughed as he reminisced about their youth!

"You still make me laugh, Fred, you're my best friend. Thirty years of marriage and we're still standing. Maybe Hong Kong can be our new adventure, to help us find each other again now we don't have youngsters to tend to or a mortgage to pay . . ."

"Thirty years! Blimey, if I'd murdered someone they'd have let me out by now!" he'd joked but that night he'd made love to his wife and Helen Devine never so much as crossed his mind.

He picked up the phone and rang through to the design room.

"Sarah, come to my office please. I want you to sit in on a meeting – you have to start sometime – it might as well be now." He replaced the handset.

Fred sighed heavily. When Helen had rung to say she couldn't move to Hong Kong, that she wanted to give him the heads-up first before contacting the Board, he'd nearly blown a gasket. Then she'd even asked him if he could put in a good word for her, see if the Board would reinstate her London position. He shook his head as he thought of those damn come-to-bed eyes of hers – they'd always been his downfall. And herein lay his quandary. He'd thought he'd wanted Helen by his side in Hong Kong – give him another crack of the whip – but what now?

She had denied any spark between them all those months ago, when everything was different. She said it was just years of banter they'd shared, nothing more. The night in Hong Kong was just a drunken mistake. Deep down, he reckoned, she did fancy him, despite her words.

He straightened himself, perking up. He made his decision then and there. He'd ring Helen first thing in the morning to break the news.

There was a rap on his door.

"Come in!" he shouted.

"There's a man outside waiting to see you, Fred," Sarah said as she walked in.

"Ah, Sarah, sit down. Helen usually helps me with these things but let's see how you get on. As you know, we've space for only one new supplier. I liked that chap, David Strong, that Helen found in Vietnam. Have you received anything from him yet?"

"Yes, I gave him the sketches and measurement as you told me to. His counter samples arrived last week. They're nicely finished and the fits are spot on."

"Good, that's what I like to hear and the fact Helen already inspected his plant saved us time and money. Plus, I like this Ethical Sourcing Campaign idea that she's suggesting – what do you think?"

Sarah looked off into the distance. "It can't do any harm, I suppose. Perhaps it'll feel good knowing we're having a positive impact through our trading?"

"Huh," Fred rubbed his mouth, "right. We'll see what this next chap has to offer – the one waiting outside. He's slightly cheaper than David Strong, but we'll have to ask about his ethics stance before we make a final decision. Call him in, will you?"

She stood but paused before opening the door. "I like David Strong's company but I think it's time I was given the opportunity to decide who I want to work with."

"Slow down, young lady. Prove yourself first but remember you have very large shoes to fill."

Sarah's cheeks burned but she kept her expression passive. She was eager to stamp her own mark in the Eden design room and the sooner the better. Fred had asked for her advice and if this next guy was better than David Strong, well, then so be it. Helen wasn't here, she was. She opened the door.

The salesman walked in. He was short, stocky and wore a pinstripe suit with a flamboyant tie. He made a beeline for Fred, shaking his hand vigorously. He barely acknowledged Sarah. Making small talk about England's great rugby win at Twickenham the previous weekend, he hung his polyurethane garment bags on a wheelie rail.

As Sarah watched him, she felt she'd met him somewhere before. What was it about today? First, there was that American caller for Helen who had sounded familiar. Now this sales rep. It was giving her that weird déjà vu feeling. She opened her eyes wide and subtly shook her head as though dissipating dark spots after staring at a light bulb for too long.

"Our sales team are here in London, we're at your beck and call and within your time zone." The rep had started to talk shop. This appeared to please Fred. "The factories we use are in Guangzhou, China. We've an office in Hong Kong also. I go back and forth all the time so you are assured I'll catch any problems before they are shipped to you."

That's it – Hong Kong! Sarah realised. The sales guy was one of the men with the prostitutes in the bar! When Sarah had brought the conversation up with Helen later in the week she'd mentioned the short stocky one had threatened her in the ladies' loo.

Bastard.

She walked over to Fred and whispered in his ear. His expression darkened. The rep continued to talk with his back to them as he fixed his samples. When he turned around, he saw an arm-folded Sarah Ross and a stern-looking Fred Giltrap.

"Were you in Hong Kong, September just past?" Fred asked.

"That's right, I'm going back again next month," the man replied, then waited to see where Fred's question was leading.

"In Abbey Road, specifically, I saw you!" Sarah jumped in, unable to restrain herself.

The salesman's knitted his brow in confusion but a barely perceptible flicker of realisation showed on his face. He smirked. He'd seen the likes of these young pretty ones before, thought they were God's gift to mankind. Give them an education and they even start to think they're as good as men. *Put her back on her leash for fuck sake, man!*

Fred touched Sarah's arm lightly. "Would you excuse us, please, Sarah?"

"But . . . I . . ." Sarah exhaled heavily, grabbed up her notebook and shot the salesman one final filthy look before turning on her heel to walk out.

He smirked at her as he rocked back and forth on his feet, his hand clasped just under his belly as though in line to receive Communion.

"I'll handle it," Fred muttered to her as she walked past him.

She paused briefly and looked at him. He winked at her and nodded towards the door. Fred had high standing in the trade and it looked as though this sales guy was going to find out all about it. Still, she closed the door loudly behind her as she made a mental note to give David Strong and his team a big helping hand to work successfully with Eden.

"Now where were we?" the salesman asked, looking as though he'd just swatted a buzzing fly.

"Abbey Road," Fred said. A stale silence hung in the air. "I believe it was you who met Eden's design director there in the ladies' bathroom of all places."

"Huh, is that who she was?" He tried to laugh it off but his breath had became shallow.

"Ah, so it *was* you."

"Honestly, Mr Giltrap, I do apologise but she was nagging at me, you know how women can be. I thought she was just another stuck-up cow. I was well tanked up I can't be held accountable – I barely even remember the night." He held his hands up. "It's not like it happened here in London."

"Sometimes though, old chap, our actions have a nasty tendency to follow us home."

He stepped forward.

This one's for you, Helen!

And he punched the salesman's lights out.

Sarah, who had remained with her ear to the other side of the door, punched the air in victory when she heard the clout. *Good old Fred, I didn't think he had the balls!* She ran as quickly as her six-inch heels could carry her to the Accounts office, with any luck Debbie wouldn't have left yet and just wait until she heard this!

Who'd have guessed being a lingerie designer could be so much fun?

63

"Rob you're early!" Helen said as Rob walked past her into her kitchen, leaving her standing at the open hall door. She swept her arm and said, "Please come in," to the empty hallway.

"I know – I waited as long as I could but it was killing me. Have you anything to eat?" he called from the kitchen, as he opened the fridge.

"Help yourself," Helen replied as she followed him in. Rob already had a large chunk of ham in his mouth. "I'm just on my way to pick up Daniel now – do you want to come?"

"No! Best if we stick to the original plan. I'll wait and you bring Danny here." He rubbed his hands together.

"'Danny', is it?"

"Yes, it seemed natural – after talking to him for a while. Christ, I'm so nervous about meeting him – what if he doesn't like me?" He scratched his freshly shaven chin.

"Of course he'll like you – anyway, didn't you speak to him on the phone and you got on grand. Stop fretting." Helen brushed crumbs off his shirt. "I won't be long – make yourself at home, why don't you?"

"Sure, thanks." He opened the fridge again, missing the humour in her tone.

Helen closed the door behind her, leaving Rob in a deadly silent house.

What now?

Usually, given an opportunity like this, he would have a rummage through the office drawers, or Helen's bedroom. He always liked going through her top shelf – there was usually something new in her treasure chest of goodies. He made to go upstairs, but stopped. It didn't seem right.

He flipped open the iBook Helen kept in the kitchen.

"Blast, she's gone and got it password-protected!" he said out loud.

JD observed Rob from his bed.

"Don't look at me like that, JD!"

The dog continued to stare at him.

"Okay, you're right – I'll stop with the password-guessing." But he still pressed enter on Helen's birth date, which he had already input. The screen shook to indicate he was wrong. He got down to the dog's level and patted his head. "I don't know, JD, this whole being-a-father thing, it has me thinking differently. I hope I'm not growing a conscience or anything."

JD licked Rob's hand.

"Less of the dog-breath, boy." Rob pulled his hand away. He brushed down his trousers when he saw dog-hair on them. "Why Helen keeps you inside, I'll never know. It's disgusting having a dog in the kitchen." He went to the sink and washed his hands with an extra pump of anti-bacterial soap.

Unable to get up to his usual tricks, due to his new-found ethical code and the watchful eye of the Golden Retriever, Rob turned on the TV and Saturday-afternoon football filled the room. Unable to sit still, he went back into the kitchen to make a sandwich. The doorbell chimed just as he was about to take the first bite. He looked down at his plate and considered whether he should answer the door or eat.

Then he opened the door, sandwich on plate in hand, to let whoever was there know they had disturbed him.

"Hello."

Great, a bloody Mormon.

"Sorry, son, we're not buying religion today, thank you." Rob closed the door, with his foot.

The bell rang again.

"Man of God or not, I'll bloody well give him an earful!" He swung the door open.

"I'm looking for Helen – Helen Devine," Jack Taylor said quickly, before the door slammed shut again.

Rob's eyes narrowed with suspicion. How did the clean-cut American know Helen's name?

"Who's asking, have you got ID?" Tanned skin, cropped blond hair, but no suit – didn't the Mormons always wear suits?

"I'm a friend, Jack Taylor." Jack thrust his hand forward, smiling – it wasn't exactly the Irish welcome he'd played out in his head.

Rob ignored the hand. "I see. She's not here at the moment, she's gone to collect our son. Can I take a message?" *Not a lie,* he justified.

Jack's smile faded. He looked confused. "Helen Devine? The lingerie designer at Eden, mother was in a car accident recently?" *There must be some mistake.*

"Yes, trust me, there's only one Helen Devine." Rob was playing with the American. He couldn't tell what made a man handsome but he was fairly sure this man had it, whatever it was.

The confusion on Jack's face was evident. Had the man really said "our son" or had Jack misunderstood his accent? Why didn't Helen mention she had a son?

"I don't think you mentioned how you know Helen?" Rob asked.

"A group of us met up in Vietnam, same boat on Halong Bay, that's all. I met Poppy as well," Jack said, playing down the connection he had with Helen – or thought he'd had.

Rob's eyes narrowed. He wanted shot of the American but he also wanted more information. Still, if he played it right, he could get both. "Why don't you come in? It's a god-awful day and you don't look like you're used to Irish weather – not if the tan is real, that is!" He laughed but he was fishing.

Jack was too shocked to notice.

"I'm Rob Lawless." He put the plate down and finally offered his handshake, now that it was on his terms.

"Helen's lawyer?"

"Yes, I'm that too." Rob smiled, tightly. *Technically, not a lie.*

Blood rushed to Jack's face. *I'm a total Jack-ass.*

"I'm sorry – I won't disturb you any further. I wanted to make sure Helen got this safely." He fished in his pocket and handed Rob a small square box containing Helen's treasured ring. "I believe her father gave it to her, I mean left it to her, when she was a girl."

Rob stared at the delicate gold ring. Helen had said she'd lost it, no idea where. She'd been devastated but had put on a brave face saying it was just a possession. In light of everything that had happened, did it really matter? But her pain had been evident.

"Anyhow, I found this after Helen had left. I was routed through Dublin, so I figured I'd drop it off in person, in case the carrier lost it. Obviously it was of great sentimental value to her." Jack shrugged.

"I see. Where are you en route to?" Rob wasn't satisfied but he couldn't outright ask the American if he'd slept with Helen.

"New York. My girlfriend lives there. Actually that's where I'm from too, New York State, Nyack. Yes, so I'm used to the cold, you see." Jack smiled. *Shut up gabbling!* He just wanted to get away now so he could crawl under a rock and die of embarrassment. Hopefully Helen would buy the story, not know he'd come all the way from the States on a whim, following his destiny, karma, synchrodestiny – is that what she'd called it? *Horseshit, more like.*

Rob relaxed slightly when he heard mention of a girlfriend.

"Jack, that's mighty decent of you, especially since you don't even really know Helen." He looked the other man in the eye, as he would when cross-questioning the opposing team in a courtroom.

"As I said, I was passing through . . ." Jack made a silly aeroplane motion with his hand. "No big deal, better than sitting at the airport for hours in a transfer lounge." He looked at his watch for added effect. "Which reminds me, I'd better be making tracks. Amy won't be too pleased if I miss my flight." He cocked his thumb, conscious he looked as though he was hitching a ride.

JD decided to investigate the voices in the hallway. He sniffed at Jack's shoes.

"Hey there, boy, what's your name? I've got a guy just like you back home." Jack rubbed the dog affectionately behind his ears. JD licked Jack's face.

"His name is Jack Daniels – I'm sorry, didn't you say your name was Jack too? Common name, I guess." Rob got his dig in.

Asshole.

"Good choice, great name for a great dog," Jack replied, not liking Helen's husband, or partner, very much.

"It's Helen's dog," Rob corrected him. He tensed when he realised the slip-up he'd made.

JD looked up with his dark, dewy eyes and wagged his tail.

"I can see that," Jack said, giving the dog a final rub.

A picture of Helen caught his eye, silver-framed. She looked younger but not that different. She had her arms around a blonde puppy – she was laughing, her face full of joy. *That's why you came to Dublin, Jack. What man wouldn't?* He noticed there were no photos of a child, or this man Rob Lawless, for that matter.

Rob was getting antsy. Helen would be back soon. The American had to go.

"We thank you again, Jack – Helen and I – for bringing back the ring. I'm sure Helen would have liked to thank you in person." Rob opened the door. But he hadn't covered all the bases, yet. "Does she have your details – an email or mobile number so she can contact you?"

"No, I'll leave my card. The details are out of date – I'm moving office but I'll write my personal email and cell number on the back so she can get in touch, if she'd like to. I'm really sorry about her mother . . . I . . . well . . ." Jack bent down on the hall table to write, his line of vision directly on the picture of Helen. *Why didn't you tell me you had a partner and son, Helen?*

"Great," Rob said tightly, taking the card from Jack, then putting it and the ring in his pocket. "Well, goodbye, Jack, nice meeting you." *Now that definitely was a lie.* "And sorry about the whole Mormon thing, didn't occur to me you'd be a friend of Helen's – Daniel's maybe but not Helen's."

Jack walked away from Helen's house. How had he misread the

situation so badly? This power-of-coincidence bullshit had him convinced there was more to it. He'd really started to believe. The whole thing was probably nothing special, just something he'd got into his head because he wanted to believe he could have more in his life – real love. He smiled to himself. Good old reliable Jack. Solid as a rock, would never do something as stupid as jump on a plane and cross the Atlantic to surprise a woman he'd only actually spent two nights with – they hadn't even made love.

He replayed the conversation he'd had with his mother when he'd said he was going to Dublin.

"Don't be a fool, Jack! You lost Amy once and now you want to throw her away again for some holiday romance!"

"Amy left me, Mom, remember? And I'm not back in a relationship with her. And this isn't a holiday romance – it's different. It's karma!"

"Did they put something in your water in Dubai? You don't sound like my educated, intelligent son!" she'd fumed.

"No, Mom, I've just woken up. I'm seeing the world for the first time without fear, following my heart instead of my head," he'd chirped.

"It'll all end in tears, mark my words, Jack."

As usual, Mom was right.

Jack Taylor's spontaneous side would go back in the box where it belonged. He pulled the collar of his jacket up around his ears and plunged his hands deep into his pockets. Damn, it was cold here. He'd noticed fishing boats and a harbour from the taxi earlier. He decided a blast of fresh air was exactly what he needed – wipe out his thoughts of Helen. He put his head down and walked quickly towards the sea. That feeling was back though, the one where something just wasn't right.

Christ stop it, Jack, look where that got you before – following your gut – freezing your balls off on a grey, Dublin day.

64

"Here's the rain." Helen flicked on the car's wiper blades, as she turned the corner for home.

A man caught her attention – and her breath.

"Jack . . ."

"Sorry?" Daniel asked.

Helen watched the figure of a man walk hurriedly in the direction of the pier. His face covered, protecting himself from the wind.

She smiled. "Nothing, I just remembered someone I used to know. Something about that man reminded me of him."

"What man?" Daniel looked around.

The man was out of sight.

"Never mind, it can't have been him, just the same gait is all. Different life, different dimension. Now, more importantly, present time, present moment – are you ready to meet your father?"

Rob looked at the card Jack had given him. Plain, good quality, white card: *Jack Taylor – Architect.*

He'd seemed like a pleasant fellow, but surely not Helen's type? Rob had always felt sure of Helen's feelings for him. Helen was like his comfort blanket in a way. Always there for him, yet independent, too bloody independent. And headstrong, Helen was too headstrong as well. She was like him in that way – maybe that's why they didn't make it in the past. Neither would admit to making a mistake.

He heard her key in the door and quickly crumpled up Jack's card and threw it in the bin, along with his uneaten lunch.

The first meeting of Rob and Daniel was a success. The boy was mature for his age and Rob actually managed to drop his airs and graces and be himself. Helen watched as father and son talked about rugby and computer war games.

"I like Wii Fit Yoga, myself, now that I can't get to my yoga class in London," Helen said, leaving out the barring bit.

If she had expected deep, meaningful conversation, she'd have been disappointed. She wished Mary was here with them and her heart gave the by now familiar tug of grief.

Helen wasn't the only one observing the scene. Although he was enjoying every moment of meeting Daniel, Rob couldn't help taking sneaky peeks at Helen – she was radiant. That American showing up with his all-white teeth and blond hair had been a wake-up call. Even if he'd been telling the truth about passing through Dublin, which Rob didn't believe, he still cared enough about Helen to go out of his way to do something for her. In the few days he'd known her, he knew the significance of the ring. Would Rob have thought about that? Would he do something like that for Helen? Probably not – and yet another man had. He'd seen something in Helen and Rob had nearly lost her to him. Nearly.

Timing had been on his side, this time.

Helen laughed at something Daniel said. Then she looked at Rob, a look that lingered a fraction of a second. Rob smiled back.

One thing he'd told that Jack Taylor was true: there was only one Helen Devine.

"That went well, don't you think?" Helen came into the living room where Rob was still sitting.

"It was fantastic – he's a great kid." Rob stretched back, interlacing his fingers behind his head. "Are you sure we shouldn't have dropped him into town though?"

"He's meeting his new college mates, Rob, what do you think?" She threw her eyes to heaven. "Surely you remember what it was like at Daniel's age?"

"True. Time for a celebration – it just so happens I've a bottle of Bollinger in the boot of my car," he said, with a glint in his eye.

"Really? Who drives around with champagne in the boot?"

"Solicitors with happy clients – besides, this is a double celebration." He disappeared before Helen could question him.

She was nervous – Rob and champagne usually equalled no knickers.

"Here we are – it's so bloody cold out, it's already chilled." He went to the kitchen, returning with champagne flutes. He handed her a glass – her father's ring wrapped on the top of his finger. She spotted it immediately.

Her hand flew to her mouth, "Oh my God, I don't believe it! How on earth? Where . . .?" Emotion caught in her throat.

"At the back of the toaster, stuck behind a coffee pot, noodle-head!" He brushed her chin with affection.

"I could have sworn the last time I had it was in Vietnam." She placed the tiny ring on her little finger, where it belonged.

"You've been through so much in the past few weeks, darling, is it any wonder you got confused?" He put a protective arm around her.

The scent of his cologne and the feel of his chest felt so familiar, she stayed there, in his arms, feeling relaxed for the first time in weeks.

"It's Saturday night, aren't you meeting your girlfriend?"

"She's not my girlfriend. Anyway, I'm not seeing her any more." Rob tightened his hold on Helen, her head on his chest listening to his heart-beat.

"Does she know that?"

Rob ignored the comment. "Is it me or do our bodies fit?" He rested his head on top of hers.

She closed her eyes and inhaled his skin – she knew exactly what he meant.

Jack checked his cell phone for the umpteenth time – it remained painfully silent. Outside his hotel window, Dublin city was gearing up for a Saturday night, laughter and music filling the air. He looked at his phone again.

Nothing.

Suddenly it shrilled, causing Jack to jump. Private number. "Hello?"

"Jack, it's Amy."

"Oh, hi."

"Contain your excitement, will you?"

"Sorry, Amy, jetlag, you know what it's like." Jack sighed heavily.

"So, did you see her?"

"No," Jack said, barely audible.

"Have you still got that blasted ring, Jack?"

"No, I left it with her husband – long-time partner, I don't know."

"Interesting."

Jack could hear the smile in Amy's voice.

More brightly, she said, "Jack, I forgive you – come home, baby – we can put this whole mess behind us."

"When did I get to be the bad guy? I don't need your forgiveness, Amy – you left me – remember?" What was it with the women in his life – were they all living in a parallel universe or maybe Andromeda as his Uncle Tom would say?

"I've apologised, like, a thousand times," she said, managing not to add – *get over it already*. Instead, she said, "When will you be home?"

"I got the last seat on the morning flight, but, Amy, I'll be honest with you: I'm taking the job in LA."

"Don't leave me, Jack! I can't lose you again!" There was panic in Amy's voice.

"Why did you throw it all away then?" Jack knew he shouldn't start this conversation, but since Amy's infidelity he'd gone over and over how he'd missed the signals. Was he a crap lover? Boring? He thought he gave her everything.

What if his best wasn't good enough for any woman?

375

"I made a stupid mistake," Amy sobbed. "We were together so long, I don't know, I guess I took you for granted – the grass was greener on the other side. I am so sorry, Jack."

And for the first time, Amy sounded like she meant it.

65

Rob kissed Helen's head and slowly moved to nibble her ear.

"Stop, you know what that does to me," she giggled.

"Exactly," Rob droned, in his Barry White voice. This made Helen laugh more.

"You're the first, the last, my everything," he continued his mime, as he playfully bit her neck and gyrated his hips.

Helen laughed and made a weak attempt to break free.

He moved his lips to meet hers. Expertly he unclasped her bra with one hand.

The sudden release of her breasts brought her back to reality. "Rob, I'm not going back there." She pulled away.

"Come on, you said it yourself, it feels right." He rubbed his groin, mimicking a seventies' porn-star.

There was no doubt, Rob was a funny guy.

"You really fancy yourself, don't you?" Helen straightened up as she looked at him.

"I fancy you – naked." He pulled her back down, moving on to his Austin Powers impersonation.

"Rob, be serious. The only part of this that works is sex, and that's not enough for me any more. We've been through all of this. There's no point rehashing it." She tried to close her bra.

"It's different now though, we've got a son."

To her amazement, he closed the bra for her.

"Just hear me out, Helen. I'm a changed man. You're right, I'm a jerk but you were never really the commitment type yourself."

It was true, and the reason why their non-relationship relationship had suited them both.

Rob persisted. "I don't know if it was turning forty –"

"That was years ago!"

"Not that long ago and you'll see what it's like yourself before you know it!" He paused. "And Daniel turning up like this, Helen: he's *our* son."

"Rob, Daniel's a young man with two parents in England that he already calls Mum and Dad."

"I know, but we did something right, didn't we?" he said, with a vulnerability she hadn't seen often.

She resisted the urge to clear the rose-tinted glasses he was wearing, by reminding him he'd walked away and gone to Vegas.

Rob let out a heavy sigh. "I know it's too late to play happy families and buy him a train-set, but it's not too late for you and me. And Daniel, well, if he continues wanting to get to know us, I don't know . . ."

"What are you trying to say, Rob?"

"On the level? The thoughts of being a parent always filled me with horror. Now that it's happened, albeit late, being someone's dad has given me a new perspective. It's what life's about, isn't it – relationships? You can have a new-reg car, the most successful company, but without someone special to share it with – what does it mean? Nothing, Helen." He took her hand and looked into her eyes.

"Sounds like you have grown up, Rob," she said softly.

"You're my some-day girl, Helen, you always have been – it just took Daniel showing up to make me realise that," he said with honesty. Although it was Jack showing up that made him realise that *some day* was today.

"Some-day girl?" she eventually asked.

"The girl you want to grow old with," he smiled. "As the saying goes, I'm HD ready!" He tickled her, chuckling at their private joke.

Helen tried to defend herself. "Helen Devine ready – but I don't know if I am."

Rob detected doubt in her voice, an opening, at last. "You don't have to make a decision right now. I tell you what, come round to my place tomorrow – I'll cook dinner for you, something from that Gordon Ramsay fellow you fancy. No sex, just dinner." He nodded, subtly getting her to agree.

Helen wasn't sure what dinner would resolve, but she agreed – these days she found it hard being alone.

With renewed energy, Rob said, "We'll start over, start dating. We'll go to movies and IKEA, do what normal couples do."

"Can't wait."

"Can I stay tonight?" He gave her puppy-dog eyes.

"What happened to starting over!"

"No sex, honestly, it's just I'm probably over the limit and I don't want to lose my licence." He cocked his head.

"Rob, you're made of Teflon, nothing sticks."

"So, I can stay then?" He snuggled into her.

"No sex?"

"Wouldn't dream of it!" He raised both hands up in surrender.

Helen nodded and hoped her own resolve wouldn't dissolve.

"A blowjob doesn't count as sex, does it?"

"Rob!" Helen hit him with a cushion and they started to laugh. Then there was silence, both of them lost in thought.

"They sell Daim Bars in IKEA. I've fancied one for days now. And I *don't* fancy Gordon Ramsay – I just admire his talent, is all." She yawned.

Now they knew they were both lying.

66

Helen woke early. Rob was snoring gently beside her. They were both fully clothed. He'd been true to his word despite the fact she'd felt his arousal through the covers several times during the night. He let her know he was available, yet honoured her wishes. A new Rob.

She crept out of the bed and went down to make coffee.

JD lay in his basket and didn't get up to greet her – instead, she got a steady stare.

"Mary will never be dead as long as you're around, JD." She gave him a rub. The dog continued to stare. "Stop looking at me like that – nothing happened. I sound like Poppy now, hey? Poppy – she'll have a field day on me when she hears that I'm starting to 'date' Rob again."

JD said nothing – but that's what dogs do.

She thought of Jack and wondered what he might be doing now. She felt guilty, but often when sitting with Mary her mind wandered to him. Once she'd even decided to contact him through his old Dubai office but the nurse had called her back into the ward and after that Sarah had called with another design-room crisis. By the time she rang it was after hours in Dubai – the office closed for the weekend. She thought it was probably for the best. It obviously wasn't meant to be.

Deciding to make the coffee strong, she opened the bin to dump the old grinds.

"Rob just doesn't get the whole recycling thing, does he, JD?" she said as she lifted Rob's old sandwich out of the paper section and threw it into the brown composting bin.

That's when she saw it, a discarded business card, crumpled, covered in mayonnaise but with the unmistakable words: *Jack Taylor – Architect*.

"Oh my God, I was just thinking about him, JD!" She pulled the card out of the bin. She was shaking.

JD perked his head up as if to say *"I told you so"*.

"Where did you get this?" Helen threw the soiled card on top of a sleeping Rob.

"What?" Rob struggled to focus.

"No more games, Rob. This business card, what was it doing in my bin, tell me?" she demanded.

But then it dawned on her: she could have put it there herself. She'd gone through her papers for the Dubai deal – clearing out the house, getting ready for her move to Hong Kong. Did Jack attach his business card when his office sent through the contracts? Could it have detached itself as she threw the papers in the recycle section of the bin, to end up in the rubbish section? She rubbed her forehead. It could easily happen. The right thing ends up in wrong place all the time. And not just with compartment bins.

Rob tried to get his brain in gear: climb out of this one.

"You didn't put it there, did you? I'm sorry – I'm an emotional fuck-up at the moment. I jumped to a silly conclusion." Helen sat, continuing to rub her brow.

"That's okay," he stammered, unsure how he'd got away with it. "It's okay, Hells – you're under a lot of stress – how about we start again? Good morning!" He pursed his lips for a platonic kiss.

"Good morning, Robert – how about some coffee?"

"Airport please." Jack climbed into the back of a taxi. It was raining heavily, the sky dark. Forty-eight hours in Ireland and it had rained solid for every one of them.

His first visit to the Emerald Isle and his last – at least now he knew why it was so green, so not a total waste of time.

"Are ya comin' or goin'?" the taxi-driver shouted back at him.

"Excuse me?"

"Are ya on holliers, goin' on holliers or goin' home?" the cabbie said, as he looked at Jack via the rear-view mirror.

"I see." Jack thought for a moment. Am I coming or going? Good question.

"I'm going. I'm going home, sir."

67

Rob was cooking breakfast as Helen sipped on her coffee.

"I think I'll give Jack a call," she said. "It's so weird his card just turning up in the bin like that."

"You can't," Rob said, a little too quickly.

"Why not?"

"Because of the time difference for a start – it's five in the morning in New York."

"How do you know he's from New York?"

Rob returned his attention to the eggs, unable to make eye contact. "What's this man to you anyway, Helen? Did you sleep with him or something?" He deployed his lawyer deflection tactic of answering a question with a question.

Now it was Helen who felt defensive. "No! Well, technically yes, but nothing happened." *But something had happened, it just wasn't sex.* Try explaining that one to Rob. "It's hard to explain – there were all these synchronicities – you know, coincidences. As if the world was just a village – our paths kept crossing."

"There's a word for people like that – stalker. Sunny-side or over?" He waited to flip the eggs.

"Over."

"It's better to put all that nonsense behind you, Helen. It's you and me now, kiddo." He darted from the grill, to the hob, to the fridge: a headless chicken.

"Why are you acting so weird and what's with the 'kiddo'?" she asked, her eyes burning through his back.

Rob laughed – his nervous reaction when he felt cornered. "Stop being silly and eat your eggs." He put the plate in front of her before setting down his own. He sat opposite her at the table but didn't look up, busying himself with eating instead.

"I don't care, I'm calling." Helen picked up the phone.

Calling Rob's bluff.

"Wait." Rob sighed as he put down his knife and fork. Helen would find out sooner or later, so he might as well admit it – shorten his time in the doghouse.

"He was here."

"When?" She pushed her chair back.

"Yesterday. He was passing through Dublin, on the way to New York, to meet his girlfriend." Rob finally looked Helen in the eye. Time for damage limitation. "He was the one who found your father's ring – he wanted to return it to you."

Helen covered her face with her hands, unable to speak.

"He's here in Dublin, so much for time difference," she said at last, looking at Rob with a new-found coldness.

"No. He's left already, Helen. Will you just sit down and let me explain before you go flying off the handle. There's more to this Jack fellow than meets the eye – too many coincidences – it's not possible in reality. I'm telling you, Helen, he's not to be trusted – he has some weird agenda."

Helen wasn't listening. Jack picked up on the third ring. She left the kitchen so Rob couldn't hear the muffled conversation. He followed her out to the hallway where she was pulling on a pair of walking wellies and a large overcoat.

"Helen, where are you going? You can't go out in your pyjamas!" he called after her, as she grabbed her car keys off the table.

Jack had agreed to meet her in a departure-area coffee shop. He didn't have long but he'd wait until his flight was called. Walking through the crowds, Helen wished she'd taken a few minutes to get dressed. She pulled the overcoat tightly around her, hoping no one would spot her PJs. As she went up the escalator, her heart pounded. There were so many people milling around, she wasn't sure she'd spot him.

Jack watched everyone as they stepped off the moving stairway, his hands wrapped tightly around a warm mug of coffee. A group of women chatted and laughed – behind them was a younger couple, arm in arm.

Then he saw her.

Just the top of her head at first, then slowly she appeared. She scanned the area, wide-eyed, looking like a lost child – or an orphan maybe.

He wanted to hold her, tell her everything would be okay. But that was the Helen he'd known in Hanoi. She had her husband or partner here.

Helen spotted Jack easily. Apart from his tanned complexion in a sea of pasty faces, he had a presence that she had a homing device for.

He waved – she waved back.

"Jack!" She rushed to give him a hug but knocked his coffee over in doing so. "I'm so sorry." She was flustered.

"That's okay, don't worry about it." He wiped the table with paper napkins. "Can I get you anything, Helen?"

He sounded stiff. Formal even.

"No, I'm fine thanks. Jack, so how are you?" She sat down.

"All good, thanks. I was sorry to hear about your mother, Helen." His face was unreadable.

"Thanks." Helen twisted the ring, now back on her little finger where it belonged. Jack's face softened. "I can't thank you enough for returning my ring – you've no idea how much I appreciate it – thank you."

"No problem." He nodded.

There was an awkward silence. This wasn't how they imagined it would be.

Jack wanted to ask why she hadn't mentioned a son or a husband. But what they had in Vietnam didn't appear to have followed them to Dublin.

Instead, he said, "I haven't got long, maybe ten minutes, max."

"Right." Helen noticed an odd look from a passer-by and pulled her coat around her to cover her nightwear. "Thought I'd do a bit of market research while I'm at the airport – see what people thought of the new Eden sleepwear range."

Jack smiled. "And here was I thinking it was a Dublin fashion statement."

"It is – for some!"

They laughed, warmth returned – a glimpse of the people they had known.

"I hope my showing up didn't cause any problems." Jack rubbed an imaginary smudge off his coffee-cup.

"No, why would you think that? Not at all. How come you're going home? I thought you were staying in Asia?"

"Amy showed up."

"Amy, as in, love-of-your-life Amy?"

"Yes." Jack didn't correct her – there was no point.

"Jack, that's fabulous news," Helen said with exaggerated enthusiasm. She swallowed hard. She wouldn't have thought it was possible, but her heart broke just a little bit more.

"I'd better get going – I've still to clear security." Jack picked up his carry-on luggage.

"Sure, I'll walk with you to the gate."

He wondered would he give her a hug, kiss her on the cheek, or shake her hand? Their short meeting had been stilted and strange.

"Well, here we are." He tapped his boarding-pass rapidly against his hand. A friendship-type hug, he decided.

"What do you think it meant, Jack? All the coincidences between us?" she suddenly asked. Now or never.

"I don't know, Helen." He was confused.

"Vietnam, it feels like a lifetime ago now, so much has happened," she said as she looked down at the floor.

Jack watched her. She had no make-up on – she was wearing some kind of flowery, pink rubber boots and a pyjama collar stuck out from under her coat. He thought she looked as beautiful as the first time he saw her.

"I don't know. Maybe, in a different life, who knows what might have been, Helen?"

A kiss, definitely a kiss.

The JFK flight announcement drowned out further conversation. People, harried with travel stress, weaved around them.

"Goodbye, Jack," Helen said, her words inaudible.

"Goodbye, Helen."

He leant down, kissing her softly on the mouth, before he disappeared through the crowds. This time, forever.

68

"What do you mean you said goodbye?" Poppy gasped.

Helen sat in Poppy's kitchen, telling her the saga of the last forty-eight hours.

"That's it – what else is there to say? He lives in America, the love of his life back in his arms, and I'm, well, here, single, unemployed and nearly forty. Why are we drinking tea anyway? Why can't I drown my sorrows in a pub like normal people?" she said flippantly, though she felt anything but.

"I don't buy it. It's the most romantic story – you've got to go after him."

Helen rolled her eyes. "And say what exactly? I'm telling you, Poppy, it was different. Whatever we had, or thought we had, in Vietnam, was gone. Have you at least got some chocolate biscuits?" She stood and went over to Poppy's goodie cupboard.

"No, you're getting a fat ass with all this sitting around, moping, and feeling sorry for yourself."

"Remind me never to go to you for counselling," Helen said to her over her shoulder as she continued to root for carbohydrates and sugar.

"Let me get this straight. Rob, who you've been shagging for years, behind my back . . ." She paused for added effect, "suddenly wants to play happy families. Jack comes all the way to Dublin, to personally deliver a ring, meets Rob, and then gets on a plane back to his ex-girlfriend." Poppy sat back and folded her arms.

Helen found a jar of peanut butter and decided that would have to do. "That's it, more or less."

"I don't know, Helen, it doesn't make any sense. I need to think. I'll get to the deception about Rob later, because I can't believe you hid that from me!"

"You'd have called me a goon!"

"Which you are!"

"The sex is good – was good. There's only so much an Ann Summer's toy can do. Oh, hi Lily, I didn't hear you come in." Helen shoved a knifeful of peanut butter into her mouth.

"I'm going to pretend I didn't hear that. Honestly, when are you two going to grow up!" Lily left the kitchen as quickly as she could.

"Sorry," Helen mouthed to Poppy.

"She's right, you know. I've started to take stock, look at my life and really decide what I want."

"Sounds ominous – I'll be doing the same, tomorrow."

"Ringing Eden back?"

"Yep, see what my options are. Fred was so furious when I told him I wasn't going to Hong Kong." Helen made a face as she remembered the conversation. "Then out of the blue he rings me at eight o'clock in the morning, says I'm right, family comes first and I should stay on in London. And they say women are moody!" She shook her head. "He hadn't wasted any time either. He said he'd sounded out Sarah Ross about going to Hong Kong in my place and that she'd jumped at the chance. She'll do well there."

"That one! I thought you said she was about as genuine as a Canal Street Chloe handbag!"

"I was annoyed with her at the time. She kept ringing about work while I was at the hospital. She's okay behind it all, just a little immature. Maybe I can stay on in London, while the company makes its transition. Even if it's only for a while – it'll buy me time. There might even be a consultancy option – that way I could even work from Dublin." She leant against the counter.

"It's not really what you want any more though – is it?" Poppy said softly.

"No, but it's a good job and I don't know what else I could do. I'm the Lingerie Woman."

"Start something up with me!" Poppy clapped her hands.

"What? A lingerie designer and a masseuse – anything we start would hardly be legal."

"Devine Power Incorporated, I like it! We'll leave it up to the Universe to sort out the details. Let's put the intention out there and see what manifests." Poppy's eyes sparkled with possibilities.

"No more!" Helen put her hands up. "I'm going back to reality – try to pick my life back up. I really had started to think there was such a thing as karma, dharma or whatever you call it."

"Where are you going?" Poppy asked as Helen started to leave.

"To see Rob – don't look at me like that." Helen pulled on a pair of long leather gloves – she sniffed the air. "I meant to ask you earlier, what's that smell, have you actually got a Sunday roast on?"

"Yes, I've started to make some changes in my life, a new healthier way of living."

"You're not running off to join the Hare Krishnas, are you?" Helen took the gloves off and sat down. "You can forget about eating roast beef if you are, you know." Helen looked at her as though talking to a naughty child. "And me just after tempting you back on the bacon butties too."

"No. It's all about balance, that's all." Poppy smiled. "I'd got so caught up in the theory of life I forgot to actually live it. You know me, I was always signing up for one weekend workshop or another – Heal your Life, Learning to Love Again, the list went on and on. Problem was it was me who couldn't accept me, not anyone else. I felt like a fraud."

Helen knew what she meant but had thought Poppy's addiction to all things alternative was what made her happy, so she'd let her at it. Now she saw it was Poppy's *thing*, just as work and status was Helen's *thing*. They'd labelled it differently but the underlying problem was the same: low self-esteem.

"I could help my clients, I was great at sorting them out but I forgot to walk my own talk." Rather than looking bashful, Poppy had an air of calm about her. "I know what works well in my life is meditation but somehow I let it go. I don't know why because it gave me balance, made life flow more easily – in synchronicity." Poppy pushed her hair behind her ears. "I keep searching for happiness outside of myself whereas I was really avoiding looking at the hollow feeling inside. I can go to all the workshops, read all the books, but until I'm ready to take the first step and make a commitment, it remains just theory."

"So you're committed?"

Poppy nodded vigorously.

"To which asylum?" Helen said.

Poppy playfully swiped her.

"I'm sorry, Pops, I couldn't help myself." She looked at Poppy and her eyes blinked softly. "You'll do great, Poppy. You're a strong, beautiful woman always looking out for everyone. Just start applying some of that Poppy magic on yourself – try some self-love – and I don't mean the other kind." She made circular motions around her privates area, saying nothing in case Lily walked in again.

They quietly giggled as they had done so often as children.

"I'm the same, you know," Helen went on. "Losing Dad and giving Daniel up left me feeling empty. I filled it with work and buying stuff I didn't need. But now I can see that I'm still afraid to move on."

"Fear of the unknown, Helen, that's natural."

"But I've always been the Lingerie Woman. I've no idea what else I could do. Can we really reinvent ourselves at our age?"

"Of course – but you've got to be open to opportunities that come your way. Stop living in fear and start trusting the Universe."

"You're right, Lily is right, there's more to life than excessive drink and sex!"

Although for the life of her Helen couldn't think what.

"You don't look too convinced, Helen."

"I'm thinking – what you said about meditation. If it helps you get back on track, maybe you'd teach me. A bit like a gym-buddy, we could do it together." She perked up at the idea but then frowned. "As long as you won't turn me into a tofu-loving hippy with hairy legs."

"You get to keep your Prada, Helen."

"I could do with a bit of balance – so, if I don't have to start hugging people or trees, I like the idea of manifesting my desires. When can I start?"

"This week." Then Poppy added casually, "I'm teaching Angelo too."

"Angelo, hey," Helen nodded.

"Shut up, you. Now go on, get out of here. See Rob, do what you've got to do." She'd had a brainwave while they were chatting and she was anxious to get started on her plan.

Helen pulled her gloves back on. Without looking up she said, "Would that be who's coming to dinner by any chance?"

"Could be," Poppy said with a blasé swipe of her hand.

"Why, Poppy, after all he's done for you?" she sighed heavily.

Poppy looked puzzled. "I know – that's why I'm cooking – to say thank you."

"I was just getting to like him too and you have go and cook him a homemade dinner. Tell him it was nice knowing him." Helen ran to the front door, laughing before Poppy could do her serious damage.

"My cooking is improving I'll have you know. Gordon Ramsay watch out! And, Helen?"

Helen had her hand on the door latch ready to leave.

"What?"

"Promise me one thing: never stop trusting the Universe."

69

Helen pulled up outside Rob's house for the Sunday dinner he'd promised her. Childhood sweethearts, now a son, they'd come a long way over the twenty years their lives had intertwined. She checked her lipstick in the rear-view mirror. She took a deep breath and wondered for a moment whether she was making the right decision.

When Rob opened the door, an amazing aroma of garlic and herbs wafted from the kitchen. He looked relieved to see her. She had run off to see the American, but she'd come back.

"Wow, smells amazing, Rob! What's cooking?"

"You, baby," Rob said, as he popped the cork.

"Champagne – again?"

"That's not all, wait until you see what I have upstairs."

He took Helen by the hand and led her up the spiral staircase of his converted mews. Rose petals were scattered and white candles lined the polished wooden steps. The flower petals led to the bed, while hundreds of tiny candles lit the bedroom, like stars in an African sky.

It took Helen's breath away.

"I told you, I'm HD ready!"

Rob looked handsome in his simple white shirt. His phone vibrated.

"So, what do you think, sweetheart, like it?" he said as he took his phone half out of his trouser pocket, to see who had texted him.

"It's fabulous, Rob. Do you want to get that?"

"Em, no, it can wait, just work," he replied, putting his phone on silent.

"Ah, but *is* it work on a Sunday evening? The thing is, Rob, with you, I'd never know, never be sure. Is it work or a woman? All this is fabulous, but it's nearly twenty years too late." Helen stayed standing at the top of the stairs.

"It's that American kid, isn't it? Do you think he fancies you, Helen? The older woman and all her sexual experience? Cop on!"

Ignoring his comments, she turned and walked down the steps.

"Where are you going? I told you I'm ready, you agreed to come to dinner. What? You were just playing with me?" He swiftly came down the stairs after her. He held his arms out wide, waiting for her explanation.

"No, Rob, you just weren't listening to me, you never are. Let's face it, we both know sooner or later you'll get bored. I'm here because I said I would be and I like to keep my word. But I also came to tell you I'm done. No more. I'll be your friend but I can't be your lover."

"Do what you like, Helen, I don't need you anyway!"

"Rob, leave your ego out of this and you'll see that I'm right. It hasn't worked until now – it's not going to work. Start thinking about what you want in life. You've been handed a gift, a son. Cherish that – you said it yourself, that when the job, the flashy cars and women are gone, all you've got is yourself and if you're lucky, your family too."

"Since when did a lingerie designer become a guru?"

"We're all gurus, Rob, just in different masks."

Rob threw his eyes to heaven. "What's this, Helen, some kind of spiritual awakening? Why do women do that, when they reach a certain age? It's not very sexy you know, this whole enlightenment crap. You're not like other women your age, Helen – you still look good. That crap is for women with divorce papers and an ever-

394

expanding waistline!" He smirked as he ran his hands through his receding hairline.

Helen took deep breath, remaining silent. He misread her calmness as submission.

"And you need to get your job back, Helen, asap, tomorrow. Come on, let's eat, I'll talk you through the legal jargon you can threaten them with. Your mother was dying when you agreed to work in Hong Kong etc. Irish law is based on English law so it's not that different."

He was back in control. He'd always managed to talk her round and tonight would be no different. He took Helen's elbow to guide her through to the kitchen.

Helen didn't budge.

"What? Why are you looking at me like that?" he asked.

"You know, Rob – you really should learn to meditate."

"What?"

Helen was surprised at herself. Had she really just said 'meditate'? As in "meditate on it" instead of "sit on it"? Yes, she had, Poppy would be so proud. She pulled on her coat. "You heard me, meditate on it."

"Medicate? What stoners have you been hanging out with now?"

"And that, my friend, is why I'm going my way and you are going yours – one letter in the difference but worlds apart."

70

One Year Later

Poppy turned the "Closed" sign and locked the door after the last customer left. Snow flakes drifted down from the night sky.

Could it be possible – a white Christmas?

She loved the stillness in the shop when everyone was gone – just her, with the massage oils, candles and lingerie. Who would have thought it possible?

There was a gentle tap on the door.

"I'm sorry, we're closed!" she said, thinking it was probably some poor unfortunate who'd no idea how to shop for Christmas and needed a last-minute present – but she had to go home at some point.

"It's me, you gobshite, open the door!" Helen stood outside, laden down with cardboard boxes.

Poppy opened up.

"Have you seen the snow, Poppy, isn't it magical? Christmas Eve and it's snowing!" She came in with a flurry of snow and excitement.

"What's all that? Don't tell me we're left with a load of Christmas gift sets!" Their first year in business, they couldn't afford to be left with unsold stock.

"Don't be daft, woman, we're all empty, I just didn't want to leave them in the car in case some idiot thought Santa'd come early, and smashed my window." She shook herself off.

"That's it then. I sold the last set about ten minutes ago. If you're saying there's none in the warehouse either, that sounds like a success to me?" Poppy looked hopefully at Helen. In their partnership, she left as much of the accounting to Helen as she could.

"Ms Power, for you, Santa has come early." Helen put the boxes out of the way and sat on one of the chaises longues that adorned the retail floor of their business.

"Okay, it's just a rough estimate – I'm no accountant but I've had a quick look. If you take the sales from the website, the shop and the wellness centre, it would appear, Poppy, that you were absolutely right – lingerie and massage is a bloody profitable mix."

Poppy took the computer print-out from Helen. She couldn't believe what she was seeing – black figures. It might be Christmas but they were no longer in the red.

"It was you who put it all together, Helen." Poppy picked up a small gift box from the display cabinet. It was their *Samara* signature collection, beautifully wrapped boxes with gift certificates, lingerie, essential oils, and candles.

"Let's celebrate. Do you fancy sparkling apple juice or champagne?" Helen asked. They both drank a lot less these days – they called it balance.

There was another gentle tap, three taps to be exact, on the door.

"Are you expecting someone?"

Poppy gave her a look of horror. "I haven't morphed into the Virgin Mary!" she said as she opened the door.

"*Buon Natale*!" Angelo held out a bottle of Prosecco and three glasses. "*Ciao, bella!*" He gave Helen his customary two kisses, from cheek to cheek.

But he kissed Poppy on the lips.

"I've cleaned everything, and locked up the café. Now it's time to take off the plug and relax." He pulled the elastic band from the nape of his neck and shook his hair out.

"That, Angelo is what I call perfect timing," Helen said.

"We've just had a look at the sales figures, Angelo – Helen has pulled it off!"

"Stop. It's the two of us together. I wouldn't know where to start with the wellness centre. Holistic lingerie – ha, makes a change from the 'hole-istic' stuff I was used to." She put her feet up and hugged a deep red velvet cushion to her body.

"It's not holistic lingerie – it's the icing on the cake. We nurture mind, soul and body. And thanks to you, it's ethically sourced, so we're even helping people on a different continent. How's that for universal synchronicity!"

"I'm glad everything worked well between Eden and David Strong's company. The PR Fred got was terrific. And we benefited from it too of course by David supplying us with our diffusion range."

"Poppy has explain it to me, Helen," said Angelo, "but I don't really understand the whole manufacturing process."

"Okay, the short version. Eden get their volume lines produced in David and Mai's factory. But the smaller runs that *we* get from them wouldn't work in a big production plant." Helen's face was radiant. "Our garments are produced by the seamstresses in their own homes. David sets them up with machines, then one of his team drops off the cut fabric and comes back to collect the finished goods. The women get to work from home so they can set their own hours and spend time with their families."

"It's truly amazing, isn't it, Angelo?" Poppy ran her hand along a deep-purple negligée, which was part of their window display.

"*Sí*, but can everything really be done in their homes?"

"Not everything. The finishing is mostly done back in the factory where it's prepared for shipment."

"Helen's designs made exclusively for us, *Samara*. We really are unique, aren't we?" Poppy smiled as a child who'd just heard her favourite Christmas Eve story.

"Yep, that's Devine Power Enterprises alright. Someone told me once that spirituality couldn't be sexy." Helen raised an eyebrow.

"Well, our bank balance proves him wrong," Poppy said with pride. "He has been good though, Rob. Helping us with the company set-up and all that red tape."

"And he's a good dad too, no?" Angelo added.

"Yes, he is. He's really bonded with Daniel." Helen rubbed the nap of the velvet she still held. She looked content.

"Prosecco time!" Angelo declared, raising up the bottle.

"I don't mean to be a party-pooper," said Poppy, "but don't you have to be at the airport, Helen?"

"I do, which reminds me, how do I look?" She stood up and smoothed down her black silk dress. "I want sexy, without tarty. I want 'I'd love to rip your clothes off but you could still bring me home to meet your mother' – how'd I do?" She did a little twirl.

"Helen, you look amazing, you've no idea – now go!"

Christmas Eve and Dublin airport was eerily quiet. Most people were already with their families, with the people they loved.

The last few flights were landing. Helen looked at the arrivals board and searched for *London Heathrow*. The magic words "*just arrived*" blinked up.

A giant snowman lit up the arrivals area and automatically sang 'Merry Christmas', as people walked by. It distracted her for a few moments – she took her eye off the arrivals door.

"Hey." The man's voice came from behind her.

She swung around. "Hey, yourself."

Jack Taylor stood before her, as he'd done over a year ago at this very airport.

But this time was different. Without hesitation, he pulled her to him and he kissed her.

"I was worried your flight would get snowbound or something." Helen felt childlike giggles bubbling up inside of her.

"There's barely an inch on the ground," Jack laughed, his arms still around her.

"You're in Ireland now – that's enough to halt the country – get used to it!" She touched his face.

"Trust me, I intend to." He kissed her again.

This time the kiss lingered.

After a moment they pulled away slightly and looked into each other's eyes. They didn't speak. Jack kissed Helen again.

And again.

And again.

71

"Exactly how many are coming to your midnight party, Helen?" Jack asked as he threw an extra log on the fire in Helen's living room before going back into the kitchen.

"Just family really. It's something we did when I was a kid – start Christmas after Midnight Mass with a slap-up Irish breakfast. I thought it'd be nice to rekindle the tradition." Helen smiled as she kissed him on the forehead. She wanted to be alone with Jack, but they could wait a few days longer.

"It looks like you're feeding an army." Jack scooped up a handful of peanuts from a bowl Helen had set out "in case people needed a few nibbles first".

Angelo rang the doorbell with the tip of his Roman nose. He tried to balance a pile of sparkling wrapped presents under his chin. Two gift bags swung from each of his hands.

Helen opened the door.

"Let me help you, Angelo. That's what we call a lazy man's load!" She reached out to help him.

"It's okay – *piano, piano!*" He concentrated, as though he was walking a tightrope.

"Piano piano?" Helen asked.

Poppy and Lily were just behind him. They carried casserole dishes.

"'It means 'slowly, slowly'. Is Daniel here?" Lily looked around.

"He's in the kitchen – reckons students should be in charge of cocktails – he's mixing them now," Helen told her.

Lily checked her make-up in a mirror and tossed her hair. "Score," she said as she disappeared into the kitchen.

Helen pressed play on Bing Crosby's "White Christmas". Lily reappeared and rapidly pressed eject. Replacing Bing with Slade, who Lily reckoned were goodies albeit they were oldies. She promptly disappeared again once the music was sorted, to rejoin Daniel.

"So, have you something to say, Helen?" Poppy asked when they'd a moment alone while Angelo and Jack finished setting the table.

"Such as?" Helen feigned innocence.

"Such as, 'Thank you, Poppy, for giving the Universe a helping hand and ringing the amazing Jack Taylor on my behalf'." Poppy raised her chin – she loved it when she was right.

"Thank you, Cupid, for completely ignoring my wishes, and ringing Jack behind my back." Helen saluted her.

"He'd already given that Amy the boot – she sounds like the female version of Rob if you ask me. Hey – there's a match made in hell – we should introduce them!"

"I think we're busy enough with *Samara,* we don't need to add a dating agency to the mix."

"Oh, I forgot to tell you. Remember Keith, the geography professor we met in Vietnam? I contacted him some time after the accident to explain why I hadn't called?"

Helen nodded.

"Well, he emailed me a few days ago. He's getting married on New Year's Eve to a girl he met at a beer stall in Hanoi!"

"No way! Is she a local?"

"That's the gas part of it. She's a maths lecturer from Coventry. He goes all the way to Asia and meets his future wife who happens to live less than a hundred miles from his home town!"

"You love happy endings, don't you, Pops?"

The doorbell rang again, "Lord, it's like Heuston Station here tonight," Helen said, slightly flustered.

"I'll get it. And by the way, yes, I do love a happy ending – doesn't everyone?" Poppy grinned.

Helen took her father's urn and placed it on the table, knife and fork either side. Lily thought it gross but Daniel declared it was cool. Helen asked him what he meant by "cool" and to her amazement it meant cool. A total miracle – teen language she understood! Lily was also quick to come around when Daniel pointed out you don't get to sit next to the ashes of a War Hero every day, so it was actually rather cool in a morbid sort of way, which made it all the better.

"Will everyone sit down, it's getting cold!" Helen shouted. "Cyril, will you pour the drinks?"

"Certainly, dear, but I thought I was needed in the kitchen?" Cyril cocked his thumb to the closed door. He looked unsure where to put himself. "I don't have to sit next to the urn, do I, Helen? It's just I reckon I'm close enough to being in one myself – I don't want to tempt fate by sitting next to one." He smiled weakly.

"Stop talking nonsense. Sit where you're comfortable – just don't forget to mix the drinks!" Helen said, winking at him. "Mum, are you coming in or what?"

"Keep your hair on, love, you'll wake the Baby Jesus himself with all that shouting." Mary Devine pushed through the kitchen door, with the aid of her grandson.

"Don't be playing the invalid card with me! Get in here, we're all waiting." Helen put a hand on her hip, but the curve of her smile gave her true feelings away.

"Will you stop fussing? Honest to God, wait until my legs are back to full strength, young lady, I'll kick your backside!" Mary took her place at the top of the table. "Now, I'd like to say Grace."

Lily and Daniel rolled their eyes, and Poppy gave them a look that said: *Don't you dare.*

"The fact that I'm here at all is a miracle, the fact that we're all here together is a blessing. I got a second chance – now I get to know my grandson and watch my virtual granddaughter grow into a beautiful woman – especially now we can see her pretty face and those dreadful black clothes are gone. And Poppy – my virtual *daughter* – if it wasn't for you, these two might never have known what they nearly walked away from." Mary raised her glass.

Helen and Jack smiled at each other.

"Cyril, to you, my love, for showing me that it's never too late to find love. To my beautiful Helen, who is terribly bossy, but she never once gave up on me. Thanks to you they didn't pull the plug on me." Mary blessed herself again.

"Welcome, Jack, thank you for spending Thanksgiving with your own family, so you could come to us, your new Irish family, for Christmas. Angelo, thank you too, for being the wonderful man you are and it's great to know we've a decent cup of coffee to look forward to after the feast – *salute!*"

A cheer went up.

"One last thing," Mary continued.

A collective groan went around the table.

"Thank you, God, the Universe, spirit, for the abundant gifts you've bestowed upon us, Amen. Let's eat!"

Lily wiped away a tear. She and her mum really did have family after all.

Later Helen sat with Mary and JD by the fire, while the others cleared the table and washed the dishes. Helen rubbed the dog's head, which lay in her lap.

"You know, I've just realised something Mum. JD, Jack Daniels, he's named after the two men in my life. The men I love. What are the chances of that?" JD looked up at Helen and licked her hand. "Thanks be to God I didn't call you Diet Coke, hey, JD!"

Mary smiled at her. "I've made a decision, Helen, if you're comfortable with it. I'd like to scatter your dad's ashes. It's time. He'll always be alive in our hearts, let's let his ashes go free."

"Are you sure, Mum, is that what you want?"

"It is. I'll keep a few and you can mix them with mine when I'm gone. But life is for living and your father wouldn't want to be cooped up in a jar. What was I thinking! Let him fly on the wind, as he always dreamed."

Mary Devine was back.

Two days after Christmas, Helen and Jack set off for Wicklow. They were alone. It was to mark the first proper night of their new life together.

"It's really beautiful around here," Jack said, taking in the scenery around him.

Helen had butterflies in her stomach. So much had happened, she'd come so far. Now, a man whom she'd met by coincidence on the other side of the world was moving his life to Ireland, to be with her. She pulled the car into the driveway of Powerscourt. The white wedding-cake building gleamed majestically in the winter sun.

"This looks amazing. I thought you weren't into decadence any more, preferred the simple things in life," Jack teased.

"This is simple," Helen grinned. "Simply divine, that is."

The lobby was adorned with crystal and brass. Bird of Paradise flowers stood tall in vases set upon marble-topped tables. In the centre hung a prism-catching chandelier, shaped like a hot air balloon.

Helen signed the register as Jack looked around, soaking it all in. He nudged Helen.

"Is that the guy from TV? The one you're always raving about?"

"Chef Ramsay, sir." The front-desk manager smiled. "He's in-house tonight, cooking for his only Irish restaurant – here at the hotel – you're in for a treat. Have a wonderful stay in Powerscourt." He handed them the key-card.

"Helen, what are the chances of that! Gordon Ramsay, cooking, the night we check in. It's destiny!" Jack grinned.

They got into the lift. Helen hadn't said anything.

"Hold that, would you?" Gordon Ramsay bounced towards the lift door.

"Hello," he smiled at Helen and Jack.

"Hello," Helen said, looking at the floor numbers flash as the lift ascended.

Jack started to say something, but Helen elbowed him.

A ping, the door slid open, Gordon Ramsay got out. The doors closed behind him.

"Why didn't you talk to him? I wanted to get an autograph for you – ask him what he'd recommend on tonight's menu." Jack looked puzzled – would he ever understand women? *Andromeda, Jack.*

Helen looked at him, holding his gaze. She subtly licked her lips. "It's not food I want, Jack."

Jack realised, no matter where she had come from one thing was for sure. The best thing in his life was – *Simply Devine.*

THE END.